EXODUS OF THE STORKS

WALID NABHAN

EXODUS OF THE

WALID NABHAN

STORKS

Translated from the Maltese by
Albert Gatt

Peter Owen
London and Chicago

Peter Owen Publishers
Conway Hall, 25 Red Lion Square, London WC1R 4RL, UK

Peter Owen books are distributed in the USA and Canada by
Independent Publishers Group/Trafalgar Square
814 North Franklin Street, Chicago, IL 60610, USA

Translated from the Maltese *L-Esodu taċ-Ċikonji*

First English-language edition published by
Peter Owen Publishers 2021

Paperback ISBN   978-0-7206-2050-4
Epub ISBN   978-0-7206-2051-1
Mobipocket ISBN   978-0-7206-2052-8
PDF ISBN   978-0-7206-2053-5

A catalogue record for this book is available from the British Library.

Typeset by Octavo Smith Publishing Services

Printed and bound by
Printworks Global Ltd, London/Hong Kong

NATIONAL
BOOK
COUNCIL

This publication was funded by the
National Book Council of Malta

To my mother and father because, before they departed,
they deliberately left the light on.

1

Nineteen years, four months, five days and I don't know how many hours, and suddenly the phone rings. On the line was my brother Mustafa who, throughout these nineteen-plus years, had always asked me to call him back because a telephone call would be much cheaper for me than it was for him, or so he thought.

The older brother is always wiser than the younger. There's no altering that sacred chain of reasoning. Mustafa knows more than I ever could about the cost of things here in Malta, even though he's never set foot on the island. That follows the rule. The words spoken by the elder are judicious and wise and are equal in value to a Qur'an handed down from the heavens.

In any case, I couldn't argue with him. On the contrary, I always agreed without quibbling – and it wasn't because of the sacred chain linking the older and the younger. I don't abide by rules and strictures of this socially oppressive kind. It's true that wisdom accrues over time, but that doesn't mean that the sediment at the bottom of the flask is invariably valuable. Truth can rise to the surface, for example, although it might be as heavy as lead.

Simon De Brincat, my friend from the city who had a clear-eyed view of such things, liked to say that truth isn't heavy at all, that when there are two conflicting versions the truth is always the lighter and simpler one. 'The one the mind can digest without the aid of any godly saliva' was how he put it with a crooked grin.

But that's not how people think. People reach for the unexplainable, as with my brother Mustafa's inexplicable belief, which he'd arrived at under his own steam, he being older than me, that things in Malta cost far less than they do in Jordan.

'I have some bad news. Our father passed away early this morning,' he said in a voice that sounded firm but full of sorrow.

'My father's dead?'

'I'm sorry . . .'

I felt suddenly as if I'd been stripped of all my clothes and everyone else was peering in, trying to catch a glimpse of my nakedness.

'We've taken care of everything. You won't make it in time, as we'll be taking him to the cemetery in a short while.'

My father was dead. The man who had brought me into the world. The man who had hurriedly put together the recipe that made me had now disappeared from the face of the earth and left me to deal with 5,048 unfixable faults – including a substantial number of problems the world has been unable or unwilling to solve for reasons that are far more complex than my father ever imagined.

I don't know if he expected me to fix what has been steadily going awry for thousands of years, ever since Moses had a chat with Elohim on the summit of Mount Sinai and somehow managed to reach an agreement with him to lead the children of Jacob into the land of milk and honey after destroying its pagan inhabitants.

The Lord, as many of us know, has always had a special fondness for the Jewish people, a fondness he himself might find it hard to explain. Maybe a father would understand it better than I can, since I've never been one.

But this preferential treatment was hard even for my own father to comprehend, who'd fathered eleven, who continued to worship the Lord in silence and in spite of everything, despite the lingering feeling that he was owed some explanation, both for the agreement reached behind his back and for all the things that had happened to him.

There was no explanation forthcoming, and I'm not sure there ever will be, not in my lifetime anyway. But if we must tell the whole truth and not find ourselves trapped like my brother Mustafa and his tendency to judge things from a distance, it must be said that it wasn't just a sentimental weakness that drove the Lord to put his name to that agreement, which sounds somewhat biased. We can't forget that the decisions taken by the gods aren't driven by the passions and occasional arrogance that drive us mortals. The way decisions are taken in heaven is far wiser. So wise that sometimes our limited intellect is unable to comprehend it.

In its final draft the agreement included a clause which stipulated that, should any of the Canaanite infidels manage to flee their homeland with their skins intact, they should thereafter be referred to as EDPs, that is, *externally displaced people,* the descendants of whom I now represent.

'The things that matter the most to you will happen in your absence,' my friend Simon used to remark when discussing the subject of Palestinian mythology, its flotsam having reached Malta's shores in the form of hostages and murder and hijacked aeroplanes and failed rescue operations and massacres of passengers at Luqa Airport. Malta, too, has suffered for Palestine. But then, who hasn't suffered because of it? She's become the world's pain in the arse. Which brings me back to the topic in hand, to that important meeting that took place in my absence 3,500 years ago on Mount Sinai, which resulted in my becoming the first refugee in the written history of humanity, and today, today after all those thousands of years, when I no longer have anything to do with El and Baal and the other false gods but adore the very same Allah who ordered my massacre, I find that I am still a refugee.

As far as anyone can make out, this business with Palestine wasn't going to reach a conclusion at the point desired by Allah, since it seems that once he'd got rid of El and Baal and their friends, other gods appeared. Some of them wore a keffiyeh and some were bald and some wore a tarboosh and some sported glasses and a necktie and some wore a turban and some had ginger complexions and some were dark and some were the colour of wheat and some were black, and every one of them laid a claim to holy Palestine, yearned for it with a passion that made them sacrifice their sons and daughters on bloodstained altars as we are about to see in what follows.

So what does Allah do in this case? What does he do when he finds himself surrounded once more by ferocious rival gods? For six days and six nights he was restless on his throne until he found the solution that would make everyone content. He made up a game. A game that would never be lost and never be won, a game that would be called 'Palestine'. He thought that would be the only way he could calm things down and, certainly up to a point, bring the situation under control until he could figure out what to do with this seething, bubbling pot. At least, should trouble break out, it would break out on earth and not in heaven. No one wants to lure the bear into their neck of the woods after all. Imagine the gods engaging in a fist fight – the shame of it! Of course, the gods do not sink so low. They issue mandates, do it by proxy, so to speak. Why get your hands dirty and your clothes rumpled – not to say ripped and torn – as you roll around with another god in the dust, especially if he happens to be as chubby as Ariel Sharon? Imagine a god with a hole in his trousers, now that's unheard of. You couldn't blame them. No one could take a god with a hole in his trousers seriously!

'Was it peaceful?' I asked, I who was fatherless for the first time.

'He died in his bed. He looked as if he was sleeping,' he replied sadly. 'He got up for morning prayers, performed them and got back under the sheets as usual until it was time for the kids to wake up, but this time he stayed asleep. Lately, he'd been talking about you a lot.'

Me? Whatever for? I began to recall the last clear picture I had of my father, nearly twenty years ago, as he stared into space while I packed my bags and prepared to leave. A scene that was endlessly replayed in our house in the Jordanian capital of Amman, which would leave an indelible impression on my life. That day he stared for a long time and then locked himself back in his cubicle.

We had all left our father, except for Mustafa who got married and continued to live with him. Throughout the haemorrhage of his children I only saw him take it badly on one occasion. It was when Muhammad left, my eldest brother. It was as if he knew he'd never see him again. Fathers can sense this apparently. Somewhere deep inside they know. Maybe in their hearts, maybe in their livers or maybe in some secret organ rooted at the bottom of their tormented paternity. The day Muhammad left, my father made up for all the tears he hadn't shed when we buried my mother under the dust of everlasting absence. The contrasting nature of my father's emotions on these two occasions convinced me that unless you yourself have ever been a father there is no way of predicting what will cause a father to cry or to make him hold back his tears.

'What did he say?' I asked.

'"Where is Nabil?" he said sometimes, or "Why's it taking him so long to pay me a visit?" That sort of thing. In his final weeks he suddenly loosened his tongue and started saying a lot of things. Some things made sense and some didn't. You remember how he was . . . Nothing to be done now. Just pray for his soul. May Allah forgive him and grant him rest.'

'May Allah forgive him and grant him rest,' I repeated numbly as the world turned its gaze on another part of my flesh that had just been laid bare.

My father was dead. The man I knew best, and the man I knew least. Closer to me than my own breath one moment, and separated from me by a limitless ocean the next. When I was young, Allah only knew how terrified I was of our physical resemblance. The same face. The same eyes. The same hair. The same forehead and nose. The same mannerisms and the same things both visible and invisible.

I've always been troubled by this close resemblance because I always felt that I was his reflection, that I would never be me. I wasn't wrong – once I started to grow up I came to resemble him in everything. Not just his face and hair and nose. His silences. The bizarre mood swings, the wild behaviour and, worse, the expressionless face that never offers any hint of where you stand. I came to resemble him so thoroughly that today I'm totally convinced that eventually every father will possess one of his sons and start to become him. To see with his eyes and taste with his tongue and smell with his nose.

I'm sure that my father chose me to continue to be him. Probably to resolve the things he couldn't. I suppose the gods know what they're doing even when they're playing games. Who doesn't like to play a little? Mind you, time isn't the same for gods as it is for humans. They're not in any hurry; they've got eternity. Which is why they probably don't wear watches and they don't hang calendars up in their kitchens. Apparently, we invented time when we accepted our first mandate from the heavens, without knowing that time was the scissors that would sever the fabric of our lives. Maybe we made it up to tell ourselves that we're not caught up in a vicious circle like a dog chasing its own tail.

When we accepted the mandate from the gods during that brief ceremony in the Garden of Eden, we forgot, on our way out, to ask about the
meaning of love and the meaning of hate. Allah seemed to be in a hurry
that day, and we couldn't take up any more of his time. He was a little
angry, too. Or worried. Maybe he was already mulling over the game he
was about to invent. Temples and crosses. Mosques and smoke. Crusades
and ships and horses. Cannon and buses and aeroplanes getting blown
up and heads going up and heads going down. Who knows what was
passing through his mind as he chased us out of his garden? It's as if we
embarrassed him. The creatures he had fashioned with his own hands.

My father was dead. The man who left Palestine and whom Palestine
never left. I remember him saying that paradise itself was only a speck
of dust in comparison. Sometimes my mind begins to wander, and I
wonder what that means. Which paradise was this that had swallowed
up my mother and father and two of my siblings and many of my friends
and which would not be satisfied until it had swallowed me as well?
Wasn't it just a land like every other corrupted land? Or are lands like
people, not all of them equal?

My father was dead – most likely after he had become me or I had
become him or we had both become one, madly pursuing an illusion
called Palestine. He had left Palestine, and Palestine had never left him,
while I had never set foot in Palestine, and Palestine had never dislodged
itself from within me. How can you love a tract of land you were not
fertilized in? How can you love trees that you've never climbed? How
can you be drawn to streets where you've never littered or got lost? How
can you love all this to death without ever having laid eyes on it? Or
would this be the same accursed fairy tale that brought the Jewish people
back to Palestine after thousands of years? Why else would there be this
chronic resemblance between me and my father? Are we really ourselves,
after all, or merely extensions of our mothers and fathers? Or did my
father do what he did because he understood that the diaspora of the
Jewish people had finally reached its culmination at the point at which
our own fairy tale began?

My father is dead, and our fairy tale continues to unfold, and no
sorcerer has yet made an appearance, and Palestine's behaviour continues

to boggle the mind. But the fairy tale would have it thus. Cows will appear who will devour other cows. Meanwhile, the gods, in fact, do nothing, except exercise their power over us. How else could Allah be Allah, and how would we take him seriously if he didn't show us plain and simple that we are his to do with as he pleases? Were it ever otherwise, if we should ever have him between our jaws, if only just the once, that would be the last time. For our knowledge of darkness far exceeds his. What does he know of the hunger and the depravities of human existence? What does he know of fear and of failed loves? What does he know of the tears shed by mothers and widows and of broken hearts? What does he know except how to toy with us for a while and then discard us?

My father was dead. After he had made me Toy Number 11. A tiny marble bead heading on a downward slide. Perhaps the only justice among life's injustices is that the slide runs downhill for everyone. The speed might vary from one bead to the next, but the direction is always the same.

'What's that you're saying, Toy Number 11? Do you call the life I gave you unfair? Truly, you are ungrateful, and you deserve not one hell but hell a thousandfold.'

'Yes, of course, life is full of injustice. Actually, I've been meaning to tell you this for a long time. Don't expect me to worship you my whole life when you give me something that will be destroyed. I'm not your toy. I'm not just a molecule of DNA that you're free to flick across generations and do with as you please.'

'Aren't you? So what are you then, Mr Human, and what else do you want?'

'I am a truly accursed human being. Although I've been banished and exiled from your zone. But I have needs, and my desires are great. As great as yours. Greater, even.'

'I see you've sprouted a tongue – and it seems to have grown very long. But let's leave that for the time being. Just to show you how merciful and tolerant I am, I shall refrain from punishing you. Indeed, I shall allow you to continue with your complaints. I'm listening.'

'I don't even know where to begin. Not because I'm mixed up and muddle headed but because the list is so long. For instance, why is it that you can see me but I can't see you? Why is it that you can hear me but I can't hear you? Why is it that you can read my thoughts while I find everything about you inscrutable? Why can you cancel my existence on a whim, in whichever way you please, while I am unable to do anything to you except express my gratitude to you for having created me without my asking you to do so? Where is the justice in all that? Today you decided – on a whim – to remove my father from the stage after he'd played his part in your pointless drama. First, you drag him out of his homeland, then you deny him his wife and children and now you've written him out of the scene altogether. And yet he never wronged you. He remained grateful to you. Me, too, when I was younger. I always worshipped you and loved you. Do you know why? Let me tell you, since we're on the subject. I loved you because I feared you. Just as I feared my father and his silence. Yes, I feared you and your silence. Because I knew you were always spying on me and eavesdropping even on the things I said to myself. Don't think I never had such thoughts when I was young. They grew up with me. From the time they started telling me about you. I used to bite my tongue and continue to love you because that is what I had been taught. If you love Allah, the love he bestows on you in return is boundless. I don't want to know if you returned my love or not, that's your business, but do you really want people to love you because they are terrified of your flames? Why don't you put those flames out and come down here among us? Just for a week. Then you'll see who truly loves you and who pretends out of fear. What did my father and mother ever do to you? As far as I know, the only thing that remained constant and intact throughout the scattered ash of our lives was their regard for you. They continued to cherish and honour and respect you above their own children, even though you abandoned and betrayed them, and you made that unjust agreement behind their backs that cost them everything they had in this life. It cost them their dignity. Do you even know what human dignity is? Come to think of it, you've never been a refugee. You've never been raped and humiliated. You, my Lord, have never . . .'

*

'Hello! Hey? Hello! . . . Hello?' Mustafa's voice brought me back from the heretical musings that tend to intensify whenever I get wind of death. 'You still there?' he scolded me, anxious because this time he was calling at his own expense. Poor man. He didn't have the stomach to ask me to hang up and call him back to tell me that our father was dead.

As for me, as I've already stated, I never argued the toss with him or tried to tell him that things in Malta were far more expensive than in Jordan, because I know that in circumstances like his he had no choice but to be thrifty in order to feed the many mouths he had surrounded himself with early in life. Eight or nine of them, praise the Lord. I'm always hearing a new name, and they always tell me that this is it, this'll be the last one, until I lost track of all the names.

Enough, I said one time. 'How many more chicks can you hatch?' He said that we hatch large broods because we die in large numbers. That scientific answer shut me up. You'd have thought he was a biologist not an electrician. We are fish that lay a lot of eggs knowing that only a few will survive. So I was never tight fisted with him, even when I heard that the little money I sent my father ended up in his pocket. After all, it was a good thing he was there to take care of my father. It's true that Omaymah, my older sister, doesn't live far away, and even Sumayyah when she's around over the summer, but you couldn't ask my father to go and stay with one of them. He'd rather end up in a casket. You needed to bring my father back to the world first before you could talk to him about his entrapment.

'I'm still here,' I said as I wiped away the tears that had welled up in the wake of my internal heretical diatribe. I was surprised that they had escaped since I didn't have a reputation for weeping and was considered pretty robust when it came to the shedding of tears, or so Nadia would accuse me. 'Men who don't cry are weaker than those who cry in public.' I was sorry when she said that because I think Nadia didn't really understand internal tears, which, unlike real tears, give no comfort and leave you in greater pain.

'I'll try to come when the forty days are up,' I said, confused. 'Don't worry about the expenses,' I added hastily, in order to put his mind at rest about the money he would have to fork out, for my father had left nothing behind but emptiness and mystery. What can an old refugee leave behind except for silence and a bitter aftertaste? Except for a repository of memories with which, unconsciously, he continues to infect his children? Until he finally chooses one of them as he chose me and transfers himself into him in order to continue to pursue those desires that still flutter in a gusty wind. True punishment is not to deny someone something they've never had but to grant it to them and let them grow fond of it and then take it away. Those who've never had Palestine will never understand me or my father, Allah forgive his sins – if he's in the mood and has the time to forgive him and purify him of his love of Palestine.

'Is there something I can do in the meantime?' I asked abruptly before hanging up and sparing him an even bigger bill that would drive him into worse grief.

'Yes,' he said with the same firm voice. 'Call your sisters and comfort them a little. You know what they're like!'

My sisters are the kind who'll make up an occasion for grief if there's none to be had. Especially Omaymah. It's as if she can't live without sadness. I can't blame them. Poor things, they were born and bred like me in a setting where sadness was a major part of their daily diet. Another ugly face in the Palestinian melodrama and the psychological trauma that came with it.

'I'll give them a call in a bit,' I said without hesitating. 'But how about I send you some money?' I returned to this point to put his mind at rest, since you only get what you pay for, as we discovered with the death of our uncle, Abdel-Rahman.

He was sick, when a bearded gentleman of the kind who frequent mosques had whispered to one of my uncle's children that the Islamic Hospital provided healthcare for a pittance. And not only that, they even had special committees to carefully scrutinize each case, so that if they discovered that you were one of the downtrodden of this world they would waive their fees and fork out a sum to support you until you could stand on your own two feet again. And they expected nothing in return for any of this. Call it charity in Allah's name. In any case, it was always better than dying in the endless queue outside a government building.

My poor cousins swallowed it whole. They rushed their sick father to the Islamic Hospital. The operation was a shortcut to his death, and the corpse of my destitute refugee uncle was held hostage for twenty days until the bill had been paid in full. Everyone pooled their money, because you couldn't leave your father or your uncle in a fridge, not even a Muslim fridge.

In life one person often takes the place of another. On a wider scale, there are nations that take the place of other nations. They take their land and their future and their sea and their trees and even their memories. That might be the reason why my father decided to possess me. To ensure his memories would live on in me. Maybe he thought that memory is the link between what you are today and what you were in the past. And even what you will be in future. I don't mean to suggest that my father had discovered something new. Nothing happens in a vacuum after all; everyone is rooted in a past. What's new in my father's case, and now in my own, is that the past of our past is so long.

'But doesn't every past have a past?'

'Yes, but for me and for my father before me, nothing from this past wants to fade away. It keeps interfering in the present and, consequently, also the future.'

'And how do you know that before 1948 there wasn't a Jewish son who told the same story about his own father who'd been thrown into the ovens in Auschwitz?'

'That might be true, but how is that my fault? And who gave this Jewish son the right to grow up and burn my own father?'

'As far as your own tongue has informed us, your father died in his own bed!'

'Yes, but what makes you think his bed didn't burn as hot as the ovens at Auschwitz?'

'Your narrative doesn't convince. It hasn't been developed enough. We're sorry about your father. But we're more sorry about the father of that Jewish boy.'

'When is a narrative developed enough?'

'When the death toll exceeds a certain figure.'

'Is that why we give birth to so many children?'
'That's your business. We're not King Herod.'
'And what does Malta have to do with all of this?'
'You tell us.'

Come to think of it, what makes a homeland? Is it geography or is it an idea? Or is it a postcard, as Palestine is? I don't know yet. Countries and cities lose their heads, just as we do. Especially when they rely on the words of their big shots, and the big shots of any country, as we know, aren't very honest.

I know that Malta has now become a European girl, slim and graceful. And I know she sometimes dyes her hair blonde and straightens it to fit in. But for me she remains a dark-complexioned Mediterranean siren. And she still resembles Palestine. The same basil, the same thyme, the same fennel and marjoram, the same obstinacy that just won't be told. And, although they might not be the most beautiful, those oranges are the tastiest in the world. I know all this, and I know that this resemblance doesn't go down well with some of her people who want her to be straight-haired and blonde at all costs, even if curls suit her, I know this as much as I know that in the course of her search for a new identity, apart from dyeing her hair and painting her face with many colours, she needed to cut certain ties and distance herself as far as she could from her own eastern Mediterranean home, from the region whose dust still coats her feet.

You can't blame her really. Who's the idiot who'd want anything to do with that ailing body? The answer is me. I'm that idiot. I'm that fool. I can't disassociate myself from that disjointed body because it's still my flesh. Even though it's been denied. Even though it has been cheapened and sullied. Malta truly resembles Palestine, no word of a lie. You can verify this with all your senses. And although you can alter your appearance and your hair and even the colour of your eyes, do anything to your exterior, what about the heart, how do you change the heart? At heart, Malta is from the east. At heart, she's Levantine. Takes things too much to heart. Loves and hates too deeply. Weeps and rejoices too much like every Mediterranean whose face is long in the morning when it doesn't see the sun high in the sky.

Where did she get her guile? Where did she get her cowardice? And me, how did she manage to hold me for nineteen years, four months, five days and I don't know how many hours beneath her merciless yoke? What is a homeland after all? A reflection of a reflection of a distant past. A geography obscured by the fog of strange religions, blemished by massacres and wars. An isolated island haunted by ghosts. I wish I had the wisdom of the gods. And their means, come to that. I would melt geography and recast it, purified of religion and the past's polluted waters.

And now that my father's dead, what should I expect? That statistically the ghosts will be augmented by one? Or will they be missing one, because my father managed to possess me before he died? From a theoretical perspective, I'm led to believe that he has no need to haunt me because his flesh is now my flesh and burdened with the scars of geography. Let's see then, maybe I'll start haunting myself. I've cast myself adrift, and yet I'm still caught up in it all. Palestine and Malta. And everything in between. Two jaws of a vice whose bite is strong enough to hold you in a state of perpetual twilight.

2

Malta. Body exposed to gales and lightning. Rising and struggling on the rough swell of the sea. Voices that it has wafted away into the unknown for thousands of years. Sometimes it feels more constricting than your own skin. And sometimes it feels as infinite as a divine confusion. Malta. Sinful and devout. Capable of tempting the Messiah himself into sin. Malta as guilty and innocent and mad as its people. As confused as the swollen sea that surrounds it; three hundred million years it's been coming and going, and it still doesn't know what it wants. Is it the sea that starts to resemble people or the people the sea?

A tepid-sounding voice reaches you over the line.

'This is Alex Attard from Seas Amidst. As an organization we focus on culture and dialogue in the Mediterranean region. Someone from your embassy gave me your number. We're going to hold a discussion about Palestine at City Gate, and we'd like to have a Palestinian to talk to members of the public and tell them about his own personal experience and what it means to live under the occupation. I've just returned from Ramallah. The situation is frightful.'

Palestine! Why is it that every time you try to get to your feet it's there to knock you back down again? Do people really not understand that it is a conflict between the gods?

You put the phone down and press the button to play that piece you've been playing ever since you and Nadia separated a year and a half ago. A year and a half listening to the same piece by Vivaldi. What's that all about?

It's aggressive, the music emitted by those violins, designed to rip you to shreds. Your besieged soul drips down a crucifix that has sprouted from some place and raised itself somehow. You turn the volume up as high as it will go so as not to have to listen to the final verdict of a love terminated. 'What'll you do? Five years . . . I can't listen to my family going on about it any longer.'

'What'll you do?' Three and a half words form the noose that strangles our love. Her eyes had been asking the question for a long time. It kept looming larger, like an avalanche hurtling down a mountain. Always growing larger and rolling until it slammed into your face, because it was *your* face it was aiming for specifically. None other.

From out of the sea of faces, a lean handsome one emerges that matches that tepid voice you heard yesterday over the phone.

'I'm Alex. It was me who called yesterday. They've got Arafat with his back to the wall,' he continues as he shakes your chapped hand. 'They expected him to choose between an offer that's worth nothing and the betrayal of his people. It was a case of refusing the offer or appearing monstrous before the entire world.'

Before you can open your mouth to reply, he continues with the same eagerness. 'Right now, it's not so much a question of who looks good and who looks monstrous. I think you're both looking monstrous right now. But somehow they want to give the occupation itself a facelift. Had Arafat accepted the "generous" offer that the world has heard so much about, he'd be booking the Palestinian cause into a cosmetic-surgery clinic, and then the occupation would continue with a new face that the whole world finds acceptable because you yourselves accepted it.'

You look at the hundreds of faces coming and going through City Gate. You try to hide your own in that sea of faces in which you'd be hard put to distinguish a Judas Iscariot from a Messiah. There was a time when you could hate an entire country or fall in love with it simply because of one single face. Now all faces look the same. Many of them ignore you just as you ignore them, while others look at you and perhaps ask themselves the same question: Judas or Messiah? Life has taught you how to be an anonymous face among faces, sometimes even rendering yourself completely invisible. Let's just say that faces don't torment you as much as they used to, although the voices are another matter. Where do you escape the clamour of voices? And Nadia's voice, which still rings in your ear 'What'll you do?' with the unspoken continuation of the question: 'Are we going to get married, or am I wasting my time with you?' Although she never actually said that last bit, it would have been the logical follow-on. A cruelty lurked in those words she never uttered but which were clearly conveyed in her silence. No one can read silence the way you can.

At last she had you in a corner. Because she herself was the corner. Her family, who for some strange reason you never wanted to meet except over the phone on a few occasions, always felt they were interacting with a ghost. They weren't so far off, one might add, since ghosts sometimes appear and make their voices heard.

What did you expect? That the mother and father who brought her into the world and raised her, taught her and provided her with love and a roof and bread, that they would enjoy watching her in the company of a ghost who had never in five years bothered to turn up with a box of chocolates? Even a ghost would call such a man a ghost.

Even though they weren't too happy about the relationship, her mother and father seemed to know exactly how it would end, never put any pressure on you because they never saw you. They only put pressure on her. And she got tired of waiting. Despite those five years, she was still confused and didn't know where she stood with you, like a ship sailing to nowhere.

Alex's club rains more blows on your head. This time his voice is devoid of all enthusiasm.

'The situation's very dangerous, Nabil. The collapse of the talks at Camp David mean we're in unknown territory, meaning the map of Palestine's been placed over a powder keg. A single spark is all it'll take to blow.'

Why is death the only alternative to talks in that part of the world?

'What'll you do then?' Five years is a long time. And, had she not pushed you, those five would have become ten and those ten twenty, and what were you thinking anyway? That there's no other creature apart from you standing on two straight legs with something dangling between them? Don't you know that all a woman needs to do is wave her hand? And then Nadia doesn't even need to wave. Just a whiff of her bewitching scent, and in no time she'll be surrounded by a flock of those creatures with their straight legs and that something dangling between them.

You admire her courage. You recall Oscar Wilde's lament that you only realize you're in love when you start working against your own interests. How would you put it? 'You know you're in love when you discover that you've ripped yourself to shreds?' See where they've got you, Oscar Wilde and Baudelaire and Rimbaud and Mahmoud Darwish and Neruda and Byron and Lorca and Alfred Sant and the whole damned lot of them.

A beard emerges from among the faces who have gathered, curious to hear about the map of Palestine that has been placed over a keg of gunpowder. You've seen that face not too long ago on television, holding forth in an academic and professional manner about the ignorance of your people, who have always failed to grab at the crumbs that fall from the table on which their own flesh is being devoured.

'Don't you think Arafat has betrayed the dreams and aspirations of your people?' he asked without waiting for a reply from you, as if expecting that the answer would be yes. 'Everyone knows', he continued with the eagerness of one who's on the winning side, 'that no other Israeli leader will make the kind of offer that Ehud Barak made him. In my opinion, Ehud Barak committed political suicide by making that offer, especially in these dark times! He certainly wasn't going to find support among Israelis, what with all the anger there is about what Hamas and Arafat's terrorist organizations are doing. And yet Ehud Barak still had the courage to offer you 90 per cent of the land in the West Bank. What more could you possibly want?'

Why didn't you tell him you wanted nothing at all? And that you, in fact, would rather let your blood go pale so that its excessively crimson colour would no longer seem so shocking, so troublesome, so off-putting to viewers around the world as they sat in front of their television sets during their leisure hours?

Why didn't you tell him that your mother's house in the north of Hebron is now inhabited by three generations of Zionists who obtained the original title deeds from heaven? Even if you did contradict this bearded type, how could you ever contradict Allah?

Why didn't you tell him that if a single spark is all that's needed to blow everything up, as Alex, fresh out of Ramallah, has just explained, then there's something pretty big hanging in the balance, something that Arafat couldn't quite swallow, although he had a tendency to swallow everything, and every time he did you always found yourselves on the road to nowhere? It was Alex who answered instead of you. 'Ninety per cent, but, as usual, the devil's in the details,' he said calmly. 'No one mentions that that 90 per cent is just 21 per cent of the land that historically belonged to Palestine. No one mentions that with the offer everyone is making such a fuss over, they were asking Arafat to hand the five million refugees, who've lived for half a century in extremes of poverty, a pill that would make them simply disappear. If there's no return for these people, there's no solution. We'd be kidding ourselves and everyone around us. Refugees are at the heart of the Palestinian cause. How can one even talk of a solution without mentioning them? It's no use talking about new realities and what have you; if there's one reality in this conflict, it's these people, because they will never be absent from the scene.'

Why do you always hide away in your own poisonous silence? Why didn't you tell him that, as a rule, the flies will swarm towards the oppressed donkey, and you people are currently the last herd of oppressed donkeys left in the world, and your skin is sometimes barely visible for all the flies that stick to it, and all of those flies are sent by the gods who want the donkey to keep suffering until the second coming of Christ, the chief sufferer?

When the talk is over, Alex, who, you've discovered, is a poet who writes about Ramallah and wants to fix the Mediterranean, tells you that, whereas this island is an insult to God himself and receives forgiveness after begging to its saints on its knees all day long and every night, no one will forgive you for the excessively crimson colour of your blood. It's as if they're all saying, 'Don't die on my doorstep. Go and die somewhere else, please.'

You collapse inside. How can you convey to him the weird ideas that have taken shape in your head over time? How can you tell him, in measured tones that won't scare him off, about the agitated gods seated, cards in hand, at their round table playing this heated game called Palestine? How can you tell him all this without provoking his laughter or forcing his pity? Since he's just returned from there, won't he have seen for himself how the knives of despair slice into the flesh of hope and sever every ray of light that might shine through a gap in a horizon darkened by the statements and divinations of rival prophets?

You could, for example, have told him that in that part of the world the past always interrogates the present and always finds it guilty.

'So, do you think the Oslo Accord was completely wrong then, right from the start?' you ask Alex at last, just for the sake of saying something, so that he won't realize on your first encounter that you're just another oddball.

'I wouldn't say that,' he replies thoughtfully. 'The talks that were led by Faisal al-Husseini and Hanan Ashrawi weren't going too badly, but let's just say that at the end of the day it was Arafat they had to come to an agreement with. The thing is that you and they have completely disparate views. You're talking about a sovereign state, while they're talking about a form of independence, something much less than statehood. Yitzhak Rabin's vision wouldn't have yielded anything but a form of independence that would depend on the mood of the generals in Tel Aviv. The problem is that every time they're faced with a choice between peace and land they'll always choose the land and dispose of the people who inhabit it. Barak's career is nearly over; he'll do anything to save it, and you know better than I do what it takes to achieve political leverage in Israel: you need to have more Palestinian blood on your hands.'

You smell the blood as it rises to your throat. You try to say goodbye and run away from the crimson colour of your blood that's used in every democratic election in the Israeli state. You think that if you run away it will let up, this Middle Eastern pain that you carry with you and which is in full view on almost every news bulletin.

'By the way, Nabil, before I go,' he interrupts your train of thought, 'I wanted to mention that we'll be holding an evening of readings for World Book Day. I'd like you to take part and read some of your own work.'

What work? Where did he get the idea you ever actually write anything? What has he seen in your eyes, this slim bespectacled poet who writes poems about Ramallah and immigrants and wants to fix the Mediterranean with his tormented pen? Or are these poets, like the prophets, sellers of dreams because they know that humanity cannot live on bread alone? He needs a warm whisper in his ear about a better tomorrow. The difference between poets and prophets is that you can't unwrap the prize of prophecy until you're dead and have turned to dust, whereas poets will give it to you on the spot, in shiny wrapping paper decorated with ribbons. You leave with a strange sense of happiness and the sweet smell of hope, and when you get home and untie the colourful ribbons and unwrap your gift you find nothing but wishes and the twittering of birds that all too quickly take wing and fly. Who knows, but maybe these poor poets, no less than the prophets, need to die before we start believing them.

A few days after that discussion at City Gate, Israeli Apaches were carrying out all that had been foretold by Alex Attard, that slim poet from Seas Amidst, the organization for peace and dialogue in the Mediterranean.

It's getting quite late when you finally leave that bar with a head heavier than a fortress. The city stops you in your tracks once more. Silence and narrowness and dim lights and desires tucked away somewhere. The city of Valletta. A tall woman fashioned out of divine wishes and other mysterious things that no one understands except her own people. It always makes you feel that behind every unknown thing there's something else unknown lying in wait. Something hidden behind those walls made ravenous by time. Behind those old doors that hide who knows how many secrets and other forbidden things. And as agitated as the gigantic sea that girdles it.

She pressed you in order to find out where she stood. She needed a reference point, something to give her her bearings. But a man who's on the run all the time? On the run from his homeland, his past and his future? Your life is made up of concentric circles, and everything's inside something else, and she, like many women, needs corners and straight lines. She needs something that has length and breadth and height. Something with a definite beginning and an end. Something real that exists on the face of the earth. What can a woman do with Metaphor Man, with a ghost who's never there when she needs him and who fades the closer she gets to him?

Had she not cornered you she'd have spent a good part of her future life dizzy, spinning in circles until her youth had drained from her and she found herself pushed aside like a rotten tomato.

You always knew Nadia wasn't going to continue to give her love indefinitely without expecting something in return. Only mothers are able to give that kind of unconditional love, and Nadia wasn't your mother and you never wanted her to be. You've had enough mothers. You know that Nadia was practical and organized in everything she did, even though she tried to convey the opposite, that she lived life day to day just like you. You knew Nadia wasn't really like that. You hated seeing your own reflection; how many repetitions of yourself could you bear to see? You told her time and again, 'Nadia, when are you going to be yourself?' So now, now that she's tried to be herself, the way you always wanted her to be, and she told you clear as crystal that this love can't be an adventure for ever, now you hold it against her and against yourself?

'So . . . ?'

'This relationship has to go somewhere, and that somewhere needs to involve marriage . . . a home . . . children.'

Silence

'I'm not asking you for John's head on a platter. All I want is to be able to enjoy the fruits of this relationship. Marriage and a home and kids. Things everybody does.'

Silence

How can someone as chaotic as you ever get married? How does a man enslaved to freedom and pain get married? Marriage means confinement. How can any woman on earth give a man a happy and peaceful home in place of a legendary lost homeland?

'Tell me, what'll you do?'

Silence

Instead of replying, you stare at the Grand Harbour wrapped in black and silence. In the dark, ports seem more mysterious. Warehouses of secrets and tears and writhing and sweat and bellowing and moaning and foolish hands waving in the emptiness and faces that leave, never to return, and others that arrive, never to go back.

You didn't see it her way. You didn't see it at all, in fact. No yes or no about it. Everything for you is grey except for marriage. Black as tar. What you perceived in that 'pitiful' situation, as you called it, was a cemetery for love and motivation. A damp fortified spot where mould slowly gathers and begins to invade the body of love wrought from fine, fragile and occasionally false emotion, until it makes it sick and it slips into a long-term coma. Within the confinement of marriage, love is the first thing to rust.

You live in a grey world where the beginning is like the end and the end is like the beginning. You remember a day at university when Professor Frendo, with his arms spread wide, stood in front of you all and uttered grey words streaked with strange wounds known only to himself. 'Nothing in life is completely black and white. Truth is always relative. And always grey.'

Truth isn't fixed and absolute. Everything can be stretched to suit power and desire. Some try to wear a truth too narrow for them, and some are already comfortable in a truth far greater than they are. You can fashion truth any way you please, so long as you have the right tools; force and maybe a sizeable coterie of intellectuals who sold their conscience in one of the moral bazaars scattered across the world. That day Professor Frendo, with his open arms and that strange respiratory device under his grey suit, managed to spread a bit more dullness over your life's greyness. Certain men, when you encounter them, make you feel as if you've met your destiny.

She discovered the crazy amorphousness of your character quite early on; so why hadn't she left? 'What do you like about me?' you once asked her, point blank, after one of those delirious battles in bed.

'I like your unpredictability,' she said. What made you ask her that? Maybe it was at that moment that you began to feel that your adventure was nearing its end, that a different kind of need was beginning to take root inside of her.

Back then, like many men, you had a high opinion of yourself and thought you knew everything about the world of women, when, in fact, you hadn't learned to spell in any of the alphabets in which women's tongues are written. Because a woman, as you would discover later, too late obviously, speaks in many tongues and writes in many alphabets, while men have a single language that can be read to any woman in the world who's capable of it. What did your knowledge of women amount to in those days, then? A curved waist you could slip your arm around? A voluptuous breast across which your lips could trace a path? A fountain of love and mercy? A river of forgiveness and zeal and, in Nadia's case, you'd need to add an elegance of thought that has since been blown away in the wind. What do men know about women? We know as much as we know about God. What do we know about God? Woman is a creator just like he is. And you, what are you able to create? She's his representative on this earth. And you, what do you represent? Not even yourself. All the secrets of the heavens are in her womb. And you, what do you know of her womb and of God's mysterious secrets? You know as much as other men know; you who have this long finger between your legs and think that finger can show the rest of the world the way.

'I like your unpredictability,' she said, flattering you. And, in order to spread further the oasis in the desert of your mind, she went on, 'I'm fascinated by the fact that you need to be discovered. Monotonous men stifle me.'

You, too, are frightened by monotony and the confinement of marriage. Isn't freedom another form of confinement? Anything that needs looking after constrains you one way or another, even life. And if you're a slave to freedom as you've always preached, what is the freedom you speak of that requires love's total destruction? Nadia never asked you where you were going nor where you came from. Maybe she knew. Did you think that a woman's eyes will always reveal her, while a man is able to hide his dirty secrets away for ever? The days and the years have shown you that a man might believe himself capable of hiding his own dirt, because the truth is that God sometimes has to close an eye and sometimes keeps his eyes shut for too long. And you, what do you know about God?

Nadia thought you'd change over time or that she would change you. She thought an intelligent woman, one way or another, might manage to change a man and direct his legs towards her straight-edged world, but after five years she'd not only failed to change you and bring you closer to her rigid lines but she watched as your dull world became ever more grey.

'My younger sister's about to get married, and I'm stuck with you; I haven't taken even one step forward.' You did not know which instrument measured the number of Nadia's steps. In life there are always two measurements and two perspectives and two disappointments, and the Mediterranean's two ugly faces that Alex Attard would love to change into a single pretty face.

Poetry is a dangerous game sometimes. Especially when it charms and placates; your anger dissipates and you are appeased with metaphor. So how would you describe Alex? As a scheming pacifist? And how's he going to fix the world if human arrogance takes on a thousand new forms a day? Christ might well be crucified daily and all for nothing.

'There's nothing wrong with injecting a bit of new blood into the withered veins of an ageing continent like Europe, is there?' Alex said, meaning to convey what he thought about immigration.

'Well south is south and north is north, you see. Facing every hunger is an obscene form of excess. The haemorrhage of the south towards the north will continue until some kind of equilibrium is reached, and maybe one day the hourglass will be turned on its head and the exodus will begin to move in the other direction.'

It's just imaginary geography. Whereas hunger and suffering are real, just like you and I are real and could even stand up for our neighbours who have come to search for a bite to eat, rifling through the bins of their oppressors. First it was invasion, slavery, colonization, colonialism and the Middle East mandates, and now it's globalization and free trade, which are much worse than military colonization because they bring the harvest right to your doorstep and you never need to get your hands dirty Globalization and free trade go hand in hand. The one spreads your legs while the other pushes his way in. How can the West expect not to have people turning up on its doorstep when it's doing everything to prop up these failed states to serve as a market? Corruption, like every kind of infidelity, needs two accomplices. He who rides and he who is ridden. He who bribes and he who is bribed.

Life has shown you very clearly that power doesn't like the company of conscience. Power prefers to hang out with arrogance. The south will probably remain the south and the north the north until the hourglass is turned over and Alex's imaginary geography goes awry.

'I have no truck with conscience, Alex, and I've no healing balm for Africa. I don't even have it for myself.'

'I understand. When you're the one taking the blows it's difficult to keep count. Do you have anyone in Palestine?'

'Two of my siblings. They made their way back on the Oslo cart,' you replied a little ashamed, as if you were sharing a family disgrace. The crazy Oslo Accord. Alex, on the other hand, thought that the most important thing about Oslo was that it shifted the battleground back to Palestine.

The pressure of his hand as he shook yours insisted once again that you should write. But, you ask yourself, taken aback, what language will you write in? In your Arabic, so that you can carry on telling your fairy tale? Your English, which is barely out of nappies? Or your Maltese, which hasn't even been born yet?

'We usually write in Maltese,' he said as if he could read your mind. 'Obviously you could write in any language you want and feel comfortable with,' he went on hurriedly so as not to appear to be forcing you to write in Maltese. You knew about this language, you already knew that it had borne its fair share of abuse, because it's a little dark skinned, the poor thing. You'd rather not let your relationship with the language sour like everything else.

'I've never written in Maltese.'

'Don't worry about the spelling, we'll give it a once-over for you,' he smiled before leaving you to face the echoes of that language which has been wafting around for thousands of years. Language is a creature of flesh and blood, it hears and sees and feels and breathes and takes offence when its own children find it wanting or feel inferior because they have to speak it. It's all very familiar. Every ex-colony shows these symptoms.

Amman, too, has its own body of people who spoke in English – but the difference is that there is plenty of space in Amman, which means you can keep away from them. In Malta, however, given its size, you can't escape them. You speak to them in their own tongue and they answer you in Anglo-Saxon, even more forcefully once they discover you're an Arab, as if they need to keep their linguistic distance and show that even Malta, small though it might be, can avoid being orientalized.

When you reach the car you realize you've left your keys behind, probably in the bar. 'What a terrible night!' you mutter in sheer disappointment. You'll have to drag yourself back.

Luckily the distance between car and keys is not far. Just across the bus terminus and the square, then a left turn. You get it into your head that something other than the drink is working against you. Something more than a curse. A secret sect, perhaps? A gang of wounded ghosts? A league of scorned women? Something's going on for sure. It's not just a simple matter of keys. Anyone can forget his keys when he's had a few. The problem isn't leaving your keys behind, the problem is leaving your entire self behind.

As you make your way back to the bar you wonder what you'll do if you can't find your keys. You don't want to have to go through the same embarrassing rigmarole as you did a few months ago when you kicked in the door at three in the morning and less than ten minutes later the police were knocking. 'Everything all right there, sir?' You briefly explain what happened. He understands. Smiles. You ask if he'd like some coffee. He says thanks but there's no need. You walk him to the veranda, and in the light of the street lamp you spot the twitching curtains across the street.

You cross the terminus with your hands in your pockets. The two drivers who were loitering at the City Gate entrance as you walked out call out to you again. You pray that you won't be needing either of them. Not that this time you'd force your way in like a thief. After that incident you began to keep a couple of spare keys handy, one in the letterbox and one hidden under the flowerpot. You can't risk waking the neighbours again, and you don't want any police officers turning up at three in the morning to question you and feel sorry for you. That time, you regretted not having spent the night in a hotel. Even one of those cheap hotels in Msida or Pietà would have served, the kind you were put off after you went to one to meet someone to collect some items your friend Musa had sent from Amman. A collection of his poems, a couple of other books, some herbs and a box of sweets from the East. There was nothing appealing about that hotel. Tasteless furniture greeted you as you walked into a haze of cigarettes and rot. A wizened face loomed through the smoke. He seemed entirely indifferent to your presence. You asked for the Jordanian's room number. He waved you to the corner where the lift was without removing the cigarette from between his lips. The stench of rot accompanied you all the way up in the lift and all the way to the room. The Jordanian said he worked in Libya.

'Libyans will buy anything. Clothes. Perfume. Knives. Toys. They'll take whatever you've got. Sometimes I shift everything while I'm still on the ship without even having to set foot in Tripoli,' he said. 'Libyans have a lot of money, but there's nothing to buy there.'

The small-time trader seemed to know his business. He said he was looking to expand and wanted to open an office in the future. He gave the impression that he'd be happy if the sanctions against Libya were never lifted. You felt that the stench in the hotel came directly from him. He offered you a job. You could act as his agent. He'd send stuff, and you'd sell it in Tripoli or Benghazi. Or even on the ship before it raised anchor. 'Believe me, we could get rich really quickly.'

You said that wasn't your line. Thanks, anyway. His expression soured a bit. Think it over carefully. He gave you his contact details and said he's here in this hotel every couple of months. You took the books and the rest of the stuff, and before you left you asked about Musa. He didn't know him, he said, he'd never met him personally. His sister's husband was the one who knew him and that's how he'd discovered someone was going to Malta. You asked him to forward your greetings, somehow. You thanked him and hurried off without asking how long he'd be in Malta and raising the possibility of ever meeting again. As you left the hotel you were accosted by a big-boned woman in a short skirt and a cigarette dangling from her lips who stood by the front door.

'Hey!' she called out eagerly. She gave off the same smell as the hotel and the Jordanian. 'Wanna fuck?'

'Thanks, no . . .' You really didn't, neither did you relish the prospect of having to go through the same performance as before, even if it meant sleeping in a landfill. That was another time. The sanctions had forced the Libyan people into poverty but had strengthened the hand of the crazy colonel. The ambitious trader had never appeared again. Maybe he'd opened that office he wanted. You didn't do so badly either because as soon as you entered the bar the waiter smiled at you. That smile was enough to reassure you that he had the keys to your car and your house and your locker at work.

3

Nabil is my name. I was born on 5 June 1967 in a refugee camp on the south-eastern fringes of Amman. Or so I was told. Eighth among my siblings; eleventh to emerge from my mother's womb. Three of the siblings who preceded me had decided to die not long after they'd come into this world, so they lost the opportunity to assist as history was assembled and disassembled in the Middle East, that holy region from which all God's spokesmen hailed.

I was the last thing to make it out of my mother's active uterus alive, since shortly after she brought me into the world she was struck by a strange and grave illness and died. I was two. In those two years, any hope she had of one day returning to Qbebe, her village in Palestine, vanished once and for all. My siblings and our neighbours and many of our relatives told me many times that this had nothing to do with my arrival. Although I did feel there must have been some link between the two events, according to them it was my twin sister who had shattered my mother's dream and inflicted upon her the fatal wound that would eventually lead to her early death.

My mother was illiterate. Her father had bequeathed many lands and fields around Qbebe to her and her siblings. It's still a matter of conjecture whether it was her beauty, the land her father had left her or a combination of the two that had made my father lose his mind over her. Those who couldn't stand my father said that what lapped at his mind was the question of land. They said my grandfather Ibrahim, my mother's father whom I never set eyes on, was known throughout Hebron. A big well-built man out of whom, as with many fathers in that part of the world, you'd be hard put to wring a smile let alone a laugh. They said he was one of those who believed that only boys should be educated because sending your daughter to school was tantamount to harbouring a snake in your underpants, which meant he deprived my mother and her two sisters of the light of education. Apparently he didn't want three snakes in his underpants. As for his three sons, he sent them all to school and they pursued their studies until the Jews arrived and swallowed up Palestine and everyone was brought down to the same level with bundles on their heads waiting for a lorry to carry them to the opposite bank of the River Jordan, where they would be referred to as EDPs.

I heard this story from my Aunt Miriam, my father's only sister. Aunt Miriam was a wellspring of information about the past. Despite her simplifications and personal convictions, I thought of her as the most sincere of all my mad relatives, half of whom had been rendered speechless by events, while the other half were deranged. My father happened to be one of those rendered speechless. He and his wife and his siblings. As for his children, the jury's still out. Fortunately one of the heads that remained relatively sane was that of my Aunt Miriam.

I confess that I often asked her things just to pull her leg and draw her out on Halimeh, my Uncle Salameh's mysterious wife, the woman with boundless eyes who turned up out of nowhere in Qbebe and crossed the river westwards with the other tribes and settled with her husband, Salameh, my father's brother, in Souf, a refugee camp in the north of Jordan, where my father sent me every summer to spend some weeks with my cousins and get some fresh country air. And despite my close proximity to Halimeh I never managed to form a concrete impression of her. I'd never have predicted that the very same Halimeh would have turned up in Malta after she discovered that my father had possessed my being so that I could resolve the issues he had never managed to and plug the million holes he'd left behind for me, including that bottomless pit called Palestine.

'They can all go fuck themselves, honey,' Aunt Miriam told me when I mentioned what some of our relatives had said about the marriage of my father and mother. 'Your father had plenty of land, and he didn't even care. He was one of the few scholars in Qbebe. While most of the other men slept in the same room as their animals and in the morning couldn't be sure whether it was his wife or the goat they'd fucked, your father had a clean house and a Dodge truck and a licence from Allah to curse the British authorities as they'd cursed us. Just for the record, your father owned the only car in Qbebe. Not even Ibrahim, your mother's father, may Allah forgive him, had one. So much for all his land and his money. He still had to lean back on a mule. That idiot Hasan who told you this, he once asked your father whether his truck was male or female – see what sort of brain *he* had! Your father said, "Why don't we roll it on its back and see what it's got below its arse crack." He made himself the laughing stock of the entire village. Before those dirty Jews turned up your father would travel back and forth between Haifa and Jaffa and Tel Aviv, always loaded down with clothes and things that Qbebe had never seen before. Before entering the village he'd honk his horn, and half the girls would come out to gaze at him – and go weak at the knees. Your mother, may Allah forgive her, was one of those. Your father took her because she was the one he wanted; he didn't give a damn about land or fields.'

On the matter of land she told me that when my aunts and uncles, my father's siblings, had divided their father's land among themselves, they had snatched half my father's share and half of hers, too. 'Your father was barely two at the time, and when he grew up and people whispered things to him, trying to put things in his head, he paid no attention and was never covetous of his brothers' properties. But after he married your mother she banged on and on about how he should ask them for what they'd stolen. He would get angry and say, "Haven't you got enough land? You own half of Qbebe and still you expect me to get into a fight with my siblings?" Your mother, may Allah forgive her, was like a shellfish when it came to land but also pernickety. If it was supposed to be a certain way, then that's the way it should be. Fair's fair, she'd say to him, but he'd still get angry and leave and wouldn't come back for two or three days. Every time she brought this up he'd just leave. Whether she kept bringing it up because the scales of justice were tilted or because of the way people gossiped about that accursed Halimeh, Salameh's wife, I couldn't tell you.'

I don't know why I kept pushing her on that occasion. I wanted to know more about Halimeh, my uncle's wife of whom so much had been said that she'd become almost legendary. No one could tell fact from fiction any more – me included, although I'd spent many of my childhood holidays running about with her children. Eating and drinking and sleeping and shitting and waking up in her house. How could I have predicted that so many years later she'd turn up again on a small island called Malta? I myself couldn't confirm or deny whether Halimeh was a real woman or a ghost dressed up as a woman with infinitely deep black eyes, who sometimes went by the name of Halimeh and sometimes Nadia.

'How does Halimeh feature in all of this, Auntie?' I remember asking her with feigned indifference.

'How *doesn't* she feature, is what you should be asking,' she said, raising her eyebrows and screwing up her face to dredge up the memories from the wells of recollection. 'Although Halimeh married your uncle, she couldn't keep her eyes off your father. Everyone knew,' she said in a voice rendered smooth by the friction of countless retellings. 'Something was going on in secret between them, that's for sure. Salameh, that idiot, never twigged, quite the opposite. "Jusef, give Halimeh a lift. Jusef, pick Halimeh up." Who knows, maybe he was unwittingly sending him to fuck her? Or maybe she was the one who ordered him to ask his brother to take her with him down to Hebron. Surely they will have stopped under a tree somewhere? Who would see them except for Allah, who's had his fill of such goings-on? Halimeh was a beautiful woman, petite and hot as a *kenur* stove. I could swear that she never had to kindle a single rotten twig in her home during the winter, and in the middle of January, when the cold could split a tree down the middle and kill half the animals in Qbebe, you never felt the chill in her house and she didn't lose a single chicken. May Allah forgive me, may the devil take me, but it's no word of a lie when I say that every time your father gave her a lift or brought her back from somewhere she always had one of her infants in tow. Anyway, your mother, may Allah forgive her, could never stomach that strange woman. She hated her until she died. With good reason, no? She was always sitting pretty next to your father while your mother only got to ride with her husband in the only car in the village once in a blue moon.'

'Where was Halimeh from?' I asked, filled with a curiosity I'd never before felt.

'Eh, who knows?' she said, even more puzzled than I. 'Halimeh was an outsider. No one knows where she came from. There weren't many women who weren't from Qbebe. A handful of other women would visit during Eid with their relatives, and they'd be invited to dinner during Ramadan. But we never saw any of Halimeh's siblings or a father or any other relatives. She was always alone.'

'What do you mean? Did she just drop out of the sky?'

'How should I know, son?' she said absently. 'All I know for sure is that Salameh once accompanied your father on a trip carrying wheat to Nablus. They're city people, the Nablusi; they never got their hands dirty with earth, but would buy the entire wheat harvest to make their sweets. When it came to sweets they were the world's greatest experts. Their sweets, as you know, are talked about to this day; they say that even the piss-pot queen of the British, may Allah give them all the misery they've inflicted upon us, liked their sweets.'

'And what then, Auntie, what happened after they went to Nablus?' I asked, to try to pull her off this new branch of the story she'd climbed upon, or she'd go on about the goodness of those sugary Nablusi sweets for two hours.

'Well,' she continued, annoyed at the interruption, 'they came back after two days, and Halimeh was with them. A shapely woman, tall and sturdy with a pair of tits that did their best to burst out of her clothes. Black eyes as wide and as deep and dark as the ocean. I thought the embroidery on her dress resembled the kind of needlework they make up north, in Safad and Senin and places around there. I said to myself, have those devils been that far? Anyway, the real devil here is your father, because Salameh couldn't wipe his own backside after taking a shit. Halimeh had just a single trunk and a mattress and two cushions, the kind you get from the market, if you know what I mean. It had the air of a marriage arranged in a hurry. Which girl would walk out of her father's house with junk like that? Not even if he were the poorest man in this accursed Palestine. Ask me how your mother left her father's house or how I left with that sack of filth who's lying in there. Three overflowing carts; six blankets and a dozen cushions, half of them quilted and the other half embroidered with every pattern and colour imaginable, and with all the kitchen utensils I'd ever need. Your uncles, even though they'd stolen half my share of our father's legacy, set me up with everything I needed, as befits a girl from Qbebe. What do you think Saleh had when he took me away? A face smeared with shit, is what he had. He didn't even have a belt on him. And he was wearing everything he owned. Your uncle Abdel-Rahman, may Allah forgive him, was the eldest of our brothers and had taken our father's place. He said our family bought men, and Saleh, who was a labourer on our land, was a man who deserved to be bought. Go and tell him how much of a man he really was, how he went limp after barely a couple of months! Saleh lived his entire life in fear of your Uncle Abdel-Rahman. He shat himself every time he heard his voice, and anyone who's scared of his wife's brother won't ever scare the wife, and if he can't scare the wife he won't even scare a mouse and will never manage to dominate her. Huh, me and my bad luck; what a waste of a life. Everyone's in mourning for Palestine, and me, I mourn the cold sheets on which that sack of straw lies snoring. I've spent my whole life feeling sorry for this body of mine becoming arid, the flesh scored with desire like the marks of a disease.'

'Poor Saleh,' I said to myself. 'Everyone's got it in for him.' Aunt Miriam had broadcast to all and sundry. Everyone knew how much of a clown and a joker she was, but when she got started on this particular subject she wasn't joking. At least that's what I felt; that's why I didn't have the guts to push her any further on the subject of Halimeh.

'Why didn't they set me up with one of our own clan?' she muttered sadly, although that question should have been answered forty years ago. 'They are real mules. The earth and their wives' sheets are all the same to them. They can plough day and night and their ploughs never wear out. I could see it in that contented glint their wives had in their eyes every morning by the water fountain, your mother, may Allah forgive her, foremost among them. She had a lot of hands to carry the water for her and she could've sat comfortably at home if she'd wanted, but she came every morning just so we could see that glint in her eye, while this poor aunt of yours was getting her water and being eaten up by jealousy and anger and a sense of doom.

'But anyway, everyone's doomed now because after we left Palestine we never caught that glint in anyone's eye any more. My curse and Halimeh's ruined us all. To cut a long story short, when we saw Halimeh climb down off your father's truck, we all thought that Jusef had gone and done one of his deeds. No one thought for a minute that she was Salameh's. Abdel-Rahman went mad; he had a fit. How could one of his brothers get married behind his back? And to a woman like this. A woman who came from who knew where. He swore he'd tear them both to pieces. "Allah will burn you. He'll burn your father and mother in their graves. You get married behind my back, and I find out like this?" Abdel-Rahman, may Allah forgive him, took it badly. He was a difficult man. You might remember him, and you might remember how hard he was on the outside, whereas on the inside he was nothing but a bale of straw. That day he came back from the fields fuming worse than a steam engine. Someone had whispered things in his ear. "Jusef! Salameh!" he bellowed like a bull. "Which one of you has gone and got married?" As soon as Salameh opened his mouth to say "Me" he hit him full in the face – you remember what hands he had, may Allah forgive him. Poor Salameh lost his left eye; he had to spend the rest of his life with one eye. See what Halimeh brought with her! Your mother was right to hate her, may Allah forgive her. And did he raise his hand to his older brother or raise his voice? No. The blood streamed out of his eye and his nose, and he just stared like a statue, like this was someone else's fight he was watching. A family gone insane, the elders first, then the younger ones. So that was the first of the curses that Halimeh brought down on us. Abdel-Rahman, once his rage died down and he came to his senses, having discovered that Salameh had lost an eye, started banging his head against the wall. When we saw the blood we were scared to death and started screaming until more men gathered and held him down, by which time he'd spattered blood all over the courtyard. A couple of weeks later he got the shakes, and they stayed on him until the end, just the way you remember him. Where she came from and how, no one knows. They kept it a secret between themselves, she, Salameh and your father, three being the accursed number and all. It's not like we didn't try to find out. They wore themselves out asking and nosing about in the villages and towns of Hebron, and even in Ramallah and Jenin and Jerusalem and Nablus itself, trying to find some trace or some news of her, but it all came to nothing. That whore either lied about her name and surname, or maybe it was as they said and she'd climbed out of the well of Sidna al-Fadl and charmed them with her evil spell.'

'How d'you mean she climbed out of the well of Sidna al-Fadl? I thought you didn't believe in that kind of nonsense,' I teased – with the intention extracting as much information as I could about Halimeh, to whose house my father insisted on sending me during the summer holidays.

'What do I know, son?' she said, confused. 'There must be some truth in it, or how do you explain that whenever the subject was broached in front of your supposedly silent father, the shakes would come over him just like they'd come over Abdel-Rahman and the devils would start dancing before his eyes? Your mother banged on about it every day until the Jews came and took everything, from the land she'd inherited from Ibrahim, her baron of a father, to the land she wanted your father to demand from his siblings. They took everything the way they found it, all set up and ready, the way Saleh, that sack lying in there, took me. Not a shot was fired in all of Qbebe. The Arab Armed Forces had given us strict commands to step aside and not interfere. According to them the uprising that had exploded in various parts of Palestine in 1947 was more of a hindrance than a help, because wars, they said, were won by organized armies with the capacity to lay plans and make tictics.'

'You mean tactics, Auntie,' I corrected her with a smile.

'Right, whatever . . . And since we didn't understand these tictics the way they did, we listened and stepped aside so we wouldn't spoil their tictic for them, and four days turned into forty years, and then there was the year in which you were born and the rest of Palestine was swallowed up. We never thought that their tictic amounted to cannon dating back to Jamal Pasha and rifles that fired backwards instead of forward. You could say the Arab armies gave Palestine away to the Jews, may Allah destroy them as they've destroyed us, all nice and ready the way Abdel-Rahman gave me away to that limp rag in there.'

Before I came to Malta, I had heard the story of Halimeh from many quarters, some of them poles apart and mired in mutual hatred, but they all agreed that her origins were a mystery. There was only one man who couldn't bear to listen to a word said against her – one of the few who knew the true story. That man was my father. The same father who died in the first chapter of this narrative. He never said a word, and the whole story remained shrouded in mystery until what happened happened and it was too late for me to understand why he sent me to visit her every summer.

Ostensibly it was to visit her children not her, and sometimes she prepared a meal for me and sat across from me and studied me with those wide eyes the like and size of which I never saw again until she turned up in Malta in the shape of a girl from Żabbar. I wonder if she saw my father in me? What were those looks and that special treatment all about? I never understood why she doted on me more than on her own children. No mother would ever do that. No mother in her right mind at any rate. But I swear that during those trips Halimeh spoiled me more than she did her children, and every morning would sit me on her lap and comb my hair with a boundless, if unjustifiable, love and tenderness, and sometimes as she combed she would sing a strange melancholy air of which I understood not a single word. I could take a binding oath that during those summer trips I was the apple of her eye, and you'd have to see for yourself just how large those eyes of hers were to understand what a rare thing it is to be the apple of such an eye. In spite of their size and the access I was inexplicably granted to them, I never understood what they wanted from me. Back then I knew nothing of the language of eyes. The whole time I thought of ways to get away from her and run around with her children, given that Musa, the imp of my childhood, wasn't around. I could never understand or explain that excess of love. Halimeh couldn't be my mother. We'd buried my mother. She couldn't have been taking advantage of me in my tender years either. I felt that she was sincere, but, rather than soften my heart, that sincerity scared me off. I saw no reason for that love, shrouded as it was in a fog of stories and fables from the past, some of them more than a thousand years old and which, somehow or other, had woven themselves around her again.

She yelled incessantly at her own children and spoke to me with kindness and delicacy. I'm sure that Halimeh's story could have been painted somewhere in her eyes, and, although I had unrestricted access to them, fear stopped me from leaning in, and so I missed my first real opportunity to learn something about the mysterious world of women. Twenty-five years later I missed my second chance before the eyes of the woman from Żabbar. It seems that love continued to scare me. Perhaps Halimeh had waited five years for my father to propose to her, and when he proposed nothing she married his brother. Isn't that what most women do? After a hurdle in a relationship they go off with the one who is closest to you. Usually your friend, the one you thought had a good grasp of moral boundaries. Was Halimeh one of those women who are willing to hurt themselves in order to hurt you? Did she decide to marry Uncle Salameh to torture my father, who then fought back by sending me to her every summer? Is it possible that I'd become a ball to be kicked around in the game of failed love, the way I had become a card in the game of the heavenly masters? What life has taught me, albeit too late, is that women who love you heart and soul are just as able to hate you heart and soul. I've also learned that you should never take a woman's love lightly, that a woman will treat everything lightly except her heart. Her emotional compass swings towards the man she loves, even if that man is under the curse and misery of the Middle East. A woman's curse falls on precisely the man who made his promise but then got cold feet or gave way before the temptation of another woman who owns land and fields. Or, like me, fell into the trap of an illusory freedom. I didn't succumb to a flash of lightning, not from another woman and not from money. It was Nadia herself who led me to the crossroads. Either you marry me or I leave. As if love couldn't survive outside the walls of marriage. And that's what she did. She left. Without so much as a backwards glance, as though she were afraid of being turned into pillar of salt.

Caught up worming my way through life, I forgot to marry her. I forgot she was a woman with specific biological needs. I forgot there are a thousand things barking at her from the inside, from the edges of a mysterious maternity. The uterus begins to send out messages and every month reminds her of her biological functions. Reminds her of creation. Of the continuation of the race. I didn't realize that woman is like the earth and the soil. Like the sun and seeds and life itself. They're all female. There's no way you could think of them as having a patriarchal etymology, since even language itself is a female invention. Language doesn't lie the way we lie, the way our prophets lie – prophets who all happened to be men, since the woman who creates them and feeds them the essence of her body and wipes the shit from their backsides can't be trusted to carry God's messages. Lest she drops them along the way. Or is accosted by Satan holding up the forbidden fruit to trick her.

So I used to give her the slip. Mainly because I wanted to be on my own. Cheating on her her with my books or just staring at nothing, like my father did. That was how I found peace, it seems; when I was at one with myself and spent my time chewing over the memory of the past. I got so used to inhabiting the past that I began to think of the suns that hadn't yet risen as already gone. It could be some kind of rare form of depression or some psychological disorder, since it's not normal to see the future as past.

Maybe it's a very serious illness. But there's no way I'm going to a psychiatrist. It's not that I don't believe that psychiatry can help. It's more that I'm afraid I'd be told that I'm right, that the future's much uglier than the past and that we, the human race, have regressed in leaps and bounds, that our world is going from bad to worse, both in terms of the environment in which we live and in terms of the figures relating to poverty and sickness and hunger and death that are completely unnecessary except to line the pockets of a few fat cats. I'm afraid he'll have me lie on his couch and then say that 'you Arabs' are mere chickens in the sultan's coop, waiting for the palace servants to chuck some chicken feed and leftovers in your general direction. And if the servants decide not to chuck anything your way, you'll eat your own shit instead, happy as long as you're in your coop and have the sultan's blessing. As a psychiatrist of a certain calibre and level of education, as someone who moves among certain classes of people who can afford him, he wouldn't use the word shit and would use filth instead, but I can tell that filth in this context means shit. I'm afraid he'll say that 'we' in the West are also chickens, but we're different. We have different feathers. You're in the sultan's coop, and we're in the devil's den. It's true we have elected democratic governments, but no one whores as much as they do, and some of them, as you well know, have stained their hands with a great deal of blood in our name. And a lot of this blood happens to be yours. 'Whose?' I was about to ask as I lay there on his couch. 'The chickens, my friend, the chickens,' he was about to answer. 'You and I and millions of pacifist citizens whose taxes go towards the human abattoirs of Baghdad and Jenin and Kandahar.' I'm scared lest this astute psychiatrist should convince me that I'm really a chicken, especially because I know I'll come out of there with my feathers plucked, perhaps even skinned and gutted.

Someone in a situation like mine has no need to visit doctors and psychiatrists, because it would be a waste of money and because I got this discourse for free from Simon De Brincat, on the bastions of Valletta, where we talked until dawn. But Simon would continue, 'In order to escape the tyrant's coop, you first have to escape the American's fist.'

'How?'

'They have to stop propping up your mummified corpses and vampires.'

That was the sort of clarity you got from Simon. Clever and well read, he knew all about life's problems. To him, the world seemed like a small screen. I found his knowledge of Palestine embarrassing, frightening sometimes. Once he mentioned al-Fadl and his mysterious well. My blood ran cold. I immediately recalled Halimeh and Nadia and their big eyes, their love that I'd refused without trying to understand it.

'What do you know about Fadl and his well?' I shot back, stunned. How could he have heard about such a little detail buried under so many layers of time? 'What do you know about Fadl?' I begged him, my curiosity gnawing at me that evening, that same uncharacteristic curiosity

I always felt whenever Halimeh was mentioned. He said he'd read that al-Fadl was a religious man who lived in ancient times and had a secret lover whom he got pregnant, but instead of shouldering responsibility for his actions he jumped into a well and for some reason or other people made him a martyr. Just then I was close to asking him, 'And what about Halimeh, what became of her?' I was like a foolish child who wasn't happy with the way the story ended. His gentle smile brought me back from the brink of that banal bit of foolishness.

'And what happened to the woman who was his lover?' I asked, feigning indifference, after I'd managed to control the thoughts that had just begun to fizz in my head. It's true that Simon read everything he laid eyes on, but who would've thought he'd manage to discover the story of that lustful hermit and the guilty woman who kept haunting my ancestors and relatives and now, possibly, me? He said that the people of the village were divided: some wanted to stone her to death and some wanted to burn her alive, so she decided to spare them the trouble of debating her fate and jumped after her priest into the well. He became a saint while she remained a whore.

I felt caught up in a plot peopled with the ghosts and spirits of victimized women, one called Halimeh, the other Nadia, with Simon as their spokesman.

'Nothing's changed since then, my friend,' he continued. 'Women are still our victims. The emancipation we granted them recently is a poisoned chalice. Everything was planned and thought out by us, with one goal in mind, which was to gain better access to what's between their legs. When you observe women today you feel pity, because she's living in conditions worse than when human trafficking was the order of the day. At least human trafficking used to be the norm; a woman who was sold at the market ended up a slave in a household where she might or might not be mistreated, whereas a woman today is still sold at the market as a slave to a thousand different things we've thought up for her ourselves. In fact, we've done nothing but liberate her body in order to dominate it. Trafficking all over again. Prostitution is a huge industry that generates money and votes. Entire countries prostitute themselves – Malta, for example. Maybe it won't be long before we hear about a new post of minister for prostitution and public whoring, because that's all that's lacking in some governments and parties, a department for lies and whoring. Who said slavery is a thing of the past? Who said piracy's gone from Malta? Who said we aren't pimping our women in this fortress of Catholic hypocrisy? A fortress built out of double-dealing and backstabbing and lies, and that includes the clergy, who shed their skins faster than lizards do. When a society pretends not to see or hear or smell, what's left of our Christian façade? How much longer can we keep applying make-up?'

We're all victims. Victims of ourselves. Victims of the lies we make up and circulate and end up believing as if they were the unvarnished truth.

I trust you'll understand why I didn't want to visit psychiatrists and doctors trained in feather plucking. Without wanting to, I now feel compelled to follow in Simon's pessimistic footsteps, even though I never wanted to look at the world through his spectacles. I had my own. But then, when you realize that everything he predicted is being fashioned into the reality before your eyes, you have no choice but to wear his spectacles over your own, and, contrary to what you expected, things don't appear out of focus but become clearer.

I'm not suggesting that I inherited all the wisdom of Simon De Brincat, but through his lens I began to see things that I couldn't see before. I don't know what kinds of books Simon read that made him come across Sidna al-Fadl, or what contacts he had with the spectres of the past. All I know for sure is that Simon, having burst into my life without warning, made his exit in the same way, without warning.

That's what men do, it seems. They leave after they've made a difference. As if their departure is the difference they make. The hole they leave behind and which no one else can fill. How many holes do we have in our lives? Simon and Nadia had stormed into my life and stormed out of it. Had they been in it together, at least as far as their decisive exits from my life went? Simon and Nadia taught me that the person in front of you, with whom you interact every day and whom you think you know as you know yourself, is the one who is best placed to betray and wound you. I have no proof that Simon and Nadia were in this together. Nor do I have any proof that my mind isn't just wittering on and whether what I'm saying, every single thing, is true or not. Could it be that I imagined it all? Did I just make up Simon and Nadia and Halimeh and let them disappear on purpose to give myself a way of explaining my own emptiness? If I'm the one who created Simon and Nadia out of the letters and consonants on the keyboard in front of me right now, what about bin Laden and Bush and Blair and Berlusconi and Saddam Hussein and Sharon and Arafat, who fit Simon's prophecies so well, did I make them up, too? And what about the dead and the mutilated and the wounded, in their hundreds of thousands, all in the name of jihad on the one hand and the War on Terror on the other, did I make those up as well? I ask you to withhold your verdict on me, at least for the time being; find out a little more, and if it turns out that there's nothing to what I've been saying, throw me into a psychiatric hospital. People who have symptoms like mine are a real danger to society, especially if that society happens to be the kind that hides its head in the sand.

4

Malta again. An enchanting siren rising from a sea of stories of the past and basking in the warm Mediterranean sun. Malta, bride of the infinite blue. A wild siren with big eyes from Żabbar. Get too close to her and she'll rip your heart out; turn your back on her and memory will claw at you. Sometimes the meaning of words lies not in what we say but in what we omit. We use words to emphasize what we won't or can't allow our tongue to express. This was hardly some glittering discovery in the pitch-black of night. For some time you had seen the invisible half of the question in her eyes, and then again for a while now Nadia had become an open book to you. Ever since she went square. Ever since she began to talk about homes and furniture and kitchen tiles.

Malta: a rocking motion that dizzies the head. An eternal bride bathing before the gaze of the unknown. 'What are you going to do?' now that love is being conditioned and encumbered and surrounded by the yapping dogs of wedlock. The five-year probation period was up, and love's contract wouldn't be renewed until you signed a new one that gave you permission to be locked in a gilded cage.

Why are women so fond of gilded cages? Why couldn't Nadia exist outside the boundaries of straight lines and squares? You didn't want to enter any social cages, however luxurious they might be. They're unbearable, those chains that bind. You didn't escape from a Jordanian dusk to lock yourself up in a Maltese dusk. 'I don't want to dilute myself in a woman; neither do I want to see a woman diluted in me.'

'Can't say I see any chains here or any dilution,' Adnan said after you brought him news of your break-up with Nadia. He scratched his scalp through what little hair he had left on his head. 'You know, life's far less complex than you make out. A partner like that – and you're just going to let her go because of these feeble obsessions of yours? Marriage crowns love, it's not the jail you make it out to be.'

Adnan wouldn't accept or even understand your doubts. Adnan had left Amman for very different reasons from yours. You're the only fugitive here, probably a fugitive for nothing. After all, when we escape we often carry the thing we're running from with us. These doubts you had, they weren't about her or about marriage as a 'contemptible' institution, as you liked to say. The doubts you had were about yourself.

'I can think of a lot of marriages without crowns or even heads,' you grumbled about his relationship with Pauline, which he thought you didn't know about since he'd never talked to you about it. 'Don't tell me there's nothing frightening about being forced to sign a few papers in order to remain entitled to love. Have you ever exchanged love for a signature?'

He scratched his head some more.

'Quite apart from that, aren't you put off by a woman who undresses before you without shame? Doesn't it bother you that she'll be taking a piss while you're shaving and talking to you about that evening's dinner as she's wiping between her legs?'

'What made you think it would be like that with Nadia?'

'It's like that already. Nadia's like a lot of other women in this world. She'll acquire something in order to kill it. Anything that's forced to exist between straight lines becomes soulless and dead.'

'Nabil, Nadia isn't some character you read about in one of your dirty books. Nadia's a normal girl who wants what is normal and natural. What is accessible to every woman in the world. Have you forgotten how you used to tell me that Nadia's beauty lay in her ordinariness? An ordinariness suffused with intelligence, as you used to put it. Why did you want to deny her those ordinary things which you liked so much in her? Is it possible that none of your dirty books contained a love story that culminated in marriage? Don't you know that every girl in the world is born with the dream of some day putting on the white veil and finding her place in society and establishing a family? If my mother or yours hadn't done that, we wouldn't be here to talk about it.'

'So what if we're here? What does that mean? Much good it's doing us! Where's the privilege in being forced into a life and forced out of it and having no choice about the arrival or the departure?'

'You're a right bundle of laughs. Simon must've really got to you. It's a wonder the poor woman stuck with you for as long as she did.'

'You're pretty well informed. Has she spoken to you then?'

'Yes.'

You try to explain that you don't want to become another entry in Nadia's list of acquisitions, nor do you want her to become one in yours.

'I have nothing, that's why I have everything.'

'Marriage isn't about acquiring and possessing. But since you prefer to use the language of business, the way I understand marriage is that it's a company, a merger of reciprocal interests. I don't mean that's all there is to marriage, especially if there's also love and respect.'

You weren't convinced. Adnan, you thought, was in no position to deliver a sermon about the morality of marriage, especially since you knew all about the skeletons in his closet. The sermon might have been acceptable from someone else, but not from a stag like Adnan.

'Since you're such an advocate for marriage, why are you sleeping with a married woman? Do you think your dick's the precious stone in the crown of this married couple?'

He was suddenly irritated. 'Pauline's a completely different matter,' he said drily, as though he didn't want to become the subject of discussion. 'My relationship with Pauline's more complex than yours. No jails, no handcuffs, none of this bizarre sophistry. I'd marry her tomorrow if I could. I swear it. I'm not like you. I don't hide behind empty illusions that only exist in your head and the books that are leading you astray.'

You remain unconvinced. Adnan could give the impression that he was a wolf when he meant to dress up as a lamb. Conversely, he could look like a lamb when he meant to be a wolf. So no one took him entirely seriously. He was a consummate liar, but a transparent one. It wasn't his lies that bothered you, because for the most part they were the kind usually referred to as white lies, at least until you started to believe him.

In spite of his lies and exaggerations, however, Adnan was always surrounded by people. A veritable social magnet. The opposite to you, in fact. He could make as many friends during one of those parties that he and Dorita liked to organize as you could in a year. You attack him once more.

'And would you continue to two-time her after you married?' you suddenly ask, now that you're on the subject of morality.

'Two-time who? What're you on about?' he stammered, annoyed.

'The fruit from the other tree's always sweeter,' you cunningly reply. 'Did you think I didn't know that you sleep with Dorita as well? Lies, we're all a bunch of liars. Me and you and Dorita and Nadia and Pauline and all the others. What happened to the platonic love that's missing from my dirty books? Forbidden fruit is always tantalizing, isn't it?'

'Malta. There's no keeping the lid on anything here.'

'Malta's like a refugee camp in that Hashemite capital of yours. Everyone gets to know the minute you've eaten a sardine. If they don't see you eating it, they'll see you when you're shitting it out, and if they don't see either of those things they'll smell it on you just the same. Everyone's a liar, but we men especially so. We declare that we're after an intelligent woman, but deep down we harbour a thousand impulses that mean we really only want her to be a body. An empty shell of a building to be divvied up according to our needs. To allow us to design corridors and staircases. And secret rooms where we think we can hide our filth. But the truth is that everybody knows it all, even before we've picked up the first bag of filth. It's only our self-importance that makes us forget sometimes that filth stinks.'

'Simon's really screwing with your head! Maybe it's true that I'm as corrupt as you say. Dorita's an old colleague I can't get rid of – or won't. Dorita brings me some comfort when I'm not with Pauline. So, let's say I'm a man-whore, why would that have anything to do with your turning Nadia into a victim? You're forcing her to throw her flesh into the arms of the first man who smiles at her.' And the moment he mentions her flesh and another man you have the stabbing sensation of a lance in your side. Now you know how Christ must have felt. That was the one thing you hadn't thought about. You imagined that Nadia would depart from your life, disappear, go somewhere far away and you'd never see her again. Get married. Wear her white veil and rings studded with precious stones to pose and have her picture taken as the light glanced off her big eyes. You'd thought of her slicing a big white cake, three metres high, surrounded by a crowd of applauding Judases. You'd thought of all this but never imagined her in the arms of another man. It never entered your mind that that body you loved so much, that you knew so well, that you adored, could hand over its secret keys to someone else.

Your male narcissism nearly made you rush to a phone to call her and say, with your tears reaching her before your voice did, 'Come back, and I'll marry you. Don't throw yourself into the arms of another man!' You came close to accepting it all, to go and sit in that corner she wanted you in, to stop that scene from unfolding. Even in your own susceptible mind. What you didn't know, however, was that the scene had already been played out and that next time it would actually happen outside your own front door. What message did Nadia want to send? You try to understand. Why did she bring this young man, the one she'd started to see a few weeks after your break-up, and start to kiss him passionately just across the street from your place? Your beloved Nadia – what had happened to that fiery mind whose maturity sometimes made you blush? Why did she do that? Why did she choose to write the final page of your story in these strange characters that only a wounded woman could decipher?

You make your excuses to Adnan and leave his place. After a long, aimless walk, your legs lead you to City Gate. You always end up there, knowing that Simon will turn up sooner or later. He just pops up, somehow. As if you two had an appointment that you'd never agreed on explicitly. His easy smile greets you. He taps you on the shoulder, and you walk towards the fountain with those three strange heads that greet you as you walk into the city through St George's Gate. Simon seemed to you to be a genuine part of the city. One of its hundreds of hidden faces. The other day he said that prophecies bathed in blood became truths. In other words, facts and realities are newly baptized in blood. A lot of blood. There's no new truth without blood, and there's no blood without truth, and truth, as you already know, can be diminished and stretched; it can always be extended at the whim of the powers that be.

If truth is bathed in blood, then blood is the worst of the godfathers at its baptism. Why did you need to see a lot of blood before you could believe that a new reality was being drawn up in the Middle East? This filthy East that seems to be a cursed magnet for invaders worldwide, from Alexander the Great to Bush Junior, the most recent crusader to the Holy Oil Wells.

You had to see the rivers of Mesopotamia flowing with blood to believe that out of all the prophets of heaven, there was one who really told the truth: Simon De Brincat. The prophet from the city shunned by his own people had foretold the future of your beloved Middle East during that hour after midnight, rendered humid and opaque by the cries of Iraqi victims who had no idea what awaited them.

Where had Simon come from? Was it Adnan who had introduced you at that party that would end in a fight? 'Dogs! Filth! Judases!' You had to calm him down and lead him away from Dorita's party after an argument with one of her guests whom you later learned was gay. She felt comfortable around gay men. Perhaps because a lot of them were more sincere than other men, at least with themselves. Adnan was definitely not gay. You'd sometimes seen Simon in the university canteen hovering on the fringes of this crowd, but you'd never spoken to him. The night of the party he was boiling over with anger.

'Everyone's free to do what they want with their arse, mate,' you said, standing outside, once you'd learned what the reason for the fight was. Dorita didn't think twice. She just kicked him out of her house.

'Everyone's free, but only up to the point where my dick begins. Didn't you see how that guy was coming on?' he said angrily. 'You can throw up all you want, just don't throw up on me.'

Simon the Radical became your somewhat ironic name for him as a nod to his reactionary views. He'd been kicked out of the party and into your life. Made his way into your calendar and immediately turned out to be a perfect fit, but why was that?

So you and Simon the Radical began to meet regularly. Almost every day. He always popped out of some corner of the city. Cut across your path with a triumphant smile the way you cut across the path of some dying animal in a narrow alleyway. He'd tap on your shoulder and you'd walk towards the fountain with those disgusting heads.

That particular night Simon was spooked. A strange fear had come over him. He said he was disgusted at the way George W. Bush had won the presidency after that muddle over votes. The words he spoke were black as pitch. He said the world was approaching another disaster and the majority of the Arabs might as well start digging graves. That acidic certainty really got to you. You still hadn't begun to understand him enough to believe in what he said. When you replied that you hoped his fears were baseless, he flashed with irritation. He started to stammer. 'When are you people going to start seeing beyond the tips of your long noses?'

'I see no difference between Bush and Gore. It's the same pig; two faces of the same monster.'

'True, it's one imperialistic face, but for one of them the skulduggery is economic, while for the other it's military. In case you didn't know, Bush was pushed to the top by a junta baying for blood.'

That night he mentioned Leo Strauss and neo-conservatism and went on about a number of blood-soaked theories. You remember what he said. Fathers of a new disaster. A new order. Creative chaos. Absolute truth and the need to remove a number of people from the world.

'Simon, don't you start . . .'

'I'm telling you the new Mughals are fast approaching and they're powerful, very powerful. When ideas formed in the jungle get into the heads of influential people with the power and the will, people like you might as well start preparing your coffins.'

'And why us?'

'Because the coming battle will be about the resources you're sitting on.'

'You think Europe will let them do what you say they're about to do?'

'Ha! What is Europe? A parastatal whore. A whore who'll fuck anyone without letting on she's cheating. Don't you see how we're all running after Europe so we can have a chance to fuck around a bit? Just look at our beaches. You'll see how wide their legs are spread, especially for foreigners. They'd better take a good look at the shit they leave behind wherever they go. It's no wonder they keep finding dark skeletons in their cupboards. Don't they know that victims come back for their killers?'

'So what are Paul Wolfowitz and his coterie after?'

'They want nothing – except your balls removed.'

And here you are at the tail end of those bloody years. Half drunk. And not far from that same disgusting fountain. But you know that Simon won't turn up out of nowhere today, because Simon decided to protest in a different way.

You walk on alone in the wind and rain and the yellow light from the street lamps. Like a dog cast out by its owner. The wind in Malta can taste salty and delicious. You hurry on to get away from a thousand things that are beating you up from the inside. When you reach the Phoenicia Hotel a car passes by at speed and soaks you with water from the puddles in the road. Someone who definitely couldn't give a fuck about you. Nothing to philosophize about there. You walk faster, trying not to replay Simon's precise analysis, which has now become a reality, baptized in a people's blood. Your people.

So who's supposed to feel pity for whom? What Simon said has come true, down to the last detail. It came true so precisely that in a desperate moment you wondered whether he'd had it all planned. You didn't swallow that one because you remember how he called you shortly after every television station around the world had broadcast the footage of the American soldier wrapping the US flag around the face of the statue of Saddam Hussein in Baghdad's Paradise Square, its thirteen red-and-white stripes and fifty stars twinkling in the corner. One state for every star. The invisible fifty-first was the state of Israel. His voice sounded feeble and passionate in its impotent rage. Other voices and noise could be heard in the background. He seemed to be calling from a phone box in the street. 'Where are the walls of Baghdad on which the new Mughals will be crucified?' he shouted. 'Guards of the Abbasid capital, good grief! Dogs, filth, Judases . . .' and he burst into tears before slamming the phone down, leaving you tongue-tied, immobile between a phone receiver, cold as ice, and the image of a victorious soldier raising Donald Rumsfeld's flag over the bent shoulders of the Arab capital that had bequeathed the first writing system to the world.

5

There's a two-year interval between each of my siblings. My mother, who remained illiterate because her father believed that that educating a daughter is like keeping snakes in one's underpants, somehow managed to maintain the two-year gap. There's a 22-year gap between myself and Muhammad, my eldest brother who stopped growing up when Palestine beckoned to him. There are ten gaps in that 22-year interval. Each gap represents a boy or a girl. Three of them chose to die before they had to witness the history of the Middle East being torn apart before their eyes.

Every one of us is two years older or younger than the next sibling. When there's no next sibling, there's something else. My eldest brother, for example, was born two years after my mother's marriage – that is, he's two years younger than her wedding and two years older than Omaymah, my eldest sister. I'm two years younger than my little sister Sumayyah, who isn't really younger than me but since she was younger than the next one up she was always referred to as 'the little one'. Since I was the last bud, destiny didn't wish to have me dangle over a chasm, two years younger than Sumayyah and two years older than my mother's untimely death.

I have spent a lot of my life trying to understand how my mother, despite all the big events and the rumblings in the region, managed to maintain that perfect interval, but I have never managed to loosen the nuts and bolts of her impeccable mathematics. Once, I decided to ask my father, since he was the other half of the recipe that had made us. 'May God take you! You and your siblings and your father,' he said. That was before he fell into his stony silence. At the time, it was his stock answer to practically every question anyone asked him. After some time I got to know that the answer wasn't exclusive to our household. It was said in every house in Jordan. A whole generation of people who couldn't offer an explanation, couldn't look at their children and tell them what had happened. They themselves had no clue what had happened. Later, I discovered that this was one of the symptoms brought about by my twin sister.

Although my twin sister didn't come out of my mother's belly the way I had, she bore an uncanny resemblance to me. Looking at me you were immediately reminded of her. She was brought up among us. She suckled at my mother's withered breast. She grew up with us, but, like all the other girls, she grew up too fast. While I remained an irrelevant little runt, she suddenly exploded and became notorious, always the subject of gossip, both in Amman and in other capitals. She even appeared on television, in books and in the news.

She was born on the same day as me, 5 June 1967. While my mother was pushing me out into the world, Israel's little army was pushing back three major Arab armies in one of the most humiliating defeats in the history of warfare. At precisely the hour, the minute, the second that I drew my first breath to fill my fragile lungs and burst into tears, millions of Arab women burst into tears with me.

For some strange reason they called me Nabil, which means noble. They called my sister, that humiliating defeat, Naksa. In Arabic that means destruction. Fall. Collapse. Disaster. In Hebrew they refer to it as Milhemet Sheshet HaYamim, the Six-Day War. A disastrous event. It took six days because back then the Israeli tanks and war machines needed time to take over that enormous tract of land. Had technology allowed them to do it faster, it might have come to be called the One-Day War or the Half-Day War. Also known as Harb Huzajran, the June War, in the space of just six days Israeli troops took the Sinai Peninsula and the Gaza Strip from Egypt, the West Bank, including Jerusalem, from Jordan and the Hills of Galilee from Syria. Only pressure from the rest of the world kept them from also taking Cairo, Damascus and Amman.

During those six days, the Arab Longnoses were buried in shit. They're buried in shit to this day. Our history teacher once said that the Germans and the Japanese, who'd come out of the Second World War broken and defeated, got back on their feet and became two of the most advanced nations in the world within twenty years, and in times of peace doubled the harvest they had failed to reap through warfare. Our history teacher failed to tell us what those two nations, whose citizens one couldn't help feeling some respect for, had that we didn't have. It can't have been resources – we had all the filthy oil. Was it geography? Skies? Rats? Dogs? Beauty? Intelligence? Or some secret mathematics? Just then I recalled the words of my ancestors: 'Everyone learns out of their own pocket.' Had I managed to learn anything, perhaps? Since I belong to this accursed race, how could I have learned anything? I wouldn't be surprised if, once I'm done with this narrative, I'll just tear it all to pieces. More likely, delete everything from my computer. I've nothing to tear except myself, as I look upon the disaster that I've brought about in the world. If this narrative should end up in someone's hands in the shape of a book, it will mean my desire to own my story – unsolicited, unbalanced and riddled with hackneyed convictions as it is – got the better of me. This writing is the prejudiced testament of a man who was born under the tent of an agency of the So-Called United Nations, a stone's throw from his homeland. And then he grew up, and Palestine just stayed there, across the way, like a magic doll in a shop window guarded by soldiers on horseback. And then, to make matters worse, Malta came to resemble it.

It's very likely that ideas never measure up to actual geography. Some geographies only exist in the mind. Like those four hundred untouched virgins. If Palestine is a fable and Malta is an idea, where does that leave me?

My father was unpredictable even in his silence. It's only recently that I've begun to understand him. What did he leave behind, anyway? A house and a car? Orange and olive groves and apple orchards that my mother took care of without knowing. that she was nurturing them and making them sweeter for some other family straight out of the pages of the Old Testament?

It's true that he was tough enough to hold his own against any character God created, but he was never a materialist. I can't remember him clutching at any of the dross of the world. Perhaps men aren't so bound to the land as women. Women grow roots. Women are wombs like the land. They nurture fruit within themselves and bring forth life. I don't mean to say that my father's material losses weren't enough to silence him for the rest of his life; in the language of numbers and figures what happened to him amounts to a financial catastrophe in every sense of the word. It's no financial joke to find yourself on the street with your entire family. It's no joke to find yourself high and dry after investing every penny in a house you thought would be your family's cradle but ended up cradling a family exiled from Europe for reasons you had nothing to do with.

Middle Eastern men devote themselves to their families and their houses. Maybe it's because they don't know how to express their love in language. Not everyone is born a poet. What can't be said is immortalized in stone. Or sacrificed to the heavens. They build palaces and gardens for their children and their beloved gods. And sometimes they build pyramids and monuments to hide their dirty secrets. In this respect, some women are not so very different from God; both are equally fragile and worthy of worship. Both offer boundless love. And both can censure endlessly. My father didn't build my mother a Taj Mahal, but from the stories I've heard, even from the likes of Uncle Hasan and his lot who hated his guts, I understood that he had a house beautiful enough to keep my mother happy, at least until Halimeh turned up.

Uncle Hasan was actually my father's cousin. I refer to him as uncle because he's my father's age, never mind that he hated him for reasons they'd probably carried with them from Palestine. He once said that my father had built my mother's house out of stones brought all the way from Jamma'in. Each and every stone. The stone in Jamma'in is considered the best in the region. As a little boy I pictured lorries driving up the Jordan Valley, piled high with stones. Stone from Jamma'in would be delivered to Syria and Iraq and Saudi Arabia. I'd no idea we exported hard-headedness. I don't know what properties can make one stone privileged, superior to another. It's all just stone as far as I'm concerned. But not the ones my father left behind in Palestine. They had walled him into his silence and his mad, grey moods. Not the material cost. Neither Liri or Jamma'in stone nor the number of trees and fields could account for my father's silence. Rather, it was memory and the voices and shadows left behind, things measurable only on the scale of the soul. My father, like any other refugee who leaves his home, left behind a substantial part of himself and of that essential something from which respect and honour grow or, at least, self-respect. It's only when you end up as a refugee that you understand that something within you has broken, and you know that when certain things, certain integrities, are broken, there's no putting them together again. They're broken and you have to live with that. Refugees and those who are strangers in their own country understand me the best, understand the origin of these doubts, and the reason for my constant disillusionment and disorientation. Simon was one of those who understood me right away. I hadn't even opened my mouth. Simon. A forgotten prophet. A fractured Messiah hanging about the streets of the city telling the world's future. He once accused me of being unable to feel loyal to any person or thing.

'How can you be a friend to all these people without being a cheat and a Judas?' he asked me as we stood in front of the Law Courts and he saw me wave to someone he couldn't stand.

'You just try to be even-handed', I said, 'and not make enemies. None of your belligerence and fanaticism. A bit of optimism is all, my friend!' He answered with a dull chuckle that I simply couldn't interpret and remained silent until we got to the top of Freedom Square. Then he suddenly stopped and said in a sardonic tone, 'Optimism about what exactly? If you have no enemies you have no friends.'

Simon was a prophet who had no followers. Hermit-like and honest, isolated and individual, as befits an honest man. His frankness left him without friends. Even his students didn't take him seriously outside the classroom and made fun of him after they'd drunk from his fount of pure science.

Simon's life, unlike my own, has only two hues: white and black. Nothing in between. No twists and turns. Maybe Simon wanted to live life the way he practised science. Sodium and chlorine make salt; always salt, never sugar or tomatoes. Simon wanted life to be a matter of yes or no. No perhapses or maybes. He was always tense.

'If you're not a lion you'll be devoured by wolves,' he sometimes said. By this definition, I was fodder for the lions and the wolves, and the dogs and flies and ants. I couldn't accept that life was all about eating or being eaten, even though I'd been gnawed to the marrow. Another time he said, 'There's only one problem you Palestinians have.' When I asked what it was, he said we weren't putting up enough of a fight.

'Fighting is a means, not an end,' I said angrily, as if he'd touched on a sensitive subject.

'You just keep waiting for something to be dropped into your laps by the Jews, then. As if they ever let anything fall!' he answered. 'And what is your *end* anyway? To get dragged by the ears into renouncing yourselves? What can a silly lamb like Arafat bring back from the lion's mouth? What choice does he have but to be devoured?'

Did I agree with him then? I don't know. Sometimes we agreed and sometimes we didn't. I was afraid to accept so much absurdity. An absurdity imbued with intolerable seriousness. Simon was able to lay out the whole of life on a plane of Cartesian coordinates and see everything in only two dimensions. He had his ways.

He'd made his calculations precisely, and, even though he made everything horizontal, I've known few people who had his depth. I tend to make everything vertical and dig deep, perhaps to hide beneath a grey crust. I was afraid to plot life on two Cartesian axes like he did. I'm still afraid of a linear relationship. I'm afraid of turning into one of the variables within it. Linear relationships require interdependence. They require commitment. Dedication. Marriage. Social cages. Children. Worship. Devotion. Slavery. I prefer to dust it all off, skirt around all that. Even around myself. Always the outsider and always running away from an eternal something I'm unable to identify. Running away and always looking over my shoulder. People who look over their shoulder are bound to smash into something in front of them. No wonder my life's full of accidents and crashes. I've injured myself and been badly hurt on occasion. And sometimes I've injured and hurt others badly. I've always managed to get to my feet and dust myself off.

As far as Simon was concerned, there were two axes in life, and the distance between them could be considerable. Animals existed on one axis; they know how to eat and reproduce without the help of doctors and books and holy scriptures. What did those things amount to on the other axis? Death? Sex? Love? Heroism? Shit? How is that other life measured exactly? With the absurd mathematics of Simon from the City of Valletta? With the yearning verse of Alex Attard and Musa al-Ghabbadi, who set out to fix the world with their weeping pens? Had I never met Simon, the roof of the Muqata'a in Ramallah would still have been torn off above Arafat's head, that sacrificial lamb, and Saddam would still have been hanged and Baghdad would still have been destroyed, as would a substantial part of Beirut and Gaza, and the So-Called United Nations would still have intervened at the eleventh hour to sweep the debris under the carpet of humanity's collective memory. Halimeh would still have appeared to me in the guise of Nadia to punish me and leave, having ground a part of me to a fine dust that nature would take care of when the time came for it to reclaim its molecules.

From a sociobiological perspective, I didn't have much to complain about. I was lucky to be of the male sex; you have no idea what an advantage it is to be born male in that part of the world. You could say I passed my first life exam. At least I was spared having to listen to that well-known phrase used whenever a newborn turns out to be a girl, 'What's sent by God is a blessing, come what may,' as if truly believing in God means you have to accept anything he sends, good or bad.

You have to accept that the heavens won't always rain gold and silver down on you. 'Oh well, a daughter will get married and leave and take the family name with her' is what her own mother will say, having forgotten that she, too, gave away her family name to be admitted into the gilded cage. I would eventually get to know the journalist Mohammed Tummaleh, who used to say that women in our part of the world choose to live life in a corner out of their own free will, and if someone were to raise them on a dais they'd climb back down to sit in the corner again. 'The problem of the Arab woman', he wrote once, 'is that she is part of the problem. She is unwittingly a burden on herself and on society. How far can a nation crawl when half of it is disabled? Which by no means implies that the other half is hale and hearty. I don't want to give the impression that I'm blaming the Arab woman for all the disasters that have occurred in our region, including the famous Six-Day Catastrophe' – he meant my twin sister – 'which will remain a black stain on the cheek of the Arab world. I'm not accusing women, because how can you accuse those who were not present? Rights, as the sociologists say, are not given away on a silver platter. You need to fight for them.'

Arab women don't put up a fight. They wait for something to drop into their laps, just like the Palestinian people. Arab women still curse themselves the moment they bring a girl into the world instead of a boy, because girls will squander their inheritance and give their family name away. Apart from that bomb ticking between her legs. Tick-tock. Tick-tock. There's no telling when it's going to blow up and shatter the honour of the Longnoses. One day, one of Musa al-Ghabbadi's female cousins eloped. 'Suddenly some distant relative shows up at our house,' Musa had said, 'a cousin of a cousin, maybe, or the nephew of I don't know who, and he says, "If you can't bring yourselves to kill her and cleanse her shame, then we will." We'll kill her, he says, as if he was talking about frying an egg or boiling some pasta.' Me, I'm blessed to have been spared all this nonsense and to have passed the first essential exam. So I couldn't complain as far as that went.

I must say that my father didn't care about these gender divides. In fact, he was closer to my sisters than he was to us, the brothers. But that changes nothing in the overall structure that is founded on those twenty grams of manly flesh hanging between his legs. A very precious appendage that you wouldn't exchange for anything in the world. It allows you to dominate others and threaten and make good on your threats and trample over your sister and mother and your mother's mother if necessary. In short, it allows you to trample over half of society. The same half that raises you to be trampled by you. That dangles a rope for you and sometimes bends down to lift you up. That continues to raise you until you're in parliament stocked with the tools and whips needed to beat women. A parliament of imbeciles except where constraining women is concerned. That's when they'll stand up to be counted, the lions in the cabinet, some of them barely able to write their own names, while the majority of the lower chamber, who are appointed by the Hashemite king on the basis of the importance of their tribe, suffer from an even graver syndrome known as structural illiteracy. Suffering from this type of illiteracy means you're apt to mistake a computer for a table. The upper chamber is the same – it refuses to change the law that says that you can get away with killing your sister, mother, wife or any female relative on the spot if you catch her in an adulterous relationship, you can even go free because you committed murder in the heat of passion and to safeguard your honour. Asked what would happen if the situation were reversed, meaning if she were to catch you in the act, lawmakers suddenly became aware of an even more crucial question: what would she be doing outdoors?

After much conflict and debate, an explanation for this ambiguous law was published: a woman's body is subject to the honour of the man while a man's body plays no part in the honour of a woman.

When I was born in 1967 there wasn't even a parliament. I don't mean the building, that's still standing, like a bruise in the middle of the people's forehead. There used to be a parliament, but King Hussein got tired of it and dissolved it on a whim. Some dervishes started to mutter that parliament was the bond between a people and its rulers, and if the ruler decided to undo this bond, that meant he didn't give a damn about his people. It sounded as if they were saying that King Hussein wasn't the responsible type and it was a good thing the West knew what stuff he was really made of. Many of these dervishes were rounded up and given a specially designed cure.

When the last Jordanian parliament was dissolved by the young Hashemite king and an infant democracy had its throat cut, they said that parliament was closed for restoration, and the people thought that maybe it needed some render and fresh paint, and, because it was quite a large building, the paint job that began in 1952 wouldn't be finished until 1989. According to some astute observers, whom I sometimes overheard whispering in the dark, thirty-seven years without an elected government meant the people had no idea what had happened throughout those thirty-seven years, as if anyone could know what was happening in a country even when there was an 'elected' government.

Where did these ministers and prime ministers come from anyway? The king has a large pack of dogs, who pounce on the bones he throws them. The strange thing I could never understand was how some of these astute observers who explained certain things to us in the dark went on to become high officials and even bigger dogs than their predecessors. Far bigger than the king himself expected.

In 1989 they inaugurated the new Jordanian parliament, having completed the restoration. The storm that had brought down the Berlin Wall and dissolved the communist empire had begun to loom over the Arab world. Jordanian democracy had to be quickly brought out of the Hashemite freezer, and the ice thawed before the eyes of the king. Lo and behold, the country was a democracy once more and it filled up with legislators, some of whom wanted to outlaw beer on the national airline. The only woman allowed among the legislators was brought before an Islamic Sharia court accused of heresy, having brazenly asked, under the canopy of democracy and before all those men, many of them heavyweight tribal leaders, for a review of the law that required a husband's signature for a woman to be granted a passport.

They said that a whore like Rania Hadidi was encouraging married women to prostitute themselves while their husbands were abroad. 'What is this review supposed to mean?' asked the director of passports and citizenship, whose place in the civil service ought to have kept him out of all controversy. 'Suppose there's a man who works in Saudi Arabia and his wife decides to go to Syria. Should we just tell her to go ahead? Just like that? How do we know this woman won't be going to "fuck around" with someone else?' I have to be honest, that 'fuck around' is my own paraphrase. I don't recall him saying those words. I don't want to lose all credibility. Credibility is as fragile as the honour concentrated between a woman's legs. I know I risk being brought before the same jury that found Rania Hadidi guilty of promoting an act that indirectly encouraged prostitution. The court said that this type of provocation amounted to heresy. When the same director was asked by a journalist, 'So suppose, sir, that she has relatives who are dying in Syria – what should a woman do in that case? Wait for her husband to return to sign the papers for her?' 'The law is clear on the matter, young man,' answered the director with a smile. 'A married woman cannot go abroad without her husband's permission. To be precise, she isn't even supposed to leave her home without permission. What has happened to everyone in this country? Have you forgotten that we're Muslims?'

When I grew up and started dabbling in life and reading books about science, I found myself associating Jordan, the country of my birth, with a certain kind of autoimmune disease. Immunology fascinates me, for being a science based on three all-important terms, self, recognition and kill, which fall in the following sequences: self + recognition = no kill, meaning a person is fine, protected, with everything under control; self + no recognition = kill, when a person is fucked. His interior army turns against him and his flesh eats away at his flesh, and if this disease affects a whole society, people start eating their own children, but rather than recognize this gravest of diseases, they blame foreigners, especially the Jews and Christians. Those devils. All they want is to exploit and plunder or expose us to that strange product they call democracy, which probably contains pork. After all, who but those nations of Christian dogs stood up for the whore Hadidi who went to parliament in a short skirt and walked among all those men? If a country allows a woman to obtain a passport without her husband's signature today, what will happen tomorrow? Isn't that what she wants, to open the door that will shift the entire country towards God's wrath and damnation?

Socio-immuno-pathology. Sometimes I think, why shouldn't it be me who brings these three sciences together? Why shouldn't I pioneer this science? It could branch out as much as you please: socio-immuno-histo-pathology, socio-immuno-endocrinology, socio-immuno-toxopathology, socio-immuno-dermato-pathology. This last involves the skin and is found in Malta as well, and the two major political parties know all about it and are doing nothing concrete to cure it. The black immigration card, according to Seas Amidst and other organizations, is used by certain people to frighten the small population into believing that their island is being overrun by Africans and Arabs. When Malta voted to join the European Union, it was whispered that if it didn't vote yes it would end up wearing a veil and obviously that meant fucking up the entire tourism industry on which the country depended. Even worse, the Maltese might mingle with blacks and have children who were half-caste. Think of all the trouble our daughters would have to go through to straighten their hair and how much we'd need to spend on hair dye to keep Malta as blonde as Scandinavia.

6

'Palestinians deserve a better leader,' is what they said about you and implied there will be nothing to talk about until you find a way to get rid of him; not to do so means you'd continue to be a failure, stuck, the way you were once spoken of by that snow-white dove Shimon Peres: 'Palestinians never fail to fail.' As expected, Camp David failed, and with it came the failure of every attempt to save the dream of your people of moving back to their original resting place, caught up in a web of vile lies and international chicanery. You still haven't dreamed enough. The Jewish people needed to dream for thousands of years. How could you expect them to give up a slice of such a slow-baked loaf?

You knew that Camp David would fail the way your love had failed. This time you didn't need to be a prophet to make predictions about the Palestinian predicament. No need to be a Simon De Brincat, who had told you to 'go and get your coffins ready' as soon as the forty-third US president and his circle came to power. 'The crazy eagles are coming with their fleets and their horses and weapons of steel and fire, and huge bombs that can sniff out human flesh even sixteen storeys underground.' Camp David failed as your love failed, and the dead restlessly began to make room for the dead that followed them. The alternative to dialogue is death. Your young people stood in queues to acquire the death uniforms needed to gain entry into heaven without any trouble. On 28 September 2000 the Second Intifada started. Two years after your love story came to an end, a campaign of blood began. The same people who chatted while seated at long tables with bottles of water in front of them, went back, took off their shirts and ties, put on their military uniforms and led their children to shed their blood. Alex isn't at all surprised.

'It's like we were saying, Nabil. They made Arafat pull out his truncheon. Carrot and stick. The eternal tools of conviction. I hope the worst isn't yet to come.'

You try to explain your oddball theory about the games of the gods, but you can't quite manage. Your mouth is sewn shut.

'The worst will come when Barak goes down, because Sharon is standing right around the corner,' Alex continues.

There's always someone standing around the corner. When your mother died there was another woman around the corner waiting for her bed to become vacant. And when you separated from Nadia there was another man around the corner waiting to build his future on what you'd left behind. That's life, all corners and queues, and people restlessly waiting to benefit from the failure of their peers.

Back to the city. Friendly as an orange. Beautiful as a freshly baked loaf in a poor man's hands. Occasionally a stranger and as strange as a bird hovering high in the sky. But, despite the spread around her waist, she always greets you with a smile and a new dress. Puts on a new perfume for you. Every time you approach her you feel agitated and enchanted. As if you were about to meet a woman at once pretty, malicious and elegant, who is waiting for you behind one of those doors, shutters slightly ajar and harbouring secrets.

The city has harboured its secrets ever since it spread its legs for the first Phoenician felucca. Simon De Brincat has nothing to say to you about his city's palaces and fortresses. Nothing about the chapels and churches riddled with corridors and gutters and the many mysteries hidden behind the stones of the past and under the flagstones of eras long past.

He never tells you where Jean Parisot de la Valette lies, the dignified hero of Africa and Asia, who won a historic victory over your faith, and after that well-deserved victory, which changed the face of Malta once and for all, laid the first stone of Catholic glory on the hill of Xebb ir-Ras and christened it with his own name. Cities are like people, they're locked up in strange names for life.

This isn't the version you would find in books. You don't find it anywhere, in fact, except coming from Simon the Radical, who doesn't give a hoot about his country's collective beliefs. Naturally you couldn't second-guess him. You're in no position to second-guess anybody, now, are you? Not that you're afraid of losing the argument. More a question of not knowing where it would lead with him. What proof do you have that heroes are in fact heroes and not criminals and murders?

So we're wallowing in your grey discourse once more. Maybe this time you'll have it your way. Depends which side you're on. Often our heroes are another person's murderers. What else could a military hero be, for example, if not a butcher? And yet we still paint him as a noble man who gave his life, or intended to give it, for us! Even though sometimes this nobility involves – implies – the destruction of another.

Nothing has changed since the time of David. To this day the same tribes continue to fight over the same patch of land. Perhaps the fight began over grazing land for farm animals. Many of the wars at the time began over things that today would be considered trivial. The Basus War, for example, which lasted forty bloody years, broke out over a camel. More precisely over where the camel was grazing. Probably a bit of grass that wouldn't have been considered trivial at the time, especially when we consider that there were precious few trees and little greenery in those parts. A bit like oil in our time. Perhaps this is what will become of Arab oil some day, an irrelevance, trivia. But how would this change people's behaviour, not to say their programming? Oil may or may not become irrelevant, but man will remain the digger of his own grave.

So Ehud Barak went down and took the snow-white dove Shimon Peres with him. The two Labour Party men sank. It wasn't that their carrot didn't have enough vitamins; it was that their stick wasn't thick enough. And now the fat guy's taken over, and he understands fat all too well. Ariel Sharon. A heroic warrior straight out of the pages of the Old Testament with his hands still covered in dust from the tablets of the Ten Commandments.

The chosen saviour, a bulldozer in David's line, sent with great urgency to lead the children of Jacob towards a safe shore and out of the dark tunnel they found themselves in as a result of meetings and discussions with the filthy Canaanites. The Canaanites, who were banished from the pages of the Old Testament, can only understand one language, that of force, and now someone has arrived who can speak this language with them fluently.

At the other extreme the regiment of martyrs from Hamas and Islamic Jihad provided support for Sharon's linguistic theory. Whether on purpose or because they were pushed by the gods around the divine round table, they began to pull what was left of the moral rug from beneath the feet of their own people. Moral superiority, the only weapon that can truly help a victim, was being eroded, and the respect garnered by the children of the First Intifada was whittled away with every young martyr who blew himself up among youngsters his own age.

The militarization of the Second Intifada was strategically, militarily and ethically a fatal error, and an enormous failure of your nation's leadership. How did a nation such as yours, which is so proud of its erudition, manage to commit suicide, both morally and literally, on such a scale? Why didn't you build on the foundations of the First Intifada, which overcame the military might of Israel and put its leaders to shame. The foundations that lent your cause urgency and prominence. Why did you fuck everything up? What were you doing, pissing about in Oslo when you had the banner of the So-Called United Nations, and why did you decide to shoot? You shot yourselves in the foot. Well done, you. Don't you know that shooting is their favourite sport? The road to Palestine remains a long and twisted one. Two years after Nadia left, Ariel Sharon arrived.

Ariel Scheinermann. The Hebrew strongman. The eleventh Israeli prime minister, on whose elastic conscience the blood of Sabra and Shatila is yet to dry. There's no joking with Sharon. At the drop of a hat he can send over some F-16s to bomb a baby with a suspicious-looking dummy in its mouth. He won't think too hard about bombing Arafat's headquarters or the wheelchair of Ahmad Yassin, the ambiguous founder of Hamas.

Sharon didn't weigh the matter for long. He immediately sent his army into Ramallah. Hamas and Arafat's al-Aqsa Brigades intensified their suicide missions. It was during those months in the year 2000 that you began to have difficulty recognizing yourself in the mirror. Alex always tries to hide a torrent of disappointment behind his thin glasses. For now, at least, he won't be fixing the Mediterranean.

He sows his sad gaze everywhere except in your eyes. He knows your exile is not a metaphor. Sometimes he casts the net of words. His net is embroidered with your pain. Every word belongs to a dream of a peaceful Mediterranean where brothers and sisters love one another. You wanted to tell him that the Mediterranean doesn't deserve poetry any more. And that everything had been said in this accursed region. From the Trojan horse to the F-16. 'The Oslo pact has brought a lot of suffering upon you. Exactly as Edward Said predicted.'

Really? How did you feel when, among the Israeli negotiators, you spotted psychiatrists and philologists and experts in geography and topology and the social sciences, all of them armed with maps and laptops while your lot had their hands in their pockets? As long as their hair was neatly combed for the cameras.

'People who go in search of a half-peace bring back half a war,' you say with a certain sadness because you know that if they could they'd lock you away in a drawer once and for all.

'You're as much a part of the truth as they are, Nabil. The truth can't be erased. You could hide it, perhaps, but you won't erase it. At the end of the day, how much longer can human conscience continue to witness cruelty and blood?'

He's used the word conscience again. What has conscience done for sub-Saharan Africans or Native Americans? In Australia and Canada they organize trips to see the surviving descendants of massacred indigenous peoples, the way you'd take a tour to see some kangaroos.

As far as Sharon and his friends in Washington are concerned, you're just dark-skinned Native Americans. Required to be wiped off the map unless you choose to melt away among the Arab nations as Chaim Weizmann and Ben-Gurion wished when they established the promised Jewish state on the lands of your fathers. The Arabs around you will absorb you, and in time you'll forget and your Palestine will be forgotten. But their wish hadn't come true. Not only that, but if the current situation persists the real confrontation with Israel won't happen with your generation but with the generation that's growing up amid the destruction and debris.

Fighting isn't a career. You've always wished that your children would be like other children around the world. Inventing games for their dolls, riding their bicycles, playing football, daydreaming about chocolate and new things to wear and their plans for tomorrow. Not playing with pistols and the shrapnel from missiles and pissing themselves at night because of the terrors they witnessed during the day. These incontinent children are your tomorrow generation.

The phone rings at 1 p.m. Only Adnan could break the spell of Vivaldi's strings, which have resounded in your ears for years. You stop the CD, resigned. The violins stop, and the knives sinking into your flesh are suddenly interrupted.

'What do you want, you women's and devil's advocate?'

He doesn't allow you to pause for breath. 'Turn on your TV and switch to CNN now.'

The knives continue to sink into your flesh without the accompaniment of Vivaldi's strings. 'Who's killed who this time then?' you ask without much interest. 'Sharon or Arafat?'

'Quick. Turn it on. I'll be over soon.'

With the knives still sticking into your flesh, you press the button on the remote control. Breaking News flashes red, making you blink. There was black smoke coming out of one of the two tall towers in New York. You ask yourself, astonished, 'What the hell is happening?' Before you go to turn on the kettle for the lawyer Judas you ask yourself again, 'Why is Breaking News red? Why isn't it green or yellow? Or brown?' You know it's a trite question, but still you answer yourself, 'Red is the colour of alarm. The colour of mysterious blood. The eternal mystery inside us. Protein and iron. No. Protein has nothing to do with it,' you correct yourself. Protein's just furniture. Faience. What really matters is iron. The atom that receives oxygen and turns from blue to red. Blue is the real colour of blood before it's shocked by oxygen and turns into a red as scandalous as your wounds, which Alex Attard noticed and which you began to compare with his impossible dreams and the wounds that won't heal of that old woman poet with the cane and the loud voice who writes to quell the fires of a love gone stale with time – unless it was born stale.

'Modern woman stands on the fascist scaffold on her own two feet,' she told you once with the confidence of one who had stood on the fascist scaffold on her own two feet.

'And don't you think that modern-day man takes a leap off the cliffs on his own two feet?' you asked with the confidence of a man at the bottom of the cliff.

'Who can snuff out fires that have burned for forty years?' she asks in pain, more to herself than to you.

'Best to just let them burn,' you say, 'until they've consumed everything.'

'And the children, aren't they memories? Should I let them burn, too?'

'Children suffer most. Love is the first thing to be consumed by the flames as the house of marriage burns down, and children are burned when it all catches fire. It's the battlefield itself that suffers most in a conflict.'

'I'm not convinced that in forty years it will have turned to ashes. There's more inside me that could catch fire,' she says with an exhausted smile.

There was nothing you could say, because you learned that we realize that we are standing on the scaffold only once we see our heads rolling along the flagstones of the execution ground. You turn to make coffee for yourself and Adnan, the feminist lawyer who doesn't really believe what he preaches. There's a shot of a passenger flight crashing into that gigantic building and, without wanting to, you scream like an ambulance siren, 'Merciful God, how did he not see that?'

Until that moment you hadn't understood what was going on. You thought it was an accident. You didn't know that on the aeroplane was a group of martyrs sent from above, from high up, by the greatest authority in the sky. Things gradually started to clear up. Did they think the Middle East couldn't go this far? How little they know. In the Middle East there is hatred and brothers tearing each other apart and Bibles and divine rocks and holy water and blessed dust trampled by many prophets who couldn't see eye to eye. Everything in that filthy East is hanging on to a single atom of iron, a blue atom that wears oxygen and immediately turns red and marches in the streets. It is in houses and shops, boards buses and coaches, and now it's in an aeroplane that you initially thought was being flown by a confused pilot who didn't spot an enormously tall building when, in fact, it was being flown by a pilot, sent on a mission by Allah, who's being awaited by four hundred virgins who have never stood under the eye of the sun.

Among all the screams and the shock and the speechlessness and the banging of Adnan at the door, another aeroplane appears and crashes straight into the second tall building of the World Trade Center. You're reminded of one of Simon's prophecies: 'You'll hand them the excuse they need. Tear the Arabs to pieces. There are traps that you've no choice but to walk straight into.'

What else did Simon know that he didn't tell you? Or had he planned it all himself?

'Ever since I learned the alphabet I haven't stopped losing. Disappointments made me wiser.'

Only he, with his many disappointments, only some of which you know about, managed to beat you at the losing game and, at the very end, despite all his losses, emerge the winner.

Simon De Brincat, the uncrowned grand master of the Knights of Malta who supped from all the bottles of human failure, tried them out one by one and threw up his innards with the poison of his fellow men who have an odd thirst for one another's blood. Simon, the failed prophet, managed to trick the entire world and emerge victorious after the last battle. Science fattened him up in order to devour him, and after it destroyed him it couldn't wipe out his sardonic smile. Sometimes a smile is the only difference between victory and loss.

'This is an attack!' you say, amazed, to Adnan, whose face crumples and whose eyes become more distant behind a thick veil of fear and disappointment as more information comes through.

'Something tells me this is the work of people from our part of the world. If that's the case, then we're done for.'

'What do you mean *we*?' you ask, confused. You no longer recognize this 'we'. Who's 'we'? The Arabs? Muslims? The people of the East? Or you and I? A couple of strangers. A Palestinian and a Jordanian who ran away from the battlefields of national failure laid out by the adventures of their dictatorial rulers. You were beyond ruined; you couldn't be ruined further. When the virus is inside you and you blame others aren't you already pitiful?

'Why are we divided?' 'Who's we?' How many thousands of times have these questions gnawed at you? How is it that in Europe nations with different languages and faiths who haven't torn each other to shreds during their various showdowns have managed to leave their differences behind and merge in a single bloc to make their continent accessible to every citizen, while you who have one God and one language, one history and one tradition, and the same ugly longish nose, still can't agree on the first day of Ramadan?

You're always dividing and spawning new divisions and hatreds for each other, while your thinkers and intellectuals blamed the imperialist dog until you rendered it responsible for all your chronic illnesses. Simon De Brincat knew, as you also knew, that the virus was inside you before the first imperialist trickster turned up in his cap and shorts. Imperialists don't just appear without a reason. It's the confusion and division and the ocean of black shit under your behinds that brought them over. This damned oil that brought no wealth but only destruction and a curse worse than you and your twin sister could bring. Why do you never stop, just once, in front of the mirror of reality to see who you really are and what you want from life? Divided and at war and confused and as ambiguous as that bloody article in the Arab League constitution that defines 'the Arab': 'The Arab is defined as the inhabitant of the Arab geography that extends from the Gulf of Aden to the Atlantic Ocean.'

This considerable expanse makes up 10 per cent of the globe. One and a half times the size of the USA, 6,566 times larger than the State of Israel. An Arab, according to this loose definition, inhabits the Arab democratic oasis above the sea of black gold. The wealth that brought US troops all the way into your women's beds. The profits from this oily gold has always been spent on bombs to rain on the heads of the living creatures who are supposed to benefit from it. A real national treasure! That definition does not address the presence of ethnic minorities because it's afraid to chip away at the geography, more so now that the world has seen how Iraq, the second largest of the Arab countries, turned out to be another Yugoslavia held together with out-of-date glue. The only thing that kept it all in one piece was the iron fist of the dictator. How many other Arab Yugoslavias might there be that you don't know about? Or don't you want to know about them because of the ethnic slippery slope and the oily gold that could be lost if you chip away at the geography?

A few hours after the 9/11 attacks the entire world got to know that the directors, engineers, executives and protagonists behind those horrible attacks on human civilization were Arab citizens with a long nose that looks like yours, and that they were all sent by Mr Osama bin Muhammad bin Awad bin Laden, the idiotic Arab prophet who gestated in the womb of the CIA and managed, with their indispensable help, to set up the first strong alliance between global imperialism and radical Islam, the blessings of God's monotheistic representatives, having worked shoulder to shoulder for a long time and having fought valiantly, free in their faith and in constant consultation with the heavens, managed to dismantle the pagan Soviet empire and open up new horizons for the wretched of the earth, and the Afghans, as expected, picked the low-hanging fruit of that campaign of jihad and Islamic meddling.

When bin Laden brought to completion his divine mission against the Russian infidel, he expanded his operations and became a point on Samuel Huntington's compass, one of the evangelists for neo-conservativism, whose adherents would, according to Simon De Brincat, use these attacks to launch a mission no less disgusting than bin Laden's own. The difference being that bin Laden still wore a prehistoric costume while they wore clean shirts and elegant jackets.

America under attack. All the stations of the world aimed their lenses at the wounded lion. The big lion. The biggest of them all. The one who, when it sneezes, gives the rest of the world a cold. You and Adnan remained rooted before the television in silence. Watching the reports as they came in, hurried and confused. You began to avoid each other's eyes as if it was you who had flown the planes into the Pentagon and the two towers in Manhattan.

What's this trap you've fallen into, and which ones can you not avoid? You think of Nadia. You'd like her to be near you. You feel a chill and an odd nostalgia. How could it fade away so completely, that beautiful dream that briefly tantalized your soul and then disappeared with the dawn? Is it true that there used to be a woman called Nadia who resembled Halimeh, the wife of your uncle who loved you when you were the apple of her eye? Did these two women really exist, or are they as illusory as your Palestine? Or is one of them real while the other is only a puff of smoke? Did you invent the memory and colour it in all those shades? What is happening in the world?

What are these aeroplane-missiles, and where has Nadia gone? Where is the woman who held your dizzy head in her lap and caressed it with those fine, angelic fingers until she wiped away your sadness, dried it with her long black hair? Nadia. You tried to find someone else like her but failed. Some women are like a rare perfume you catch an enchanting whiff of somewhere then search for but fail to find. Nadia. The woman who went out with you to discover what she didn't know, while you were trying to forget what you knew; she took on board what she didn't know, but you're still unable to cure yourself of what you do know. She had to leave, as her eyes informed you that strange evening when she turned you into her past. She disappeared behind the glass walls of a marriage, and you continued to twirl around in dizzy circles, expecting the world to hear and understand your silence; pretending that you didn't know that the world is like Nadia, giving herself to the strong, to the one who takes her hand and leads her in the direction of life.

'That's all the Arab world needs,' Adnan said finally, when everything pointed to the fact that the nineteen martyred protagonists were all of Arab origin. They were identified so quickly that it all seemed to have been agreed upon in advance. By evening their photographs and their profiles and everything about them had been aired as if they'd long ago applied for this swift martyrdom that in just a few moments could transport you to the halls of a heaven thronging with impatient virgins. Even manuals explaining how aeroplanes could be blown up were found in the cars they left behind in the car parks from where their sacred mission began.

'They created this monster themselves. It used to be a pet they pampered. They fed it and fattened it until it got out of control and now it's turned on them,' you told Adnan, horrified.

'These are words you share with me or I tell you. But memories are short these days. There's a lot of political amnesia. From now on you and me and everyone who has a long nose will be the target of American weapons.'

'When have we ever not been their target? Isn't everyone in the region their vassal? Starting with Israel and continuing with the oil pharaohs and kings.'

'There won't be any agents and vassals this time. It'll be a new Vietnam.'

A new Vietnam. He said it with the same certainty as Simon. You know they used to be friends and Simon can't stop chattering. So far, so good. You can understand that Simon and Adnan are friends, but how could Halimeh and Nadia have been in cahoots? And what was al-Qaeda? What did bin Laden feed them? What could explain this psychological will to kill and be killed in such a spectacular fashion? The two New York piles gave way under the sheer weight of the surprise. Beneath them was buried the life of thousands of innocent souls. Adnan got a text from Pauline, and he went to meet her somewhere. 'I feel like shit, stopping to buy a bottle of wine while the world is ablaze,' he said as he left your place, as if to say that he was going unwillingly. You had no doubt that he was going unwillingly.

You didn't sleep a wink that mad night. You weren't the only one who got no sleep. Millions of speechless viewers continued to watch the biggest lion of all moaning from the pain caused by those nineteen brave men hypnotized by a powerful Islamic spell.

That night you pictured the passengers on those planes burning to cinders. The people who were working in those offices above the clouds.

Those who came from the other side of the world to give their children a view of New York from the tops of those monster towers were turned to ash in seconds along with their children, ashes floating on the September breeze. As you pictured Sharon's tanks in Ramallah and Jenin, flattening anything that found itself under their tracks. And Nadia, writhing in pleasure on top of another man. The slippery slope of life and the divine table. Simon De Brincat and those long, strong arms that were never visible but could move and upturn everything. And you saw yourself as you moaned in silence like a sick bear who'd fallen into a pit.

It was that very night of 9/11, Tuesday 11 September 2001, not long after the the prophecies of Samuel Huntington. A few hours after Adnan went to fuck Pauline against his will. A few hours after Giuliani, the mayor of New York, declared from among the debris that anyone wearing a nappy on his head would have to answer for this. A few hours after you convinced yourself once and for all that there's a large, secret society working to ruin your life. A few hours after the history of humanity broke into two pieces. What came before 9/11 and what came after. A few hours after the population of the world was broken into two camps: those who were with them and those who were against them. A few hours after that night of madness soaked in blood and riddled with debris and smoke and pieces of human flesh, the real Halimeh appeared to you. Your uncle's wife. In the flesh, her hair as black as night. She appeared in the living room of your house in Swieqi, where Adnan had been sitting with his gloomy countenance smoking one cigarette after another. Her eyes as black as ink, as wide as a riverbank, just as your Aunt Miriam had described them twenty years before. With the swell of her breasts beneath her Canaanite dress with the mysterious al-Karmil embroidery. On her left cheek she had the same large beauty spot as Nadia. When she saw you from her armchair coming from the kitchen and opened her arms and said, 'Come into my arms, my lovely. Come here, darling.'

7

From a timing perspective, things didn't look too good. Quite the opposite. My arrival was always associated with that humiliating loss of 5 June 1967. At the precise moment I appeared, the entire region was glued to the radio, listening to the reports from Cairo and the news directly from the battlefront.

On that day the only permissible noise was the din of battle. The radio transmitted news of the historic victory being won by the Arab armies. My siblings' faces were drier than the wooden box to which their ears were glued and which never left my father's hands. He wouldn't let go of it for a second, like a little boy holding a toy surrounded by children who wanted to snatch it from him. My siblings were still as statues, watching the expressions on his face intently, hard as Italian marble. My brothers' and sisters' faces mirrored that of my father. If he smiled, they smiled; if he closed his eyes and screwed them tight, they did the same. My father hadn't shaved in more than fifteen days. According to my mother this had never happened before, except when they had left Palestine nineteen years earlier. My father greeted me with a face prickly after fifteen days of not shaving, fifteen days that would alter the map of the Middle East for ever.

The voice of Ahmed Said coming out of the radio. Authoritative, full of bravura and enthusiasm, not stopping to dust off the debris of battle. A little broadcasting, a little playing of martial tunes. Tunes that filled you with longing and nationalism and pride, made you want to drop everything and sign up with the victorious army. The word going around was of a single decisive victory that would cleanse the region of the 'Jewish pigs'. They should be thrown into the sea, some said. Others would rather let them leave in peace. 'After all we are so much better than them. We have morality while they have nothing of the sort.' A chasm was about to open in the Arab world, between those who were for forgiveness and those who were for throwing them into the sea.

Statement followed statement. '*Allahu akbar*, we've downed forty of the enemy's planes.' '*Allahu akbar*, the Arab armies have reached Tel Aviv.' '*Allahu akbar*, our forces are laying siege to the Jews in every corner of the land, and there is fighting from street to street and from foxhole to foxhole.'

'That means they're in the cleaning-up stage,' my father told my older siblings with his eyes wide. 'That's what they call it in military jargon.' Then he suddenly switched his pronouns and began to use 'we' to identify us with the victorious soldiers who were cleaning the cowardly Jews off the streets and alleyways of Palestine. 'We think of it as a cleansing. You cleanse the lands you've just taken from the enemy. In the army you've only acquired land when you have boots on the ground. A million aeroplanes won't acquire an inch of land. It's the soldier's feet that make the difference. The long black boot on the ground, and since the battle's happening from one foxhole to the next, that means the Arab armies are cleansing the liberated territories of the enemy, you see?'

'*Allahu akbar* we've downed another hundred of their planes.' '*Allahu akbar* the Jews are running away from battle like frightened mice.' '*Allahu akbar* they are leaving Palestine.' '*Allahu akbar* we've downed countless more planes.'

When the battle was over we discovered we'd apparently downed more planes than their air force actually owned.

'*Allahu akbar* they're jumping into the sea.' '*Allahu akbar* stay tuned for more developments.'

Father steps out into the yard for a bit. One of my siblings keeps watch by the radio that for fifteen days has been tuned to 'This is the voice of the Arabs, all the Arabs, from Cairo'. And what could be more beautiful than to be a part of this noble race that won't be deterred from fighting to restore its rights? All the other stations were lying. 'They're just dogs who want to defend the Jews.' My father, like millions of other Arab fathers, had made it clear that he would strangle anyone who so much as touched the radio's dial. My mother and my siblings obeyed. From time to time he'd step out into the yard for a cigarette and exchange a word or two with the man next door. Once he told him that they'd come here with two children but now had to go back with a whole litter. 'Ja, Abu Muhammad,' the other replied. 'It's all a blessing from God. Don't forget that we will return to our houses, not to the unknown. We're tired of these tents and tin roofs. If the house is your own home, there is room for a hundred. Indeed, they lighten your load. God sent us Nasser to deliver us from this misery.'

'God bless him and keep him victorious, at last a real man has emerged from this race,' said my father thoughtfully.

And then Ahmad Said faded away from 'This is the voice of the Arabs from Cairo', and my father's face took on several other expressions that bore no resemblance to the one from the first three days of war. His smoking increased, and the breaks he took in the yard with the man next door became longer. The conversation with Abu Ibrahim took place in increasingly lowered voices until it couldn't be heard any more. Before, he would raise his voice so that we could all hear what we needed to do once the battle was over. 'We need to move as fast as possible to be among the first.' 'Oh to be in Palestine at last,' my mother said from behind her tear-soaked handkerchief. He tells her to prepare, gather together whatever she needs. 'We need to move fast before the roads fill up. You understand?'

On 8 June the announcements on 'This is the voice of the Arabs from Cairo' became even shorter and drier. The news was confusing and riddled with rumour, vague words and many lengthy intervals. The statements became fewer and further between, and people began to avoid looking each other in the face. Some even took the risk of shifting the radio's dial to the Arabic-language broadcasts from London.

'Voice of London', the Arabic broadcast from London, reported a version of the story quite different from ours and Ahmed Said's. My father became angry and shouted at my siblings, 'Who the fuck tuned in to this shitty station?' when it was he himself who'd done it. 'They're lying, isn't it obvious? Aren't they the ones who brought the odious Jews to Palestine? What else would you expect from them once they'd shifted their filth on us?' After every news bulletin he'd tell us that the English were simply lying, but we could see the tears in his eyes. They came and went, welling up and waiting for the right time to burst forth. On the fifth day, 9 June, Ahmad Said reappeared. His voice suggested he hadn't slept in a long time, hadn't eaten in a long time, hadn't drunk in a long time and hadn't seen the light of God in a long time. That voice of bronze erupting into your ear now seeped out like water issuing from a forgotten cranny, and with a few words dripping with bitterness he confirmed the arrival of my twin sister: 'Oh, Arabs, you still have Allah.'

When the dust from the battle had settled, we discovered that we had been losing since day one. That the entire world had known what was happening except for us. That the Egyptian Air Force had been decimated before they'd even taken off; 7 per cent of the Egyptian Army had been destroyed completely. Jordan and Syria had lost land and soldiers, and the number of tents and makeshift shelters had increased by hundreds of thousands.

Utter defeat. Beyond any reasonable or unreasonable doubt, the biggest defeat was that of the Arab lands. Israel, the country that would be wiped off the map and driven into the sea, had suddenly tripled in size.

Later, on the night of 9 June, Nasser made an appearance on Egyptian television, which was broadcast on 'This is the voice of the Arabs, all the Arabs, from Cairo', during which he announced the dramatic defeat and handed in his resignation. A few minutes after he resigned the streets of Cairo thronged with millions of people weeping and wailing and begging Nasser to stay on to captain the sinking Arab ship. Two days later, on 11 June 1967, Moshe Dayan, the Israeli commander with one eye and a long history of bloodshed, was strolling through the centre of Jerusalem with a smile. That same day, the So-Called United Nations announced a cessation of hostilities, and five months later, on 22 November 1967, the UN Security Council issued its famous Resolution 242, which ordered Israel to effect an immediate retreat from the territories it had occupied in June 1967 and allow the new Palestinian refugees who had to flee their land because of the war to return to their homes.

So why did a boy come into the world during this time of lunacy?

What is a child beside such an enormous loss? Nasser had been broken and the Arabs had been crushed, too. We were broken and our land was broken and everyone was wearing the robes of shame. 'The worst isn't losing a battle,' my father said. 'Battles are lost and won. Human history is made of victories and losses, and sometimes a victory can compensate for ten losses, and sometimes one loss wipes out twenty victories. The worst is when you lose a battle and lose your honour at the same time. With the battle and the land went not only the respect of the whole world but our self-respect, too.'

Nasser was broken, and with him the project for an Arab nation was broken, which had been built on past illusions. A leader with big dreams. So big that the wounded Arab body could not contain them. Nasser tried to heal, but he was administering the wrong medicine. Instead of healing the sick body, he pushed it into a permanent coma. Wars and battles aren't won by romantic visions and empty hollering. Battles and wars are won using different means, known to the colonels and heroes of the Six-Day War, six days that would disrupt the Arab geography and throw its people into the darkest of mines.

Why did a boy enter the world at a time when everyone wished to leave it? I was coming out of my mother's womb when everyone else was entering the deepest shame. I was coming out of the darkness of her womb into the darkness of the Middle East. Darkness to darkness. From liquid darkness to airy darkness. From a darkness the size of a watermelon to one spanning two continents. You understand the darkness of the womb because your eyes are closed, but you can never understand the darkness of the Middle East because, although your eyes are wide open, they are unseeing.

Toy Number 11. I came into the world when love had dried up and patience and mercy had come to an end and the father did everything he could to stay away from home to avoid holding one of his children and looking directly into his or her eyes. Father had suddenly aged fifteen years. Mother lost interest in everything around her, including the house with its shouting, noisy occupants and their demanding mouths.

After the arrival of my twin sister my father suddenly stopped working and took up playing cards. He would go out in the morning and not return before midnight. He didn't bet with money because neither he nor the other men he played with ever had a penny in their pockets. The man who owned the first car in Qbebe, who at one time wouldn't be seen dead in a pair of unpressed trousers, even in his own yard, had now been wearing the same clothes for more than a month and had stopped shaving. When my mother scolded him and told him to go to work he flew into a terrible rage and started smashing everything within reach. Suddenly, as he banged and smashed, he noticed that the radio was playing a song by the Egyptian singer Mohammed Abdel Wahab: 'All that happened is because of your eyes.' He picked up the radio, which he normally would never let anyone else touch, raised it above his head and smashed it to the floor, shouting 'Whores, the lot of them. A bunch of whores!' And he went out cursing and raging, and no one saw him for two whole days. That box of light-coloured wood that he loved so dearly and had brought from Baghdad and would sometimes take to bed with him had been smashed to pieces, bits of its mechanism finding their way underfoot in every room of the house.

In 1967 inside every house in Amman was a broken radio and a lot of open-mouthed children and a father who had lost all interest in life and hadn't shaved for more than a month and never came home to avoid holding his children and looking them in the eyes, and so the distance began to grow between a generation who had lost without understanding why they had lost and another who drank the bitterness of a loss for which they were not to blame. Between a generation who didn't get to their feet and start building anew but rather threw themselves into the lap of despair and a generation who opened their eyes and found themselves living in tin huts with no one to pick them up and embrace them. A generation whose father was never at home and only stared vacantly into space if he did happen to be there, and who would shout and thump the table if you so much as spoke to him, and a mother who observed everything in silence and only opened her mouth to pray to Allah to take her from this world.

They wanted me to crawl through all that darkness with my legs amputated and my arms bandaged in the wake of lost wars that I had done nothing to inflame. They wanted me to bring back the lost land and lost honour, and I was torn by fear as I watched my father, whenever someone asked him for anything, hurl his glass at the ceiling, which was already in need of a new roof over it to stop it leaking during winter. They wanted me, this child of water, a few days old and fragile, to take history back, open it and fix the mistakes that had been made. As if they didn't know that history does not open its pages to the losers. They wanted me to reinstate the honour that had been lost by begging at the door of the So-Called United Nations, which hurried to distribute oil and flour to the second wave of refugees, who thronged the pavements in Amman and Beirut and Damascus. The second wave of people whose loss of dignity was displayed like an open sewer that showed their excrement for all the world to see. No one can mislead anybody and no one has any reason to hide anything from anybody, especially if everyone knows what everyone else has eaten.

They wanted me to explain on the night of the Naksa, when my twin sister and I were born. Abdel Hakim Amer, the commander of the Arab army and intimate friend of Nasser, was so certain and confident of victory that he decided to spend the night of the decisive battle fucking his model wife, because a fuck tastes heavenly when it accompanies victory. Another theory runs that he went for his usual fuck because he didn't know the war had even started.

How am I supposed to explain anything? And to whom? An army defeated in one of the most decisive battles of the Middle East while its commander is having a good time in one of his secret villas. The night of the Naksa, the commander of the army had a glass of revolutionary whisky in one hand and a shisha with marijuana in the other, with Berlenti Abdel Hamid half undressed swinging her shapely and ample backside for him.

They wanted an explanation for why some Jordanian regiments, armed to the teeth, didn't make it on to the battlefield after two days of marching but instead found themselves in the Saudi Arabian desert like a herd of goats without a goatherd. They nearly died of hunger and thirst. Their rusty compasses had misdirected them, pointing in the direction of shame rather than glory. How did they get lost in a country whose border with Palestine was 360 kilometres long? Almost any direction you chose to walk in would lead you to Palestine. There's just a single downhill route between Amman and Jerusalem, which takes no longer than three-quarters of an hour. If you go to the summit of the mountains in al-Salt you can see the whole of Palestine laid out with its Canaanite dress intact.

They wanted me to explain how the hills of Galilee had surrendered, when they are thirteen hundred metres north of Israel. Hills you could defend with stones. Had they left the residents to defend their homes Israel wouldn't have taken as much as a centimetre. How can I explain all of this, and what can I say about the tribunals in Damascus for the soldiers and the patriotic generals who defied orders and kept fighting until the last bullet?

Who owes an explanation to whom? I and my generation who inherited all this bounty, or our fathers who built a legendary army out of empty words and fantasy? Because the Arab armies were in a parlous state when compared with the Israeli ones. Their leaders were drunks, their weapons were outdated and rusty, the soldiers weren't trained and some of them had never fired an actual shot in their lives, and yet all the reports insisted that the Arabs were at their peak, and no one could stand up to them. Arab firepower consisted of the ink used by mendacious newspapers. *Al-Joumhouria, al-Akhbar, al-Ahram, Tishreen, The Revolution, al-Ra'i* and hundreds of other newspapers that circulated the lies made up in rooms choked with hashish smoke and the sweat of dancing women. If only we'd fought the way we danced none of this would ever have happened. If only we'd fought as much as we spilled mendacious ink, as much as we'd tricked ourselves and our children, none of this would ever have happened. How can you win glory when all you have reaped is fantasy and empty words that couldn't hurt a fly? How can the sun rise in the lands of darkness where humans are the cheapest commodity? Lands where the jails outnumber the schools and the police headquarters outnumber all the hospitals and churches and mosques put together? How can you win a war when you're defeated from the inside?

After the '67 war ended and with the Arab body lying injured on the ground, the people wept themselves blind. Some of them, seeing the greatness of the body now covered in wounds and how small the enemy was that had rained blows down upon it, chose to stop believing in God. Others said that paying too little attention to God was what had brought us to this pass, that Islam is the only curative medicine and that the Arab nationalists didn't know what to do because their romantic project was now lying there losing a great deal of irreplaceable blood. Arguments and shouting, and 100,000 scalpels to operate on the prone body. More jails and arrests and shooting at citizens and political adversaries, while the wounded body slipped into a permanent coma.

In the midst of all this, on the first anniversary of my birth and that of my twin sister, my mother stopped talking. For a while she had been speaking less, but now she stopped altogether. She didn't answer when spoken to, as if she were deaf. Twenty years before her eyes had lost their lustre, and now her lips stopped moving. She kept her words and her sadness and pity and anger and confusion within and locked them up behind thick doors of silence. My father didn't insist on seeking help for her, as if he knew there was no cure. He just kept staring vacantly as usual, as if nothing had happened to her. In the little time he spent at home he stared into his personal unknown. Every now and then he'd throw her a glance and just as quickly shift his faltering gaze from her, as though he knew what was waiting for her beyond the silent hallway.

On 14 July 1969, two years after 9 June and my mother's silence, at exactly two o'clock in the morning, my mother died at the age of forty-four. The woman who was once said to be pretty and whom no one could remember ever smiling died shrouded in her silence. The Naksa and I had just been weaned off her breast. At first, the doctors from the UNRWA, the agency of the So-Called United Nations set up to help the Palestinian refugees in the Near East, concluded from the tests they conducted on my mother that while I was in her arms suckling the little milk she had left, my twin sister, Naksa, was injecting some rare poison into her veins, which wrought grievous harm.

The Scandinavian doctors from the UNRWA paid even closer attention when they noticed that many people in the refugee camps were dying without any sign of chronic illness, and the majority had suddenly stopped talking after their lips set firm. The Scandinavian and Belgian doctors became anxious and nearly went mad, because when they tested the living and the dead they discovered traces of the same poison in my twin sister. The doctors sent for more advanced equipment, but it was all for nothing. Despite the many biopsies and instruments and samples and microscopes and professors coming and going, no one managed to establish the link between my twin sister's poison and the silence that sealed the lips of the Palestinian refugees who had spread to the four corners of Syria and Lebanon and Jordan. Huge sums of money were spent, but the mystery persisted until two Norwegian students turned up who were conducting anthropological research, and, after some investigation and a few visits to the tin houses, they concluded that these people all had something in common, something that no professor, no pill, machine, instrument or equipment could ever heal.

The emotional tie and the metabolic tie to my mother had been broken. My mother left just when I needed her most, and the world would continue to mock me when, twenty years later, other women would turn up in my life who wanted to play her part. How can a woman be understood? One hormone can render her a slave. One hormone can bring about a mysterious transformation. The palms of the hands become tools for caresses, the legs become pillows and the breasts become bottles of wholesome milk, the nipple a soft comforter to absorb pain and hunger and sadness and tears.

On 14 July 1969 I lost the mother I'd never had. I lost a mother who had been dead since 1948. My Aunt Safija, her sister, insisted that it wasn't true, that my mother had clung on to hope until 1967. 'People who have hope do not die, my dear,' my aunt said. Perhaps that's the reason why my father had never even taken a peek at me, never learned the shape of my face – which would, much later, become a perfect copy of his own. He must have associated me with the loss of Palestine, which had led to the loss of his wife before his very eyes, as he looked on impotently, following her in her silence until she packed her bags and departed peacefully.

My mother was buried eighteen metres away from her sister Sarah who had died thirteen days before her. Between them, in the same row, were another seven fresh graves, three of whose residents were relatives of mine and whose cause of death was probably related to the destruction I had brought with me into the world. No wonder I felt responsible for a long time for the ever-growing number of holes in the ground.

In 1967 Umm al-Hiran, the isolated cemetery in the south-west of Amman, was still small and nearly empty. By 1970 it was declared full and couldn't take another cadaver, and the unelected Hashemite government was forced to locate another cemetery to serve the residents of Amman. The residents grumbled because the new place allotted by the unelected government was quite a distance outside of Amman, and they would now have a long trip to bury their dead or visit their loved ones. Apart from that, the real Jordanian dead, those who were actually from the place, were none too pleased with the presence of the refugees lying by their side and stinking to high heaven. When was the last time they'd washed? What was worse, they'd probably washed using the cooking-oil soap provided by the So-Called United Nations.

So first we took up space on their land and now we were even bothering them in the earth's womb. The unelected government was more bothered by the living militants who had begun to operate in the west of the country, firing on Israel. The unelected Jordanian government got into the habit of saying that it lived in a glass house, and you can't throw stones if your house is made of glass – especially if the people doing the shooting were squatters. The unelected Jordanian government decided that there was no way the Palestinians, having sold their land to the Jews and pocketed the money, could shoot from within the fragile kingdom, never mind that the West Bank, including East Jerusalem, was under the Hashemite crown. The West Bank and the East Bank were considered to be Jordan's lungs, but the king suddenly realized that it was better to live on a single lung. King Hussein was a master of the art of survival in that forest of rifles.

Despite the complaints of the indigenous Jordanian people, the government nevertheless allocated a large tract of land for a new cemetery in the south-east of Amman in a place called Sahab, at the edge of the desert that threatens Amman from the south, where thirty-five years later I would go in search of my father's grave, spending hours going around and around, lost in a cemetery that for a while seemed to me to be bigger than the country itself. That cemetery managed to halt the determined onslaught of the wild desert that spread from Hijaz to Tabuk in Saudi Arabia, from where the Arab Prophet came, and his acolytes after him, to reign in their strange robes over half the ancient world. Perhaps they reigned at a time when they all shared a single head, as opposed to scores of heads with no clear shape or design, which sometimes take on the guise of wolf heads and sometimes the heads of sheep, although lately they seem to me like the heads of ageing reptiles. Some of them resemble those strange creatures in *Jurassic Park*.

The government said that its house was made of glass and people in glass houses can't throw stones at others who might throw stones in return and smash everything to pieces. Apart from the shooting, the unelected government kept saying that the Palestinians were becoming a real problem, and that they were abusing the generous hospitality offered to them and were probably mistaking kindness for weakness. 'The Palestinians', it went on to say with some justification, 'are becoming an authority within an authority. They are stopping and interrogating and arresting whoever they want to, and even using their own twisted language. This can't go on. We need to remember that a lot of them are Freemasons and communists of the kind who sleep with their own siblings, and therefore are not only an abomination in the eyes of God, but also in the eyes of the Americans who, let us not forget, are much more powerful than God.'

Under the irresistible pressure of the USA and many other countries who were fed up with the way the Palestinians in Jordan were behaving and the way they taunted Israel, allowing it no peace, the unelected Jordanian government, against its better judgement, was forced to decimate the Palestinian resistance on 17 September 1970. The Hashemite Army, which had been unable to fire a shot in the right direction to defend Jerusalem in 1967, suddenly became a fearless, ferocious lion, and in less than fifteen days it killed a large number of Palestinians. As usual the final figures were kept under wraps. While the Palestinians said they had lost more than five thousand, Jordanian officials insisted that the number was no more than three hundred. The difference, as we can see, is negligible. Because those 4,700 people will in any case be forgotten. The exact figure, as everyone knows, will remain buried beneath the dust.

The 1970 tragedy came to be known as Black September. If we have a descriptive, resonant name, we have all we need. At the age of three I was already reeling under the weight of three major wars – the Nakba and the Naksa and Black September. And the worst was yet to come. Three years and three major tragedies, the last two of which, as you can see, I had brought with me into the world. No wonder my mother decided to pack her bags and leave this world before she had to witness brothers murdering brothers and relatives chopping up relatives and the dead dying with strange questions in their eyes, questions that probably have no answers. That your enemy should kill you is understandable, but how can you understand your own brother killing you? As the cheap Arab blood flowed once more, the Arab League held an urgent meeting. Arafat, whose bones were still tender and who hadn't yet smeared himself properly with the shit of politics, had to disguise himself as a woman to get out of Amman and into Syria and then to Cairo to attend that summit of enraged Arabs at which it was decided that hostilities among the 'brothers' should cease immediately until they had all figured out what to do with the militants and refugees whose shouts and hunger and din had filled the Arab capitals.

It was said that on his way to that important summit, King Hussein received a telex from the Americans telling him to bear in mind that if he wanted to continue reigning on the Hashemite throne, not a single shot from Jordan could be fired in the direction of Israel. In 1977 Bob Woodward revealed that King Hussein ibn Talal ibn Abdullah ibn 'al Sharif' Hissein bin Ali and so on and so forth until the sequence rolls its way into the face of the Prophet himself, as the sacred royal family tree shows, had, since 1957, been receiving monthly payments from the CIA amounting to millions. No one paid any attention to Woodward.

On the 28th day of that same Black September in 1970 Nasser died.

The very day after that tempestuous summit, during which Nasser accused King Hussein of wanting to destroy the Palestinian resistance and letting Russian-backed Syrian troops amass in the north of Jordan. Meanwhile, the US Sixth Fleet was on its way to the region to protect the throne of 'Mr Beef', as the CIA referred to King Hussein. Major muscles were about to be flexed and another catastrophe of world proportions was about to be unleashed on the Arab territories, which already had no shortage of pits and cemeteries. Jamal Abdel Nasser, the legendary Arab leader who still had a place in the hearts of all Arabs despite that humiliating defeat of 1967, died. His picture hung in every house and shop and from every drainpipe, looking into the horizon with eyes full of longing and hope. True, Nasser hadn't won a single military battle, not even that of the Suez Canal in 1956 on which his popularity had been founded, but at least he had provoked a real feeling of unity in an Arab world divided up with a rule and pencil by the victors of the First World War.

Millions of people walked through the streets to mourn the mighty leader. The only leader that the people had loved with all their hearts and in whose empty talk they continued to believe until his final breath. They saw him as a hero, a symbol of unity and salvation. They saw in him a dream that could never be realized, the dream of becoming a single nation, a single body with a single beating heart.

Surprisingly, my father was among those who mourned him. We had thought he had become a statue since my mother's death. A statue in his own image. We couldn't believe that this man still had enough liquid left in his eyes. He'd been saving it up for Nasser's early death. Everything in that region comes early. Everyone's in a hurry; even the grass and fruit grow in a hurry. He hadn't even cried for my mother. For Muhammad he cried a torrent. I don't know whether all men are hard to understand or if it's just my father. When I stare for a long time at the Middle East, I still can't understand why father cried so much for Nasser, and why millions of Arabs mourned him, from Morocco to Yemen. Maybe some men are of a kind that don't show up too often in the world. They are born once in a blue moon. What Nasser's mourners didn't know, however, was that his legacy would be buried with him.

Every last bit of it. All the patriotism, unity, nationalism, productivity, cultural renaissance and romanticism, it would all be buried alongside him, except for one thing that he had started together with his junta and which had spread like an epidemic throughout the Arab world: the military coup.

8

The night was humid, and you didn't feel like counting the dead. They do say it's bad to count the dead in the small hours. That very night, while Simon De Brincat was ranting in the face of the French grand master who engraved his name in gold on the forehead of his Valletta bride, Colin Powell, the handsome US foreign secretary, stood before the microphones of the Security Council of the So-Called United Nations, telling the world they had solid proof of Saddam Hussein's nuclear programme. Lying doesn't suit a man like Colin Powell. Or does it? Does it suit him or not to stain his hands with the blood of the children of Baghdad the way he'd stained his hands with the blood of the children of Mai Lai in Vietnam?

Weakness has a price. Everything suggest that if you're not a wolf, you'll be devoured by the other wolves, as Simon predicted. They'll devour you and tell you it's for your own good as they're chewing on your flesh. Help is invariably the word used by invaders and imperialists. Cruelty is always dressed up as aid.

A few days after that hilarious presentation, which failed to convince even Powell's own wife, the US navy of death, followed by its faithful British sister, lay at anchor off the shores of Arabia.

At two o'clock in the morning of 20 March 2004 the first of the fires and smokescreens began to tear the curtains of night in Baghdad. This time they hadn't come to pull out her teeth. These global dentists had long since thrown her teeth into the bin. The big countries didn't want Baghdad to have any teeth. She might use her teeth to bite, and they wanted to force her to swallow.

This time they had come to flay the flesh off her bones. And when they failed to find any weapons of mass destruction they were forced to play a different tune. A tune celebrating the human rights they had never given a damn about, especially while the dictator was their friend. They began to play the tune everyone had come to expect, the one about democracy and incredible wealth and liberties, civility, investment, prosperity, reconstruction, capital that would flow in of its own accord and billions pumped into Iraqi veins by the US Congress. Charity reminiscent of the Islamic hospital. They thought Baghdad didn't know that for every dollar they forked out they would rake in a thousand. Baghdad knows this very well but doesn't know if she should speak out. What does it matter to a sheep whether it's skinned by its own master or by someone more professional?

'Where are the fucking bastions from which you'll hang these new Mughals? Dogs! Filth! Traitors!' Simon barked in your ear. What did he expect from the feeble Iraqi people? What did he expect from an oppressed people, a people milked, exhausted and crucified, who, despite the oil reserves under its feet, had to spend half a day queueing just to buy a kilo of sugar? What did Simon expect from the feeble soldier whose pay packet was barely enough to buy milk for his infant child let alone a chicken. Bread comes before dignity. Without bread the body gives up. It bends over and loses the will to resist. The reason Baghdad didn't put up a fight was that she wanted revenge on her pharaoh. For years the Iraqi people had been deprived of oxygen. What is there to defend when your father's dead, your brother is a refugee or under arrest, and your children have no bread or milk or medicine? Is it rock and earth that make a home, or is it what takes place on that rock and earth?

Did Simon expect the Iraqis to defend the monster who'd sullied every Iraqi household with the blood he spilled? The tyrant who had left every Iraqi family in needless mourning, wearing black? Simon had predicted and known in advance, down to the last detail, what the mad conservative hawks would do when they swooped down at top speed, borne by their infinite power and science and with the wind and the sun at their back, so why did he still expect the oppressed Iraqi people to hang the new Mughals from the walls of their heartbroken capital?

'The oppressed are unable to mount a defence.'

'If you do the occupier's bidding, you'll pay an even higher price.

Ten years searching under their blankets and their beds and even in the places where Saddam goes to take a dump. Even Genghis Khan didn't do that.'

'Don't tell me that you expected the famished Iraqis to stop these well-armed hordes equipped with the latest death-dealing technology.'

'They could at least make their lives hell once they got there. But you need a writer's pen to make people realize this. Where are the Iraqi intellectuals?' he asked bitterly, and for a brief moment you couldn't remember which of you was the Arab and which the Maltese.

'No one in the history of humanity has taken such a negative view of their own people and country as the Iraqi intellectuals,' he continued. 'Their position is in itself a tragedy, a tragedy unfolding alongside the other major tragedy. They've come across in the worst way a person could come across. They've come across as people without honour, without will and without conscience. Hypnotized like idiotic lambs chuckling as they're led to the slaughter. Some of them parroting the same idiocies they heard from their invading masters. The same phrases that laid the grounds for the destruction of their country. How can they unashamedly repeat them when the Americans themselves have been so clear and consistent in talking about their imperialist project? The harm that certain Iraqi intellectuals have done to humanity can never be forgotten or forgiven. Their poisonous behaviour is a stain on the principles of humane, decent living, not only of their own people but the entire world. When Paris was occupied, Sartre and Camus and Aragon didn't stand by to mull over the crap thrown up by the Germans. They didn't turn away to continue talking about existence and whatnot. They exchanged their pens for rifles and went out to defend their country. How can you sleep alone for a single hour if your land is occupied and your identity has been stolen? How can you close your eyes without being woken up a thousand times by nightmares? Not agreeing with Saddam is one thing, riding into your own country on armoured tanks whose tracks are still stained with the blood of your people is quite another. It's macabre. It beggars belief.'

'There's the resistance, isn't there?'

'It doesn't sting enough, Nabil.'

'Resistance can never be certain of its own victory. Don't forget that resistance is born out of defeat and needs time to gain strength.'

'One or two soldiers or even a hundred won't hurt a monster of planetary proportions with more than six hundred military bases around the world. An imperialist octopus. You can't stab empires in the heart – because they have no heart, my friend. You only hurt them through their pockets. If the resistance doesn't cost them a fortune, nothing will come out of it, mate.'

'Hasn't it always been there, this huge octopus trying to envelop everything before it? Not to mention the dogs running alongside it? What's new? Me and you and the Iraqis, what could we possibly do in the face of these instruments of death that soar through the sky at the touch of a button and find their mark with absolute precision? Isn't it wiser just to hunker down until the storm has blown over?'

'Rubbish. The words of a coward. You and I and every decent person can refuse to be fodder for the octopus. We can even cut off its tentacles. The brave die only once, but cowards like you who wet themselves die a thousand times a day.'

That night you wept together. What were you weeping for exactly? And how could you ever keep up with all that mourning spreading around the world? First Halimeh and Nadia and now Ramallah and Basra and Baghdad and the Tomahawks that could wipe out a village in a second.

During the three weeks of Baghdad's dramatic fall you were visited by a multitude of ghosts. They visited often. As if they wanted to mock you. Ghosts are quite unforgiving when you're under their influence. Baghdad didn't go out to defend its caliph and didn't hang a single rotten Mughal from its walls. Indeed, it left its doors ajar and greeted Hulagu Khan with open arms. Baghdad knows how to get its own back. It knows how to reduce a man, a sultan reigning alone with his golden sceptre, to a frightened rat in flight, flea ridden, confused and hiding in a hole in the ground. Baghdad is able to give you a dose of your own medicine, the one you fed her for twenty-five years. It knows how to march you up to the gallows you forced her to build and hang you by your own rope. Baghdad is like Halimeh and Nadia. They don't care whether they jump into a deep well or into the shallows or even into the arms of strangers.

Baghdad knew it all and didn't say a word. She knew they'd say that she hadn't fired a single shot. And that she hadn't hung a single Mughal. She knows. She knows they'll say she left the door to her temple ajar for Hulagu Khan. They'll also say she went out to greet him in a skimpy dress. They'll say she went down on her knees and begged him to free her from the Nebuchadnezzar of Tikrit. They'll say she gave away all her treasures to Khan before the very eyes of al-Kut, where the Furat and the Tigris join in an embrace. They'll say this and they'll say that and they'll say more, but Baghdad doesn't give a fuck about what they say or what you'll say to your children or what history will write about her.

If Baghdad's flaw is the beauty of its eyes and Jerusalem's flaw is the holiness of its womb, which has spawned numerous prophets, what then is Simon's flaw? If Baghdad and Jerusalem have always been implicated in the chronic suffering of the Arabs, what then of Simon's suffering? And Halimeh's and Nadia's? And why did they all suddenly gather within you in a secret society bent on your destruction? Simon knew everything. He knew what the knights of the West were about even though they always preached supreme values. He knew there would always be a huge octopus, and that one day, when it had devoured everything, it would find nothing to swallow and would begin to consume itself. He knew there would be another octopus getting fatter, getting ready to take its place. Athens, Rome, Persia, Constantinople, Mongolia, London, Washington . . . what did Baghdad's teat secrete? Simon knew that one day your heart would become like his, a gallery of revenge and mutilation. You will always remember his words. You'll remember his words because they're shorn of any metaphor or verbiage. You'll remember his words not because they drip truth and sting like a spear in your side but because what we remember most is what we most wish to forget.

You spend the best part of the night tossing under your blankets staring at the ceiling. Where is sleep going to come from? One minute you were surrounded by all sorts of people; the next you were surrounded by no one. Except for the ghosts and the arrogant spirits of the past.

Those have every right to haunt you because they have many bills and IOUs to settle with you. Except that you can't do anything for them. You declared yourself bankrupt a long time ago. Both morally and emotionally. Which gives them all the more reason to haunt you. But what can they do? Tie a rope around your neck and drag you away? Who said you're not one of them already? At least that's how you were with Nadia and her parents, a ghost. It's the living we're talking about here, the ones you drove away from you.

Was it really you who drove them away? There was Adnan, after all, who went to England of his own accord after he met an English widow who was loaded.

'Come with me,' he said. 'There's nothing for us in Malta. We're just going around in circles for nothing. What have we done to ourselves? The years are charging by.'

'And will the years stop to wait for us once we're in England?'

'England is a big country. There's more space and more opportunity. At least we'll have turned a page, if not with our environment and the people around us then at least with ourselves, and you more than me, Nabil. You really need to turn the page.'

He was right. You really need a new page, except it had to be a page on which you were not present. It seems that in order for your life to succeed you need to leave the life you are living now.

You couldn't go with Adnan. You knew you'd just take it all with you. And you know the problem isn't London. Or Malta. Or Amman. It's not any city. The problem lies in you. Adnan wasn't willing to understand your motives. He wasn't willing to understand how and why you ended up carrying Palestine wherever you went, despite having been born in Jordan. And now Malta. It might seem a small cross to bear, but it isn't. It's true that some crosses are simply dictated by geography, but geography doesn't determine their size. That's up to you. You need to decide on the measurements and the size of certain crosses on which you'll bleed to death. Unlike you, Adnan didn't see any crosses in life. Not only that, he was capable of taking those two wooden beams and turning them into rungs on a ladder. The ladder he had climbed was constructed from various disassembled crosses, the majority of them female.

'Maybe you were right. The problem isn't how to meet a woman, the problem is how to get rid of her.'

'So what about Pauline and Dorita and all the others on the list? Were they just provisional loves or wooden stairs to climb up?'

'You could call it bilateral deception. If it wasn't me they'd have found someone else. I'm as guilty as they are, especially since I happened to fit their specifications. It could've been someone else who happened along instead of me. Janette told me that when I walked into the Reef Bar with my friends they were just about to leave. Timing is everything. Happenstance. Four minutes can make all the difference. Had I gone there five minutes later I wouldn't have met her and nothing would've happened. Who'd have thought that five minutes could alter the course of your life?'

'How do you know your future life will be determined by those five minutes?'

'Come on, you know we've bought the rings!'

'Didn't you tell me once that it's never a good idea to marry an older woman?'

'Seven years don't mean anything for a couple in love. Don't you know the Prophet married a woman fifteen years his senior?'

'She was a widow, too, from one of the biggest merchant families in Mecca. How's that for coincidence!'

'Come on. Janette may not be the most powerful businesswoman in London, but she's not badly off, and she's eight years younger than the Prophet's wife, and she's blonde. Someone the Prophet himself wouldn't have turned away, wouldn't you say?'

Where could these exchanges with Adnan lead? Adnan seemed to know what he wanted to get out of life. Maybe Janette was a shortcut to what he wanted. Or he was for her. Hadn't he said that marriage is a company set up to protect joint interests? Maybe he wasn't far wrong, but you weren't about to start a fresh page. Not in London and not in Kuala Lumpur. In fact, you continue to be amazed at those who do start afresh with such ease, like opening a fresh packet of Twistees. As if life's pages allowed you to turn them over as and when you pleased, instead of turning you over to find everything already scribbled for you in advance. Just a matter of dissolving into the recipe prepared for you without consent, as Simon once said, 'What really concerns you happens when you're not around.'

Adnan wasn't keen on this kind of psychotic chirping. Adnan didn't have a lens through which he saw more than was absolutely necessary or more than he wished to see. What good did those bloody books do you that Adnan harangued you about? What did they do, except increase your sense of uncertainty and doubt? Let's be clear about this, without beating about the bush, without any of your grey opacity. What happens to you when you read a good book? You just feel as if ten people are screwing you up the arse, don't you? Who writes books except lunatics and cowards and eunuchs? What is a writer except an unwanted stranger that cries under the endless lashes, many of which are unnecessary but which the writer nevertheless encourages? Adnan had no use for whips and clubs, or for anyone to poke around in his flesh. Could that be the reason why he found it so easy to pack up and float off like a cloud? As if Malta had never existed and had never tormented him. As if he'd never contracted geographic measles.

Adnan believed he'd finally made it with that English widow. Perhaps it was true, after all Adnan wasn't demanding the impossible like you. Neither did he want to fix all of creation. 'I don't give a damn,' he liked to say. That's how he viewed the conflict and debauchery in the world.

'That's how the world works, what d'you want to go fucking around in it for? It's designed to keep conflicts going. There's no peace if there's no conflict. There's no light if there's no darkness. Each thing to its opposite. We don't need Karl Marx to tell us about dialectics and whatnot. My mother and your mother used to say that even the guts in our bellies get in a tangle. Me, I don't want to get into a tangle. Actually, I just want more. I want to wring as much as I can out of the bounty that God created for us – including women obviously – because those are a special kind of bounty. Every new day is a party for me. Especially because I don't know what and who I'm going to encounter. I don't care if one day I'll be getting my just deserts. Nabil, do you know there are millions upon millions who don't know we exist and couldn't care less?'

All you could do was wish him well and hope he'd find his fortune in the fog of east London. At the airport he 'admitted' to you, as he shook your limp hand, that he did sometimes read a few books behind your back. You smiled and embraced him. The affluent north lured him far away from you. The north always defeats you. Adnan came from the north of Jordan. The opposite point of the compass from Musa al-Ghabbadi, who would later help shape your life. That son of the parched south. But Musa is another story. Musa is the twin of your stoned soul. Musa is the mirror of everything within. With all its beauty and madness. Musa resembles no one except Musa. Irbid is in the opposite direction. Irbid is Adnan's city. The bride of the north. Half its people in the army and the other half spying on them. That's why it's considered the city most loyal to the palace. One aspect fleshed out of that loyalty is an odd intolerance and a smattering of hatred towards the Palestinians, the uninvited guests.

Within a few days you were already missing Adnan terribly, even though he didn't convince you and nor did you convince him. You learned from him that it's not important to convince someone, especially on matters on which no one is ever convinced. The day Adnan left, you drove around aimlessly until evening along the roads of Malta, which had started to feel empty, even though they were crowded with cars and people. You found consolation in Adnan and forgave Irbid its obstinacy because, while the heart softens over time, the head does not. Whether we're made of stone or clay, whether we're toys or beads, whether or not we're a herd of goats driven towards the unknown, whatever we are, the fact remains that Adnan, with everything about him that was pleasant and unpleasant, with what little hair he had left on his skull, will remain one of those whose absence you will feel, another thing missing in your incoherent life.

9

Blood can either bind or separate. It binds whenever a marriage creates a mixture and someone you never knew existed suddenly becomes your father or your uncle. It separates when it is spilled, and once spilled it's hard to staunch the flow. In the Middle East the blood flows from strong arms and legs, inherited from the times of Hammurabi. The Middle East rises to its feet and walks, even after five thousand years. It seeks to bathe itself, but the only thing it can bathe in is blood. The Code of Hammurabi. An eye for an eye and a tooth for a tooth.

In the desert capitals there's no forgiving anyone. Forgiveness is weakness and weakness is shameful, and shame is the foulest of scourges. You split open the head of the man who split open yours, and if his head is not within reach you split his brother's, and if he has no brother you seek out his cousin, and if he happens to be a child we'll wait until he's older, as long as someone's head is eventually split. People in those parts don't really forgive or forget. Never mind that Allah has told them countless times to forgive and has sent them a succession of messengers to reinforce this message. When some of the prophets tried to suspend the laws of Hammurabi it was too late; by then it had wormed its way into the people's DNA. Prophets who persisted were crucified and stoned under Allah's very gaze, and there was nothing he could do except crucify those who'd crucified them and stone those who had stoned them and burn those who'd burned them. Allah himself was caught in Hammurabi's trap.

Division crept into Jordan in the wake of Black September, and you could see hatred peeking out of every door and window and from every balcony. Neighbours began to avoid their neighbours. It was as if Jordan was no longer Jordan, and the people weren't the same people, and blood mixed through marriage began to churn as if it wanted to separate itself and was cursing itself, and children from mixed marriages felt as if they were the filthy product of a misapprehension. A mother would curse the father and the father would curse the hour he'd set eyes on the mother, and aunts and uncles began to hate their nephews because of the aunts and uncles on the other side of the family and vice versa. Following the Naksa and the death of my mother and Black September and the death of Nasser, the refugees lost all hope that they would one day be able to return to something, especially after the king of Jordan decided, without consultation, to make them Jordanian citizens. The ray of light they'd seen in the military resistance led by the Palestine Liberation Organization, the PLO, quickly evaporated after the expulsion of Arafat and George Habash and their allies to the south of Lebanon, where they would wallow in Lebanese filth for another twenty-two years before being expelled and dumped in Tunis and from Tunis to the powder keg of Oslo.

My father remained a broken, demoralized man who preferred the company of trees. He had no country and no job and no wife. Only his tears suggested he was still alive, uncontrollable tears he wept on the eve of Nasser's death and when Muhammad left to pursue his studies in Yugoslavia. That day he burst into tears and again showed signs of life. I will always remember Muhammad's brown suitcase on the doorstep, and my own vague glance, that of a tow-haired four-year-old boy, brushing against people's legs, his father an old man, or one who has suddenly grown old, who hasn't lifted him in his arms or kissed him since the day he was born.

Muhammad waved and left carrying his brown suitcase. No one could imagine what was hidden behind that wave. No one even knew that the rest of my siblings would one day stand on the same doorstep and wave their hands and leave, one after the other, especially after my father returned one day in the company of a slender woman. He told us she was his wife and she'd be living with us and no one needed to call her mother. My siblings seemed to interpret that as an invitation to leave if they'd rather not call her mother. A brother or a sister slipped away every couple of years. Some of them married, and others went abroad to study. Sami joined the resistance, annoying Golda Meir in the south of Lebanon and poking his nose into the shit of Lebanese sectarianism, taking sides in an Arab country that floated on a sea of dynamite.

Meanwhile my father, having decided that Palestine was no more, had found a job as a driver. 'Since there's no man of Nasser's stature, there'll be no Palestine' were the last words he uttered before he stopped listening to the news. He spent what little free time he had tending to the few trees my mother had planted in the little patch of land she'd walled and made her own when the people of the camp started spreading out in all directions. It was a stroke of luck that we lived at the edge of the camp, because we acquired a fertile patch of soil. It was my mother who acquired it, because my father still believed or thought that this was all temporary. At first he wouldn't lift a finger to help with the soil, but, as time passed, in the wake of those momentous events, he seemed to realize that the temporary would last a long time and that five trees on a patch of land were worth more than the paradise in his head. At length he began to bring trees and other plants to place in the soil. Within two or three years the little garden became the most beautiful of orchards.

During these years it might seem as if he were coming back to life, but if you got close to him you'd realize he wasn't coming back to life at all; instead, he was turning into a tree. I'm sure I sometimes heard him talking to the trees, and it seemed as if they were talking back. My siblings laughed at me when I told them. They'd decided my father had simply gone mute, but that wasn't the case at all. Once I thought I heard him call out to me from the garden, and when I went to him I found him staring vacantly. 'Did you call, Dad?' I asked, confused. He just stood there, staring into his personal void. 'Daad!' I begged once more, and suddenly he stared at me in astonishment, as though seeing me for the first time. He tilted his head and continued to stare vacantly, and when I finally gave up and walked away, he said, 'Listen, do you think this woman has invaded your mother's bed, too?' That brought me up short. In part it was his voice, since I'd forgotten when last I'd heard it, but it was also that poisonous question. It wasn't a question you put to a boy of six or seven. You wouldn't even ask it of a twenty-year-old. Or even to me now, since I still can't explain how it feels when you see another woman slipping between your mother's blankets. Even when your mother's in the ground. And on the other hand there's your father's life, and you can't expect him to wage constant war on two fronts, one against memory and another against testosterone.

'Has she invaded your mother's bed?' Hardly a question you ask a boy who's still feeding on his mother's absence. Apparently some of my siblings, especially the girls, blamed my father for remarrying after my mother's 'predictable' death. As if they would never forgive him for that. In the Middle East the only thing you can do with forgiveness is to wipe your arse with it. You can't forgive if Allah would never forgive. So when my father brought me up short with that question on a Tuesday in 1973, after many speechless months, I, no less speechless than he, just said, 'Yes, of course she's invaded my mother's bed. She's sleeping in her room.' Three days after my verdict he helped that slender woman up into his truck with the two suitcases she had brought with her and drove her away without a word, and that was the last time I set eyes on that waif. She had come into my father's life and left it without leaving a single mark on his crowded features, where all the marks had been etched already. Fifteen days after I'd beheaded my second maternal victim, a new war broke out in the region.

On 6 October 1973 my father came home suddenly and rushed to the new radio that we, or rather his new wife, had forced him to acquire. He immediately tuned in to 'This is London'. The resonant voice from London said that at around two o'clock in the afternoon on Yom Kippur, the Jewish people's day of atonement and forgiveness, which happened to be the tenth day of Ramadan for the Arab Muslim people still reeling from the drunkenness of 1967, Egyptian and Syrian troops had launched a surprise attack on the fortified military bases of the Sinai and the hills of Galilee annexed by Israel during those six spectacular days. Preliminary reports, the voice continued, indicated that the Egyptian troops had managed to cross the canal into the Sinai having penetrated the defensive line at Bar Lev, while the Syrian troops had made 'significant' advances into one of the occupied cities in the hills of Galilee.

'Who'd have thought?' my father said unexpectedly. 'What's this lunatic son of a bitch on about?' And when I asked what son of a bitch meant he said, 'Someone who trades his manhood for a comfortable chair.' He was referring to Anwar el-Sadat, the Egyptian leader who had scooped the country out of the bubbling socialist pot and thrown it into the white-hot American frying pan. As a demonstration of his loyalty towards his new master, in the space of a week he had expelled thousands of Soviet military experts. Having realized that American bait tasted nicer and was healthier than that of the Russian socialists, he drove the largest Arab state into the embrace of Uncle Sam, who was waiting to bag a big fish. The vitamins provided by Henry Kissinger would cause a new outbreak of diarrhoea that we still suffer from to this day.

Despite this, during that unexpected war the USA put together an air force to support Israel with their weapons, as if using the conflict to wage a proxy war against the Soviets.

After a few days the scales began to tip away from the two Arab armies. For the first and effectively the last time the Gulf states used their damned oil as a political weapon; they reduced their filthy production by 5 per cent and caused the famous oil crisis of 1973.

Kissinger, the special envoy to the region, spent those three hot weeks yo-yoing backwards and forwards until he finally managed to convince all three armies to stop fighting and each to declare victory. And that's exactly what they did. Only Kissinger could explain the unexplainable. Only Kissinger could explain how, to this very day, all three of the aforementioned countries still celebrate the victory of 6 October.

The biggest victors were the Americans. A few months after the war they swallowed up Egypt, and it wasn't long before it served as a huge archway through which the latest army to occupy the Arab world could make its way.

After the 'Glorious War' of October 1973 a major event began to brew, far bigger than that strange trio of victories. On the surface everything stayed the same, except that Kissinger kept shuttling to and fro and sprinkling new herbs into the mix. Anwar el-Sadat, who came to be known as the Hero of the Crossing, began to dismantle everything his friend Nasser had constructed to prepare the country for its new betrothal. This time the new ring would cost a lot of money because it was bought by the Oval Office in Washington. My father gave himself over completely to the few trees he and my mother had planted. He sheared and snipped and dug and sowed plants and vines and other vegetables. My mother's little allotment with its four little trees became an earthly paradise. Everything he touched turned green and scented, whispering 'good morning' as you left home for school.

Following the glorious war, which was also a holy war, my father stopped paying attention to politics or talking about it. Once in a blue moon he'd listen out for news of Sami. We'd had no news of him since he joined the resistance in the south of Lebanon. We didn't even know whether he was alive or dead. My father had a major upset when he found out that that Muhammad, after finishing his studies, had made his way over to the PLO.

'They won't rest until they've killed everyone's children,' he said, referring to Arafat and his friends. 'Soon one of them will return in a casket.'

Meanwhile Omaymah had got married, but she still dropped by every day. She warned us not to say a word in his presence about the caskets that were already returning from the battlefield. 'If any of you utters a word I'll rip his tongue out,' she warned. We tended to listen to Omaymah and obey her because she was as good as her word. Those harsh years had baked her pretty hard. She'd had to grow older and tougher abruptly, and, perhaps without even realizing it, she had begun to pull the paternal carpet out from under my father's feet, while he without objection ceded his authority to her, as if he'd long since grown tired of being a father. Omaymah suddenly found herself in charge of two families, a silent father and two missing siblings.

We still had received no word of our siblings. Every time she heard that someone had secretly come back from Lebanon, Omaymah would rush over with their photos, because the air in Amman was very murky and the Hashemite prisons couldn't keep up with all the residents and guests, especially those like my brother Sami who were associated with the Marxist George Habash and the convert Nayef Hawatmeh. 'Do please check carefully. Maybe you crossed paths with one of them in Beirut or wherever it is you were.' The answer always came back negative. 'I'll ask as soon as I get back,' they said, but she never heard from them again. 'If only I could find someone to take care of you I'd go and look for them myself,' she would mutter to us. She didn't have to, because a letter arrived from our cousin after a few weeks. Enclosed with the letter were two photos of my older siblings in Beirut, their arms draped over each other's shoulders. Although he passed no comment on the photos my father's wizened features did show some signs of relief.

My cousin brought a great deal of joy and happiness. Joy hadn't visited our house since my twin sister and I were born. He spent a week with us before taking off again in secret, the way he'd come, towards Sidon in southern Lebanon. During that whirlwind of a week, he badgered everyone but especially my father. 'You just ran away like lambs,' he said to him once, and in order to tease him even more he would turn on the radio and tune in to the 'Voice of the Palestinian Revolution', which was banned in Jordan. During that week he was both among us and not among us, and he softened the parched atmosphere of the house with his happiness and his banter. Nevertheless we sometimes caught him muttering to himself like an idiot, and on the last day we found him using a little key to scratch something on to the radio's wooden surface. When he left we read the following words: 'I'm on the road . . . Oh, land, wait for me.' A few months after he etched these words in the radio's wooden casing, my cousin came back, except this time he was in one of those long boxes that brought heartache with them.

The main thing churning away under the still surface of life, a thing about which we knew nothing, took the form of a heightened US diplomatic presence in the region. According to Omaymah those US diplomats were like the crows that appeared in times of disaster and tragedy. Omaymah didn't need US diplomats or crows to make her wallow in odd superstitions and sow the seeds of her melancholy in every one of us.

One year after the Glorious Crossing, the Nasserites and communists and members of the Egyptian left all ended up behind the bars of Anwar el-Sadat's new corrective politics, which he'd discovered shortly after the arrival of Kissinger. The country and the entire region were getting ready for something quite big. Mr Beef's frequent presence and that of the Americans in Cairo were confirmation that this something had to be quite major. In 1993, once documents from the archives of the British, the Americans and even the Israelis were made available for research, we learned that twenty-four hours before the surprise attacks on the Sinai and Galilee during Glorious October, King Hussein flew to Tel Aviv and warned Golda Meir and her army chiefs about the attacks being planned by the Egyptians and Syrians. The Jewish leaders would for ever regret that they hadn't treated that amorphous Arab king with more seriousness. Who would have thought it? Jewish leaders, even those who hadn't been anointed yet, would soon realize that a king like this was worth his weight not in gold but in diamonds, and from then on he would become the apple of the eye of all peoples, much as I was the apple of Halimeh's eye.

Three years after my cousin arrived in an elongated wooden box, three years after the Yom Kippur War that was won by all three countries, Anwar el-Sadat, speaking from the dais of the Council of the Egyptian People, declared that he was willing to visit the Jews in their own home, that is, Tel Aviv, to sign a decisive peace accord. The Egyptian parliament erupted in a round of applause that lasted for several minutes. One of those who applauded for a long time after the declaration that lifted Egypt out of the Arab flock and threw it into the American gutter was Yasser Arafat. At once confused and enthusiastic, Arafat that day demonstrated in his pompous way just how paranoid and politically infantile we still were. In 1977, four years after the Glorious October, the Arab world sat open-mouthed before its television channels and watched the Egyptian presidential plane land at Ben-Gurion Airport near the enemy's capital.

The Hero of the Crossing was given a warm welcome, despite the fact that, like Mr Beef, he'd turned up uninvited. The major thing that had been brewing under the backside of the Arab world had at last taken shape and took the form of the first Camp David Accord, whereby Sinai, which the Jews had so deservedly conquered during the Six-Day War, was returned to Egypt with a host of conditions you needed a month to read through, including an exchange of diplomats to pave the way for negotiations and normalization of relations between the two neighbouring peoples. That agreement took the Egyptians out of the game, although not entirely, but they could only pull off what they managed to pull off by cutting out the Palestinians, who opposed an appendix in the agreement that would grant them a form of autonomy. Go and weep somewhere else out of earshot, they told Arafat as they kicked him out of Cairo. Meanwhile, Israel could focus more on the pain in the arse to the north, in the south of Lebanon, where the Palestinian guerrillas were based, among them two of my brothers.

In the wake of Camp David, Egypt was suspended from the Arab League, which was well known for its spectacular impotence. While he was riding roughshod over public opinion, while he was chucking Nasserites and communists underground, Anwar el-Sadat, the Hero of the Crossing, who had now added a new title to his list, had forgotten that in a volatile region such as this you couldn't trust anybody much, not even your own mother or siblings.

While he eliminated the left-wingers by taking care of the right-wingers, that controversial leader didn't realize he was nurturing a bearded monster in his lap, far worse than the snakes of our grandfather's lore, a monster that would eventually swallow him up at dawn on 6 October 1981, on the anniversary of the very crossing he was commemorating. That glorious morning he was attacked by Islamist members of the Egyptian Army during the annual victory parade as it was going out live on television. They shot him 189 times, thirty-four of them in his chest and his head. A few hours after that spectacular assassination, the birth of Islamic Jihad, the first of radical Islam's offspring, was announced, which would later spawn many more and join bin Laden to form the Tanzim al-Qaeda, which declared open war against the American infidels. The new Tanzimat led by architect bin Laden and surgeon Ayman al-Zawahiri led to a series of bloody attacks against the USA that peaked in 2001 when they flew three passenger planes straight into American icons, including the Pentagon, the general headquarters of the mighty US Department of Defense, and very nearly managed to blow up a plane over the White House, to crown their mockery of the Americans in the eyes of the world. Apparently bin Laden and the surgeon Ayman al-Zawahiri weren't too concerned about who would pay the price for this spectacle: hundreds of thousands of innocent citizens, some of whom had barely heard of a sizeable country called the United States of America.

The televised assassination of Anwar el-Sadat, the Hero of the Crossing, gave rise to hopes that Egypt would find its way back into the Arab flock. Some of the residents of Jordan, especially the refugees, handed out sweets on the street on receiving confirmation of the death of the erstwhile hero. There's no making sense of anything in this region. Not the rulers and not their flocks. In the meantime my father was following it all without uttering a single word. He had travelled a fair distance into that silent world where my mother had strayed, never to return.

After a few days Muhammad Hosni Sayyid Mubarak was announced as the fourth president of the Egyptian Arab Republic. Mubarak wasn't at all *mabruk*, blessed. Instead of taking Egypt back into the Arab fold, he drove the entire Arab flock into the hen house of the sons of Jacob and fattened himself in the stables of Uncle Sam. Meanwhile the smell of gunpowder was in the background. Sometimes it came from the south-east, sometimes from the north and sometimes from above. Yes, from the sky. Everything in that land depends on the moods of the gods, who still hover around Hammurabi's trap.

10

In Vittoriosa you spot Alex in a crowd of people, among them a woman with a loud voice carrying a walking stick. No need to be told they're writers. Many of them are well known, especially the one with the loud voice and the walking stick. You are the only nameless one. You are the only one without an address, and you are the only one without a warm country waiting for you to return to so it can say, 'What took you so long?' You are the only one who expected nothing from the silent mobile phone deep in the pocket of your cold jacket.

Alex's radiant smile makes you forget the pain that flowed through you all the way from Swieqi to Vittoriosa.

He starts to introduce you to the other writers, and you realize there's plenty of pain flowing, pain not quite the same as yours but not dissimilar. You think you can see a wound that has been bleeding for a long time and another that has opened more recently – but which glistens, just like yours, under the fine pattering rain that has begun to taunt the shy walls of Vittoriosa, a fragile picture-postcard town you still can't believe managed to withstand the cannon of Mustafa Pasha for ninety days, when those same weapons had destroyed half of the defensive walls around Vienna. The cannon of the Ottoman Empire and Dragut's swords that had caused terror throughout the entire Mediterranean could do nothing before the magic of Vittoriosa. Some cities defend themselves with their beauty. Vittoriosa, a town that to this very day celebrates its victory over your creed, you always feel as if you could fold it and carry it home with you every time you leave the bar where you slump unseen in a dark corner to drink until you can no longer see yourself and can no longer hear Simon's cracked voice barking 'Dogs, filth, traitors . . .' at you.

As the mayor of Vittoriosa takes you on a guided tour, you notice dreams and tears and desires coursing from the auberge of the Knights of Malta to the square and from the square to the other villages and from the villages to the capital and hidden cities far away from the shores of tiny Malta. The island had come into the world behind the backs of two vast continents engaged during a wild moment of agony in a brutal struggle for a foothold among the deep-seated cliffs at the bottom of the dark titanic ocean three million years ago, resulting in the Caesarean incision that gave us Europe and Africa with the Mediterranean to divide and conquer between them. Two enormous continents and tiny Malta in between. A little child without a mother to rock its cradle, without a father to defend it and give it his family name. Three million years, and Malta struggles between two mothers, yearning for adoption and identity in a cruel sea that still insists on dividing. Pretty little Malta, which had to wait all those millions of years to receive an identity card after she was forced to bare her tits and show her behind.

'My name is Jane. Jane Busuttil,' says a woman wrapped in strange clothes as she shakes your cold hand. Her curly hair is hastily gathered into a ponytail and the scarf draped over her shoulders is far too long. Her eyes sparkle with intelligence from behind a pair of glasses no less strange than her clothes. A dark-coloured, floor-length skirt, creased and billowing, and a coat with large buttons. You shake her hand, which is as cold as her nose looks, reddened by the chill of an evening that had begun to receive the first drops of rain pushed along by the north-easterly wind.

'Alex has talked about you. He said he'd met this Palestinian. So how're you doing?'

'It's not hard to meet a Palestinian. They're all over the place – except where they ought to be.'

'Very good . . .' she laughs. 'Your case will never be decided. Not a chance. Maybe one day, if you become as strong as they are, maybe then you'll be able to fix something. Otherwise you might as well forget it.'

Her words immediately remind you of the gods around their divine round table. Instead of answering her, you turn your perplexed gaze towards the square where the writers have met to discuss some issues that you, certainly, have nothing to do with. Who knows, maybe that's why the woman in the strange clothes came to talk to you; she noticed your scandalous loneliness and thought you shouldn't be left alone. You try to push aside the sadness that grips you – you don't need a Jane Busuttil to remind you of that – and observe the car across the street that has been struggling to slot into a parking space between two other cars. The space is wide enough for two cars, but the driver, whose face you can't see in the dark, is backing into it at completely the wrong angle.

That evening you can't face having another autopsy performed on your person. You are about to tell her to leave the surgical knives and scalpels for another occasion. You make an effort to change the subject. That fool of a driver hasn't managed to park yet.

'Looks like even the Maltese writer is impoverished and a stranger among his own people. I used to think it was only our writers who live in solitude and exile.'

'Don't worry,' she answers, her eyes bright with intelligence behind her strange glasses, 'I can assure you that the situation for writers in Malta is pretty pathetic, too. It won't be long before you discover that here the people who write are the same ones who read. During these literary evenings that we organize, you'll always see the same faces. You'll get to know them well, all of them, because they're the only ones you'll see. We're like a small circle travelling from hall to hall and square to square. If your writers live in solitude, ours fare no better. They're like an ice-cream van in the middle of the desert.'

After the fourth or fifth attempt, the driver finally parks his car in that generous space, which is wide enough for two large vehicles. The driver gets out of the car and walks around it to check that everything is in order, but after a while gets back in, starts the engine and manoeuvres the car this way and that until it is in the exact position he has in mind. He gets out slowly, as if he can't bear to be parted from it. Checks the doors one by one to make sure they are all locked and any troublemakers wouldn't have it easy.

'Do you think there's a crisis in writing or in reading?' You're trying to gauge her intelligence.

'Both!' she shrieks, as if she knew exactly what you were about to say. 'The reader is spoiled and lazy, and there are two kinds of writers: schizophrenics, like the one you see before you, and business people who import books pre-packaged. And, as you know, the spoiled brat prefers a product to be ready made.'

You confirm the two impressions you had when you changed subject on purpose so as not to offer her a glimpse of your internal organs splayed out on a table. All of a sudden you realize that all subjects lead to your own autopsy. Once again you observe that suspicious-looking driver who had reached the top of the street leading to the auberges only to return to his vehicle to fold in the side mirrors.

Jane must have genuine talent, just so long as she resists the temptations of the market. You decide to share the second of your impressions with her. 'It looks like the writer's sickness is universal. But, in addition to that illness, one should add that many people in the Arab world can barely afford to put food on the table; it's hard to imagine them buying books and finding the time to read them.'

'And you think we don't have such people here?' she answers brusquely. 'I work in a school, and I know they exist. They not only exist, they're steadily increasing in number.'

'What're you two chatting about?' Alex interrupts with his enthusiastic laugh, patting your shoulder in a friendly gesture.

'The state of writing,' she answers with a sardonic glance that makes you realize they've discussed this subject among themselves many times. 'We're talking about how much the Maltese read and how highly respected and appreciated we are in this country.'

'But I don't agree with you, Jane,' he answers, as if he's been eavesdropping on your conversation from the very beginning. 'Those who read are, generally speaking, a small percentage the world over, and this trend is even more pronounced with poetry than other forms of writing. Find me a country where people go to sleep clutching a book against their chest. Malta's no exception; we're just part of the world.'

'I know you don't believe there's a crisis of writing. You seem happy if you sell fifty copies.'

'There is a crisis, Jane. I'm not saying it's all rosy, I just don't think the situation's as bad as you make it out to be. When I compare the state of reading and writing in Malta with that in other countries, I don't feel we come out bottom of the rankings. For all that they say about Alexandria and its famous library, I was recently invited there for some literary event, and I'm not lying when I say that there were barely ten people present that evening. So, considering that we're just a handful of people in this country and can draw a crowd of fifty, that's pretty successful when compared with a country of eighty million in a place famed for its 2,000-year history where you can't even pull in ten.'

Finally, the driver regretfully determines he'll have to leave the car parked on the road overnight in that space between two cars across the square in the centre of Vittoriosa. Having folded in the side mirrors and checked countless times that all the doors are properly locked, he crosses the square with heavy footsteps and disappears up the street that leads to the heart of Vittoriosa, the buildings of which absorb the pale light bouncing off the sea before reflecting it back out on to the water, which is ruffled by the chill north-easterly wind.

'The matter of a lack of reading', Alex continues, 'is rather open to interpretation. A great deal of research could be undertaken on that. One strand of the story has to do with one's daily bread and the censor's scissors; the other strand involves the writers themselves. Many writers are like dogs chasing their own tails. You can't just stay within your own personal frame and call yourself a good writer. You need to find your way into social spaces, have your finger on the pulse of the man in the street. Give them stories, prophecies, advice, comfort, rock them in their cradles and sometimes gently spank their bottoms.'

'Why not breastfeed them, too, while you're at it, Alex?' she replies angrily, no longer caring whether you're listening or not. 'This nation has enough gods and fathers, and you know we've not made much headway with them. Whose cradle d'you want to rock? Rather than spoil people, you need to rain down the blows.' Suddenly she turns her face to you, saying, 'Unless you charge like a bull on to the scene no one will pay any attention to you.'

'And what do you mean by charging?' you ask, interested.

'You need to tell the blind man to his face that he's blind. And to the lame, you need to say, you there, you're lame, you little shit. You don't need to be some wily politician fondling the backsides of all and sundry.'

'This won't get us anywhere, Jane,' Alex replies calmly without the slightest hint that her words have done anything to change his views. 'It's true that writing is an indispensable tool, but don't forget that ultimately it's an art and it's about bearing witness, and art doesn't always need to have claws. Not even when it's duty bound to bring about change. What do you think, Nabil?' he asks, hoping to find some support in this complicated discussion that you opened to get away from Palestine.

'I used to think that, one way or another, all art was about change. Maybe change is the only constant in life, otherwise no one would have started writing, painting, sculpting, no one would have ended up with their back broken under the yoke of a creative soul that yearns for change. I believe that every genuinely creative person who hasn't come on to the scene through the back door feels this weight on his soul. People in our parts of the world have lost faith in writing and in writers. Previously, when there was talk about a big Arab project, there were people who went hungry in order to be able to afford a book. People felt that writing was part of that shake-up, because back then a lot of pens were still clean. Today everything is dirty and corrupt. The Arab citizen is desperate and has no hope, and if he goes without food he still can't afford a book, and if he could somehow afford it he'd have to choose one of those books that have made it past the censor. And yet he doesn't protest or rebel. It's as if we've gone through a process of complete domestication. Whatever you might be, our system can turn you into a lamb.'

'Will you listen to this guy!' says Jane in the same sarcastic tone tinged with a hint of anger. 'Don't even think that there are no sheep and chickens over here. If your lot was domesticated through threats and jails, here there are other means to poison your daily bread. We've become the same as you to all intents and purposes. At least in your case everyone knows what kind of governments you've got, but everything with us happens under the cloak of democracy.'

'What I mean to say is that there are several ways to make your message heard through art. You could write a novel or a poem and use it to attack and criticize, but there are also those who paint a flower and are also protesting and rebelling just as loudly and angrily. The important thing is to look through your people's eyes and listen through their ears and smell with their nose.

'I completely agree with you,' answers Alex, 'and for the most part, when you are looking and listening and feeling and tasting with your own senses, you're considered a fool from a marketing perspective, not to say an ass when it comes to seizing opportunities, and you might call that making a social bargain. Sometimes I'm envious of musicians and painters. Their creativity is cut from a different cloth from that of the writer.'

'The choice is yours,' you reply. 'It's up to you whether you become a fish swimming freely in an open sea or a fish with its head cut off in a sardine can. A writer shouldn't go home with a lot of money and food and other people's rubbish! You and Jane are disagreeing only on which words to use. Jane prefers claws that can draw blood.'

'Isn't that right, though?' she says, smiling. 'What's the use of shooting at invisible targets that no one can see?'

'Even poets', you say, trying to grasp the stick from its middle, 'have their own ways of drawing the blood of society and cleansing the wound. The important thing is that what they see and feel are at one with the masses, and he's not addressing the inhabitants of Pluto!'

'People, shall we?' a voice asks from behind the curtain of chilly rain that is starting to get increasingly heavy.

'Yes, we should make a move,' Alex declares with that poet's voice that for some reason always draws your sympathy. 'Nabil, I'm adding you to the list of authors who will be reading. Jane and I have discussed this already.'

He seems certain that you'll come up with something in Maltese, this language that resembles your own and yet is completely different.

If he is confident it's because he's seen something in your eyes, because he knows that writing can also be an accumulation of pain. Let's be honest. Sometimes you feel that you need to feel pain in order to be able to write – except for the times when happiness takes you by surprise and you're left with a mysterious delivery: contentment. Alex did see something. Something is still visible, it seems, beneath the wreckage you carry from one corner to the other – as if you were the only condemned man in that wide region with enough space to accommodate everyone except you. First, they expelled you from the Bible, and now they want you outside of geography. Will they succeed? It's not that the ins and outs of politics can't pull off what the Bible hasn't managed to. But you lot breed like mice. The heads of ten siblings peek out of every hovel, all of them close in age, as if to act as a reminder that the authors of the Bible got it wrong. 'We're still there,' the heads say. 'One thousand fables, and we're still here, and we're going to stay. We don't want to argue or mock your words or embarrass you in front of the evangelists and other authors. Far from it. We don't engage in that sort of thing. We're no good at twisting the facts and making up sacred stories to prove we're inseparable from this earth. Although we are, in fact, inseparable from it. We were here, and here we will stay, for the simple reason that we've got nowhere else to go. Even those refugees you kicked out, even they have nowhere left to go. Look at them. Look closely at them to see how they still encircle Palestine as a cat encircles its litter. We know that ruined Palestine isn't the most beautiful of lands and isn't the kindest of mothers, but she's the only one we have, the only one, and so we'll keep multiplying like rabbits and mice because no one is happier in a hole in the ground than rabbits and mice.'

Those heads remind you of Mustafa's words: 'We breed so often because we die so often.' Palestinian women have so much to bear! Not only do they have to bear their own handicap, now you want them to prepare the demographic bomb. The children of Jacob ended up importing people from Manipur in India on the grounds that they belonged to the twelve tribes of Israel, dispersed for thousands of years and now suddenly rediscovered on the shores of the Gulf of Bengal. Even the Indians of Mizoram and Manipur have a sacred right to your mother's patch of land. All they need is a bit of sanding down to get them into the right shape to fit the mythology.

*

After the discussion you go to that bar just off the square in Vittoriosa. The rain becomes heavier. You find your inconspicuous spot and start drinking as if you could quench fire with fire. After a few shots the heart grows warmer and the veins begin to glow. You know the real problem isn't with writing or with readers. The problem is within you. With this world that has lost its head. With this race of people who are probably programmed to self-destruct. The problem is with the divine table. With Adnan and Pauline. With Halimeh and Nadia. With your own head. With the secret and dangerous cult conspiring against you. With the ghosts that pursue you. What the hell did Halimeh and your father get up to for you to turn into him and to cause her to cross the Mediterranean Sea to ruin your life, a life that had been ruined already? Ever since the heavenly game began. The first time she appeared was on 9/11 when the world was burning and cracks were appearing in Alex Attard's dream. When Adnan was fucking against his will. When the Afghans and Iraqis began to gather in their hundreds of thousands to find their place beneath the dust. She thought you were your father, and you thought she was her. The same mysterious embroidery. The same big eyes that used to scrutinize you thirty years ago, as you diffidently nibbled at the food she had prepared. The same breasts she would press hungrily against you as she combed your untidy hair in the yard between the two tin huts in Souf.

After that infamous date that changed the world she appeared to you frequently. Whenever she felt like it. Especially, though, when you were in pain. The pain you felt when the aeroplanes flew through metal and glass and the tower became a pillar of fire. Or when Nadia taunted you by spending an evening with someone else just across the street from your own front door the night of the dramatic fall of Baghdad. Nadia and Baghdad fell on the same bizarre night. One fell into the hands of the new Mughals, the other fell to a depth you cannot fathom and which no one can fathom except perhaps a woman whose heart has been wounded. Except for a Halimeh, who prefers to appear to you when you're wracked with pain. As if to poke fun at you, to rub salt into your wounds. Or to make you drink some poisonous medicine that courses through her. Who knows what medicine your father made her drink?

Who knows what medicine life made you drink as it passed you the rusty keys of a disfigured Arab empire that could no longer tell its arse from its elbow? Who knows what your people made you drink to stop you from growing up like any normal child in any other part of the world, turning you instead into an odd, ruthless creature that would turn aeroplanes into bombs and missiles and blow himself up on trains and in bus stations? What could you do with an empire torn into twenty-two separate Arab entities, each guarded by thousands of dogs with tails that extended from the edge of the Arabian Peninsula to Washington?

What sort of medicine did you make Nadia drink after life gave you a taste of every type of poison? What kind of security could you have given her when there is no knife, there is no sword, there is no bomb, no cannon, no epidemic that hasn't scarred your face? What could you give her when today there's no weapon on the market that hasn't first been tested on your flesh? She began to look square to you. Always talking about houses, stones and ceilings, kitchens and bathrooms and their colour schemes. A square world. Her face, eyes, mouth, tongue, teeth, nose, even her soft breasts that could engulf a man in seconds, now felt hard and square. Everything went square and the dogs of marriage barked from every corner of the world. You began to feel as if you'd been squeezed into a square suitcase and Nadia was trying to force it shut. There wasn't much you could do except slip away. Except run away from the square altar. Leap off the parvis and escape the square city. Nadia would never be the same. She would never again be fathomable. The dogs of marriage wouldn't let her, just as the dogs of the Arabian Peninsula wouldn't leave you alone. They would pursue you until they'd caught you, bled you dry, distilled your blood, bottled it and sent it on ships to the vampires in the Oval Office to guzzle during their extravagant soirées, just like you guzzled the memories and counted the losses and failed loves on a wet night in Vittoriosa.

No matter how much you drink, you cannot stop the rain. To you it looks like yellow wheat cascading from the sky. The north-easterly grabs at you as you exit the drinking hole. You're not completely dead yet.

There's more for the dogs of the desert and the Valley of the Nile to squeeze out of you yet. As you cross the square you're gripped by a strange desire to smash the windows of that crazy man's car or at least scratch it. You almost do so, but suddenly you spot a woman's form at the side of the square, almost exactly at the spot where you're parked. She wears a dark floor-length dress. She has no umbrella. Her hands are laid across her chest and her hair is soaked. Your first thought is that she might be high or lost or waiting for someone, but, when you start walking slowly towards her, those ravishing eyes shining under the yellow lamplight, like twin windows on to a brightly lit purgatory, seem familiar. As soon as she sees you approaching she walks into the damp alley. You hurry after her. Again you catch sight of her in the alley, under the curtain of golden wheat coming down from the dark sky. Your heart is beating fast, but you keep following her. Suddenly she stops before one of the doors. Rummaging briefly in her soaking-wet pockets she draws out a key. She inserts it into the lock and turns it. She wipes her feet on the mat, pushes the door open and goes inside.

11

The year 1973, which brought so much madness and destruction and so many political earthquakes, was also my first year at school. The six-year-old boy bearing the weight of three major wars on his shoulders stood in a queue of new pupils, many of them refugees, carrying a large exercise book he'd acquired from his older siblings and whose drawings he knew by heart.

'From now on you're my responsibility. Make sure you keep this place quiet and in order and, most importantly, clean, because this school will become your second home,' we were told by a huge heavily made-up woman brandishing a cane. 'Those who stick to the rules will find love and encouragement; if you have other ideas you'll have to deal with this.' She swished the cane through the air. 'Do you understand, children?'

Everyone understood, because everyone in that gathering of taut flesh had heard of Miss Jinan and her moods, even though we'd never set eyes on her before. We'd heard a lot about her, or rather about her beatings, from our predecessors. Sometimes from the mothers of children who went home with red backsides. The name was enough to make you shit yourself. Who knows, maybe over time we actually come to resemble our own names. *Jinan* sounds like the Arabic word for madness, which is no surprise really. Let's assume for the time being that it meant madness in the abstract, not the madness that drives you to the Mount Carmel loony bin. What is mad after all? Going by the Arabic etymology, madness (*jinun*), genie (*aljaniu*), foetus (*jinin*), all mean something you can't actually see, which also includes heaven (*aljana*)! Goodness, we were going to leave that one out! Such an important word! Perhaps it's *aljana* because it drives you *jinun* with its beauty (*jamal*)! It causes you to take leave of your senses, and you end up invisible. Or it drives you mad, wailing under the strokes of its cane. I have to declare that Miss Jinan, before whom we stood all stiff and straight and pretty on 24 September 1973, a few days before the Glorious War of Ramadan, represented both types of madness. Once again I would be the one to discover, after only a few days, that this tall statuesque woman, who painted herself in the seven colours of the rainbow and whose very glance made everyone shit themselves, was actually two women in one. One of them hated children with a vengeance; the other couldn't live without them. For as long as I attended that school she was never sick and never took a day off and never had an errand to run and never failed to grease herself with the seven colours of God's bow. But will you listen to me? It's as if I've discovered the missing link in life's spinning top! What do two women in one imply after all? Aren't all mothers like that? They curse the day they brought us into being, and then they're utterly content to wipe the shit from between our legs. And the majority of teachers simultaneously both hate and love the children in their care. I've added nothing new to the social or scholastic narrative. All mothers are trained to wipe shit, not just their children's but also that of the children's fathers.

Miss Jinan handed out beatings, some of which went down in history. But that wasn't what drove me mad about her. What drove me mad was the way she could look you straight in the eye and know whether or not you were lying. Was that child abuse? Or is a child never supposed to lie? Not even if it was born and raised in a cradle of lies and horrific fabrications and the hollow declarations of Ahmad Said, which had won us the war for five days straight only to lose it on the sixth like an athlete who collapses four metres before the finish line? But in order not to cast a shadow over Miss Jinan – who knows what's become of her? – I have to admit that her piercing glances never failed. Not once. Her look was a precision instrument – and that's why she never punished anyone who didn't deserve it, once the system had given her a stick in addition to a licence. Needless to say we're talking about a rotten totalitarian and patriarchal system founded on fear and intimidation and threats and the sacred order of the big and the small, which had placed Jordan at the peak of civilization.

On the other hand, we also need to remind the reader that there are always those children who simply drive you nuts, and the only thing that can control them is the cane. I must also admit that, despite the good marks I used to get and the astute mind I thought I'd acquired during those few years chock full of big events, I was still one of those who frequently found himself on the receiving end of her cane after she'd interrogated me with her glance and promptly pronounced her sentence before the guilt could die down. And I swear that while under her cane I could see a mysterious love in her eyes.

According to Omaymah I lost my way the day I hooked up with Musa al-Ghabbadi, the boy from the nomad family that lived at the top of our street. She thought Musa was possessed because his mother and father were possessed and they hated Palestinians.

'Stay away from that filthy family. The Jews have more mercy than they do,' she told me. Musa, too, received similar admonishments from his own mother. The air was pretty thick between the two peoples. One had breached the bounds of hospitality while the other lived in a glass house. Musa and I weren't interested in the hospitality or political glass that everyone else prattled on about, and the more they advised us against spending time together the stronger our friendship became.

He and I were descended from the same pack of lies, stamped with the downfall of 1967. He had a dictatorial mother and a father who was always sloshed, while I had a dictatorial sister and a father who was always silent. Being silent and being sloshed are close enough. Both entail a flight from reality and duty.

Few members of the generation that preceded ours had refused the national anaesthetic like my martyr cousin, whose smiles and happiness had once filled our house while he was in hiding from the Jordanian intelligence services, which had launched a ruthless campaign against anyone connected to the PLO or anyone who hadn't buried their head in the sand or a sack of chicken feed.

Musa al-Ghabbadi and I began to fertilize ourselves on that land and awaken the demons inside us. Perhaps because we were so restricted indoors, we let loose outdoors, among the stones and the dust and the drainpipes and people and animals and birds in the trees. There was nothing and nobody we wouldn't poke fun at, and they would all report back to Miss Jinan, the big headmistress whose hand weighed three rotolos.

Together we were an explosive presence, and after just a month we had to be put in different classes, because even Miss Jinan's cane couldn't keep us in our place, while the threats and admonitions of his mother and Omaymah didn't diminish our mutual friendship one bit. Despite the constant orders not to talk to each other we were joined at the hip. The pure refugee boy spent his time with the pure Bedouin boy. One whose father was a tree and the other whose father was a bottle.

'That's what you get from the son of a drunkard,' Omaymah muttered the day the school called her in following an incident in which we had managed to break a window.

'Your son, madam, and that devil, with all their wild behaviour and throwing things about, they smashed a window in the classroom. If it happens again he won't be allowed back. Do I make myself clear?'

'Go ahead and break his fingers, madam,' Omaymah said angrily. 'I hereby give you permission. I've no idea what's possessed him. He was never like this, I swear. It's only since he's been hanging around with that filthy boy.'

'It's the fault of that stinking refugee with the dumb father,' said Musa's mother when they sent for her as they'd sent for my eldest sister, who had matured so much over those seven years that they thought she was my mother.

Musa was just like me. On his own he was an angel, but when two quiet types get together it's as if the fusion releases a massive amount of energy that has to be spent somehow: by picking on other kids, especially girls, jumping over walls, climbing trees and drainpipes and lamp-posts. We even climbed the pole bearing the Hashemite flag in the middle of our school playground.

'What are you? A pair of dressed-up monkeys?' Miss Jinan barked at us as she beat us with her cane in front of the whole school. The morning beating had become more or less routine for us. Not a week went by without complaint, and, if the complaint was about only one of us, the other would get it, too, because Miss Jinan was never convinced that one boy could single-handedly cause all that trouble. In any case, her glance never failed. That's why she put us in separate classes on the advice of the three other teachers, Miss Widad, Miss Majida and Miss Salwa. They all wore perfume and warpaint, and they all agreed that Musa and I were disrupting lessons.

That separation felt worse to me than all the wars in the region. In retrospect it might seem as if they were right to keep us separated, but people like us were really a gift, for it was knots like ours that forced people to come to their senses. Knots and friendships like ours that began to bring King Hussein around to the realization that the new generation couldn't be lied to and told that communists and their ilk stamp on the Qur'an and sleep with their sisters. Because the generation that was growing up hadn't fallen from Saturn like George Habash and the convert Nayef Hawatmey and the Ba'athists and the other nationalist Freemasons who were driving the Arab flock towards an abyss.

King Hussein was no fool, and he could smell what was brewing. After all, in 1970 he had realized that a Palestinian military presence would become a huge headache and might even topple the Hashemite throne to which he had ascended after his mother, Queen Zein, had locked up his father, Talal bin Abdullah, in a mental hospital. In private, some of the Bedouins with palace connections had denied that King Talal was mentally unstable and told a completely different story, one that probably involved horns and the stench of cuckoldry.

According to the Bedouins with palace connections, Talal had caught his wife Queen Zein al-Sharif in bed in the arms of Sir John Bagot Glubb, better known as Glubb Pasha and among the insiders as Abu Hunaik which means 'Little Jaw'. Now, Little Jaw was the commander of the Arab Hashemite Army from 1939 to 1956, precisely during the period when the first sizeable chunk of Palestine was swallowed up. Does this mean that this English general was leading the Hashemite Arab army against the Jews that his own government had allowed in? 'Unbelievable!' my father had said, back when he still had a tongue. 'What a bunch of idiots we are. We expected Little Jaw – who takes his orders from the very same London that coordinated the largest Jewish emigration to

Palestine – to send them back to Europe where they came from when Europe did all it could to get rid of them, even burned them alive.'

According to the palace, he'd been christened Abu Hunaik because he had a long chin, but, according to the Bedouin gossips with palace connections, he earned the nickname because when King Talal caught him with the queen in the royal bed he shot him twice. One shot hit the pillow but the other hit him in the jaw, which subsequently hung open and couldn't be put back into position, so he became known as Abu Hunaik. And between a *hunaik* and a jaw some Arab land was lost because it was handed to the Jews on a plate, as my Aunt Miriam, who knew nothing of the tactics of the Arab army led by the English colonel, once put it.

King Hussein realized that it was relationships like mine with Musa al-Ghabbadi that could screw him up and that if he didn't do something about them he would quickly lose his hold over a kingdom surrounded on all fronts by voracious neighbours. King Hussein was no fool. Actually he was a very clever ruler who'd been educated at Harrow and Sandhurst, the famous military academy. They say that many who walk the corridors of these Machiavellian hothouses become big shots in their own countries – kings, political leaders and so on. Who knows what they feed them there to make them so great?

Under severe pressure from my friendship with Musa al-Ghabbadi, the clever king had to relax his fist and reduce the speed with which anyone with different views was hunted down. This inseparable friendship between a Palestinian refugee with a dumbstruck father and a pure Jordanian with a drunken father forced him to launch a publicity campaign to improve his image at home. His reflection in the mirrors of Washington and Tel Aviv already showed a handsome visage; all he needed was to burnish it a little at home – I mean with me and Musa al-Ghabbadi, who knew nothing of political mirrors and double dealings but who nevertheless forced him to descend to the street to meet us, with me and Musa and those in whose name he went to beg, claiming they were his people.

We had been standing since morning. It was a burning hot day. The dazzling sun over our heads was as scorching hot as the calibrated voice of Miss Jinan and her colleagues, who were daubed with even more colourful make-up than usual. We were still young, like ducklings by the roadside. There were soldiers and police everywhere – at the crossroads, on the rooftops of hotels and houses and shops and even in the minarets of mosques. An incredible heaving confusion. The teachers were like frightened cats anxiously weaving among us. Miss Jinan waved her cane as she paced between the rows of ducklings in a heightened state, soaked with sweat, and she kept up the exhortations she'd thrown in our faces since early morning. 'Careful now, children. Wave your hands when the king drives past, wave as hard as you can. Understand?'

My mind wasn't on the king but on my friend Musa, how to find him in that horde of ducklings and pacing teachers, with a policeman or soldier aiming a rifle at you every time you glanced upwards.

They had brought out all the schools in the country to give the king a warm welcome on his return from Damascus. I don't remember what the welcome was for exactly – it could well have been that Syria and Jordan had suddenly, without warning, become friends again. That's how it goes in that part of the world. You never know when and how and why they pick a fight, and the same goes for when and how and why they make friends. All you need to worry about is how you're going to dance to the tunes.

Suddenly there was the sound of drums and trumpets, French horns and bagpipes and other instruments, the names of which I didn't know. After a few seconds a lot of motorcycles and shiny black cars appeared. Soldiers and armed officials ran alongside them, some of them literally being dragged along. More motorcycles, cars and soldiers. More soldiers, cars and motorcycles and then . . . the king . . . the king himself. As large as life and smiling from behind the glass of a roofless car. He waved at us, and we waved back with our nervous, sweaty little palms. It all happened in the blink of an eye. They'd been preparing us for that historic blink of an eye for fifteen days, and then it was over like a sudden flash of light. Valuable or historical moments always pass by in a flash. And we like to think that life's major events take decades to brew in the pot of human history. Not so, since every event has its precise moment of birth. As for me, with my mind on my friend Musa rather than the king, I didn't know that during that precious time I was being written into the pages of Arab history, one of the lucky few who got to see a real live king at such a tender age. Because, let's face it, how many kings is anyone likely to see in a lifetime? And what are the chances for a filthy refugee like me, who had been responsible for so much harm in the world? After the convoy passed by everything got tangled up, and the geometric lines of drenched ducklings and teachers pacing among them turned into one giant gaggle rolling along behind the royal convoy on its way to one of the palaces scattered around the hills of the Hashemite capital. I tried to extricate myself from that gigantic mass of people to look for Musa, but someone pushed me, and I tripped and ended up on the ground. No one helped me up because no one was paying any attention to me; in fact, no one was paying any attention to anyone else. They were all focused on the king; at least that's what I thought before I discovered that at the crossroads of the main thoroughfare they'd slaughtered some camels to make the welcoming gesture more auspicious for the king returning from Damascus, and for some reason or another, as soon as the parade was over, the people stampeded towards the camel meat, and the little ducklings like me ended up under the feet of the adults. I don't know how many feet and shoes trampled me, and I've no idea how long I struggled to free myself from that human flood under all those feet and shoes, some of which had holes in their soles.

After a great deal of effort I managed to extricate myself. Musa was nowhere to be found. I dragged myself home with my hair in an unruly tangle, my clothes and body caked in dust and sweat, and as soon as I arrived my sister emitted one of her loud shrieks. 'What the hell have you been up to? Go and take those clothes off and wash or I'll be giving you a piece of my mind. Move!' I ran into the bedroom panting and went straight to the mirror stuck inside the door of the wardrobe to take a look at myself; there, instead of my own face, the face of the boy that I was, there was a face of a large lizard staring back at me from the mirror.

The slow haemorrhage continued from our house in Amman. The fourth of my siblings left for Czechoslovakia, which would later spawn two European member states. By that time my father had turned into a tree. He didn't pay any attention to those who'd departed and those who remained behind.

Omaymah was torn between her husband and children on the one hand and her siblings and father on the other. She, too, without knowing it, began to lose some of her toughness, and gradually her authority started to slip. The more she let go, the more the street beckoned to me. The looser her fist became, the more I got smeared with grime from the street. In the ensuing years Omaymah became so weak that the street won me over completely and became my mother and father. I now understand that it was the street that brought me up, despite Omaymah's efforts to divide herself into two mothers and despite the fact that they sent me every summer to spend some weeks in the custody of Halimeh. Because there, too, I would roll in the dust just as, despite my desperate efforts to find my childhood friend, I had tumbled in the dirt beneath the feet of the masses hurrying to get their share of meat from the king's auspicious welcome in Prince Muhammad Road, the main artery of the old city of Amman.

That parade would be etched on my memory in big letters. Musa, too, said he'd had his share of kickings as he looked for me while I was searching for him. Who knows? Maybe it was at that moment that our little minds began to conceive of the same elusive and difficult question: why are we at the bottom? Sometimes the question is more important than the answer. The answer might be for someone else to find, the main thing is to ask. The elusive question gave rise to even fiercer and more aggressive behaviour.

There were times when we terrorized the whole street. At school, sometimes even at the police station, parents and relatives of other children kept coming in to complain about us. All of which contributed to the morning beatings at the hands of Miss Jinan. The early-morning beating became the routine under the Hashemite flag that was raised every day to billow in contrived glory.

Despite the fact that we wore her out during those hellish three years, on our last day of school Miss Jinan told us she wished us well and advised us to be careful of male teachers, because male teachers, she said, weren't nearly as patient and gentle as she and her colleagues. Despite the demons riding on our shoulders, she added, Musa and I had brains, and it would be a shame if our silly shenanigans were to get us expelled from school. The school, she said, wouldn't tolerate the damage we did, both on and off the premises, for much longer. 'One more time, and you'll be thrown out of our school, and you'll end up shining shoes on the pavement.' As if we weren't already on the pavement polishing our poverty and hunger. The hunger that had made the shoes of the citizenry walk on us, upon their own children, the same citizens who had just given a warm welcome to their king on his return from Syria.

I didn't know then that my fragile consciousness, which had recorded all the details of the greatest welcome it had ever witnessed, had as yet seen nothing of what life had in store. There was much more it needed to absorb and gaze upon in wonder – in much the same way as the entire world stopped to gawp at the million and a half Iraqi graves that were dug after the arrival of the Americans. I didn't know that my mother's haemorrhage and my father's would continue to bleed out within me and that life would finally turn me into a big open wound, a wound with the features of a man who sometimes stood before the mirror and couldn't recognize himself because he still saw the lizard that had replaced his own features after that important meeting with the Hashemite king.

In the boys' school Musa and I were separated again. This time the separation was decisive: not only were we not put in the same class we weren't even on the same shift. He was on the morning shift, and I was on the afternoon one. Evidently Miss Jinan had sent word about us.

'Those whose names are called out should stand on this side,' a pot-bellied man with a cigarette in his mouth said on the first day of school. A sheaf of papers suddenly appeared in one hand and a cane in the other. Every now and then he'd swing it against his leg as he read out names, as if to send an early warning about what awaited us at the new school. He read from his list, and the children who heard their names crossed from one side to the other. My name was one of those that crossed to the other side while Musa's was not read out. When the pot-bellied man reached the end of the list of names, he told the others, including Musa, to stay where they were, and told us to go home and return the next day at eleven in the morning.

Finally they had managed to separate us. Who had we upset? It seemed that no one wanted our friendship to survive. A friendship between two children who had everything and nothing in common. One whose father was a bottle and the other whose father was a tree. The only thing they had in common, as fathers, was that they were both absent.

When we're young we have no idea how adults think. But what they tell us, when they tell us anything, we tend to take with the utmost seriousness. The problem is that our fathers never told us anything. They always cursed our presence, if not with their tongues then with their stony silence. There's nothing worse than the silence of a father in his own house. Sometimes even a single cough at night is enough to calm a boy who can't get to sleep between his sheets.

How is my generation to blame, a generation that inherited all manner of things: lost battles and accursed wars, bills that haven't been paid for thousands of years? Many of these bills are divine and form part of the game of the gods.

Musa and I went wild when the state separated us on Miss Jinan's recommendation, the woman who, after 783 early-morning beatings over three school years, had declared that we were a pair of good students and that she wouldn't want to see us one day sitting on the pavement with a box of polish shining people's shoes for a pittance. She wasn't making it up, since the majority of children who left or were expelled from school did end up as street vendors or else as doormats in factories and sweatshops on which people could wipe their feet as they came and went. That was the fate of Musa's cousin Muhammad, whose father took him out of school and dumped him in a garage to absorb a trade at a young age, and he ended up absorbing nothing, since he immediately became a servant for the boss and his clients. 'Son, a pack of cigarettes. Muhammad, three teas. Muhammad, go to that bloke's, see if he's got a nut shaped like this one. On your way back, drop by that arsehole's, check if he's finished that bloody pump for us . . .'

After a week at the boys' school Musa couldn't take it any longer.

He began to threaten his mother, telling her that he'd drop out unless she got his shift changed so he could be with me. One time as he nagged at her, his father barged in from the other room carrying straps and a whisky bottle and began to shout, 'Go. Get out, then. You'll end up getting fucked in a garage like your cousin and your uncles and your father, too. An entire country bent over to get fucked. Ptuh! I spit on you and those who brought you into this world.' He vented like an exhausted whore. After that family discussion Musa's father never interfered again, not in his life or in anyone else's. He continued to drink until he'd worn out his liver and died a few weeks after that winter, the winter that turned Musa al-Ghabbadi into a vendor of bread and lemonade in front of the Passport Office, where such a crowd gathered you'd think the entire populace wanted to flee the country.

While I kept my nose in the books and exercise books that I knew by heart from my older siblings, Musa had to keep his nose among the people and their filth, and that's why he matured before I did. Musa found himself responsible for a lot of mouths, which were kept shut by the few crumbs his father earned working as a gardener for some rich people, having been expelled for idleness and insubordination from the army during a phase in Black September when the kingdom was being disinfected of Palestinian scum. Those who showed the parasites even a little bit of compassion were discharged post-haste, especially those who, like Musa's father, wore a uniform. Because within that august institution the opportunists and the ambitious had started hatching their plans.

Coups and rebellions are always being cooked up in military kitchens, and King Hussein, as we know, was no dummy. Quite the opposite. He knew all too well how far the military could go if its claws weren't trimmed every now and then. Apart from the fact that he himself had an army background, he'd seen with his own eyes what had happened to the monarchies in Egypt and Iraq in the 1950s.

He couldn't forget, for example, the bitter experience of his royal cousins in Baghdad. They had been literally torn to pieces, and some of their corpses had been tied to cars and dragged along the main thoroughfares of Mesopotamia. King Hussein, having witnessed what befell his relatives in Baghdad, swore he would draw blood from every house in that city. I can't confirm or deny these reports, but I can confirm that after three major wars, none of which had anything to do with Palestine, every house in Baghdad was bleeding.

From 1958 on, binding and dragging enemy corpses became an Iraqi tradition at which they excelled. The nationalists dragged the monarchists, and the communists dragged the nationalists, and then the Ba'athists came and dragged everyone. Fifty-five years later the tradition was revived in the al-Adhamiyah district of Baghdad. This time it was the corpses of young US soldiers, probably from poor families, who'd been dispatched on an ambiguous mission, the name of which kept changing, only to end up murdered and mutilated and dragged through the streets of al-Adhamiyah and Fallujah.

King Hussein had the right medicine for every ailment. Let's not forget he was the product of the British military establishment, which never misses a thing, especially when it involves a king as important as ours. The recipe was simple: destroy the middle class, the engine of ambition and creativity. Because of this, the Hashemite Army had to be built from scratch in a way that reflected the country's social strata, which now consisted of a few very fat cats and the famished masses chasing their illusory daily bread.

The early death of Musa's father and the bread Musa began to earn for his family in his father's stead gave him a newfound authority in that household. His mother, who used to lay into him because he spent his time with me, no longer said anything when she saw us together. Not only that, she sometimes even invited me in for a meal, especially when I helped Musa carry his things back after a day's work. By the end of that summer Musa's mother was welcoming me with a smile and treating me like her own son. As soon as I went into their house I discovered that, although they owned the place – I mean they weren't EDPs, like us – their circumstances were no better than ours. It might even have been worse, because one way or the other, between what my father made whenever he did any work and the aid we got from the refugee agency, we made ends meet. At least we could fill our bellies and multiply.

Jordan continued to suffer an acute haemorrhage. The best people invariably left while the fat cats and dogs increased in number and became more aggressive, and every time a new cat or dog arrived on the scene they brought into existence hundreds of families like ours and Musa al-Ghabbadi's.

12

'I heard you were engaged,' she said the first time you went out together. Their resemblance couldn't possibly be a coincidence. Halimeh as a young woman.

'How did you hear about that before you'd even set eyes on me?'

'The ear gets curious before the eye.' You turn away, not wanting to show her the marks left by the fingers of her malice. Intelligence and beauty and the big eyes from Żabbar and breasts made to envelop you. Finally the hour of your execution has arrived. Every man steps out to his own cliff edge, and if he fails to go the cliff will come to him. Before those Żabbar eyes there's no turning back. You need to choose between execution and . . . execution.

'Yes, I was engaged. I was betrothed to wounds and darkness, and I haven't yet recovered from the injuries I suffered under various religions. Despite what the prophets say, love is always the loser. They asked me to change my religion the way you change a shirt or a pair of socks. But how is it possible to simply declare that from now on you will no longer be yourself? And you, where are you on the arc of life?'

'No better. I'm looking for the gallows. I'll welcome anyone who comes along.'

Gallows, did she say? Yes, gallows, and here you were. From the blows of the biblical cudgels to blows inflicted by wide eyes and a hungry breast that could swallow a good-sized man just like that.

Gallows! Did you know the gallows would welcome you? And that a welcome is the first step up to the platform raised between heaven and earth on which your ancestors trod and left behind their features and the depth of her eyes, the explosions of language and the seeds of a lunacy that five thousand years later would appear as this shapely

Phoenician bride here before you and inviting you to your execution. An execution that you yourself would be in charge of, so that she wouldn't need to stain the tips of her fingers with the Phoenician purple of your ancestors? Did you know that before those big Żabbar eyes there was nothing for it but to bid farewell? Farewell to yourself and the heart weaving its own shroud with every beat, without realizing that it was the clothing you'd wear at your final farewell.

'My great grandfather was an Arab or a Turk.'

'Those sacrificial eyes must have come from somewhere.'

'A poet, too!'

You need to verify whether she is, in fact, Halimeh. 'Do you know who I am?'

'I do. I know more about you than you think.'

'Do you know that Palestine borders on sorrow to the east? And the alienated sea to the west and to the north the ladder the prophets climbed towards heaven?'

'Isn't that why I'm looking for the gallows?'

The gallows! And here was your head. She climbed up the ropes of welcome. 'I'll welcome anyone who comes along', and here you were. Welcome. You arrived after many religious battles, all of which you lost with the intervention of the Christ child who had to pitch in in favour of his people and at the last moment rescue those who were poised to become your victims, to save them and leave you with a broken heart dripping questions.

'Would you like to watch the sunset over a coffee?' That was how you asked her on your first date, the first step to the Hangman's Square.

'How could I possibly resist a poet's gaze?' she replied maliciously. Accused of poetry! Better to be accused of a couple of verses than a thousand other things. You were in no position to deny the accusations, especially those brought against your eyes caught gazing at her breasts.

You make your way home in a daze. You ring your own doorbell. Expect someone to open the door until you remember that you live alone and have a key. You apologize to yourself and turn the key in the lock and go inside.

How could you still be so weak as to fall for the same game of hearts that deep down you know very well will end in your own sacrifice? Have you become so addicted that you cannot live without the pressure of a blade against your veins? What are you anyway? Prey or predator? Always swinging over the edge of the wound. You who, until this very day, were half here and half on the far side of this confused sea. In Gozo with another Maltese woman who not so long ago plucked your heart out through your ribs only to present it back to you wrapped in bandages, saying as she wept, 'I'm sorry. The parish priest spat in my mother's face this morning. Please take your heart back and go back where you came from.' You did all you could to nail love in place, but you weren't to know that her parish priest in Gozo had more authority than God himself. 'Ha, have you no shame? How can you allow your daughter to be with that heathen?'

'Heathen?'

'Nabil, I can't take it any more. Ever since I started going out with you our house has become like a funeral parlour. I get the blame for everything that goes wrong. Please go back where you came from. Gozo is too small for our love. I'll never forget you. The heart will always remember the first blade that inscribed on it.'

'Heathen?'

'Go, in the name of our love. I can't look at my mother's cheeks running with the spittle from heaven. Have mercy on me. I'll never forget you. How can I forget a knight like you?'

'Heathen?'

'I wanted to show you a Christian heart, but the heart can't bear to look at you. We wanted the impossible. Go, Nabil. You're not about to drop the manhood you've always shown me, are you?'

Go, you godless knight. Manliness requires that you exit your happiness. Tear the shirt of love and leave. Or did you think you'd merge the Bible and the Qur'an into one little booklet? If they wanted to divide the sky in two, how will you manage to make it one? Do you have to hang on to the ropes of the impossible? Real manliness demands that you take your bandaged heart and tear it to pieces. That's what the godless knight would do. The tears of love will be dried by the parish priest; yours will be dried by the handkerchief of time. The heathen knight has put on a mask, taken his sword and scimitar and torn his own heart to pieces, and now, many years after he left the parish of Gozo celebrating the return of its prodigal daughter whom Christ had pulled out of the clutches of the Dragut of the Middle East, now he's just hours away from the big eyes of a woman from Żabbar and her hungry breast, which could lay waste to an entire army without losing any of its voluptuousness.

Simon had no truck with the colour blue. The colour of exile and alienation, he called it. According to him, it was the most deceptive thing of all. He once told you something about blue eyes, Kristina's to be exact, because after he saw her he told you something and said there was no future for that relationship, but you never paid any heed to his warnings until what had to happen happened.

'I knew you would come back carrying sacks of nothing,' he said when you returned from Gozo, banished from Christ's pastures.

'It wasn't nothing, Simon. We make our own nothing.'

Perhaps his own failure with Klara, whose eyes happened to be blue like Kristina's, drove him to a similar conclusion about my relationship. 'You can't send the same postcard to the same address,' you had told him. 'You and Klara broke up simply because you weren't spiritually compatible, not because she has blue eyes!'

Where could a failed scientist meet a girl who was obsessed with basil and mint and Chinese herbs and Vietnamese spices? They didn't have a single thing in common. And what the hell did her blue eyes have to do with anything? Klara was obsessed with plants and the mint she grew in who knows how many varieties, while Simon was fixated on his fanciful theories. Simon was never happy to merely watch and observe things from the outside, even when they were obvious. He was always on the lookout for the hidden, dabbling in the obscure. You, on the other hand, had no intention of regarding a flower as merely a bunch of cells fighting to absorb one form of light and keep out another. A flower was a flower, that was all. Colour and delicacy and beauty that had no need to explain itself. You didn't want to see cells and reflected rays of light. After all, when was a story written in flowers? Especially in your Middle East. What did Kristina and her parish priest gain when they kicked you out of the garden of Christ? Did the heavenly postman arrive bearing boxes of gifts and sweets to thank them and say that Christ was weeping with happiness?

'You've no idea how much more extreme we are where religious bigotry is concerned. We're second to none. Remember when you introduced us to Kristina? I noticed she made the sign of the cross. My poor friend's heart, I thought, it will wallow in the mysteries of the colour blue. Don't say that I didn't warn you.'

'But will you tell me what bloody blue has to do with anything?' you chided him that day.

'You'll find out in your own good time. You'll learn that happiness and disappointment and failure have their own colours. Everything has a colour.' He left it at that, left you half drenched in the mystery of his words, which seemed to have no logic. If only you were able to look at things through his lens back then, you would have seen how right he was, how he was able to see things you couldn't see; you could have discovered that there are colours and shades far worse than your own grey.

After a bit of literary vomiting they made you a writer. Alex especially. 'The Pen of a Thousand Rifles' he liked to call you to remind you that your cause didn't have a military solution. When Ariel Sharon reappeared on the battlefield riding a biblical horse, George W. Bush, that other knight, described him as a man of peace. At least he didn't call him an honest man, because he knew he wasn't an honest man. Because he was like him, a man with a divine mission. A man doing God's bidding. You didn't joke around with men like that, men with a mission – in fact, you had to understand and respect them. Even as they killed you. Even as they peeled the flesh from your bones, you needed to understand and sympathize with them. These men are like bin Laden and his acolytes; they have strict orders, and you can't screw them around.

After penning a few lines they said you were a writer, without knowing what it was that Palestine had managed to turn you into. Without knowing what they turned you into, Nadia and Halimeh and Rukayyah and Baghdad and the Arab empire divided along straight lines drawn by the colonialists and held in place by your siblings, who still maintain them lovingly. They don't know that whatever flowed from your pen was mere vomit. Pure vomit. If you didn't let it all out in writing it would have had to come out in some other form; a shot to the head, perhaps, or a suicide mission. What are writers after all but maniacs who shoot themselves and the people around them in the head? What are writers? What is writing, and what does it take to write? The beauty of nature and a tragedy, Musa liked to say. One to force you to observe and the other to bleed you out. One to open the valves of your senses and the other to inject acid.

Tragedy and the countryside. You were brought up in the midst of both. Nothing to complain about as far as that goes. True, Amman is no Riviera, but at least it has birds. It has its flycatchers and herons. Swallows and grouse. Hoopoes. Butterflies and poppies and ears of corn. Ponds and springs and woods. Valleys and caves and the retreats of obscure saints and others long forgotten and abandoned. It had everything to make you light-headed, to make you forget all about food, from morning till evening. If Palestine had not been just across the valley it could have been the most beautiful of cities and the most beautiful of childhoods. No headaches or queasiness, no exile, no solitude, no writing. Not even writing, do you hear that, you bastard? Do you know how peaceful and comfortable life can be without writing? This whorish masochistic desire that took root in you as you made your escape from your domestic doldrums to find release among the frogs of Amman. It took root in you during those long hours with a pencil copying stories from the humble school library in order to have your own collection. It took root in you as you moaned and wept in the empty valleys of Amman, with no one to hear you and no one to answer except your own confused echoes. As you told yourself the stories you copied. As you recited your pain to the stones and trees and insects and rain. Every bird, every cloud, every tree and every stone in Amman knows your pain. It took root in you with the regret you felt whenever you spotted books in shop windows. As you collected cuttings from newspapers and old books. As you borrowed and cadged and stole. As you scribbled the poetry of Mahmoud Darwish on the front of your exercise book: 'My country is not a suitcase. I am not a traveller.' As you discovered the narrow worlds of Naguib Mahfouz and Kafka or the steamy voice of García Márquez. As you compared Zorba, Robert Jordan and the rebellious bastards of Hemingway with the fisherman in Hanna Mina's novel. As you went crazy for Rimbaud and Oscar Wilde. As you nourished yourself on pre-Islamic poetry in the morning, leaving Qabbani, Neruda, Lamartine and Pound for the evening.

It took root in you as you tossed and turned in bed. As you watched familiar faces looking out from silent wooden boxes draped in Palestinian colours. As you struggled to understand why we put our lives at risk for a ragged piece of soiled cloth. As you woke up frightened in the night and got up from tangled sweat-drenched sheets to go outside into the garden, your father, a living mute, kept alive. As you spied on the golden owl perched on the orange tree your mother planted. A small queen with gilded eyes. When your father still had his wits about him he once said the owl is the farmer's best friend; it clears the fields of mice and other rodents.

As you brought out your notebook to start drawing the owl. As she stood calm, as if she felt your pencil caressing her feathers. As you rediscovered her the next day and the day after that and every night throughout that autumn, always on the same branch of the orange tree. As you wondered why she suddenly stopped coming and never returned. As you waited for her night after night, writing letter after letter to her which she never came to collect. Who knows, you said to yourself, maybe she's found another tree or her young have grown big enough that she doesn't need to hunt for them any more or, as so often happens in life, she has become the hunted. The weak, the strong and then the strongest. The unwritten law of life. The law of peace and war. The law of powerful countries able to swallow up less powerful countries. Through the mandates of international organizations, a desire to set human history straight and put the right people in the right place. Empty words piled upon empty words. Lies. Diplomacy was all lies, international law was all lies, embassies and ambassadors were lies; mediators, special guests and envoys, even the original heavenly documents, they were all lies piled upon lies.

You never expected that the same whorish writing instinct would take root in you under Alex Attard's insistent gaze. His gaze reminded you of the boy who kept waiting for the golden owl that had disappeared in the early November showers. You had avoided the pen because you knew that the moment you picked it up you'd be digging deep into yourself. Like Alex and his friends. Like that venerable tortured woman poet with so much intelligence except where matters of the heart were concerned. Betrayal only tortures us the first time; for the rest we torture ourselves. Sometimes in the name of disappointment, sometimes in the name of the wretched. Who said the pen isn't a knife? Who said letters aren't shots that are first fired in the writer's own head? Who said poetry isn't a Molotov cocktail that can burn your house down and put the lives of your wife and children at risk, as happened to Alex Attard? Who said Malta's still Malta? Who said this world was ever sane?

Alex's house was burned down in a series of attacks against refugees and the Jesuit Refugee Service and anyone connected to them, like Alex himself. He still kept writing and standing up for the rights of Palestinians and black people. He appeared to have steeled his resolve even more, and his poems became more beautiful. Poets don't waste their spittle. It's not mere spittle anyway; sometimes it's a cause. The patriots who had put his wife and children's lives at risk remained free to roam in a society that proclaimed its disgust at their actions. And yet the Maltese still didn't want you in their midst. They wanted black Africans even less. They stain and muddy the genetic homogeneity of this Catholic island that, like the rest of the fair-complexioned continent, paints Christ as a handsome white man with pale eyes, like someone born in Strasbourg who has never been scorched by the Palestinian sun. No one believes you're a descendant of Christ, although he grew up and came to manhood a stone's throw from your mother's house.

Malta is vexing, but you love it to the point of exhaustion. As if you had a choice. When it becomes too constricting and you board a plane to get away for a while, you regret the decision and feel like a baby torn from the breast as soon as the wheels leave the ground. You regard it from the skies. It shimmers like a playful sea bream. What is Malta really? A fish or an escaped Phoenician bride? Or a bewitched siren? Or the icon of a forgotten saint? Or the place where the final Armageddon of your life will unfold? Deep down you know that destiny is unable to wipe the snot from its own nose or walk a single inch without man's helping hand. You're reminded of Simon De Brincat. 'In life there's no such thing as destiny or any of that nonsense. There's mathematics, and then there are our own actions.' How absurd Simon was! And how hard you always tried to prove that you weren't won over by him. When you look out through the aeroplane window once more, Malta has already disappeared beneath clouds and fog and an indifferent wind.

On 11 November 2004 Arafat died. He died lying down, without a pistol or medals or badges, without Palestine by his side to wipe the sweat from his brow with the edge of its keffiyeh. Who knows? Maybe what helped God kill him was the same invisible hand, the same illness that killed your mother and father and your siblings and will probably kill you, too.

Many world leaders, especially those who expressed great sorrow at the loss of Arafat, were secretly relieved because they thought the world would be less chaotic and perhaps less difficult without him. They weren't far wrong, at least as far as their second thought was concerned, because Arafat's successors, including the hand that probably poisoned him, immediately began to sharpen their knives to divide among themselves what was already divided, to get a slice of the imaginary pie. Before the dust had even settled on Arafat, Ramallah was overrun with Mercedes and BMWs and men with elegant ties flapping against the fat bellies of his orphaned children.

In a mutilated society there was nothing new about the exchange of conscience for a bit of chicken or rabbit feed, even though the mules who were born castrated sometimes protested by throwing themselves off the mountainous heights, burden and all. Who knows, maybe in Hemingway's case it was also those mules, which he said had made him so angry, that made him protest with a shot to the head, the same head that had dazzled the world with its beauty.

Sometimes to continue writing means you have to replenish your pen from Hemingway's mad stream, since the alternative is to fill your lungs with subsidized fodder whose consumption brings about this sort of schizophrenia and masochism, where the victim begins to tear the flesh of the victim who stands beside him, the first taunting the second because his wounds are not so deep. In a society like this people eat their own children and become creatures addicted to humiliation, where the victim cannot live without pain and torture. Who knows how many tyrants, sadists and murderers your people have created? You gave birth to them on purpose, fashioned them from your own skin, so that you could labour under their yoke and feed on their humiliation.

In Gaza you began to see many princes of darkness with well-tended symmetrical beards who told you what you could and couldn't do, as if Arafat had to die for you all to discover how ugly you really were and how little you agreed among yourselves. The imaginary pie began to be sliced and handed around through elections meant to institutionalize division. The Palestinian entity looked weaker than ever, like a chair attacked by woodworm and held together with cheap glue. The international community didn't even acknowledge the elections! It just went on negotiating with those slick ties in Ramallah, in the meantime hardening its fist against Hamas, who had contested the elections despite declaring ten thousand times that they had no faith in the entire political process but now found themselves in the imaginary seat of power.

Dark black clouds continued to build up on the already stormy horizon. Musa once told you that his father called him into the shelter where he liked to drink alone in silence and told him a story about a person who asked the pharaoh how he had become pharaoh, that is, a tyrant, to which he replied, 'There was no one to stand in my way.' You were too young to understand exactly what this meant and to conclude that it wasn't really drink that had killed Musa's father; there were many things that can consume your liver without a single drop of alcohol. The night after Musa told you the story of his father and the pharaoh, you dreamed that you were holding a bottle of alcohol, and there were corpses all around, as you drunkenly said to yourself, 'Yes. In life there are many things that burn hotter.' A few months after Arafat's death Palestinians were standing on rooftops and hills shooting at Palestinians. And what do you know? Once again all the dead were Palestinians.

13

Musa's absence from school was one of the most bitter experiences of my life. School seemed like one vast exile, and the other children were like monsters. Although Musa and I were on two different shifts, we would at least meet for a short while at changeover. Shifts alternated from month to month: one month we went to school between seven and eleven and the following month eleven to three. Four hours was all we had, and if you left out breaks and time-wasting and errands and delays and the teachers' moods, we received barely two hours of schooling in a day. During those two hours we were meant to learn Arabic and science and geography and history and mathematics and English and religion and social studies and PE and art. Ten subjects, about which we ultimately learned nothing meaningful.

The education system was overstretched, and sometimes there were forty-five children crammed into a single classroom like sardines in a tin. We sat three to a desk, and if you moved your elbow you were likely to dig someone in the ribs. After the war of 1967 the population of Amman had suddenly doubled, and education was hardly a priority for a series of unelected governments in a young state focused on maintaining order and steadying a shaky throne. Half the money they made by begging, often using the refugees as leverage, was spent on the security apparatus – soldiers, police, headquarters, intelligence and new jails – while the other half was squandered on the eccentric whims of the king and his coterie.

Although Omaymah felt sorry for Musa's father, she seemed relieved when she discovered that Musa wouldn't be exerting his bad influence on me as much as before. 'Good riddance,' I once heard her tell the woman who lived next door. No one knew I still visited him every day and stayed with him while he sold bread and lemonade until closing time at the Passport Office. I told Omaymah I was staying out longer to play football. She was already much weaker, mostly because of the children she gave birth to every year like an unneutered cat. One child at her breast and two in her lap with another forming inside her. These days, as I mull over my past, I realize that in all my memories of my sister Omaymah she is always pregnant, actually pregnant and breast-feeding, and sometimes pregnant and sweeping and scouring and cooking and chatting to the neighbours and, above all, shouting at me to take my clothes off. I don't know what it was about the clothes I wore that annoyed her so much. The second she set eyes on me she'd start shouting at me to take them off. I remember I once won a prize for elegance and cleanliness. We were still in Miss Jinan's school. Miss Widad, who was our teaching assistant, had decided that on that particular day I was the cleanest in the class. They put a medal with ribbons on our chests to show how neat and clean we were, at least on one particular day. We were on top of the world. I went home intending to show off that medal, which was the first and actually the last recognition I would ever receive from the state. But I had barely stepped over the doorstep when Omaymah screamed, 'Go get those filthy clothes off!'

Musa didn't excel at his studies, but physically he was three times as strong as I was and about six times as brave. He had an innate courage. It was genetic. I've never met anyone as brave as he was, especially considering his life's many mishaps. His tremendous physical strength nourished and protected me and allowed me to hide the vulnerabilities I had from the thousands of defects I'd inherited from my mother and father.

Musa's family were Bedouins who had emigrated towards the centre in the 1950s when Amman began to take shape as the capital and many new jobs were being created, mostly in the police and the army and the various sectors connected to them. A police officer and a soldier need to dress and eat and drink and shit and have their hair cut. Every police officer and every soldier had five or six other invisibles clustered around his back end, only to find himself lost in the deserts of Saudi Arabia when battle finally starts.

According to official figures, which we'll assume haven't been doctored, in 1948 Amman had a population approaching sixty thousand – although when the state says approaching sixty it really means it was barely half that number – but let's go with sixty thousand, even though that pales into insignificance when compared with Cairo or Damascus or Baghdad, which already counted their populations in millions. Sixty thousand was the size of King Farouk's entourage when he went for a shit or hunting in the Nile Delta. It took our thinkers a lot of head-banging to figure out that Jordan had been set up by the British colonial authorities shortly before the Palestinian melodrama to serve as a sponge to suck up refugees kicked out of their towns and villages. How else could one explain the presence of Little Jaw at the helm of the Arab army valiantly defending Jerusalem? Neither does it take much education to understand the dangers inherent in King Hussein's decision to make refugees citizens in one fell swoop, thereby avoiding the risk of some smart alec coming along fifty years later to tell them about Palestine and whatnot.

They thought the love for Palestine would abate over time. They thought it would dry up and harden and die, as Ben-Gurion wished when he announced the birth of a nation state for the Jewish people built on the land and property and blood of another people. 'Do you want a throne and a country and a population? Just shut up and obey our orders.' That's probably what they told King Abdullah, the grandfather of King Hussein and the founder of the Hashemite kingdom, as he made his way with two regiments to warn off the French. His brother Faisal had just been removed from the throne of Damascus where he'd crowned himself king of Syria in 1920.

The British intercepted Abdullah in the city of Ma'an in southern Jordan and put to him a proposal that would mean he wouldn't come out of the partitioning of the Arab world empty-handed like his father Sharif Hussein ibn Ali – on the condition he kept quiet and did as he was told. That was the plan, according to the British archives: to establish a new country that would absorb the refugees arising out of that other agreement made with the Jews, and who would in future be granted a new space and a new identity so that Palestine would be forgotten eventually.

Typical British skulduggery. But my father screwed them. He kept on working in silence, secretly, as a tree that nourishes the soil. Secretly, until he had transformed himself completely into that tree, and now their problem was with me and not with my father who lay beneath the dust.

Anyway, Musa's family were among those Bedouins who divorced the desert early on. They came to settle in Amman in the 1950s because the father landed a job with the army. They arrived around the time that my mother and father were uprooted for the second time, from Bir Zeit to the River Jordan and then to Amman, where they would be granted a new identity on condition that they be realistic and forget about the cities and villages and cemeteries they had left behind.

As far as I could make out, Musa's father had joined the army in 1953. He started as a soldier in the mechanical artillery and rose through the ranks to sergeant. However, during Black September in 1970 he refused to order his troops to open fire on Baqa'a, another refugee camp close to Amman, which was probably housing a military base for Arafat and his gang of Freemasons and Marxists. I had heard the story from Musa more than a thousand times, of how his father had refused orders and watched as the tanks from other divisions mercilessly bombarded the densely populated camp. His father told him that the Jordanian troops had herded those fleeing the camp and told them to beg for mercy from King Hussein as if they were praying to Allah, and as soon as that sacrilegious ceremony was over they took a few of the men and threw them under the tracks of their armoured tanks, telling the terrified remainder to applaud as King Hussein's tanks flattened their brothers and perhaps their children like pitta dough. Musa's father told him that when he saw those scenes unfolding before his eyes he threw away the insignia of the kingdom and the rank he had worked like a dog for twenty years to obtain and simply left, and from that day forward he stopped believing in the kingdom and the army and Arabism and even in the God who had failed to descend from on high to defend the weak.

Apart from his great physical strength that had been baked in the desert sands, it seems that Musa had inherited other qualities from his father, who would always remain jobless unless he was tinkering with some used car he'd bought after he'd sold off his wife's gold. One day they came to his house to arrest him. It was an event to remember. Musa said his father had argued with a traffic policeman who had stopped him and asked for his licence. He refused, and the policeman became annoyed and said he was obliged to give it up because he, the officer, represented the state, but Musa's father, who might have been a little tipsy, just said he didn't give a fuck about any state or those who governed it. 'Are you insulting His Majesty?' the policeman said angrily, as though he couldn't believe his own ears. Rather than accept the gravity of what he'd just said Musa's father got out of the car and attacked the officer with a metal pipe. The way his son told me the story, he grabbed him by the neck and told him in front of the sizeable crowd that had gathered around them, 'Go and tell your king that I, Hasan Rajab Salem al-Ghabbadi, who live by al-Wihdat, al-Muhajrin Street, do not give a fuck about him or any of his minions, starting with you. See this? This is my dick.' And he took it out right there on the street. That was the wrong thing for him to have said, because in less than an hour the street on which we lived thronged with police and cars and jeeps. Sirens screamed and lights flashed and walkie-talkies crackled, as if some major mafia boss was about to be seized. That day even the dogs and cats came out to witness the proceedings. At first the neighbours thought Musa's father had been made a minister or the head of something truly important, but when the police climbed up to the roof and surrounded the house they all realized that Musa's father had done something serious. Some people muttered under their breath that they'd always thought he was a bit shady. Others insisted that he probably headed a secret organization working to undermine the throne and disrupt the regime. They said he was dangerous and armed, that when he was in the army he stole weapons for his secret society. One old woman said he was a drunk who didn't know what he was doing and, as Allah had said in his book, 'Drunkards should not be taken seriously.' Never mind the fact that in subsequent days I studied the Qur'an from cover to cover and couldn't find that verse about drunkards, at that moment one of the policemen, a ranking officer, told her to keep her mouth shut and step back. Suddenly

Musa's father came out on to the balcony in a singlet. He held a half-litre whisky bottle, the kind shaped like a hip flask. He looked down on the scene amazed, raised the bottle to his mouth and downed the dregs before saying with a smile, '*Allahu akbar!* I had no idea my dick could cause such pandemonium in this country.'

The year 1981 was when my father completed his transformation into a tree, and as a tree he gradually began to channel himself into me.

It was the morning of Tuesday 17 March when a man with long hair and a light beard turned up asking for my father. We told him he was at work and that he'd be back later. Although that young man with curly hair down to his shoulders and that light beard seemed handsome and educated, I sensed there was something hard about him. I didn't have to wonder for too long, because Omaymah turned up from somewhere and shouted to him to wait a minute. She seemed to have smelled a rat. The outsider realized she suspected there was news, probably bad news. He lowered his eyes as if he were carefully weighing the difficult words he had come to say. Before he could even open his mouth, Omaymah was already weeping. The man with the light beard and long hair said nothing to calm her down or deny whatever she suspected. He stared confusedly at her and said, 'Sami . . . condolences.' Omaymah threw herself to the floor in front of the door and began to weep and wail and roll her eyes as if she'd gone mad. I stared at her stunned, wondering what to do, as if I had nothing to do with this Sami whose death the man with the light beard and curly hair had just announced. Omaymah became hysterical, pulling at her hair and slapping her own cheeks. The street quickly filled with people from all directions. Some women lifted my sister off the ground and dragged her indoors and tried to comfort her by wailing and slapping their own cheeks just as she was. The man with the light beard approached me and said my brother had died 'an honourable death in a fierce battle with the Zionists. He died standing up, rifle in hand, as he'd always wished.' He told me that we should get in touch with the PLO office in Damascus to arrange for his corpse to be brought home from Lebanon. He handed me a piece of paper with some contacts and numbers and said other things, but I could hear nothing of what he was saying. What difference could it make that he had died a martyr? What could comfort my siblings, watching stunned, or my sister and the women around her who tore their clothes and danced the Canaanite dance of death in our backyard in Amman? What would comfort the old man-tree who seemed to have known that we would have to go through all these rituals? That's why he decided to turn into a tree. To make himself strong for when the time came. My father received the news of Sami's death without reacting. His face remained like parchment, his eyes were glass, as if he did not know the deceased, and I, who had not known Sami at all well, never felt such hatred for Palestine as I did that day, except when they carried in my other brother, Muhammad, in another wooden casket less than a year later.

I had only seen Muhammad once since he had left to study in Yugoslavia and returned to join the PLO. In 1975 he was in Damascus. Members of the PLO and any of their associates couldn't get into Jordan for fear of ending up behind Hashemite bars. We all visited him, with the exception of my father. Muhammad rented an apartment for us in the heart of the Umayyad capital where I spent the best two weeks of my childhood. He took us to see the Barada river and the gigantic Umayyad mosque and the enormous souk. During those two weeks I realized Amman was a tiny insect compared to the vastness of Damascus with its ancient broad squares. The Damascus International Fair was on at the time, and Muhammad took us to see a film in the open air on a large screen raised over the Barada, which was decorated with fountains spraying jets of water illuminated from below with multi-coloured lights. The fountains were like a cordial made from all kinds of fruit. The bridges over the magical river thronged with vendors selling pistachios and ice cream and all kinds of sweets that would have made the Nablusi envious – unless the Nablusi were actually Damascenes. The Nablusi and the Damascenes resemble each other in their surnames, the fluidity of their accent, their mechanical religiosity, their stupendous sweets, their diligence and hard work, their stinginess, the avidity with which they set money aside. All of which can't be a coincidence, just as it was no coincidence that the Nablusi who crossed the River Jordan with the rest of the EDPs would within a few years came to dominate the sweet market across the entire kingdom.

Muhammad seemed to know he didn't have much longer to live. He wouldn't leave us for a second, as if to compensate for what was to come, and for me especially – the young one, the youngest, supposedly the spoiled brat – he bought trinkets and sweets. He spoiled me and my sisters. Several times he asked why my father hadn't come, why he'd preferred to remain hunkered down behind the doors of his silent world. My father had taken it badly when he discovered that Muhammad, having completed his studies in political science, had joined the PLO, in particular the Fatah movement led by Arafat, whom my father hated with a passion. He believed that Arafat and his antics would destroy everyone's children. 'That's right, keep following that buffoon. We'll see where it gets you,' he would say back when his tongue still wagged. I don't know if my father expected other people, or perhaps aliens from space, to fight on behalf of Palestine. Or maybe he had a premonition, as a father, that he would end up sacrificing two of his children on its bloody altar and would have to bury them instead of their burying him. At least that's all he lost. There were some who lost all of their children, there were even entire families that were wiped out. Back then I'd listen to my father grumbling and wonder: What does he expect? That other people shed blood in our fight for Palestine? First they teach us to love Palestine to the death, and then they blame us when we give up our lives for it. Isn't that what a destructive love will bring? Isn't that what Palestine is about, his Palestine to which no vault of heaven could compare? Isn't that the holy land that so many angels and prophets and saints shat on? The land everyone wanted but which apparently belonged to no one. Isn't it the same land that Halimeh hailed from, only to appear to me twenty years later in Malta to scoff at the wounds I had inherited from my father? Or was that not the case? When my older brother was brought home in a box draped in the Palestinian flag I felt like pulling off that flag, spitting on it and tearing it to pieces. I saw only lies, lies within lies. Palestine was a lie and the world was a lie. We are lies and flags are lies; we make them up to make the deaths of our siblings and our children acceptable with a lying pride.

As far as I could make out, Arafat made Muhammad his cultural attaché to Bulgaria, commissioning him to establish contact with the

Americans, who until then wouldn't recognize the Palestinian nation. To them we were, and perhaps still are, a bunch of savage wolves. The Americans understand the vagaries of language and what definitions can bring to life. When you recognize a people you recognize the territory lying under their feet. Since the territory in question had been taken by their friends, they could only disavow us. The best thing to do in a case like this is to close your eyes. That way you see neither people nor territory. To me it made no difference; in fact, the less the Americans saw of me the more air there was for me to breathe. But for Arafat it did seem to make a difference. My poor brother. Apparently Israel was not very impressed with the dialogue he had secretly initiated in Bulgaria. They wanted to send a message, both for Arafat and for their excessively optimistic American friends: 'Nothing can happen behind Israel's back.'

On the night of Saturday 9 January 1982 a group of professional killers from Mossad intercepted my brother in front of his apartment in Sofia and shot him fifteen times through the heart with a silenced firearm. We, however, heard the sound. It echoed off the walls of our house. Inside my father's ribcage. In the bitter hearts of my siblings still mourning for Sami. In Omaymah's breast. She would now be mistaken for my grandmother were she to visit my school. In fact, Omaymah never recovered. She went into an advanced state of mourning and hallucination in which she stayed until the end; she always wore black and was always exhausted and would wrap a headscarf around her aching head. For months on end talking was an effort for her, and when she did talk half the words she uttered couldn't be understood. It's impossible to suffer two blows of that magnitude and remain the same. In fact, nothing in our lives remained the same, not Omaymah, not my father, not my other siblings, not even me. We all turned into different creatures. Creatures with a complicated relationship with death and consequently also with life. Unnecessary laughter and smiles were banned from our house. Those were an insult and a betrayal of the memory of our martyred brothers. No music or television. The mourning we imposed on ourselves was social and cultural; it even affected the way we communicated among ourselves. I can't blame Omaymah for that, although her bearing always brought to mind what we had been through. It all remained etched on her face and her vacant eyes, which had once been so hawkish and alert. Because of the poor woman's composite role in our lives, the loss she suffered was far greater than ours. If we had lost our brothers, she'd lost brothers who were also in large measure her children.

As he had done at Sami's funeral, my father followed everything in complete silence without a single word or tear. As if it didn't concern him. I don't know if he was like his son, preferring to weep inwardly, or if he had cut himself off from reality and was spared the whole thing. How to understand my father? It's not enough to be a father to be able to understand my father. It's not enough to have lost your land and your honour and your wife and your children. It's not enough to suddenly marry a slim woman whom you banish just as abruptly after your youngest son says she has invaded his mother's bed. It's not enough to have betrayed Halimeh who came to the funerals of all your loved ones just to have the chance to sneer at you and dance the Canaanite dance of death over your children. In order to understand my father, you have to be a father who turned into a tree.

Not all fathers are the same, that's what life has taught me. Some of them laugh and joke around, some of them are quiet and tearful. There are the dictatorial types, while others are bottles or trees, like my father was until he was resurrected during his final days, when he began calling me often, to check if the transformation was complete, to check if it had been executed properly. That bills have to be paid in blood is not important. The Arab empire is not important, although it has been chopped up and is suffering from thousands of grave illnesses that won't respond to conventional medical treatment, at least not the kind I know of. That Halimeh would begin to appear to me, to ascertain that my life was ruined like my father's and would always be swept clean of all happiness, is not important. What is important for my father is that the transformation happened and that I became him, with his flab and his chin, his hair, his posture, his stubble, his fossilized eyes, his fleshy nose and – let's not forget it – that ambiguous grey that could break your head open if you struggled with it in order to understand yourself. The complete recipe for me to eventually become a tree, just like him.

One that seems to be dead but isn't, seems to be alive and isn't that either. One that isn't anything it appears to be.

Because of the drastic metamorphosis he underwent, my father became impossible to understand, and even if you thought you understood him he wouldn't understand you. After every funeral I would look at him and see his face transform into something that was most decidedly not my father's face. Looking at how thin he was becoming I would ask myself fearfully, 'What more can life do to a man like this?' As for me, what impact would this bony face have on me? What other scars would my father's silent struggle with life leave on me? Sometimes I saw my father as a burden on life's shoulders, and sometimes I saw life as a heavier burden on his. I was the heir of the father and all his burdens. I inherited the memories and the extensions of those memories. Everything that my father had accumulated would explode within me. After all, what are our children but ships to carry our freight of poison? I decided I didn't want any children. I did not want to pass on my own poison and that of my ancestors. I did not want to explain what I had brought into this world. I did not want to lift them up and look into their eyes and find I had no stories for them. I did not want to smash a radio to pieces and shout, 'Whores! Queers! A bunch of queers and whores!' I did not want to answer their inquisitive gaze and their questions about my sister the Naksa. I did not want to explain to them how far human hatred could reach and why in 2001 aeroplanes collided with the twin towers of New York and reduced them to rubble; how Baghdad, one bizarre morning, threw in the towel without strangling a single invader and how the only head dangling from its walls was that of the caliph himself, who deserved to be hanged, along with twenty-one others, all of whom had broken our eggs without ever cooking us an omelette.

A few months after the assassination of my brother Muhammad, on 6 June 1982 to be exact, Israel launched the greatest operation in its military history. This time it happened in the north, in order to excise the tumour known as the PLO from the south of Lebanon. Back then Lebanon was one big carnival of blood. Everyone was killing everyone else, and everyone blamed everyone else. Sunnis and Shiites and Druze and Catholics, Maronites and refugees and Syrians, Israelis and French, US and Iranian secret agents, they shot at each other, but no one was to blame except the Palestinians. Since they bore my curse, they caused a great deal of harm wherever they went. There were more sects and assassins in Lebanon than in the rest of the world. Killing happened based on your identity card. On the basis of culture, religion and even language. To catch a Palestinian in Lebanon you produced a tomato and asked him what it was. If he said *bandoura* rather than *banadoura* you could shoot him without compunction, as the Maronite Phalangists did at the checkpoints to their ethno-religious districts. Every district was led by a demi-god who took orders from a slightly bigger puppet. When Sharon, the young and ambitious minister of defence, arrived on the scene leading an army of a hundred thousand well-trained soldiers, backed by the best air force in the region, he found that half his work was already done. The vice was half closed. All he needed was to tighten it a little. Between his enormous military machine on one side and the Christian Kataeb militia with their allies on the other, the Palestinians found themselves caught in the middle. They cut off their water and electricity supply and all access to aid and began to bombard western Beirut, where Arafat and his friends were located, from all directions, from the land and the sea and the air, until Beirut looked worse than Leningrad. For three months Beirut, the bride of the Arabs, was a ball of flame, and the other twenty-one caliphs, some of them supplying the very oil that powered the killing machines, expected Ronald Reagan, the paranoid cowboy who consulted the stars before taking a shit, to have a change of heart and order a ceasefire for at least a few hours so that people could get some water and bury their dead. And yet, little Beirut, the friendly doll of the east, despite its tiny size, despite having no artillery or aeroplanes or walls, despite having nothing at its back, managed in those seventy-six days of hell to hang seven hundred invading soldiers from its non-existent walls.

Certain cities, like Vittoriosa, can mount a defence with their eyelashes. Beirut didn't give in; it continued to defend itself with its hands and legs and hair and nose and teeth. It resisted and fought, down to the last pair of stones still standing on top of each other. The Israeli aeroplanes began to fly back with their bombs intact because there was nothing left to blow up, yet they still couldn't set foot in Beirut.

During those last days of madness, American crows, which, according to Omaymah, tended to appear in times of great disaster, reappeared to see what they could pick from the debris and the dead bodies. When the bloody expedition had gone on for too long and the body count became embarrassing for Israel and its allies, Henry Kissinger turned up once more with another diplomat who was just as wolfish, if not more so. Philip Habib was no *habib* (which means 'friend'), even though his grandparents were Lebanese. Like Sharon, they insisted at first on the total annihilation of the PLO, but, when they realized that the PLO wasn't defending Beirut on its own but with all the Lebanese nationalist movements behind it, the minimum condition of a successful campaign was for Arafat and his friends to leave Beirut. The Arab nations eagerly welcomed this proposal like a gift from heaven, if only to calm their own streets, which seemed to be waking up from the numbness of the World Cup to realize that something odd was happening next door.

To make matters worse, during that World Cup, Algeria, who had beaten West Germany and Chile and looked set to make it out of the group, were fucked over by the West Germans and Austrians who appeared to fix their last match. The Arab leaders kicked the ball between the goalposts of Arafat and his friends. They told them the Israelis were determined and that they had the go-ahead from the US to destroy the PLO once and for all, whatever it took; they didn't care about public opinion around the world, since they manufactured that anyway. They told him he'd better leave; it was in the interests of Beirut and its people and everyone else. The pressure on Arafat increased until finally he and his thirteen thousand members evacuated the city with their light weaponry, escorted by the Multinational Force in Lebanon whose barracks would later be blown up by a truckload of dynamite.

Their new destination was Tunisia and Yemen. Two Arab countries very far from Palestine. 'Where are you going now?' the journalists asked Arafat as he boarded the ship to his new unknown. 'To Palestine!' he said, smiling among the tears and flowers and waving hands of the refugee families gathered to bid farewell to Arafat and his warriors who together with the nationalist Lebanese forces had stopped the powerful Israeli Army from entering Beirut. Philip Habib, who was no *habib*, had given a guarantee to the Palestinians and the Arab countries that no one would touch the refugees. But barely a week later, on the night of 16 September 1982, the Israeli Army surrounded Sabra and Shatila, two Palestinian refugee camps in Beirut, and coordinated the entry of the rabid Maronite Phalangists, who would commit one of the most appalling massacres in the history of humanity. They pierced the bellies of pregnant women with pickaxes and cut out the organs of children and old people with knives. They shot anything that moved, even cats and pigeons. They raped girls and shot them naked, danced and drank and pissed on the naked corpses. The killing spree went on for three days and nights, with the Israeli Army always keeping watch, stopping up any gaps in the two destroyed camps and shooting flares into the night sky to light up the streets and alleyways for the murderers. The outside world began to notice the stench of mutilated corpses and the hungry wild dogs.

As usual the actual number of mutilated victims is disputed to this day. Some say hundreds and some say thousands. The So-called United Nations was supposedly shocked by the massacre, putting the figure at between two thousand and three thousand, most of them women and children and old people. No one was ever found guilty for this avalanche of human souls. Elie Hobeika, the commander of the Christian Phalangists who led the bloody operation, would go on to become a minister, while Sharon, the fierce biblical hero, became prime minister of Israel and in 2003 broke the roof of the Muqata'a over Arafat's head before poisoning him and sending him on his way to meet his friends from Sabra and Shatila.

In spite of the drama of those months, my father and Omaymah remained unchanged. One was a tree and the other always wore black, her head wrapped tightly in a scarf, weeping all the time, brooding over the loss of the two brothers who were like sons to her. The bloody chapter that unfolded in Beirut didn't help her to forget any of her personal mourning. After Sami and Muhammad it was as if the world had come to an end for her. As if she didn't want to hear news of any more dead. One day, almost three years later, Mustafa brought a television home, and he and I spent a whole day fiddling with the aerial on the roof until we got a fuzzy picture. It was enough for us, if only to soften the sad, hard atmosphere in the house. At one point Omaymah came into the room without warning, pulled the wire out of the socket and screamed tearfully, 'Your brothers' blood has barely dried, and you're already in the mood for happiness and partying! What are you, bloodless?'

And she burst into tears as if they'd died only the day before. On seeing her sister cry, Sumayyah burst into tears as well, while Mustafa and I just stared like two traitors accusing each other. Now, when I think back to those strange times, I realize that the hand that had assassinated Muhammad had also assassinated many things in our lives, including our ability to be ourselves. To be normal, to eat and drink and shit normally. To wear clothes and be happy and reproduce like normal people. We began to see everything through the lens of a Palestinian dusk, blurred like the picture on Mustafa's television. Like our muddy relations with the Arab world that Nasser thought he'd unify with the peasant recipe he had stowed away in his revolutionary pocket. When he died the revolution died with him. And the world looks upon us: a bunch of terrorists who jump ships, kidnap athletes and hijack planes.

One morning towards the end of November we awoke and saw the sky over Amman teeming with storks. Hundreds if not thousands of the huge birds were darkening the sky high above us as they flew north. The scene reminded me of a verse in the Qur'an that describes how Allah sent mysterious birds to save the Kaaba from the elephants of the Aksumite king, Abraha al-Ashram, in the year 570, the year of the birth of Prophet Muhammad.

'Allah will protect al-Bayt,' said Abd al-Muttalib, the Prophet's grandfather, when he received the news of the march of the ambitious king who, like Sharon, headed an army of 100,000 soldiers. The Qur'an says that Allah, with his mysterious birds, indeed saved his al-Bayt, the Kaaba. The emigrating storks of Amman obviously had no intention of saving anything but their own feathers. In any case, it was too late to save anyone, especially in our house and in Beirut. That morning, while the blood of my brothers and that of the refugees was still wet, we went up to the veranda to follow that incredible scene, which has remained in my memory as one of the most beautiful things I've ever seen in my life. When we got down from the roof Omaymah was curled up in her usual place in the yard, and you'd have thought she'd hardly noticed the racket or glanced up at the sky. When she saw us coming down she tightened the scarf around her head and muttered under her breath, 'Even the birds want to get away from the Arab world.'

14

Three-quarters of an hour before your appointment with the eyes of the woman from Żabbar, you pour yourself a glass of wine to face the sunset. You raise it and drink to your heart's health, the heart banished from the table of the apostles. You listen to its slow beat, unbutton your ribs and observe signs of life.

> In the name of the son and the father and the soul
> I declare my heart still has love as its goal
> Welcome, heart returning from the land of lack
> Welcome, heart sailing with the wind in its bandages
> One woman to draw from me death
> Another woman to draw from me life renewed.

Just imagine if you had to tell your heart that it was coming back to life to walk towards its own end. The final steps of the resurrected before death. It's enough for your hopes with Kristina to have been dashed. One cliff isn't enough for a heart so enamoured of heights. If only we could see the future we would accept the present. And if only we could see the present we'd be content with just the past.

Just three-quarters of an hour to go before you meet the woman who emerged from the well of the past with the intention of pulling you back into it. You'll be meeting her at the same table across the same Grand Harbour before the same shame-faced sunset that five years later will bear witness to the bizarre conclusion to a love you thought was for ever. Love that lasts for ever is one that ends with the death of the protagonist. Did you know you have to die to be allowed into the immortal tent of love?

You get there before her. When it comes to keeping appointments with women, men always get there first. It's only when it comes to wise decisions that they always turn up late and sometimes never get there at all. And you, whose life has been one long late arrival, couldn't you have turned up late one more time? Sometimes five minutes is all it that's required to alter the direction that things take, as Adnan said before he set off to take a bite out of the British pie. What if you had turned up late for her? Perhaps she would have felt offended by your negligence and turned up her nose and left. Perhaps she would have read the signs and made her calculations and discovered that this wouldn't work out for her. Nadia was one of those women who keep their calculators handy, you know that. Women calculate. Only men take shots in the dark. Like many women, Nadia calculated and measured and compared. Multiplied and added and subtracted and took stock of the odds, whether they were weighted in favour of security or not. Security: the essence of the calculations made by the absolute majority of women. Always in search of shelter and security, whatever that might mean.

So you get there early. Back then there were no F-16s or Apaches directed by the Old Testament to rain death down upon your family and no Western conservative hawks in elegant suits and ties cut from the finest cloth sitting on comfortable armchairs and swivel chairs ordering the death of your Iraqi brothers at a distance of exactly 11,172 kilometres. Distance matters. These elegant people are the same ones from whom you need to learn the moral alphabet of humanity, who have always criticized your people's treatment of your pets and your womenfolk. How can you be human when you have no respect for the basic needs of a dog, if you can't stroke your pet cat's fur? After a day's work, which might well include a ceremony of mass killing, these people go back home, play with their dog and cat, whistle to their budgerigar and feed him out of the palm of their hand, and when their daughter comes back from piano lessons they hold her in their arms, hug and kiss her and throw her up into the air, whoooeeeee, whoooeeeee. It is this merciful father, who has just ordered the death of God knows how many people, many of them his daughter's age, from whom you have to learn about respect for the lives of dogs and cats – not to mention human beings! Back then, her noose and Halimeh's curse weren't yet in play, and neither was it ordained that your head should roll along the flagstones of the temple of failed loves, failures as abject as the Palestinian national project. You were still a man without too many lacunas. No one could see through your flesh. And no enemy of the Enlightenment had yet burned Alex's home while his wife and kids slept between the sheets of a clean conscience, and Simon from Valletta, Simon the prophet rejected by his own people, hadn't yet slammed the receiver in your face and burst into tears in Republic Street after seeing the US tanks rolling beneath the palms of Baghdad, and then, one year and five months after the arrival of Paul Bremer, the new mayor of the oldest Arab capital, Simon would say to hell with this life and abandon you like a filthy stray dog running in the street with its tongue hanging out, hungry and thirsty, shunned by everyone.

Back then, none of these drill bits were boring into your brain. Back then, you were just a picture trying to become relevant and hoping to find a frame. You thought a frame would make you whole, because so many paintings lacked meaning, they were just the mad reflections in the painter's mind before a frame gave them consequence. A frame conveys a name and surname. A frame is as much of an accomplice as a brush and paints, if not more so, and now, if you were to take a good look at yourself, you would discover that you're still a grotesque painting after all, and you still have no frame and no signature, not even a wall to hang on. Now you're grotesque and riddled with holes and wounds. Perhaps doctors and professors might examine you and find you in good health, but you know well enough that you carry a thousand diseases, including a virulent one called Palestine.

You picked a table in a corner. Five years later the same table would be the surface on which your love, having reached its end, would be smashed to pieces. Far off to the north-east the gulls were wailing. A mysterious bird that never tires of calling and travelling; it seemed as if its tormented cries were warning you not to step deeper into this love that so resembles Palestine.

She sat on a chair beside you and began to tell you about her life. Her transparent, childlike face made you want to hug her. She wanted to tell you the story of her life in its minutest details. She was like a stripper on a stage slowly taking her clothes off until she stood completely naked. You remained silent, absorbing the tender pain of a love you didn't yet know would be stillborn. Just as you did five years later when she sat you down in the same fateful corner at the same table across the Grand Harbour and asked you to choose between desolation and exile, and you opted for both.

You didn't share much about yourself. You filled the silent intervals with another silence. She claimed she knew a lot about you, but even Halimeh herself isn't aware of all of your troubles. Not even when she changes shape and inhabits this young Żabbari woman. She actually knew little and got to know little and would know little even five years down the line when she picked up love's luggage and left for good. The only thing she could be certain of was that you were a fishing line that was all knotted and tangled, that the only solution was to pick up a pair of scissors and start snipping. So that's what she did: she reached for her scissors and snipped.

How many steps did Nadia need to descend into your churning depths to discover that, as men go, you were as run-of-the-mill as a war in the Middle East? That you drank all of this silence in Amman after you witnessed its transformation into a permanent way station for refugees who thought they wouldn't have to stay away from their homes for longer than fifteen days?

How many chains, how many keys, how many rusty padlocks did Nadia have to open to be able to learn something about the man she loved and to whom she gave herself? She gave herself to you unfurnished so you could fit her out to your own design. Up to that point Nadia had been as honest as a loaf of bread. As pure as a cup of innocence. As rare as truth with a beauty as abrasive as granite. At that point you wished you could hold her flesh against your soul. How rare they are, those women who smell of youth and its inexplicable happiness when you meet them for the first time. Those women with whom you begin to feel the hands of a mysterious femininity caressing your face and hair with infinite tenderness. Their fingers are petals descending along your spine, holding you against their delicious flesh. In the lap of warmth and shelter. You are overtaken by an immense desire to bury your head in that lap to hide away from the cold and the wind and the prying eyes of strangers.

And suddenly she said, 'How I love winter. I'm looking forward to it.' Who had taught her to love the rain? Who had coloured her eyes with such happiness as she mentioned the rain? Her statement was enough to drive you to declarations of love, to give the rain the right to pursue you for the rest of your life.

'What about you? What kind of relationship do you have with the rain? Are you in love at least a little?' She continued to bewitch you with her little flurries of curiosity. You were caught off guard by a strange happiness despite the mysterious cries of the gulls in the distance.

'If I told you how much I adore the rain you might think I was mad and leave, or think I was one of those who are unable to see any beauty in life unless they're underneath an umbrella or behind a curtain of rain.'

Her eyes lit up as if she'd just won a bet. That was the moment you saw the first transformation in her black eyes. You hadn't known that one black could become another. A black olive shining on the silvery drops as they slid slowly down. 'Winter can never come soon enough for me,' she said, as she handed you one of the keys to her heart. 'I'm like parched soil.'

'I love the winter, too. Each winter manages to surprise and renew me, and it always manages to give me a ride on a rainbow and take me back to intimate times.'

'What beautiful words! Maybe you're like me, you don't want to leave your childhood behind,' she answered, charmed. 'I have my reasons for not wanting to grow up. What do you have against the present?'

'Nothing!'

'I wouldn't want to be as cowardly as you,' she says with a smile.

'What makes you think I'm a coward?'

'I, too, don't much like the present, but I believe there are blank pages on which we can scribble something of our own.'

'Don't tell me you're one of those romantic dreamers for whom a glass is half full.'

'Your vocabulary is totally escapist. Why do you prefer half empty to half full?'

'Because I don't know what it's full of, whether it's full of nectar or poison. Or both at once. I've learned not to loosen the belt of happiness too much or I might get caught with my trousers down. Even when I see that the glass is half full. Beauty can sometimes hide a lot of cruelty.'

'Fifty years of failure are no joke. Don't take this personally, though, but part of your failure is homemade. You brought it on yourselves.'

You turn your eyes away from her sharp intelligence to a far-off point in the north-east. The screeching of the gulls has doubled as they hover around a boat probably on its way back from a fishing trip. What were they so happy about, the boat or the smell of fish that made them hungry? Those birds want something. All creatures know what they want except for your kind. Your national compass doesn't yet know which way to turn. Part of you runs in pursuit of an oasis in the desert and another part runs to throw itself into the arms of death, like those whales that commit a collective suicide.

You, too, have learned to celebrate death as much as life. Mothers would greet the blood of their children with chants, as if they were on their way to a wedding rather than that cruel hole in the ground. What nation is this, which values death over life? When will you understand that death is the opposite, the absolute destruction of life? A battle like yours isn't won with explosive belts fastened around the waist of desperate children. Perhaps you need a Palestinian Gandhi. Someone who's able to air his dirty linen in public better than Arafat and his friends.

Simon thought differently. 'You're always asking the world for sympathy, yet the world has clearly shown you that it doesn't want anyone on its doorstep. The world respects the victim who resists. The one who dies on his feet. Fight, damn it. The lives of your children are at stake. What the fuck are you waiting for?'

So whose view do you endorse? Dr Jekyll's or Mr Hyde's? Whose view do you endorse when all of them are right, when their proposals all lead to the same suicide? Bombs have got you nowhere. Talks haven't either. There must be a mistake somewhere. Simon kept insisting that those who whisper in the sultan's ear are worse than the sultan. 'Where could the Camp David talks have got you when nine of Bill Clinton's consultants were Jewish? Sandy Berger, Madeleine Albright – the US's first female secretary of state, who woke up one morning and discovered she was Jewish – Dennis Ross . . . The only non-Jewish American at Camp David was Clinton himself. How can you understand these people, and what kind of peace can you expect from them?'

Waking up from this unscheduled autopsy you're surprised by the presence of this young woman from Żabbar with eyes like big black olives shining with the light of love. Where did all that beauty come from? The question is painful. How many women are there in this world with whom, on a first date, you could discuss your chronic illness which, with increasing regularity as time goes by, splatters people's TV screens with crimson?

Where did this bewitching woman come from who can open the drawers of your pain and take off, leaving them open, with questions dangling from their innards like the guts of a bizarre half-eaten animal?

After the coffee and the screeching of the gulls – which did eventually disappear along with that old boat – you went down to the shore where she handed you her magical keys. Nadia. The Phoenician princess. All she lacked was a crown. As you were basking in her beauty she whispered in your ear, 'Do you know how long I've been waiting for you, descendent of Goliath?'

'How long?' you murmured, lost in that yielding flesh.

'For ever, since before I'd even set eyes on you.'

'How do you know I'm me and not someone else?' you asked as you buried your spinning head in her tender breasts.

'Because I made you up. Your nose. Mouth. Eyes. Lips. Chin. Hair sprinkled with the dust of bygone battles. I designed it all. Let me dust the past off you. The dust of battles won and lost.'

'There are no battles won and all the others lost. Every battle has been lost,' you said as she folded herself into your arms. 'Every moment of glory is stained with blood and tears and with someone else's remains. History spits on victim and killer in equal measure and continues on its way.'

She blinked in the moonlight that pressed its face against the car windows to spy on her breasts, trembling in your embrace like a terrified bird. The same breasts that moments ago were about to swallow you up as they peeked from beneath the mad fabric of the autumn dress she was wearing before you tore it off her. Those youthful breasts that seemed so confident began to tremble and shy away from you when you touched them. You put your ear to them; they whispered the first words in the mysterious language of woman. There are women who are able to make you understand immediately what makes them women. They unfurl their sails and say, 'Onwards, captain.' Nadia was one of those who never had to explain that she was a woman, an angel, a fragile creature, soluble, absorbable. A weaver of merriment and joy. That alien joy that takes over when you're struggling to breathe in her arms.

Nadia was one of those. One of those women who could even seduce the nephew of Zechariah. One of those women whom you desire more of with every sip you take. Because they make you even thirstier. A mad thirst that nothing can quench except for two round fountains above the navel. The navel that feeds you for nine months before you're weaned off one tit and put on another. Actually two. You wanted her all the time. Even in your dreams. You begin to want her again as soon as you're done. As soon as you come away from each other's delicious slippery embrace. You want her as she's putting on her clothes. As she's slipping on her high-heeled shoes. As she's arranging her hair. As she's hunting for her earring in the candlelight. As she prepares her key. As she plants a contented kiss on your cheek. You want her as she pulls the door shut. As she starts her car and leaves. As she makes you wait once more like a dazed Shahryar eagerly waiting for Scheherazade to take him for a ride on her magic carpet around the minarets of Baghdad. The same Baghdad that the wolves of Washington have smashed. The new conservatives who believe in creative chaos and want the world to become a gigantic supermarket. Nadia, who has turned into Scheherazade, leaving you giddy with her beauty and her stories. A Scheherazade whose head you deferred taking for a thousand nights and who took your own on the thousand and first. She got her dues and Kristina's and Halimeh's, your mother's and your father's skinny wife, all the women whose head you took because they got closer to you than your lungs could bear.

After five years Scheherazade ran out of stories, and her magic carpet was worn. During the night she was seen rolling off it. The night of the fall of Baghdad. There were women wrapped in black. Minarets weeping. Smoke everywhere, and Muhammad Saeed al-Sahhaf, the Iraqi minister for media and foreign affairs, informing journalists that the plan drawn up by the Revolutionary Council was to let the coalition forces advance as far as they could into Iraqi territory and, once they had formed a long line, take them by surprise and hack into them the way you hack at a snake with a Japanese sword. 'You could say that the war against these calves and pigs starts now.' Minister Muhammad Saeed al-Sahhaf. His name immediately reminds you of Ahmad Said, the buffoon from 'This is the Voice of the Arabs, all Arabs, from Cairo' back in 1967. It turns out that until then the minister for media and foreign affairs hadn't realized that the long snake he intended to hack into who knows how many thousands of pieces was already coiled beneath him, but it wasn't resting quietly, it was in al-Rashid Square right in front of the Ministry of Information. On the banks of the Tigris.

Scheherazade from Żabbar descended from her magic carpet. There was no magic any more. 'I need to get up for work tomorrow. After work I have to go to choose a bathroom. What colour would you prefer?' Grey, obviously. You didn't say it out loud but, as usual, with your silence. 'I quite like peach or even something turquoise . . . white is in, too . . . Goodness, the moment you see one you forget the last one you saw . . .'

You didn't see anything, so you had no need to see one and forget the other. In your case it's all forgotten right from the start. Everything is in the past. Scheherazade had long since begun to hold back, preparing to descend from the magic carpet. Those heights had given her vertigo. She'd been looking for something with which to occupy herself and make her a normal woman. She couldn't do that with you. Do what? There's a difference between being everyday and being normal. Assuming you don't suffer from vertigo. But that wasn't the case. How much longer did you expect her to stay on this stupid carpet? Everyone has the right to lie down. Even prophets and stars have a right to lie down and take a rest. Don't they? Simon liked to say that icons have no right to take a day off. 'They have to remain up there on their pedestals. If they descend even once we're done with them and will no longer love them.' Maybe that's why we choose our icons once they're dead. So they won't ever open their mouths or protest about something they don't like. After all we've made three-quarters of their stories up ourselves.

But Nadia was no icon, and she was not dead, and she was no Scheherazade either. Go and find your Scheherazade somewhere else. See if you can find her in your dirty books. Nadia was a normal woman. Never mind how you define normal or not normal and what counts as common or rare. The only thing that matters is what society has agreed upon. You could call it a dictatorship if you wish. Call it whatever you like, the fact is that no one pays attention. Nadia was a normal woman like all the women in the world. She cooked and ate and drank and shat and longed to become pregnant and give birth and nurse children. She did all this while thinking ahead. In the direction of life and photosynthesis. There was no future for you. In your case the future was already behind you. And you didn't want an extension of yourself. You didn't want a little boy to pull on your beard. Everyone has the instinctive knowledge that everything will come to an end. Flesh. Hair. Eyes. Nose. Holiness. Even divine forbearance, already a scarce commodity, will one day come to an end. And yet what choice does humanity have except to carry on eating and drinking and shitting and reproducing and pretending they know what they're doing on this godforsaken planet? Does that mean that only Nadia appeared to know what she was doing as she drew the straight lines in your life and invited you to choose a bathroom? Ironically what she wanted was the one thing you couldn't give her. It took her five years to arrive at the greatest disappointment of her life, when she understood that you didn't want children or a bathroom. You had unshakeable views on that. In fact, it was the only thing in your life you could call unshakeable or solid. The rest was all liquefied, full of air bubbles, rising and popping.

During those five years you watched as Nadia changed into fifty different kinds of woman, none of whom could understand you because you couldn't understand yourself, and you had never intended to explain to anyone what you yourself couldn't understand. You did tell her that fantastic proverb of your ancestors that one can learn only out of one's own pocket and not out of the pockets of others. You told her that your people had woken up and realized you didn't have any pockets at all, and so you fell asleep again and woke up to find yourselves as bare as skeletons who could do nothing but criticize and complain and irritate people even as they tried to make them understand. At least you were conscious that you were in no position to understand or make anyone else understand. It was too late. That's why you chose silence. So as not to become a bore. So that it could be the cloak beneath which you hid the shortcomings you could never explain.

It took her a while to discover your discomfort. Not because it wasn't clear that you were damaged and delinquent; you even smelled that way. Your smell was sour enough to convey a clear message to her that you were nothing but an errant soul haunted by ghosts from the past and that no prayer, no icon, no entreaty could save your soul from the cowardice of that past. You wished to tell her all of this and many other things, including that the greatest cowardice is that which a man imposes upon himself. But communication between you had long since come to an end. You were in no position to preach and she was unwilling to listen for a minute longer. Nadia became square and was no longer interested in who had killed whom or who had embraced whom, who had defeated whom and who had surrendered to whom. Nadia was only interested in one thing. One square thing connected to bathrooms and their elusive colours. Those rooms that made you forget one the moment you saw another.

15

Musa and I became increasingly involved in Amman's underbelly. Every city has an upper and a lower dimension; it shows you one thing in daylight and a thousand other things after dark. Every city has its accessible and inaccessible sides. Every city reveals itself within certain parameters, although as a stranger you hold a mysterious advantage over its sons, because cities, like women, prefer to open their hearts and their legs to strangers. Not Valletta, though; she doesn't open up to you at all, not her heart, not her legs, not her lips. Amman was beautiful when it was light. Even though it had no sea and no shoreline. Even though it had no rivers or gulls. No sea urchins and limpets. She was beautiful because she was small and quiet, surrounded by fresh air and virgin mountains on all sides. I could smell saffron and fennel on her clothes every morning when I woke up and got ready to start my chaotic day while she got ready to start hers. Amman was beautiful and small, even though, like every Arab capital, it was inhabited by poverty and hunger and religious faith. By dogs with a royal bearing prowling behind windows and low walls. By fear and paranoia and autoimmune disorders. Inhabited by those strange wide-eyed creatures we once called our fathers.

Musa had been saving up without his mother's knowledge. Or maybe she knew but said nothing about it, since she seemed to get along with him far better than his father, who guzzled everything away with the whisky that would eventually send him wherever it was that he eventually went. Maybe it was where he wanted to go, who knows? You never know what these Eastern men are thinking. Musa hadn't yet become a habitual drinker like his father, but he was on that path. A drunkard but a free one. Brave and gentle, with a mind divorced from fable and faith and all the baggage attached to that. It's true that life had made him a street vendor, but his heart in its unrest kept up its enquiry and pursuit. A creative heart will never be still, it seems. Sometimes he bought books and passed them on to me after he'd read them. Often we discussed them, and for the most part he would surprise me with his insights. He had razor-sharp instincts, which came from the desert. Then there was the way he spoke: a rich Arabic, warm and spicy, baked in the oven of pre-Islamic poetry.

Although, like me, he'd been born and raised in Amman, his accent was pure desert Arabic as if he'd spent his entire life there, baking his consonants in the hot sand. Why am I surprised? Haven't I also ended up talking in a Hebron dialect although I've never set foot in Hebron? In Amman there were some very interesting linguistic distinctions. You could tell where someone came from as soon as they opened their mouth. Not all mouths are the same. There are the big and the tiny ones. There are ones that have been sewn up like my father's, and loose ones. There are eastern and western mouths. The ones from the south, the centre and the north. Not to mention those of the minorities and EDPs, which doubled the number of wide-eyed, vacant citizens in that stunned capital. Musa and I weren't a linguistic exception. He had his baggage, and I had mine. You could tell right away where we were from and even who we were. In Amman there was none of the homogeneity that would allow its inhabitants to merge with the crowd.

In Amman everyone locked themselves up in their own accents. Some families and tribes surrounded themselves with bastions and locked the gates. Black September continued to function as social cement. Some families kept refusing to intermarry with others who were not of their linguistic flock. The concept of citizenship never developed in that country devoid of happiness, since neither the citizens nor the state itself knew what citizenship was. The state was too busy pulling strings to maintain the balance of refugees and tribes. There were ongoing tensions between the major tribes from the south and those from the north and even people from the central regions, not to mention the country's ambitious Circassian minority. Meanwhile, when it came to the pulling of strings and ropes, no one could compete with King Hussein. The same Arab king who had waved to me as a child and to whom I'd waved back without knowing that he had grassed on his brothers on the night of Yom Kippur.

King Hussein was well aware of the demographic implications of those tensions. There was no government member who wasn't appointed by him. No cabinet, no army or police chief he hadn't handpicked the way you'd pick half a kilo of cucumbers at Joe the Greengrocer's. To maintain the delicate balance that secured his place on the Hashemite throne, King Hussein had to pick the spoiled and wormy cucumbers, too.

Needless to say, Musa and I were at the bottom of the linguistic classification. Our dialects were rough compared with the softly spoken masters of modernity and the builders of the rosy future. A Bedouin and a refugee peasant; you could tell from their voices that they belonged to the shattered class. The rich classes had a language all their own. They had their own designated zones and spaces. They had their own shops, swimming pools and bridges. In other words, there was another Amman just for them. An Amman that never consorted with ours.

Some time after the spectacular sight of the migrating storks a squad of armed soldiers began to keep watch outside the house of Ejad Abu Rumman, one of my friends who lived on our street and whose family was considered liberal because their mother didn't wear a headscarf and the sisters often went about in figure-hugging jeans. After some nosing about we discovered that the soldiers were guarding that 'liberal' family from possible retaliatory attacks after a cousin of theirs had shot and killed a man in their village eighty-five kilometres outside of Amman. For many people, especially the older generation, this seemed quite normal. Not the guarding of someone's house but the killing of an innocent man and the revenge it necessitated. That's why many Arab capitals can never become cosmopolitan, despite the billions upon billions they spend on them. Perhaps they needed to invest in people first. In enlightening primitive minds that believe in an eye for an eye rather than in building the biggest gallery or the tallest skyscraper erected on unstable sand and artificial pebbles in the desert, where the tribal hierarchy is strongly valued. The ruler is the leader of the tribe, the sheikh, the lone monarch whose farts dictate politics and economics and the future of the country. It all depends on what he's eaten, drunk and shat and which woman he's fucked. On what he's decided to order during those obscene evenings in his court. Amman expanded without a distinctive accent and its linguistic web continued to reflect huge social divisions. The drama of Ejad's family came to an end after two months, not through the judiciary system of the country that insists it is completely upright but through a tribal tribunal set up to deal with such matters the way our Arab ancestors dealt with them 2,500 years ago. Forget magistrates and judges, forget courts and books of law. The sight of those armed soldiers changing shift on Abu Rumman's veranda was enough to make anyone realize that nothing had changed since the time of the Prophet Muhammad; we were still tribal aggregations who hated each other but who were happy to yield under the baton of Byzantium and Persia.

Musa spent the money he'd saved on his friends and on anyone he took a fancy to. He wasn't the type to buy something for himself. A pair of shoes or a shirt, for example. No way. He had an 'I' that was collective. It included all comers. A heart as big as the ocean. As big as the whole Arab geography lying in wait for some legendary hero to wake it from its perpetual slumber. Musa was that hero. It was a relief to have him around during those months of darkness during which my brothers and the majority of residents of Beirut and Sabra and Shatila died. In my darkest moments he was there for me, every bit of him. Brimming with sympathy and consolation. He was like the switch that lit up the world. I never meant to show him my tears or to see his, but Amman, cunning Amman, insists on baring all. He cried so much for my brothers that I was confused. For a moment I imagined they were his brothers and that I was the one who should be consoling him.

Musa had nothing to hide. Not even his tears. A person with only one face. Whichever angle you looked at him you always saw the same face. That dark, bony face weathered by the open-heartedness of the desert. He acted and moved through life courageously; he didn't wait for life's events to reach him but leaped at them as they approached. I didn't have to dig deep before I discovered where he'd inherited all those genuine characteristics. One visit to his relatives in the desert was enough. I once accompanied him to Wadi Musa. The valley had given him his name. It was where his family were born and where his father wanted to be buried beside his Nabataean ancestors who had dominated the south and founded Petra, the Rose City that forced Athens back into its shell for five centuries before it opened its legs to Rome's advances 105 years after Christ's birth. We turned up unannounced, as our ancestors would have 2,500 years ago. His aunt's surprise quickly gave way to happiness at the sight of us; she overwhelmed us with kisses and hugs as if we were a pair of angels. Their humble tent suddenly took on the appearance of a large palace. In a moment the harsh everyday bed sheets were replaced in our minds with thick colourful mattresses and pillows.

'Rest your legs, my son.' She insisted that we stretch our legs out on the sheets as we leaned our elbows on the clean, comfortable cushions. 'Rest them or she won't stop telling you to,' said Musa when he saw me stretch them out and pull them back towards my stomach as if I were ashamed to expose them in front of a Nabataean lady.

After a while Musa's cousins arrived and took him into their arms, then they hugged me with the same warmth without knowing or wanting to know whether I was a refugee. An EDP. One of those who had lost their land beyond the river and now shared their air and their cemeteries.

They brewed coffee on the coals from the fire their mother had lit to welcome us. They say you can tell how gentle a Bedouin is by the fire he stokes. The generous always have their fire on while the tight-fisted put it out right away to avoid unwanted visitors looking for food and drink and gossip to take into the desert. Especially the poets with their long tongues, those who know how to play with language.

Arab history has many stories of large tribes who ended up humiliated and isolated or had to leave their precious dominions because of a couple of verses. One I can never forget is from Jarir, the satirical Umayyad poet, in which he insults his friend, al-Farazdaq. Whenever they heard the dogs bark, al-Farazdaq's mother would piss on the fire: being that mean, she never fully relieved herself in case someone else should turn up unannounced and she would be caught with no piss to put the fire out again. Not the sort of scene one would want to witness, but the eloquence is chilling. Frightening. Had the Umayyad era not marked the start of the Arab golden age I would have believed that our sword has always had a longer reach than our arms, and one of our chronic illnesses is that our tongue is far weightier than our ambiguous aspirations.

The fire kindled by Musa's aunt and the coffee her children brewed bore no relationship to the behaviour of al-Farazdaq and his parsimonious mother. At one point his aunt whispered something in the ear of one of her children, who nodded and rushed out of the tent. Musa, with his typical incisive Bedouin instinct, guessed what was about to happen. 'Don't bother to make anything, Aunty, we can't stay long,' he said at once. 'We always welcome our loved ones, so stretch your legs, son, stretch them out. Don't be shy,' she responded, paying no attention to his protestations. 'Guess we'll be staying the night, my friend. There's no changing her mind,' he whispered to me. He tried to convince her and tell her that we hadn't told anyone we'd be sleeping out. There were no telephones in Wadi Musa. 'Your mother will know,' she said as calmly as a princess whose word is the only law of the land. 'Stretch your legs, son. Relax. You're in your own home, with your family.'

She'd sent her son to slaughter one of their two sheep, and this was served for dinner, as if she thought we were poets and was afraid of our wagging tongues. We spent the night in the embrace of Bedouin kindness and generosity. A true, uncomplicated kindness and goodness. The desert is harsh but clean. It is swept clean every morning and washed every evening. Unlike filthy Amman. Devious Amman. Rabbath Ammon, who hasn't bathed since she was crowned goddess of the Ammonites.

They say that Amman was built on seven big hills. Seventeen, according to some. I don't care. I've never counted them, but I know every one of their peaks. Street by street and hill by hill. I know every stone in Amman, and I know what each stone is doing in its place. Musa and I trod every one of its streets, explored every cranny and alleyway, climbed every gutter and drainpipe, squeezed into every nook. We ate and got drunk and danced and laughed on every step. We threw up and pissed and cried under every archway and in every corner. We even ate and shat in the intact Roman theatre. We even traipsed over and shat in that other world, the forbidden world of the rich who lived with us only in a physical sense. We made fools of ourselves. Climbed their trees and scaled their defences. Picked and ate their cherries and pears and loquats and spied on the women wearing bikinis and sunglasses lounging beside their pools and reading papers and magazines from London and Paris. We watched them rubbing cream and aromatic oil into their sagging breasts. Saw them touching themselves. Even witnessed them inviting the dog to nuzzle between their oiled legs, wagging its tail as if it had found a jug of gravy. We watched their barbeques and luxurious parties.

We watched them pile their tables with all kinds of fish and meat, including people's flesh. We watched them clink their glasses of marvellous wine distilled from the blood of citizens and the poor.

We watched them open their imported champagne and accompany it with snorts of white dust. Watched as they gambled away their cash or threw it under the feet of singers and dancing whores. Watched them get dizzy and exchange their wives. Watched as they raped their maids and servants. We watched as the entire country was dismantled, broken into little pieces, twisted, squeezed, distilled and distributed in bottles and small packets to be drunk and smoked at national orgies. Once, during one of those orgies, we saw the minister of defence and the minister for dowries and religious affairs with glasses of halal champagne in their hands, celebrating the liberation of holy shrines from Zionist clutches.

This is Amman. This is the Philadelphia that shows you all sorts of things, from the shit of refugees to the shit of the privileged. 'Most people aren't like that,' Musa said as he struggled against the emotion tightening his throat. 'The world is us. You and me and Omaymah and my aunt. Your mother and my mother and the neighbours. People in the fields and quarries and factories. Those who queue for hours for a loaf of bread, an honest loaf, even if it's been kneaded out of sweat and blood. One day the world will sweep them away. It will throw them up as a pregnant woman throws up to confirm the new life in her womb.'

Musa was well versed, perhaps too well versed, but he had a heart of gold open to life and its joys. He never gave up and never stopped hoping, even after he'd acquired his father's habit and become a slave to the bottle. He remained a happy, optimistic drunkard. The opposite of what I was. When I drink I have to weep. I weep inwardly. My tears come from a place into which Nadia could never peer. I remained grey and doubtful, like a shadow, a shadow walking in Musa's shadow, in the shadow of his certainty. He must have got his determination from somewhere. Maybe it was his desert roots. The dry and distant south. Or the street where he had to slum it to earn an honest crust. Apparently eating honest food keeps you honest. You can only get dirty once. That single time implies that the ribbon's been cut. Another slippery slope. Everything's a slippery slope. That's why there are things in life you should never do. Not once. Not even half a single time. Because the minute you set one foot there the chain will pull you over and take you down, and then you're no longer a hero. Heroes, like Simon's icons, cannot afford to lower themselves by even a millimetre, can't get a single speck of dirt on themselves. They need to stay aloof. High up by the distant stars where we've put them. Maybe Musa was an exception. One of those up above, even though he lived down below. A hero without medals or badges. Even though he had to wake up at the crack of dawn to get ice and lemonade to soften the queuing mouths of the storks leaving the country of their birth.

Musa watched the country being drained of blood every day, and yet he continued to believe in it. He believed that the Arab soul was like all other souls: drawn to the light and the air. That's why he lit candles instead of crying and cursing the darkness. Sometimes he even caused flashes of lightning, like that 1982 invasion, when he was arrested by the River Jordan as he tried to cross to the other side to join the Palestinian resistance. The king's police officers couldn't believe their eyes. 'Just say you were running after a lamb that went astray. Say you shot a bird and were going to retrieve it,' they instructed him to say during the interrogation once they'd discovered that his uncle was someone high up in the southern Jordanian army. One of those thick cords, shall we say, in the hands of King Hussein bin Talal, Talal the mad king. One of those whom King Hussein had to appoint against his will on Machiavelli's advice.

Like his father, Musa got off lightly. He spent two days at headquarters and left without signing anything, he said, although he did get a firm scolding from his uncle the colonel. 'Your father's behaviour and now yours are embarrassing me mightily. Do you know that all kinds of ministers and shit were involved in this? If they kick me out on my arse who will look out for you? You do something like this again and you'll rot in jail, because I'll issue a statement saying I don't know you any more and you're no longer related to me,' he told him in front of his mother, while Musa pretended to listen. 'They can both go fuck themselves, him and his king,' he said to me, smiling.

'So now we're starting to hide stuff from each other?' I said, hurt and shocked that he'd planned and carried it all out behind my back without telling me a thing. I felt truly betrayed. That the only time he hid anything from me it had to be something of this magnitude. He could have disappeared for good. Had he not been caught by the Jordanian guards he'd have been riddled with holes by the Israeli snipers spread along the border.

'You need to concentrate on your studies,' he said, sounding paternal. That made me even angrier.

'And you, don't you have mouths to feed? Who the fuck said you should die instead of me?' I said furiously.

He laughed and replied, 'In birth and in death, my friend, we don't need permission. Next time we'll go together so we can die together. How about that?'

Musa. The shape of childhood and adolescence. It would take me ages to paint his portrait accurately. Ink wouldn't suffice. Not even photos. You needed to catch Musa in action. You need to have spent your childhood running after him. The Zorba of the desert. Hard-working, he gave the impression of being in multiple places at any given time. Dancing in one place, reading in another and selling lemonade in front of the Passport Office, and all the while eating from the same honest loaf. Even though he'd become an insider in that department. Anyone else would have pocketed whatever they could and in no time be behind the wheel of a Mercedes or a BMW of the kind that lower-grade employees were all suddenly driving. Everyone said it was an economic bubble. Some of them couldn't even spell the word luxury let alone pick its ripe fruit, which is usually found high up, right at the top where no one can reach except for the long and powerful arms of major plunderers.

The economic bubble of the 1980s was no bubble, it was just a bit of opportunistic capital from Lebanon that made it to Amman after the destruction of Beirut. The bubble didn't last long; it quickly moved on to Dubai, which was preparing to become the world's biggest brothel. Let's just say there was a bubble and that Amman, as it always had, made a killing off the wounds of Beirut. Let's just say that cities are like women; they get jealous of each other. Let's assume men aren't as jealous, but, even so, how would that explain the fact that a minor messenger in a small department who knows nothing of bubbles or their economic foam is suddenly driving a Mercedes Benz and discussing the stock exchange?

I had to find out. If these minor employees had done so well for themselves, just how well had their bosses done? I had to know. I had to find out exactly what was happening. What was really being sold in a poor country without resources? I had to find out so as not to get dizzy. The entire country, citizens and all, was being sold cheaply on the wholesale market. We were told that privatization was inevitable without being told why it was inevitable. No one knew who had sold, who had bought and who had grabbed or when and how the sale had taken place. Everyone was in a daze; no one knew what was going on. A few months would pass, and we would have to buy, at twice the original price, the same products and services we'd been forced to sell for our own good. Only the packaging had changed and the logo on the receipts and bills. This is my Amman and Musa's and Philadelphus' – a cow that eats its children and is milked by its neighbours.

Meanwhile, many refugees continued the process of domestication. Many of them turned into trees and chickens and lambs and goats and cows and lizards and dogs, both domestic and hunting dogs, and even racing dogs.

The refugee camps continued to expand in the heart and peripheries of Amman and other towns in the kingdom. Tents made out of thick fabric became tin huts – very interesting in winter to those who are fascinated by musical sounds – and the tin huts developed into rooms built haphazardly out of bricks and cement, often following the joining of families through marriage.

Polygamy began to rear its head as the number of widows increased, especially among the young and beautiful. Widows who had barely started out in life. Another of the fruits borne by the trees of war. 'Marriage is a cloak,' people began to say because of the ticking bomb between the legs of every widow. 'Better the shadow of a man than the shadow of a wall.' Families wanted to get rid of extra mouths to feed, and men wanted what was best for the appendage between their own legs. What else was there to do, seeing as the only way to protect a young widow in Muslim society was to fuck her? Many of these women were assaulted and persecuted in the PLO offices that had once again sprouted throughout Amman after King Hussein and Arafat had made up – as usual with no warning.

King Hussein would never have given Arafat the red-carpet treatment at Amman International Airport without having consulted – let's not say taken orders from – his US friends. This is where the road to Oslo began. On that red carpet which made Arafat's eyes pop out of his head like a frog dazzled by all the glory that awaited him.

Meanwhile, our house had more or less achieved its final state – having been almost emptied of inhabitants. The last two of my brothers had left, one to Czechoslovakia and the other to Baghdad. Needless to say, both ended up wallowing in political shit. Arafat's, to be precise, since he wouldn't rest until he'd destroyed the children of his people, as my father said.

Meanwhile, my father's irrelevance had long since engulfed him, and he'd stopped working completely. Why do I say stopped instead of using the exact words? There's quite a difference between stopping and being fired. Yes, he was fired. No one wants to employ a man who is dumb and vacant, not to say barely in his right mind. When you avoid people, people avoid you in return. And when you put life aside life puts you aside and turns its back on you. It might also show you its arse and make an obscene gesture.

One day I got home and found him building a rough hut in a corner of our garden. Right beneath the orange tree my mother had planted, where the golden owl used to sit for me while I drew her. The walls completed, he was fashioning a roof out of wood and some other junk he'd scavenged. Sumayyah stood in the doorway and shrugged at my questioning stare. I walked up to him and greeted him as usual without expecting him to greet me back. I wanted to understand the purpose of the little room he was building. 'Are you going to breed chickens, Dad?' I asked. He was too busy pottering about and hammering away to notice me. Occasionally he'd wipe the sweat from his hollow temples with the end of the keffiyeh he wore summer and winter. Suddenly, as I watched him, he hit his finger with the hammer by mistake. He threw down the hammer and held his injured finger in his other hand. I looked at his face to see if I could catch an expression of pain, agony, anger or any other emotion that would prove that this man was still alive, could still be hurt by a blow from a hammer.

He held his injured finger in his other hand as if it wasn't his own. Like one of the logs and planks he was chopping. Always with that face like parchment that life couldn't fossilize any further. 'Dinner, Nabil!' Sumayyah suddenly shrieked from the kitchen at the other end of the house.

What kind of father was this man who could no longer be hurt by a hammer? Or at the least hid his pain from his youngest child? The youngest whom he had never lifted in his arms and never hugged or kissed and whose birth he was perhaps even only vaguely aware of. After all, no one was paying much attention when he was born. Not just his father, even his mother who spat him out from between her legs and hurried off. Everyone's mind was on the wars. On Nasser and on Arab glory. On Ahmad Said and the drip of his poison. I dragged myself off to eat. As soon as I got to the yard a cat jumped out and stared at me in surprise. I looked at the frightened cat and back at my father, still standing stiffly like a statue made of salt. Unruffled by the wind or by death or even by a blow from a hammer. I turned my gaze between my father and the cat.

'It's getting cold. Are you coming or not?' Sumayyah yelled.

'Yes,' I called back as I shooed the cat away, muttering, 'We aren't the only ones who don't know why we're here.'

16

The Upper Barrakka Gardens lie shrouded in fog and darkness. At its edge, the lights struggle against the curtain of salty fog exhaled by the sea below its thighs. You're on high alert as you enter, like a thief trying not to wake the garden from its languid torpor, because you know that in a little while it will have to rouse itself to resume its endless watch.

There was a time when the Barrakka would share its doubts and secrets with another tormented denizen of Valletta. Another city dweller who left many entries in the ledger of your conscience. Rużar Briffa, who, the moment you picked up his poetry collection, became the first Maltese poet with whom you felt a kinship. He felt like a father, an uncle, a cousin, a brother or a son; poets and the afflicted and the sidelined are all your kin. Even the brooms that sweep the streets are your kin. Rużar Briffa. The Barrakka would wait for him to show up at her entrance, running to throw herself into his arms as soon as she saw him, and as she embraced him she would surreptitiously take his shoulder bag, empty it of ointments and syringes and bandages and fill it with roses and sweet-smelling grasses and melodies. And what melodies are you expecting to receive from her? What melody could reattach your flayed flesh, your twisting riot of ghosts and spirits? You're like a carriage driven by a frightened horse. You could never have imagined that Simon would register his protest in such a terrible manner. You did not expect a betrayal of that magnitude from him. Had you forgotten? Had you forgotten that Simon is a scientist and scientists have no limits? Simon isn't just a talker. He doesn't worship your greyness. There's no grey in science. That's only in your head. In Professor Frendo's head. In the heads of leaders and lawyers and those who know how to stretch the facts and twist them. Simon, on the other hand, is like every honest scientist – he follows through. Takes the experiment through to the end until a conclusion is reached, until every shade of grey has been eliminated. The last time you meet he issues a final declaration: 'Whoever it was that designed and made us, I'd like to tell him that his project failed, and I am the greatest proof of that.'

How much more clarity did you need? It's not true that Simon's actions came out of nowhere. You just didn't notice because your head is weighed down by the dust of the past. Your sight is clouded by the salt of religions. You are cursed from your head to the soles of your feet. It's not just Palestine, not just Simon and not just Nadia, but everything: each and every one of the things you touch, you ruin. Every single thing, even your toothbrush suddenly seems to bear a grudge against you and has turned into a weapon. But Simon's not a weapon, Simon's not a truncheon or a nightstick. Simon's not a dagger or a lance piercing your flank. Simon's the rock of Sisyphus, which you'll need to carry for the rest of your life, which will keep forcing you back down from the mountaintop.

The Upper Barrakka doesn't greet you at its entrance. It doesn't even notice that you're there. It remains ensconced in its gentle sleep. You're no Rużar Briffa, my friend. You're no Alex Attard. And she won't be waiting for you freshly bathed with a towel around her waist, she won't be taking you by the hand the moment she spots you in the fog, to hug you against her breasts, against that tender, wholesome flesh, laced with inexplicable perfumes, the smell of mercy that will wash away all your exhaustion and put you back into the orbit of life and oxygen. When you visit the Barrakka at night it's not the first time you feel a shiver and a huge desire to bury your head in the breasts of a woman who is a stranger to you. A mysterious woman like the Barrakka herself, hidden behind the curtains of night and fog exhaled by the sea. A woman who resembles your mother. Who resembles Nadia before she went square. Or Halimeh, who travelled across shores and bays to pursue you because of some ancient debt she owed your father.

'You've really done it this time, haven't you, you dog, you coward, you whore.' The Barrakka doesn't stir. Doesn't open her eyes. Doesn't move her head on the pillows of the humid night. 'Even in death you beat me at everything! Even as you lie in the Christian tomb that I know for certain you didn't want. Who gave you permission, and how will I ever cure myself of you? How many thousands of things do I need to cure myself of? Did you not know how many cadavers and skeletons pursue me? Why did you have to add one more? Who shall I report you to now? To Allah, who never sticks up for refugees and doesn't even come down to defend his own title? To your mother and father whose hearts will be broken for the rest of their days? Or to the basil and mint that Klara has neglected, Klara who has ballooned to five times her original size since we received the news? It's almost as if she was waiting until after your death to grow fat. And what if they were to listen to me, what could I tell them? That you betrayed me and got away in secret, and now you're looking down on me and laughing from somewhere up there and saying to yourself, 'Stay down there, in your own personal hell.' Or should I tell them that you'd given up swimming in the global maelstrom? If you were a coward, how are we to blame, you dog?'

The Barrakka lies beneath night's sheets softened with dew. A princess who achieves her fullness in sleep. She doesn't rock you from side to side. Neither sweetly nor roughly. Yet the life-enhancing scent of her breasts is like that of a sliced apple. That odd desire to bury your head in a woman's breasts grows. You slip into her arms as if you were sliding between the sheets of a sailor's wife dreaming of her husband's return. Beside the small circular pond you glimpse the shadow of something moving. The shadow takes fright. It panics when it senses the sound of your footsteps. You hurry in its direction, but the shadow has dissolved into nothing. You wander from one column to the next, looking around you and rubbing your eyes and wondering whether you are going mad. The ghost is nowhere to be seen. You drag yourself towards the balustrade, slowly, like an aged wolf. From behind the parapet wet with salty dew, the lights of Vittoriosa wink across the bay. They seem pale and distant. Struggling against the harsh night, they leave a little reflection on the belly of the dark monster.

'That day I thought I had begun to understand you. I apologize, my friend. Wrong again. I apologize, and not just to you. I apologize to the whole world but especially to you because I never imagined that your declaration was also your final verdict. I thought it was just another wound, open for discussion. Another open wound for us to pick at with our scientific instruments. For us to pull the wound open, infect it with our futile questions, which become more insistent as death waits for you just around the corner.'

Vittoriosa is directly opposite. Sending out her light to lay a band of glorious gold on the cheeks of the sleeping Middle Sea. Vittoriosa is an orange, intact, unsqueezed. A Christian jewel wrapped in the luxurious robes of a 500-year-old victory. How good the robes of victory always look! Victory always suits one, doesn't it? It remains compelling. Decisive. Glorious and warm as if it had happened only yesterday. It stays warm because we keep remembering it and reminding ourselves of it. Commemorating and celebrating it as is only appropriate. We celebrate when man overcomes man. When cannon defeat cannon. When faith in God rips faith in God to shreds.

'I thought I'd understood you, my friend. But the intellectual just packed up and left without giving notice. He took the final decision after a silent battle with himself. The scientist-intellectual decided to betray his friend after he himself was betrayed by the calendar of life. Existence and its supreme values betrayed him, and the mottos he had adopted without knowing that they were far heavier than he was. Heavier than his failed Palestinian friend. I thought I'd understood you, but Sinbad the city dweller set sail for the seas of no return to challenge the suns of nothingness and the moons of the unknown.'

Suddenly, at the end of the parapet over the port side, you see a shapely woman standing and watching you, her arms crossed over her chest. You recognize her immediately.

'Haven't you avenged yourself enough over me?'

Silence

'Haven't you had your share of my blood?'

Silence

'What else will you do to me?'

Silence

The woman with big eyes says nothing. She gives you a strangely pitying look, just as she used to do in the remote past whenever she put a plate of food down in front of you out in the yard and looked on while you hurriedly pecked at it, as confused as a cat expecting a beating.

'You know that my mother and father and lover and siblings and friends and country and Baghdad and Simon and Adnan have all left me. They've all jumped into the well for your sake. What more do you want from me?'

Silence

'Why did you come here, now that the earth is earth no longer and the sky is sky no longer and the sea is sea no longer and we are no longer ourselves? Why did you come here?'

Silence

'I'm not myself any more, you know. I don't even resemble my father any more. I've actually become uglier than he was. Look closely at me! What do you see? What do you see but the remains of a man who was knocked down by the winds and lightning and trees and newspapers and cannon and wrinkles and the betrayal of his friends and the cursed blood and ancient shame? Look closely at me. If there's one thing that's left in its place just go ahead and ruin it. Destroy it now or else, just to be completely sure, throw me over. I promise I won't whimper any more. Even when I crash against the rock-hard bottom. By now I'm used to dying without uttering a cry of pain, because even cries of pain have betrayed me, you know. Show me what you're made of, and throw me over the parapet now. Don't just stand there staring at me; big eyes can only kill you once.'

'Throw you? Throw you? Don't you know how much I love you?' the woman with the big eyes finally says, approaching calmly, spreading her arms wide to welcome you into her flesh.

'I've been dead since before I was born. Before you even dreamed of me. Before I was formed in your flesh. I've been dead since I plucked your first victim from the hands of God and threw him into a bottomless well of sin. Since you tempted him to climb that mad tree to bring you the only fruit that God had warned him not to touch.'

'So obstinate, just like him, exactly the same!' the woman with big eyes says as she locks you in the tenderness of her flesh. Were it not for

the beating of her heart you would think she was a ghost. Boom-boom.
Boom-boom. Ghosts don't have hearts as far as you know. At least not
one this big. Not one that beats at this speed. Not in three dimensions.
As far as you know, the heart of spirits and ghosts is flat and unable to
pump. It's unable to dance the mad antagonistic dance. Boom-boom.
Boom-boom. Halimeh holds you against her flesh. She strokes your
hair and plants a warm kiss on your temple. You're tired . . . tired . . .
so tired, alone, defeated and sad as a branch torn from its tree.

You never expected it from Simon. You never expected it from Nadia.
You never expected it from Baghdad. You didn't expect it from anyone.
But why, Simon? 'Why? You have to tell me,' you shouted at the silent
coffin in the packed church, half of whom didn't even like Simon. Then
a pair of grey suits turned up and politely led you outside. Grey once
more. This time in matters relating to your friend's death. You howled
in the church parvis like a bitch who's lost her litter.

'You're not the only one who's harvested disappointment. You're
not the only Messiah to be betrayed and sacrificed before God. There
are other messiahs; they're there in their thousands, in graves and on
the streets, on pavements and before brothels and bars. In their damp
rooms. In a cell with Musa al-Ghabbadi. In the poetry of Alex Attard.
Behind the cannon of Ariel Sharon. Under the bombs raining down
on Fallujah. Before the embassies and in the squares. Behind screens
and on altars and minarets. They're all there, but none of them has given
up or jumped into the well. They offer resistance as a respectable victim
should. Aren't these your own words, you clown? Why are you giving
up now and going against the very grain of what you said? Why? Tell
me why.' And you weep inwardly, tearlessly, succumbing to one of those
fits of weeping that Nadia could never comprehend.

'Don't worry, darling, I'm here for you,' the woman says as she
continues to plant kisses in your hair, tousled with sweat and exhaustion,
with the salt of night and the futile walk through the streets of the city
mourning its son who never worshipped its heroes or its saints.

'Do you know how tired I am?' you sob as you bury your head into
the softness of those welcoming breasts.

'Come with me, my darling, come,' she says, raising you up in her arms as light as a cotton cloud. She lays you down in her lap as she leans her back against the arches. The air grows colder. Vittoriosa lies just across the bay from that WELCOME sign guarded by the Barrakka cannon, with the medals of victory sparkling on her chest. The melody becomes more upbeat. You weren't expecting the melody. Not from the Barrakka or from Halimeh. Boom-boom. Boom-boom. The anaesthetic goes gradually to your head. The eager, voluptuous breast invites your chapped lips. The shivering lips slide over the curve of the tender flesh. They find the cherry-like swelling. You begin to suck at Halimeh's breasts, your uncle's wife. The wholesome anaesthetic travels to the weary heart. The weary heart pumps it back up towards the tired head. Halimeh hugs you even tighter against her flesh. 'Rest now, darling, rest, my love,' she says as she teases your ear with the tip of her tongue and spreads her coal-black hair over the entire Barrakka, turning the night into a blanket.

During the night your mother visits your dreams. Beautiful. Fresh. Scented and joyous. She hums a tune as she works henna into her hair. The air is suddenly full of the scent of motherhood. If motherhood smells like anything, it must smell like that. At once strong, comforting and piercing.

> Dear mother, if only you knew
> of your son's tribulations
> since he left his home
> and was taken from you!

You request Ružar Briffa's permission. He immediately welcomes your proposal. After all, poetry is an open wound.

> Why, dear mother,
> did you push me away
> and leave me, a child
> exiled from your lap?
> How do you know, dear mother,
> that I'm not the same child
> still hankering after you?

How do you know, dear mother,
that the man on the cross
is not your son?

You ask her why she went away and left you behind when you were so fragile, but she doesn't reply. Maybe she didn't hear you. She sings to herself as she smears her hair with the reddish paste. Suddenly Halimeh appears. You're a baby again. Soon your father appears, and the dream begins to get murky. The Barrakka isn't the Barrakka any more and Vittoriosa is no longer Vittoriosa. They begin to look like Qbebe. Your parents began to argue, and you, a baby, are stuck in the middle, gasping through your tears, but no one takes any notice. Your mother is hitting herself in the face and clawing and pulling at her hair, when only a little while earlier she had been singing to herself contentedly and gently rubbing henna into her locks. Your father begins to knock his head against the wall. Suddenly men with long beards appear and throw stones at Halimeh, calling her a *sharmuta*, a whore. The stones that miss her hit you instead, but you feel no pain, while she, instead of running away, rushes over and protects you with her body. You feel something warm and sticky dripping against your skin.

You wake up with a start, bathed in sweat. There is a tremor in your fingers and knees. You try to weep, but you can't. The fingers of approaching dawn and the birdsong in the Barrakka calm you, but still you wonder how you've found yourself in the lap of the void instead of in her lap. You wake up in a heap, fully clothed in a public garden like a mad man.

What do you call someone who sleeps on the street? A 'rough sleeper'? Let's just say that the Upper Barrakka isn't the street, but it's not your bed either. But then who said that those who sleep in their own beds achieve a restful sleep? They might sleep comfortably, but rest is something else, and it has nothing to do with the thickness of a mattress or the feathers in a pillow. Rest is another thing you've never known. But the problem for you isn't a bed and a pillow. If that were it, you could just buy new ones and be done with it. How much can a bed cost? Isn't it better than being picked up and taken to the nuthouse? There'd be no point explaining to them and swearing that there's nothing wrong with you. They wouldn't believe you since everyone who ends up in that place will rattle on in the same manner, maintaining that, really, they're fine, it's the world that's sick.

What would you say? That your head's fine but the world is out of alignment? Even more reason to be carted off. It's never a good idea to claim that you're fine and the rest of the world's gone mad, because they'll stone you the way they stoned Halimeh all those years ago. What was it the Arabs of old used to say? 'When your people lose their heads what else can you do with yours?' But what does it matter what they said or didn't say since they never had pockets? According to you, all they had was a piggy bank with a hole in it. That's why they've learned nothing from life's lessons. What would you say before the doctor on duty at Mount Carmel? Would you tell him you're fine and it was really quite simple: you decided to lie down and get some air? He'd ask you what that means, simply lying down to get some air. No. The first thing he'd ask for is your name and surname, then we'd get into the psychological details. And as soon as he hears how unfamiliar your name and surname are he'll find himself asking you where you're from and what your nationality is. There we are. What will you say? Best to just keep quiet. It's true that silence doesn't work in your favour in situations like this, but isn't it in any case better than telling him that you don't even know how to define yourself? Not on the map and not even on the platform of everyday life? What will you tell him about the friends who've abandoned you, one after the other? Those who died, those who went abroad and those who hanged themselves? Will you also tell him about the betrayal of Nadia and Baghdad? And the ghosts that visit you during evenings fogged over with steam from the past? Will you tell him about the secret cabal that works behind the scenes to ruin your life?

If you were the doctor on duty, what would you do? Be honest now. Before you stands a dishevelled man with untidy hair who clearly hasn't shaved in more than a fortnight. Picked up because he was sleeping on the street. 'Come on, the Barrakka isn't the street!' you try to say. 'Shh,' an inner voice will urge. Opening your mouth will only make it worse. These psychiatrists have software designed to make you slip up as soon as you start talking. 'Here are some pills. Take one before bed. Don't worry. Half the Maltese population is on them.' So, obviously you will say nothing. What does it matter if the number of rats increases by one? It's as if he were saying, 'Take these because half of the Maltese population consists of lab mice.' And what about the other half, what are they? Cats and rams? Or professors and consultants and lawyers and financial controllers who experiment on the mice?

'I'll tell you about this country, Doctor, sir. And what I'm about to tell you has nothing to do with the pill you're about to prescribe. I mean, it's got nothing to do with the receiver you're about to plant in my head that will allow you to control me from now on. And make sure from time to time that my pockets have been cleaned out. Before they picked me up and brought me to you I was at the dentist's. And last week I got my electricity bill. You can understand, Doctor, why I'm feeling a little dizzy. It's not only you that I blame. Don't you worry about that. I can assure you it's not just your receiver. I've lost count of the number I've planted in this confused head of mine, and who knows what you're adding to my food and drink to keep me under control. According to you, half the people in this country are mice while the other half are cats. You forgot to mention crocodiles, Doctor. Crocodiles with wings and ambitious spirits. Possibly like your own, Doctor. Just because we trust you with our bodies you claim the right to sell our organs on the market. You're like a spider's web. Whoever walks into your net will never get away again – unless it's to the grave. And they still need your signature for that. There have been times when you've charged me seventy euros just for a couple of words. Do you know how many hours I have to work to make seventy euros, Doctor? And, if you want, I can prove to you that the work I do is far more important than yours or even your prime minister's. In fact, the same goes for all leaders and premiers. We put our trust in those, too, when it comes to our daily bread, and they've assumed they can go ahead and sell our children's future. It seems that everyone sprouts claws once they have the people behind them, but that's not what's brought me to you, Doctor. What brought me here are other things that Your Excellency has not studied. You could write a new thesis about me if you wanted, and if you're in a hurry, as you people usually are, you could maybe submit an article about me to the *Journal of Psychiatric Research* announcing that you've discovered a new form of schizophrenia. All it takes is for you to scribble a few lines that even God, for all his linguistic knowledge, would be unable to read. Maybe that's why he needs a pharmacist by his side to help him decipher them . . . ha-ha . . . ha-ha.'

Naturally, you won't be telling the duty doctor any of this. No chance! Where would you end up then? But even if we set aside the doctors and psychiatrists and discuss things from the perspective of a homemaker or a clerk in public service who has an ounce of conscience and some love for his country, they would all tell you the same thing: 'If you sleep in the Barrakka, whether Upper or Lower, you'd be showing us all up if you were spotted by any tourist who'd followed the sun's course as it emerged from its cradle. Why should they get a fright seeing you sprawled on the ground like a corpse? What the fuck does this country care whether Baghdad threw in the towel or Nadia left or your friend hanged himself? There's no holiness to be had in death. All holiness is in life, and life must go on.'

But can life indeed go on without Simon and Nadia and Baghdad? 'Life must go on, isn't that true?' the patriotic clerk will harangue you. 'True, true,' you'll nod to show you agree that you're unstable, and if not quite mad – because that is rather a strong term – definitely not quite all there. Doctors like to avoid it as far as possible. Professional ethics, don't you know. You don't call a madman mad to his face. Better to say out of sorts, tired, exhausted or distracted. Language is very important and not just in this particular domain but in any domain, especially in those occupations that depend on honeyed words. No need to mention politicians and poets and lawyers. When language slides off the tongue of one of those, it really turns into a whore. Perhaps this is the reason why what they all have in common is the need for some form of therapy. But no one is as well versed as you when it comes to the whoring of language.

You resurface once more, feeling groggy. You look around the Barrakka. It's completely deserted except for the birds bidding each other good morning. You feel a little calmer. Thank God there are no doctors or psychiatrists or frightened tourists. Not even prime ministers or civil servants. There's a sudden movement in the air. Beside that same small circular pond you spot a blonde woman in a dark dress carrying a dark-coloured handbag. The sun's fully risen now, and there's no more room for phantoms. Could this be the same ghost you frightened last night? As if on cue a flock of wild pigeons gather to greet her arrival. The pigeons strut and coo merrily around her feet as she scatters feed on the ground.

Suddenly the blonde woman notices your presence. She smiles and scatters more feed around the pond. The pigeons are going mad with joy. You wish you were one of them. They're pacifists and always congenial. They don't even have proper claws with which to scratch anyone. They don't eat beyond their hunger and don't hoard either. That keeps them light. How else would they fly? Unlike humans, always shoving their hands into the mouths of others, even when they have a full plate in front of them.

They say that male pigeons don't distinguish between females. They're all equally beautiful to them. All Nadias. They also say that when the pigeons grow up they no longer recognize their own mothers and fathers. The flock comes first and second and third. No individualism and no airs. Everyone shops at the pound store, and that's that. And if God decides to provide something worth a bit of cash, then everyone will sooner or later manage to peck at it, and whatever's left is pickings for the other birds unless it gets dragged away by the ants. They wouldn't throw it into the sea to keep the prices stable, would they? So it must be true that pigeons can't open secret bank accounts in Switzerland!

Meanwhile, the blonde woman sits down on a bench by the pond. Taking out a sheaf of papers and a biro, she begins to rifle through them until she seems to have found the point where she left off. Holding the biro between her teeth, she goes off into another world. Perhaps the world of pigeons where the males don't distinguish between females, not because all females will satisfy equally but because all pigeons are equally beautiful and simple. Men and women. If only you'd come into this world as pigeons. You wouldn't need to bury your head in the sand or bury your siblings and friends. Or even your mother and father who have been dead since the Palestinian sun hid behind the eleven stars of Yahweh!

After some reflection, the blonde woman begins scribbling on the papers on her lap. Staring one moment and writing the next, while the pigeons around her are busy pecking away. Contrary to what the clerk thought, no one is put off by your presence. Except for that vague smile, they didn't even pay any attention to you. You think of the storks from your childhood: how far away they seemed up there! They were one with the clouds. If only you could have joined them or they were a little closer, you would have thrown them a soft tomato or a hunk of bread. You think of the aluminium antenna you had begun to mend in order to receive the first hazy picture in a lifetime of hazy pictures. You think of Omaymah with her head always covered in black. You think of the pall-bearers and the stream of coffins coming from the damned north. All of them youngsters who gave up their lives for bugger all. For the bugger all of history that has no eye for fine details.

You think of Simon being lowered into a tomb. Like the dead, all tombs look the same. Any one of them can swallow you up, process you and turn you into a remote past. What is the past but an enormous ever-expanding hole? Expanding around you, in particular, perhaps. How can that be? Everyone's just a grain of sand in the same hourglass.

You decide to leave the scene in peace. Perhaps the woman is a poet and comes to feed the pigeons, and the pigeons feed her imagination. Perhaps she's Rużar Briffa's granddaughter, who comes here to smell the aroma of her grandfather. Perhaps this whole scene, with you and the woman and the pigeons and the Barrakka and the dawn, is just an excerpt from a poem that Rużar wanted to write. Would you mind so much if you were a stanza in a poem? But why would Rużar Briffa want to put you in his writings when his writings are so beautiful without you? 'It's true!' You admit that you would only have been a hindrance to the poem. All the more reason to leave before you ruin the poem. You quicken your pace to get out of the Barrakka. You skulk along the edges, exercising the same caution as when you came during the night. The blonde woman is still lost in her scribbling and the pigeons that are still making merry at her feet.

17

My father took some of his belongings from the house and moved into the hut we thought he had built for rabbits or whichever animal he'd dreamed of – assuming dreams are possible in the world of silence. We never understood his motives for leaving his room. We never stepped into that room. Not even when we were like squashed macaroni, sharing a single bedsheet that always left one end of the bed uncovered whenever a sibling tugged at it. Communication between siblings indeed. The refugee brothers constantly came to blows as they nibbled from a single plate like squabbling cats. During our first years under Omaymah's sceptre we all tucked our tails between our legs and chewed quietly. Once Omaymah became weaker and stopped coming over so often, Sumayyah took her place, but by then it was too late. Not only for Sumayyah but for everyone else. Authority had long since been eroded in that house. At her age Sumayyah couldn't scare an ant. She was frightened of her own shadow. In the hierarchy, I was the only one younger, and I still wasn't afraid of her. Mustafa had acquired a shred of authority because of the salary he had begun to earn, while Sumayyah acquired another because of the washing and cooking and chores she performed. I, too, acquired a shred of a shred since, after Omaymah's reign was destroyed through the death of Sami and Muhammad, I stopped taking orders from anyone. Even Allah. Except what I heard in my own head or from the kids on the street. Mustafa tried to play the role of father on many occasions, but it was far too late for him, too. It was also too late from a demographic perspective, since only four were left of what was once a sizeable refugee family: Mustafa, me, Sumayyah and my father – whom I might as well exclude.

Among the things he took to the hut was that tattered book of ancient poems from which he would, on evenings long past, occasionally recite. One day Sumayyah swore she heard him arguing with a woman while he was in there. Mustafa rebuked her roughly. 'You, too, are you losing your head? A family of lunatics!' he said after she burst into tears, thus proving that what she had heard was true.

We felt bad about our father's actions, not least because we never understood what it was that had upset him so much in his own home. Omaymah was quick to blame the rest of us. 'You must have done something, and now he doesn't want to stay under the same roof as you,' she said tearfully. 'I'll take him with me if he's such a burden to you,' she went on, as if she didn't know exactly what state her father was in. As if she didn't know he'd turned into a tree, a fossilized tree, in fact, because a healthy tree speaks to you at least once a year through its leaves and fruit and blossoms. As if she didn't know that no one could ever understand her father. Even when he was at the peak of his mental powers. In any case, there was no substance to her words. Although Mustafa and I didn't spend as much time around the house as we used to, we always kept our eyes on him and treated him with respect, imagining he was still vigorous, even though he never reacted to anything we did. Neither positively nor negatively.

Sumayyah, too, did her best to make sure he didn't want for anything. There were times when she would warm up his food five times in a single day. And sometimes she would cook something from scratch if he hadn't touched the food she'd made. And all this despite the fact that the poor woman had had to shoulder these responsibilities so suddenly. She never enjoyed any of the fruits of childhood. Well, she did, of course! She saw everything that I saw. She saw the stars and the planets collide and bring forth hatred and blood and war. She saw her mother hurrying to leave this world before she could witness her children covered in their own blood once they had been prepared to be sacrificed on the altar of Palestine. We might have forgotten to inform the reader that according to Muslim custom the bodies of those who are considered martyrs are not washed. They are buried as they are, stained with their own blood, which is supposed to light their path and perfume their presence in Allah's court. She saw her brothers shrouded in certificates. Two metres of fabric. Black and white and green and what else? Red, perhaps? What was it? A sizeable triangle the colour of hate. The colour of Goliath's blood. What else had Sumayyah seen? For a long time she wet the bed, even into adolescence. The images and fear of Black September continued to torment her even in her sleep.

When the fighting intensified in our neighbourhood, we would hear the whine of missiles before they blew up somewhere near by, sometimes just across the road from our house. The entire world would tremble above our heads. And we would squeeze under the table, face down like those flat fish with eyes on the tops of their heads. Omaymah had warned us, as she squeezed us under the table, to stick to the bottom or we wouldn't have a head on our necks any more. She wasn't exaggerating. One time, as we fooled around under the table, the house gave a sudden shake, and a hole opened up in the wall. We felt our ears popping and saw that the room was about to collapse on to our heads. A bit of metal whizzed through Mustafa's hair where he sat squashed against me. The smell of his singed hair is still in my nostrils. Maybe that's why I hate barbecues. I don't want to be reminded of a scorched past. Of the smell of death barely a millimetre away from me and of the skull of my brother as he pressed against me. I don't want to be reminded of Omaymah's screams in the debris and dust and smoke.

'This is where the Arabs want to bury us! Under the rubble of shame and dishonour. How is this heap of flesh to blame? Where has your mercy gone, Allah?' she wept as she hugged us to her body, washed in tears and dust. At the time my father was caught up somewhere outside the capital. He couldn't get back to us because Amman had been declared a closed military zone. No one could get in or out of that hell. My father was always far away from us. Even when we were a few centimetres from incineration. That day we, too, wept and wailed and begged for the mercy of Allah, whom we hadn't wronged in any way as far as I knew, except for the fact that we were refugees.

After the tremors and the shooting died down, Omaymah told us to get out from under the table and harangued us. 'Either we get out of this wreck of a house or it will become our tomb.' Sumayyah had a large stain on her clothes. A stain that would continue to pursue her. I have to admit that, in the more relaxed times to come, it would earn her the nickname Peewee. I'd use it every time she got on our nerves, even if it earned me a beating from Omaymah. After the beating I'd slip away and bark at her through the cracks in the garden wall, 'Peewee!' She would retaliate by calling me a mule and a brute and say she didn't know where they'd found me. Omaymah heard her once and really hauled her over the coals. I actually felt sorry for her that day. Omaymah nearly pulled her hair out. 'I'll rip your tongue out if I ever hear that filth coming out of your mouth again,' she said as she pushed her to the floor.

Our Peewee had to grow up and start taking care of her dismembered family – what was left of it. Making sure something entered our mouths before we went out. Meanwhile, my father picked at it in silence. When he didn't like his food he'd leave it outside the door for her. Sometimes she'd put it before him and observe him the way Halimeh used to observe me to see if I liked her food or was just forcing it down.

Using my mother's death as an excuse, Halimeh started visiting us again. Omaymah didn't greet her cordially. She had inherited her mother's hatred of her. She'd pass snide remarks that Halimeh would take meekly, as if she had no strength of her own. Her eyes would sometimes turn unblinkingly to me. And when my father was around she'd divide her gaze between the two of us. My father would lower his eyes to the ground, and at the end of her visit he'd drive her to the bus station, the way they used to do in Hebron forty years before, away from the prying eyes of the neighbours and my mother. Omaymah's tongue could be quite sharp: 'There's no keeping this owlish whore away!'

Musa had started courting a certain Rukayyah, a Jordanian girl who lived at the top of a long flight of steps that divided our district down the middle like the zipper on a travel bag. Rukayyah was the youngest of seven sisters from two different mothers. Her father had taken her mother as his second wife in the hope that she'd give him a little ruffian after his first wife brought forth four girls, all of whom were fat like their mother. The silly father, who didn't know that women lack a Y chromosome, that golden chromosome that's worth so much, blamed the mother, who, in turn, blamed herself and encouraged him to remarry after she'd squandered a lot of money to-ing and fro-ing among seers and peddlers of lies hidden in verses of the Qur'an. According to certain unreliable sources, she fed her husband all kinds of recipes and forced all manner of junk down his throat, and by the time he found out it was too late for his balding head.

The bald father didn't think the proposal of remarriage over for long. An offer like that! He immediately found a relatively young woman and married her, but, to his great disappointment, she brought forth three more girls, the last of whom was Rukayyah.

The bald father took the disappointment of Rukayyah's birth badly. He packed up and left for Kuwait, leaving behind nine female mouths who depended on the cheques he grudgingly sent back.

Unlike their siblings from the first wife, Rukayyah and her two biological sisters grew up to be as thin as broomsticks. The two women and their seven daughters, fat and thin, lived in the same house and ate and drank from the salary of the bald runaway who, rumour had it, had remarried in Kuwait and fathered another family of females. When I left, they were all still around; none had married, probably because of the family's reputation for not bearing sons.

Rukayyah was the most hard-working and studious of all her siblings. While she studied, the other six stayed home plucking chickens and peeling potatoes and devouring the stews they concocted during the day with the bald man's money, always hoping that one day some knight would turn up on a white horse and take one of them off to his grand palace. The only brave knight who stepped into their territory – and he still failed – was my friend Musa, who had just opened the small cafeteria near the Passport Office, a few steps away from the girls' secondary school that Rukayyah attended.

Within a few weeks Musa had completely lost his head over Rukayyah. She lost her head over him twice over. Something between them clicked. After all, Rukayyah wasn't a bad find. True, she was thin as a rake, but she had a certain bearing, a way of walking and behaving and a particular feminine grace and, above all, her eyes were beautiful enough to draw any man's attention.

She was two years our senior. Just starting out on her first and what turned out to be her last job after a two-year course in Arabic literature that brought her to the point she had always dreamed of: a teacher of Arabic in a forgotten village at the south-eastern limits of Amman.

As Musa put it to me, Rukayyah was a sea of poems. Apart from memorizing thousands of poems, she wrote her own poetry, too. 'She eats and drinks and breathes poetry. There isn't a verse that's been spoken that she doesn't know, Nabil,' he said as he justified a love that was ultimately stillborn because as soon as the two families got to know of the affair they did everything in their power to stop it.

'Are you mad? Are you going to marry a woman who could be your mother?' was the first reaction from his own mother, who didn't care much for the family of too many girls.

'She might as well be. She's the same age as you, mother,' he replied angrily.

His mother's face became a stony sculpture of pain. 'Oh, where are you, Hasan? Come and see how your son is losing his mind,' she said as she pummelled her own cheeks and broke into a wail that reminded me of Omaymah receiving news of the death of her brothers. But the real reason lay elsewhere. 'You take that one and we'll be overrun with girls, and you'll end up a bald runaway like her father,' she said angrily with tears in her eyes.

'It's my life to do with as I please,' her son shouted back. 'If it's a mother I take – whether or not I have my hair – it's my life, and no one has the right to interfere and map it out for me. Not even you. No one interfered when you chose that drunkard,' he told her as he went out and slammed the door.

'I'll calm him down. Don't take it too hard,' I said as I opened the door Musa had slammed and chased after his angry footsteps.

'I feel like celebrating something mysterious. Are you coming?' he told me as he gazed at the horizon.

'Let's go,' I said, although I had no idea what he had in mind.

'They're so ignorant, though. How they label you and shun you before even having met you! It just makes me want her all the more,' he said, putting a cigarette in his mouth and trembling as he lit it.

'Easy, Musa,' I said. 'The only way to resolve these matters is to do so calmly.'

'They can remain unresolved for all I care. She's the one I want,' he replied firmly. Until then, Musa had not yet heard the other side of the story, that of Rukayyah's family. Despite having spent their lives waiting for someone to knock on their door and take one of the daughters away in the hope that she'd deliver a miserable little boy and finally lift the curse that hung over their heads, Rukayyah's family were not overly fond of Musa. The sisters were suddenly jealous and made trouble. 'This is unacceptable. A man with little education expecting to marry a teacher! How dare he?' they said of Musa.

'As long as he works and he respects you, that's the most important thing, darling,' her mother said more encouragingly.

But the position the mother took was not enough to move things along. Even the consent of the other nine women put together would probably not have done the trick. What ultimately mattered was the word of the bald man. 'She wants to do what?' he said on the phone when they called to let him know that Musa had asked for her hand. 'Marry that illiterate ignoramus? That's all we need! I've spent thousands on her. If she can't find someone worthy of her I'll come and burn her alive in the street and burn you all with her.'

After Musa's argument with his mother we went straight to a bar he knew, and there I had my first drop of the fermented poison that would dog me like a shadow for the rest of my days. Musa was hurt and depressed, knowing that the current was strong, very strong, and that the first love of his life would be summarily executed on the altar of Ammani ignorance.

'How do you feel?' he asked after I'd had the first drink of my life. At first the alcohol tasted as bitter as tar. I was amazed that there were people who became slaves to such bitterness. As if life wasn't bitter enough already. But, once my veins had expanded properly, I felt happy and my tongue loosened.

'Prepare yourself to fight an unwinnable battle, Don Quixote,' I said.

'Your mother's just a small windmill among thousands of windmills, and for thousands of years they've been crushing voices and throttling desires and scattering them to the four winds.'

Musa waved to the bartender to pour us another shot. 'If there was a single person with Don Quixote's intentions in every house, it would be enough to bring us all out of the cocoon,' he said, a smile plastered all over his lips.

'Don't dream too much, my friend,' I said with the same plastered smile. 'The fact that you're threatening to have it your way is proof enough that we won't be coming out of any cocoon. I know that one way or the other you'll argue with your mother and maybe bring her round, but this isn't what you'd call persuasion. It's tyranny. You'll need to draw the same weapons every father wields in his own house. The swords of patriarchy. Money and yelling and even blows. And in place of one broken windmill you'll erect an even bigger one. From a kindly Don Quixote you'll turn into a cruel Don Quixote, a dog, a tyrant and an accomplice . . .'

He waved to the bartender for the third time. 'Right you are. But at least I'll have tried,' he said and threw a despairing glance outside at the fine darkness slowly descending on the hunched shoulders of Amman.

Rukayyah's father ordered her to stop working immediately and stay at home with her sisters, otherwise he'd come and break her legs. For Rukayyah, quite apart from not being able to see Musa again, there was no worse punishment than being deprived of the oxygen of education. Musa and school were the two lungs that allowed her to breathe and make it through life. Now she suddenly found herself behind a double lock and thick walls guarded by eight female windmills, all of them set in motion by the hot air blown by a fugitive father hiding somewhere in the Persian Gulf.

'No school and no outings. No open windows or balconies.' Her mother had the sword of divorce dangling over her head, and there was no news. Musa had sent his sister to scout a little on his behalf. They refused to open the door to her. From behind their high walls they told her never to come back. The letters he sent with her were returned to him to remind him of those spinning windmills, of the limitations that were his, ours, the individual's whenever he sang outside the choir.

Rukayyah wasn't as steadfast as Musa. Rukayyah was fashioned out of the freedom of poetry. Out of oxygen and rays of light. Transparent spirits that cannot be locked behind the thickness of walls. Rukayyah was dedicated, delicate and quick in her thinking. If there's no Musa and no school, then there's no life. No purgatory intervened in the middle. No zone between darkness and light. Between oxygen and carbon dioxide. Rukayyah was an almond tree that loved life but had been smothered with sulphur. Rukayyah was a scented Arab flower surrounded by the thorns of the southern peninsula. A Friday at dawn with a clear sky. Rukayyah, wearing a white dress, climbed on to the parapet on the roof of the house and jumped, falling as straight as the zipper on a travel bag. The Arab bride turned into a poetic stanza, a huge blemish on the cheek of the Allah of the East.

Like Simon De Brincat, Rukayyah wanted to break out of a cocoon that had been imposed upon her. She rode the vertical wind to a destination of her choosing. That thin body, elegant in a white dress decorated with bloodstains, was just the shell Rukayyah left behind before she flapped her wings.

Musa ran to her with the others but fell to his knees, alone. Took her head in his hands and wailed like a wounded bear. My curse had descended again and struck Musa once more. My friend Musa, a partner in life and joy and death, a witness to laughter and tears and all kinds of childish pranks. Musa holding her against his skin, his tears, with his mouth open in shock. Rukayyah, finally happy, happy as a bird in its nest, as the first stanza of a poem. It was sunny that morning, bright sunshine, so bright you felt you could almost take hold of the light.

18

'Do you understand Maltese?' the thin inspector asks impatiently as he flicks through your papers. His mobile phone hasn't stopped making noises. Messages and calls keep coming in.

There are two others in the room. One of them is staring vacantly. He has a long face and must be well over fifty. You decide that he must be a sergeant or someone of a slightly higher rank but definitely not above sergeant major. The third person is a young policewoman with blue eyes and generous breasts restrained by the stiff fabric of her uniform. You're under the impression that you've seen her somewhere, but who knows? The stern face she puts on seems false in the presence of her superiors. Her general appearance, especially her eyes, is too sympathetic for them. Her sympathy exceeds the quota set by the police. You began to wonder how they didn't notice that those eyes were simply not made to be a police officer's.

How could they have noticed? They say sympathy shows up in your urine. In your urine? How did you come up with that? What would show up in yours? The extent of your derangement and naivety? What a cruel dog, what a terrorist you are! There'll be a kit laid out for you, won't there? Don't you know that governments have everything at their disposal? From toilet paper to accusations of terrorism? And even when they have none of that they'll come up with something. Just like they always have. They've even gone so far as to create a Sacred Chosen People for your sake. It wasn't easy but still they pulled it off. Hats off. Not just for this but for the entire sequence of things they pulled off so well in your lifetime.

'Nabil? Is that your first name or your surname?' barks the inspector as he turns your identification papers over and over.

Silence

'Is Jordan a nice place?' he asks, this time with a bit too much familiarity, maybe because he's seen the place of your birth. 'You had that king, he was all right. What was his name?'

Silence

'Anyway, I can't remember, but he spoke pretty good English,' he says, pulling up a chair and sitting down in front of you. Nose to nose. 'How about you tell us something about yourself, sir?'

Silence

The sergeant – or, rather, the one you decided must be a sergeant – is all over the place. Here and not here. His eyes, despite the constant noise coming from the inspector and his phone, remain blank. Maybe he's thinking about his pension. 'Bring it on.' Or the opposite. 'May the day never arrive.' Maybe he's tired or sick of the job and has nothing left to give. Or maybe he isn't tired, doesn't even want to retire because his heart belongs to the police force and he's finding it hard to get used to the idea that from being a veteran sergeant major who trained half the inspectors in the Maltese police he is destined to babysit for his grandchildren.

But how did you decide that? Maybe he's not a sergeant and maybe he never married and never had children and none of this is true, the clothes you're designing and in which you're dressing him up. More likely this is just your mind on a roll, pointlessly musing and analysing. What are these? Symptoms of illness? Of exhaustion? Derangement? Total disintegration? And what of this silence? What is this silence? Don't you know it's worse if you don't talk? What happened when you went quiet? The entire world became a wagging tongue. A tongue that not only wagged against you, it even gave false witness after taking a hefty oath to tell the truth, the whole truth and nothing but the truth, although it knew that this truth was hazy and elusive and cunning and sometimes put personal interests before the blood and breath and flesh of many citizens of the world.

'Can you tell us what day it is today or maybe where you are right now?'

Silence

216

'Guy's obviously nuts,' he tells his colleagues, one of whom is himself not quite all there.

'Have you been drinking or taking something?'

Silence

'What the fuck is wrong with you? Are you dumb? You're not helping yourself, sir, and you're not helping us either,' he says, annoyed. 'If you refuse to talk, we'll have to get in touch with your embassy and let them decide what to do with you. I've got enough shit to deal with.'

Silence

'There's no Jordanian embassy, sir,' the young policewoman pipes up with some authority. 'We've checked. There's a consulate with someone called Portanier in charge.'

You wonder why policewomen aren't allowed to look attractive in their uniforms. But you understand that this police officer is a personification of the law, and the law can't be sexy, otherwise everyone would screw it, you included.

Fifteen days sleeping in the Barrakka. Why, when you have somewhere to live? So they finally picked you up. Don't say you didn't know or weren't asking for this. They just did what they had to do to keep their island clean and pretty. Let's not forget that this island lives off tourism. There was a time when Malta was swarming with lunatics and beggars. That time is long gone and no one remembers it. Maybe it's because no one wants to remember that it was Mintoff, the man wearing the belt buckle, who cleared Malta of such displays of the national viscera. But that chapter has nothing to do with your personal pain, so we won't open it here or we'll be operating on two different bodies, both evidently sick. Yours and Malta's. Malta's wounds, in which you've been sticking your nose, although no one asked you to do that. And it's not enough to say that many of its wounds and much of its pus resemble your own. How dare you? You shouldn't say that even if it were true. Let them see to it. They won't be asking for your advice. Advice from a dirty Arab? Not to mention a filthy EDP. The kind who would even make soap dirty. Do you know what you're saying, Toy Number 11? I hope you do. Otherwise, mate, we have a problem. Otherwise we're just talking to the wall. They're just wasting their breath on you. It seems you haven't understood anything about the European vision. Apart from your mental problem, you've got a problem with your sight. Before we talk, you'd better go and get yourself some glasses. Then you'll be able to see exactly where you are. It's important to see clearly before you start damaging a sector so vital to Malta. Understood, Toy Number 11?

The young policewoman begins to explain that according to their investigations you landed in Malta for the first time in August 1990. At 22.14 on 19 August, to be precise, on a flight from Rome. Rome that hadn't allowed you to set foot there, kept you behind the glass of the transit area for thirty-three hours, craning your neck to catch a glimpse; Rome that had been scared of you, although you'd never done anything to it except want to see it because you'd always heard your people say that he who has not seen Rome has not seen the world. You had to come to Malta without seeing the world. Oh well! There wasn't much that you could do. It was useless to protest at the glass window of the Italian *sbirri*. Quite apart from the fact that they understood nothing of your schizoid English and you understood nothing of their Italian, the issue wasn't linguistic. You just didn't know how undesirable you really were. The issue facing you was that you wanted to see Rome – that is, the world – but the world didn't want to see you.

According to the young woman, the Maltese police also discovered that you entered the country as a student. And that you've always renewed your visa on time except for one occasion. You forgot to apply. Your mind must surely have been occupied with some war. It might even have been one of Saddam's. Might? You mean you're not even sure? And you expect these very busy people to wait around until you manage to remember? Admit it, Nabil. Your mind's exhausted. Totally exhausted, it would seem. No wonder you've been picked up. Police officers in democratic countries don't pick people up for no reason. The application you forgot to submit eighteen years ago to extend your residency by a further three months could have cost you your studies. 'This is to certify that Mr Nabil Yusef Zitawi is . . . blah blah blah.'

Those were the words they needed to hear. That you're studying and aren't planning to blow up an embassy or a hotel during some important conference. They sent for you from the police HQ that day. Let you in through the back entrance. You never knew the HQ had a back entrance through which suspects and criminals were let in. That's how highly they regarded you. They kept you waiting. One, two, three hours. Was that enough to make you feel humiliated? Not for them. 'Next time I'll have you kicked out, even if you're about to graduate the next day,' that giant of an inspector yelled angrily. Later you got to know he was the head of the Drug Squad! You had no drugs. Hadn't ever set eyes on the stuff. You tried to explain that there was a war in Iraq, the third or fourth one, you couldn't remember, your head wasn't clear, and that one of your brothers was caught up in it. Not caught up. He was there because he chose to be. Because he was another idiot like the cousins who thought the road to Palestine began in Basra and the Negev. You tried to explain that you'd already lost two of your brothers and couldn't afford to lose a third because Omaymah's heart would be unable to bear another piece of bad news. By the time you left she was already stuffed full of pills and crap and looked like an old woman.

Arguing with the head of the Drug Squad was useless. Rather than having a change of heart he stood up angrily and began to lay into you. 'I don't give a damn about any of that. I'm sick of being lied to. You listen to me, my friend, I'm a man of my word. Ask around, you'll see. I'll tell you one thing. If your file ever lands on my desk again you can be sure you'll be on the first available plane out of here. That's a promise.' You had to admit that he would be as good as his word. He had those carnivorous features, more pronounced than those of any other police officer you'd encountered before, including those in the Hashemite kingdom.

The policewoman adds that after you graduated you found a job and ever since then you've always been a regular guy, and your record, according to their investigations, is completely clean.

'So what happened? They wait till they're in this frigging country to go nuts. As if we didn't have enough lunatics of our own! Here's what we'll do. Call the refugee centre in Ħal Far, see if they'll take him in until we figure out what to do with him.'

'Ħal Far?' says the policewoman with the excessively kind eyes, stunned. 'It doesn't look like he's one of those, sir . . .'

'One of those what?' he asks indifferently, rummaging among the papers on his untidy desk. The mobile phone continues its merry jig. It rings, and he hangs up, cursing occasionally under his breath.

'I mean these types who come over, sir. I mean the *klandestini*,' she says, looking at you, full of sympathy. Her sympathy is the last thing you feel you need. Actually you have no idea what you need. Like your father, you've long since given up on acting on your needs. There's no point telling them that in the world of silence the only thing you feel you need is more silence.

'Yes, but, Scicluna, we need to hold this tongue-tied fellow somewhere. You're not expecting me to take him home, are you? If you've taken some sort of liking to him, go ahead and take him. I don't need him around here!'

'What I mean to say, sir,' she says, taken aback, 'is that he's been in this country for so long and never broken any laws or been in any trouble . . .'

'How d'you know he's never been in trouble? Why would he be here then?'

'That's not what I meant, sir . . . It just looks like something's happened to him . . .'

'Then what was it you meant, Scicluna?' he snaps. 'D'you want me to book him a room at the Radisson? Don't you know I can't keep him here without bringing charges against him or sending him over there? What charges could I bring against this man – neglecting to shave? Sleeping in the Barrakka while renting his own place? I mean, for fuck's sake, aren't there people who choose to sleep at a farm or on yachts? People who sleep in the car? I can't figure these fuckers out. So much for all their certificates and shit. If it's a public place, I can't stop anyone from being there, for God's sake. Terrorism . . . ? That's all Malta needs. And that idiotic mayor! Had to go and kick up a fuss over nothing. And to make matters worse this guy's not saying anything to help himself or us. Someone must've bitten his tongue off. Just my luck. What was on his computer?'

'Nothing special,' says the young officer promptly.

'Nothing special meaning what? Why's he got a computer then?' he asks irritably.

'Nothing that could lead to any charges. Some poems and other writings. Some of them really good. He seems to know Maltese pretty well. He also has a lot of stuff written in his own language.'

'Those are the ones I want to look at. See if you can find an interpreter. Call that Egyptian guy if you have to. I'm mainly interested in his mail. His contacts. Check what he's written and to whom. Look at the entire history. Check against the server if necessary.' The mobile phone stops ringing. Apparently the caller has finally given up. Maybe ended up cursing like the inspector.

'If it were up to me I'd send him to the nuthouse. He doesn't look very interesting to me. He'd be more interesting to the guys in white. Or maybe to you, Scicluna?' he says smiling. 'Hey,' he adds, 'you can't put anything past these Arabs. Don't trust them. They can surprise you at every turn, whatever your calculations. Remember the heroes of 9/11 were all pilots and engineers. Don't be fooled by appearances, Scicluna. When I get back I don't want to see his face still here. Get it? Otherwise I'll have him deported.'

'Leave it to me, sir,' the blonde police officer says eagerly. The elderly sergeant finally wakes up and nods in agreement, giving the impression that he hasn't followed a single word that's been said in this room. Meanwhile the thin inspector collects his keys and other stuff from his chaotic desk. His mobile erupts again. 'Here's what this shitty country's come to. We're taking care of idiots and lunatics!' he mutters, checking the caller's number. Finally, he decides to answer. 'Hey, I'm nearly there! Where the fuck are you?'

That's it then! Someone reported you for sleeping in the Barrakka. And your clothes are dishevelled and dirty and your hair is matted and, probably even worse, you haven't shaved. The young officer, full of eagerness and passion, genuinely seems to be trying to help you. But how? She won't be taking you home, that's for sure. Maybe she doesn't want to dump you in Ħal Safi or Ħal Far. Or even Mount Carmel. Why Mount Carmel? You'd never be able to get out of that place. It's King Talal's story all over again, the father of your own king. After they dumped him in the loony bin no one wanted to hear his complaints. It wasn't because only one in a thousand who were admitted to that place ever made it out of there. Or even because mental institutions are often neglected by God himself, never mind governments. It was just that you were incurable. You couldn't be cured by the pill that half of Malta's population was on or by the jab used by the other half. They could force as many pills down your throat and jab you as much as they pleased, there'd be no cure for you. We know what we're saying. There's no cure for you. Not even at the hands of the best doctors and consultants. Not even at the hands of God himself. At best you'd be resurrected for two or three days, like your father, and begin to search for a tree or a son to possess. To examine the process of resurrection. To keep pursuing that whore named Palestine.

Meanwhile, the blonde officer has found the number and phoned Mr Portanier, consul for Jordan, in whose office you once saw a blown-up portrait of your king hanging over his head. Mr Bully Beef. The spy king of the Hashemites, the man himself. Smiling in the photograph as he smiled at you thirty-three years ago from behind the glass of his open-top Land Rover. Remember that? Does Portanier know he represents a spy? Someone who spies on his own people, no less? What difference would it make to him? As long as he's receiving his pay cheque. Maybe the cheque was drawn out of that other cheque! The million-dollar cheque that Jimmy Carter decided to sign without really understanding what he was doing. Even men of the stature of Carter can make mistakes, although they're surrounded by consultants and thinkers. Good thing King Hussein had other ways of making money. A million dollars a month are bound to be noticed. Especially if he'd already committed himself to certain duties and responsibilities that affected the comfort and well-being of the Jordanian family – Portanier's salary, for example. They, too, could be called expenses, could they not?

Portanier says there isn't much he can do. But given the urgency of the case he'll speak to the embassy in Rome as soon as possible and let them take the lead. He says he's never come across a case like yours. They sometimes made arrangements to transport a corpse but not a whole live mad human being. Maybe he doesn't actually say mad. At least not literally. No one uses the word mad just like that, off the cuff, and anyhow no consul would, especially with all his education and his thank-yous! This matter of madness, no one's mentioning it except you and that confused inspector. But your problem isn't solved for all that. They still don't know what to do with you until the embassy in Rome replies. You've become a nuisance in a country already sick of the foreigners who fall in your category – at least, according to a poll taken by the biggest local newspaper, published in a language that wasn't the language of the locals.

'Should we take him back to his home? This man must have some relatives and friends, surely?' the police officer wonders confused, staring at you with pity. Maybe she doesn't know that you had them once but destroyed them. She doesn't know you have a family and a woman and friends and a country of birth – not one but three – and you went and fucked them all up. Forced them to betray you. Turned them all into Brutus so you could play the victim. Turned them all into Judas Iscariot to play the Messiah. A Messiah whose tongue was bitten off by events. Like his father. A Messiah abandoned even by himself.

What can these people, neat and tidy in their police uniforms, do for you? They all have their own families for whose sake they wear these stiff fabrics. What do you have on this planet? Your ancestors used to say: when your people lose their heads, what can you do with your own head? These Arabs, they're always leaving something behind. And when you lose your head what can you do with your own people? And when you all lose your heads what can the world do for you? What could these people do to bring your lost head back? And your people? Who would bring your people back? Who would bring Simon back? What was life worth without him? Simon, who always appeared to you as mysterious as the flights of steps in his city. Those steps whose beginning and end you can't understand unless you've been steeped in the agonies of Valletta. Every alley leads to a path and every path to a staircase and every staircase goes through to Simon and Simon leads to the unknown.

He would double up in pain at the things he witnessed and couldn't change or stop. A prophet without a scripture. Without holiness. Without cherubim and seraphim. He was never believed because he never promised paradise and never brought manna from heaven. Or walked on water or had forty virgin dolls under his tent waiting impatiently for the sperm of the first martyr to blow himself up in a crowd.

'I'm worried about you, Nabil. Simon's got a hold on you that frightens me,' Adnan said during your last phone conversation; he had called from England to offer his condolences following your father's death.

'You've no reason to fear the influence of an enlightened man.'

'Nabil, Simon was an extremist. Extremism blinds you, it blinds even the most enlightened. Don't be so desperate. There's still a lot of room in life. There are lots of beautiful things we can do.' He sounded happy. But maybe not as much as he had expected. What do you know of his expectations anyway? When you asked him how things were he said, 'Life's a struggle everywhere, isn't it?' Struggle didn't sound right to you. You immediately interpreted that to mean he wasn't happy. Adnan didn't like to struggle. Unless life had pushed him down one of its manholes.

'Better not to take on responsibilities, love. You can get into all kinds of mess,' says the sergeant to the policewoman, the one you thought was a sergeant, who'd been asleep or buried in thoughts far deeper than yours. 'Take my advice, love, dump him where he told you to. I'm of the same mind as you. He doesn't look dangerous, but who can tell? In our job we can't make mistakes. Can't take risks just because it feels right. That's not the reason society places its trust in us. Society watches us even more closely than it does criminals. They never tell you that at the academy. You learn it. As you look people in the eye. The eyes of suspects and innocents and murderers. As you look into the eyes of those who are lost, like this man whose mind gave out before he reached the end, poor guy. Now suppose you took him home and he was found somewhere the next day, hanged or beneath some cliff, what'll you say then? That it felt right? Or that you didn't expect it, judging by the look of him? Don't think these things have never happened. Just go down to the archives and you'll see. Why go to such lengths when all it takes is a phone call? Take my advice, love, and stick to procedure. Call social services. They'll know what to do.'

The young officer, her mind only half made up, looks confusedly from you to the sergeant. Perhaps she feels she holds your destiny in her hands? What destiny? Her face reminds you of that blonde woman feeding the pigeons in the Barrakka. Could she be the same person? Ružar Briffa's granddaughter. Maybe that's why she was struck by the scribblings on your computer. Will she publish it or just throw it all away? She wouldn't want to anger her grandfather! What would she call it? *A False Narrative? Mutterings from a Stranger? Vomit of a Mute? Of a Man Exhausted? Of a Man Stunned, Overcome by Life's Realities and Events?*

The elderly sergeant said you could easily be found hanged. You want to pity him. Despite the fact that he's a veteran, despite the breadth of his experience, he clearly knows nothing about men standing at the edge of the abyss. After all, he's trained half the inspectors in the force, some of whom still go to him for advice. The last piece of advice was the one he gave that young officer, sitting on the fence with the dictates of procedure on one side and her hunch that you are not mad on the other. But police officers can't take too many risks. There's the sword of order and discipline to be reckoned with. There's the scimitar of rank and strict obedience. The fabric of neutrality. The police keep the same distance from everyone, including those who are invisible or sleep in the Barrakka. Finally the young officer reluctantly picks up the receiver and calls social services to ask them to come and get you.

19

In life there are crosses from which you never manage to climb down. You're born with them the way you're born with ears and hair and a nose. The very fact that we're born is already a major cross to bear, if not the biggest of them all. It's debatable. I'd rather say it's debatable because some people consider their birth to be the best thing that's happened to them. I don't want to rain on their parades. Who am I, after all, to daub all life with my own grey brush? This is why I could never become a painter or have any appreciation for art that involves lots of colours – impressionist or realist. I'm not sure whether I should also apologize to Van Gogh and his friends who became famous for the wild and colourful pictures they left behind.

There are crosses you aren't born with but which you are hoisted on to later in life. Contracted crosses. Because you contract them like a contagious disease? Never mind. You get used to them, too, the way you get used to your name and surname. The way you get used to your own skin.

Then there's a third kind of cross. I still don't know what these are called, but I know we nail ourselves to them. Whether or not we climbed up of our own accord, what difference does it make once we are up there bleeding and are unable to climb down? Or is it that we don't want to get down? Maybe we've got used to the height and the fresh air. Or want to argue with the Creator and point out the extent to which we've become victims of his plan.

'I'm no longer involved. I cursed you only once. And drove you out of my paradise only once.'

'True. But which paradise, Lord, would ever let me back in when I've been driven out of yours?'

'Not true, stop making things up. I'm sick of you playing the victim. I've not interfered since I had you deported from my paradise. Not even when you decided to pollute the new paradise I had promptly given you. Not even when you angered and enraged me.'

'But didn't you summarily condemn me as soon as I made my first mistake, without even listening to what I had to say? You didn't give me a chance to explain or to defend myself, did you? Do you know I never recovered from that? I had to make up the science of laws and build halls and wide courts. I had to endow them with a pair of scales and big columns like your own and create the role of lawyer – which you don't seem to believe in. Do you know why I invented lawyers? Because I never recovered from the hurt your hasty decisions inflicted upon me.'

'Are you going to keep on with this? As I've said already, I proved how just I am by never interfering in your paradise.'

'Because you know you didn't have to pursue me once you turned me into a little marble and set me rolling downhill.'

'What did you expect, Mr Human? For me to build you a ladder so you could climb up and eavesdrop and see what I'm up to? Anyway, I shouldn't be surprised if you weren't waiting for the right moment to jump in and take my place.'

'Come on, Lord. How could you think that? As if I have the talent and the power to take your place.'

'Ha-ha . . . that's funny. It's true you don't have the talent or the power, but you certainly have the desire.'

'You see, you're judging me again without even –'

'Ha-ha-ha. Funny again, Mr Human. Of course, I can judge you whenever and in any way I choose. Want to know why?'

'Why?'

'Because I know exactly what it is that I've fashioned with my own hands. Ha-ha . . . ha-ha.'

*

So what type of cross did you place Rukayyah on? Is it the same as Halimeh's or Simon's? Didn't she take the leap just like they did? It's true it wasn't into stagnant and dark water or even into the cold vacuum of a room but on to a flight of steps. Two steps on that flight, to be precise: one to smash her ribs and the other to crack her head. But, mathematically, it's the same relation. Always vertical and subject to the law of gravity. The one involving the apple. I'm not trying to say that when we take a leap or hang ourselves we're not committing an enormous mistake, that we're just obeying the laws of nature. Nature doesn't tell you to hang yourself instead of that apple or to carry a pair of scissors around with you. I don't want to judge.

After all, who am I to pass judgement on life's grey moments? All I'm interested in is that piece of wood in the middle. The upright pole of the cross. The new cross that appeared in Musa's life. After the cross of Rukayyah, Musa was no longer Musa. Musa turned into his father. Wearing a singlet and a bottle of whisky in hand as he insulted people, anyone who crossed him, traffic wardens in particular.

During the first months following the drama of Rukayyah I would collect him every day from her graveside. He'd be drunk and reading poetry to her. He had completely let himself go and let his hair and beard grow long, and the neighbours had begun to call him a drunk.

'Do you know they're calling you a drunk, you drunk?'

'If it wasn't me or my father they'd have to invent one. Everyone in this bloody city needs a saint and a whore and a drunk. Every street needs its oddball and its bad guy and killer and miser and even its madman to ride the donkey backwards – as if the whole country hasn't turned its face towards the donkey's arse and will keep facing the donkey's arse until Rukayyah comes back from the grave.'

Rukayyah wasn't coming back from the grave. She would remain the poem she had always aspired to be, and Musa would just have to accept that. Even the dead start to distance themselves over time. They gradually withdraw from our lives. Maybe it's because they love us too much. Or pity us too much. Or they find us too disgusting. One day we'll find out. The important thing was for Musa to come back to life. The important thing was the skin that time grows over the wound of memory. Maybe that's where the dead play a role in so far as they're willing to help us forget them. In so far as they are willing to transform themselves from flesh and blood into ghosts and shades moving about in the distant backwaters of memory. They say time heals, but how long does it take time to heal, and how many marks and bruises will it leave in the depths of one's consciousness

I had no doubt that Musa would finally come out of it because life would demand it. But he would be changed into a member of another species. An angry species. Volatile. Drunk. Critical but creative. Apparently the poems he recited at Rukayyah's graveside reopened all his wounds. They reopened his mysterious desert repository. What repository does a desert Bedouin have but that of the wounds inflicted by the moon and the sun and the wind? How odd and macabre that we need a fist, or an acquisitive hand like that of death, to unlock our creativity! When Musa dedicated himself to drink he also dedicated himself to poetry. Just like that. As if it were already in his head. All he needed to do was open the tap.

> Your love
> Was never a sin
> The fault is all mine
> Because I am who I am
> A mad Easterner
> Wearing desert and confusion
> And the fist of the past pursues me
> To divest me of the shirt of happiness
> The uneaten loaf from the hands of the orphan
> I apologize for being me
> A knight without a sword
> Or a palm tree's shade
> And my horse is tired
> I carry the bones of truth
> Once its flesh has been gnawed before the eyes of heaven
> My face is grimy with the dust of shame
> I've lost all my battles and emerged bloodless
> From vein to vein
> And the desert serpent

Laps at my blood and there's nothing I can do
Because I am so defeated
The desert's punishment
For all who dare defy the tribal code.

When I heard that for the first time I hurried to show it to Muhammad al-Mashni, the teacher of Arabic who had helped me publish a couple of short stories in a newspaper that no one bought. In my mind that fortnightly newspaper had become more famous than the *Daily Telegraph* or the *New York Times*. When I saw my name printed beneath that first short story I felt more important than Gabriel García Márquez. That man didn't stand any taller than my crotch. It was the first time I saw my name printed anywhere, since it wasn't even printed on my identity card or examination certificates, which were still written by hand.

I would carry those two issues with me everywhere I went, and I swear I showed them to half the inhabitants of Amman, except for my father who was tucked away in his hut. He had no time to look at my face or at the name of his son who would fill the world with his writing and his glory. I have to say that I, too, once thought I'd heard some voices coming from his hovel. When I approached to check, the voices abruptly stopped. I knocked and waited but in vain. I began to imagine that, like Sumayyah, I had started making up stories. I decided to keep everything to myself in order not to make us all an even greater laughing stock. It was bad enough that we'd become like a hit record, constantly on people's lips, once they'd learned of my father's latest exile. Mustafa and I, and even Sumayyah to some extent, had become known as the family 'who locked up their father'. In a chicken coop, for shame! Omaymah never tried to understand or forgive. She kept accusing us of having done something to him. 'If someone comes along to ask for your sister's hand, what will you tell him? That your father's buried alive in that shithole?' She was right, but what could we do for him? Tie him up in the living-room so that he could greet the guests in silence? Or lock him up in his bedroom so we could claim he lived in his own house?

Before long someone did show up. He was another EDP. An

accountant who worked in Saudi Arabia. Who knows, maybe Omaymah sent him, because they seemed to be in agreement on a number of points, among them that my father should not be mentioned. The conversation skirted around him as if he'd never been a part of our lives or the life of the bride-to-be, whom, unlike most fathers, he had never taken anywhere. At first Sumayyah seemed confused and didn't know what to do. Part of her wanted to stay and take care of us, but, like many women, she also wanted a family of her own. She knew there would be no opportunity for further study after secondary school even though she'd achieved excellent grades. She had to abandon everything to take care of her siblings and her father, who between them would have been unable even to rinse a sock. Apart from the fact that there just weren't any resources. Not even for me, and I was nearing the end of secondary school. The universities and government colleges of the realm cost money – and they still do. Money that few could afford. Only the children of the privileged could go there, which kept everyone in their place. Cats remained cats, and mice remained mice.

Sumayyah needed to think it over. Omaymah encouraged her. 'What's there to think over, silly? He's got money and a future and he's building a place in New Amman. What do you want? To remain a spinster? To spend your life slaving away inside this miserable pile of bricks?' The accountant sent his mother, and they began to apply pressure. They wanted a quick response before his summer holidays were over. In doubt, Sumayyah wept before my father's hovel, the father who would never take her by the arm as she made the transition from his surname and his custody to that of another man about whom we knew little.

Her father never gave his consent. He didn't bless her or kiss her or wipe away a single tear from her cheeks. Tears and death and marriage and birth and the hammer blow, they all had the same quiet rhythm for her father. None of them hurt or comforted, and none was enough to bring him back from the land of ghosts. As Mustafa and I left the house with her Sumayyah suddenly stopped and looked back at the hovel at the far end of the garden. Maybe she was expecting or hoping or imagining that her father would come out and wave to her one last time or trace a kiss on the palm of his hand and blow it in her direction to escort her on her way and shade her from the heat of sultry afternoons and evenings in Saudi Arabia. Sumayyah burst out crying and nearly brought us and the relatives and guests to tears, even the chauffeurs. So much for her dress and make-up and other preparations that the women had made without us. I knew that all girls cried when they left their father's house. I also knew that Sumayyah's tears just then were more than the tears of a girl leaving behind her memories for marriage. When she got into the taxi I gave her a sudden smile. Mustafa was busy herding the guests and relatives into cars. I bent down by the window of the car, all done up with balloons and ribbons and flowers, and looked at my sister. I'd never seen her wearing make-up, even though it was now smudged with her tears. Omaymah considered make-up to be a deadly sin. Everything in that house was prohibited out of respect for her dead brothers. Sometimes I was ashamed to shave in her presence. She might think I was some kind of traitor. I took Sumayyah's hands through the car window and squeezed them between my own chapped hands. I kissed each finger. A thousand times. Her hands were as cold as ice. Her face was masked by embarrassment and tears and the traces of her make-up. And yet she was beautiful. Very beautiful. Why had I never noticed that my sister was so beautiful? Palestine had managed to blind us to everything. We'd become unable to see even the beauty of our own siblings and children. That's why the accountant had gone crazy when he set eyes on her. Because she was so beautiful and fragile he wanted to take her and run away with her before she changed her mind, or we did. Or before her father woke up. Just then, despite the fact that my heart was breaking, I smiled and for a brief moment felt like her father or something resembling a father. When the car started I kissed her once again on her forehead, took her by the shoulders and said, 'Make sure you write, Peewee.'

On Muhammad al-Mashni's advice I encouraged Musa to send his poems to the same paper that had published my stories. They published them immediately. Within a few days we began to feel like star writers, even though no one knew about us except for the few friends whom we'd bored to death with our scribbles and who sometimes made fun of us and probably even pitied us.

But now that our work had been published Musa and I, with a confidence that was excessive but also somewhat fragile, began to frequent the Central Café, the literary café in the heart of Amman, where ambitious journalists, failed writers and unknown artists gathered. There were usually a few alienated types keeping them company. There were all kinds at the Central Café. The merely curious, the genuine articles and the liars. The original and the woebegone. Drivers and riders and over-reachers. Talent and foam, even the sick and the marginalized, those who blame the world for not understanding them and claim that future generations would show them the appreciation and acclaim they deserved.

At the Central Café it was always said that no one in Jordan ever read and the few who actually did preferred Allah's book or the biography of his Prophet or some pre-Islamic poem about chivalry. 'Because people are in search of icons and heroes in the mythologies and fables of the past,' a man with a voluminous black beard once said, as he explained the gravity of this type of 'social miscarriage', as he called it.

'When a nation has no contemporary heroes it begins to prod the corpse of the past. And when you bury your head too deep in the past you end up blind to the present, and so you also miss the train into the future,' the man with the disorderly beard continued. His voice became firmer when he noticed we were listening. I have to say we were enchanted by his words. We moved our chairs closer and continued to listen to him to the end. Until he declared that all art was useless in a society with its head in the sand. 'It's just like blowing into a punctured bagpipe,' he went on.

When he had finished his disquisition he shook our hands and introduced himself. Over the next few visits we became friends. His name was Muhammad Tummaleh, and he would soon become the most important correspondent in Jordan because of the controversial articles he wrote every day for *ad-Dustour*, considered the largest Jordanian newspaper both for the size of its sheets and its circulation. But, because of Muhammad's pen, it was forced to shut its mouth and its doors several times. I have to admit that *ad-Dustour*, despite a board of directors that, according to Muhammad, was appointed by the regime, probably directly by the head of public intelligence, was marginally more liberal than other newspapers. Sometimes its tongue got a little loose, but according to Muhammad Tummaleh this wasn't because it had liberal leanings but because its board of directors wasn't very good at censorship, because they didn't read much and understood little of what they did read.

Tummaleh was a cunning lizard. He did write between the lines, but everyone understood what he meant except the board of executives of the government newspaper that declares its independence every morning just below its masthead. Once he told us that those executives didn't have the brains to think about anything except two subjects: their bellies and their dicks. Their involvement with Tummaleh became hugely significant because sales had exploded since they employed him, as the figures showed. When, on one occasion, they suspended him, no one bought the newspaper any more. That said, we're not talking about Switzerland here. Muhammad eventually had to be fired from *ad-Dustour*, and they had to watch as their readers shifted to *Shaa'b*, the paper Muhammad started writing for and whose popularity began to soar until it finally outsold *ad-Dustour*. Once it outsold *ad-Dustour* Muhammad was fired again, and the newspaper was suspended. He kept getting fired by newspapers and even spent time in jail, until finally he ended up writing for the paper that really suited him, *The Pavement*.

Tummaleh had a certain charm, and the sweet smell of success wafted off him. His language was humorous but could burn like hydrochloric acid. He could make you laugh and cry at the same time. You'd laugh at the macabre idiocies he would come up with and cry because you'd realize you were laughing at yourself. Because Tummaleh had grown up among ordinary people he was one of them. One of the masses. He felt the citizens' pain and addressed it directly, even though he came from a privileged background. When the price of bread went up he wrote about bread, and when the price of cooking gas went up he wrote about cooking gas. He wasn't one of those schizophrenic journalists who wrote about the beauty of Sophia Loren's lips when there wasn't a grain of sugar to be had in the entire country.

Muhammad had published two collections of short stories. One of them had clouded the country's stagnant literary waters. His stories were short but controversial and provided a great deal of food for thought. One of his characters still makes me uncomfortable to this day. It was a man who couldn't sleep at night because of a tap dripping in his kitchen. He spent the night tossing in bed, and as soon as it got light he went to buy washers to repair it. But he found the entire country queueing up outside ironmongers' shops to buy washers for their taps; women, men, old people and hungry children. Some of them had been waiting for three days to buy a piece of rubber.

If Muhammad Tummaleh hadn't been completely focused on journalism he could have become one of the finest novelists in the Arab world. But the need to earn his daily bread enslaved him, and he was pinned down by the newspaper column. This sucked all the energy out of him, and he couldn't get away.

Tummaleh gave us access to the literary pages of every newspaper he worked for. We would read him our work in the Central Café, and he'd take it and get it published. He wasn't too complimentary. 'Indian rice!' he said once when I read him a short story after we'd become friends. 'Do you know what I mean by Indian rice?' he asked sardonically. When I said I didn't he said it was multi-coloured rice. 'You use a lot of linguistic embellishments but have no content,' he explained, when he saw me trying to make the connection between my writing and colourful Indian rice. 'Eloquence doesn't create events, Nabil,' he said. 'Your characters are buried under far too many superfluous linguistic frills. You need to give them air to breathe and move. The fact that you created them doesn't mean you should ride them and impose your will upon them. Out of this whole story I'd keep half a page,' he said bluntly, without losing the self-satisfied smile on that face overgrown with the wild black beard. Musa's poetry, on the other hand, didn't cause as much damage. He needed to fix a few details and grammatical trivia here and there, but the body of his poem was always saved from Tummaleh's axe. 'What strikes me most about your poetry is that it isn't forced,' he told him. 'Poetry that's forced feels like the shit you force out when you're constipated, dry and desperate, with nothing to leave a scratch on your conscience.'

Musa's morale rose to the heavens. He began to write one poem after the other. Each one was more mature than its predecessor. 'My aim is to dismantle the world and immortalize Rukayyah.'

> Now I feel I'm about to leave
> while my heart returns on the smoke from this ship.
> One day I'll die in some far-off corner
> Without a single flower that matches your eyes,
> Asking the heart that returns with the fog,
> Why could I never forget you?
> Why could I never follow you?
> Why, whenever I set eyes on you,
> Did I see my own end in your eyes?
> One day I'll die in some far-off corner
> or by a precipice smudged with memories
> and no one will see me
> and no one will forgive me.
> I will die a stranger
> the way I have lived, a stranger,
> since the day I loved you.

With a lot of help from Tummaleh, Musa, at the age of nineteen, published his first volume of poetry dedicated to Rukayyah, *As Your Eyes Migrate to the South*.

> All I want from the sun
> is an orange
> with a twin at her breast
> slowly undressing before me
> telling me, 'I am yours.'
> Squeeze me tenderly,
> drink me with the fondness of a prince
> who knows how to set your blood on fire
> and quench the flames.

All I want from the sun
is a scented orange
always in sight
embracing me, passionately,
whispering . . . 'I am yours.'

Musa's poetry was well received. At least in the Central Café, where
a fair amount of literary discussion took place, led for the most part by
those with nothing to do except criticize the work of one writer or
another while wishing they'd published it themselves.

'Everyone . . . !' As usual, the Central Café was crowded. Writers and
pseudo-writers. Critics and pseudo-critics. Painters and journalists and
photographers and a lot of their hangers-on. The air was heavy and
stuffy with loud voices and curses and the smoke from cigarettes and
pipes and shisha. 'Your attention, please!' Tummaleh shouted. Suddenly,
an unexpected calm descended. 'Today a shining star is born in this
dark sky,' he continued as he stood with his arm around Musa's shoulder,
holding it against his own, with Musa's book in his free hand. Musa
looked down, humbled and ashamed as if he'd done something wrong.
'Today one of the finest Nabati poets is born. The kind you don't get
too often. The kind you, or if not you, your children, will be writing
books about. Let's celebrate his birth, my friends. Let us praise the desert
for giving us this man. For nourishing a beautiful flower like Musa in
spite of its cruel drought,' he continued merrily, his eyes brimming with
a strange happiness, while his dark features remained shrunk, as though
they were hiding under the black beard. The Central Café unexpectedly
broke out into loud applause for Musa. That made him retreat even
further into his shell in embarrassment.

After the applause a cough was heard from the café owner, who then
said to Tummaleh, 'Hadn't you better clear your tab first? How much
longer are you going to be drinking on credit?'

What sort of man was Muhammad Tummaleh? I didn't think he was
too different from me or Musa. He was of an older generation, so maybe
he'd seen more hardships in life. And that beard lent him the appearance
of a hermit, perhaps. Maybe he was mad!

They said he was born with a silver spoon in his mouth, his father a major businessman, although they never saw eye to eye. Muhammad's imprudence and coldness had apparently resulted in his being kicked out of the family home. The father, said to be a brusque disciplinarian, seeing that his son was a hindrance rather than a help, didn't think twice. He just kicked him out on to the street, which was probably where he wanted to be anyway.

No one knew his address or where he lived exactly. Now he was at this friend's house, now at that friend's, now at that woman's. Maybe the only real address he had was the Central Café. That was where he could always be found. Otherwise you had to look for him on the street, among the drivers, workmen and merchants. Sometimes he disappeared for the whole night, and then you could bet he had a tryst with one of his lovers. I was always amazed at how, despite the dense, black, prickly beard, which was probably not altogether hygienic, and despite the fact that he always wore the same clothes, he was always sought out by women. Could it be because he was mad? Or because they knew that at the end of the day all his father's wealth would land in his lap? After all, Muhammad was his mother and father's only male offspring. Indeed, his mother still secretly supported him. Maybe his father knew but turned a blind eye.

Apparently his father was one of those businessmen who counted every last penny. But it doesn't take much to know what's coming and going from your pockets, especially when your wife, like Muhammad's mother, isn't employed. Based on rumour, and on the fact that Muhammad never spoke of his father for good or ill, I'd made up my mind that his father was one of those with a head like granite, quite willing to cut off their own balls if that's what it took to spite their wives. Why not? He was an Arab father after all. Everything worked in his favour: culture, law, the sky, the wind and the sun. And no one could challenge him. His property belonged to him and him alone. There'd been a challenge to the system once, from a parliament 'whore' who had tried to raise her head above the parapet, but the people's deputies had dealt with her forthwith. 'A headless country,' Muhammad commented on the verdict that found her guilty of inciting heresy.

'Be happy, you sniper, because the bullet didn't embed itself in your flesh but in mine,' he wrote in one of the major papers. 'The only woman who was ever elected in this country has now been branded a whore.' Maybe that was the article that opened the doors to the world of journalism for him, since after that his work began to appear in many newspapers and periodicals. It was as if he had a lot of work backed up waiting to come out. After a while he took on the most important column in *ad-Dustour*. The public would eagerly await his column in the morning, the way you wait for your breakfast in some fancy restaurant. They always started the day with him. Even though he rubbed salt into their wounds. Apparently people like to have mud and poison thrown at them.

Or was this just a tactic on the part of an unelected government? Back then an unelected government surely needed a few articles by a secular author to leaven a dry political scene dominated by the Muslim Brotherhood, which had taken a parliamentary majority in the first elections, elections one could call free despite a great deal of interference, some of which we know about and some of which we don't. It's not enough to dismiss the editors of the largest government-controlled newspaper by saying they didn't read. I think they do read and read intelligently, because they're like the people on television, they're chosen with great political care. What they didn't know, perhaps, is how far they should allow Muhammad to go. Whenever they miscalculated it cost them their heads. In fact, almost every time Muhammad was fired from a newspaper his boss was also fired. Why? The rule was very clear. You can say what you like as long as you don't touch the king and his friends. We'll still do as we like anyway. So much for the semblance of a democracy. Within a few weeks the clotheslines were hung with dirty linen. Just don't go anywhere near the palace. The problem is never the king. Everyone knows he's infallible and above criticism.

'We've burned our fingers – my brothers, my children – with the misdirected use of democracy.' The king intervened to explain how a real democracy should be handled. 'We need to keep in mind that democracy doesn't mean every man for himself or that we can insult this man or that man.' As if it wasn't he himself who was letting the dogs out to fight his rivals. 'Democracy, my brothers, my children, is first and foremost about tolerance built on an understanding of the other. Understanding that leads to the equality we aspire to in this country. Let's also not forget that democracy has claws and knows how to defend itself, knows how to defend itself well,' he warned us, to keep us from burning our hands completely and force us to embrace the democracy freely bequeathed by the palace. For now, all we've burnt is our fingers; why don't we burn what's between our legs!

The king had to be right, as all the newspapers insisted in the morning. The newspapers invariably agreed with what he said; his words were important, enlightened, brilliant, mature, considered, wise, historic.

'We won't do it again,' Muhammad wrote. 'Do forgive us, sire. We didn't know this bitch of a democracy could get so hot. What is this thing with its claws? A cat or an owl? Or a bat? To be honest with you, sire, we've never seen democracy up close except in photos taken abroad. After you suspended parliamentary life thirty-seven years ago and told us democracy probably contains pork, we immediately set it aside. You know, we are for the most part a Muslim people. Do you know what pork means to us? Thirty-seven years are enough to make you forget, sire. You forget whether it was a cat or a hawk and how and when it sprouted claws. You tend to ask more urgent questions like why does it burn so much given that it was frozen. Thirty-seven years are enough to make you forget, sire, not only what this thing was all about but also your own children.'

Had Muhammad really been his father's son maybe he wouldn't have been able to identify the wound or have the courage to put his finger on it. I always wondered where he found the words. It's no joke writing a column every day. Even once a week would be hard. But Muhammad seemed to do it effortlessly. He would go to the newspaper offices for half an hour a day, scribble down his article and bugger off. What sort of man was he? What demons controlled him? Now, after all this time, after all this distance, all this rolling and sliding, I sometimes picture him but can't quite hold the details of his face in my mind. I feel a pressure in my chest. He was a great man. Full of encouragement and praise but not for everyone. He could be harsh and critical with me, but he never cut me off completely. He had that something that could get you back on your feet and make you write. And then you had to write, if only just for him, if only to shut him up and show him that you were as worthy of madness as he was. He liked to say that he was able to sniff out a poet right away. 'Poets stink because poetry thrives on slovenliness and bravery. If you accept the poet as a knight you have to live with his stink.'

We joked about Musa's stink, although he insisted he washed every day. Musa had come back to life. Was it because of the poetry Rukayyah had left behind for him? 'Better a present absence than an absent presence' were the last words she had written to him. Rukayyah's absence seemed to have given a huge presence to Musa, who would in the future become the famous poet Musa. The same naughty boy who used to be my classmate, who'd goad me into beating up some guy or other and to climb up drainpipes and vault over walls. When I left Jordan after the First Intifada Musa was preparing his second collection, *The Stones of the Boy from Galandja*.

20

Your fingers stiffen as you wait for your luggage to appear on the big oval conveyor belt. They feel moist even though they're as cold as ice. What are you afraid of exactly? That no one will recognize you? Or that you'll recognize no one? Or both at the same time? Or are you afraid that you'll be greeted as a madman, as the Maltese doctors and psychiatrists claimed in the report that got here before you?

Well, in that report – written in English, obviously – no one actually said you were mad. Not even that fuzzy-headed inspector; it wasn't his job. So no one actually called you a lunatic, but you know that hallucinations and poor emotional responsiveness mean 'not all there'. You know that bizarre delusions and social and occupational dysfunction mean you're unfit to be among people. Not even among animals, to be quite honest, whether they're domestic or wild, because you also need to have your wits about you to care for such creatures. Who would trust them with someone like you? Or trust you with them? At best, you might be fit to live in a hovel like your father's. Could it still be standing? Or did Mustafa have it removed after his death? He probably dismantled it right away, otherwise it would remain a lasting monument to those who locked their father up. Otherwise it would remain a minaret towering over the family's dishonour, a lantern illuminating the total disintegration of your chaotic life before it had even begun.

What were the words you heard that night twenty years ago? They weren't the howling of the wind. They weren't the prattling of desperate spirits or the mutterings of disturbed ghosts. What were they then? Were they another birth certificate for you? Or a death certificate? Could they have been the poison with which you exited not only Amman but all of life itself? Why are you taking it out on the world when the world is not to blame? Not at all. Not in this matter, at least. It even tried its best to help you. Both at the personal and at the national level. And you must have been in a really grave condition if so many heads had to be involved. Commissioners and doctors and psychiatrists and consuls and ambassadors and lawyers. It's a wonder Henry Kissinger didn't show up as well.

We know you won't believe that the world tried to help you as best it could. It's up to you! We won't get into pointless arguments with you. We know how obstinate you are. In any case, you could shed some light on the matter yourself. Enlighten us. Tell us how a man can be helped who won't help himself. Who doesn't even give the professionals a single word to go on, even though some sincerely wished to help him. But you didn't collaborate at all, did you? And your body didn't respond to the pill that's been prescribed to half of Malta or the jab that's prescribed to the other half. You can't say that during the period before your embassy responded, a period of a year if not longer, they didn't try everything within their power to cure you. They even tried an MRI scan and electroconvulsive therapy, but in vain. Neuropsychiatry finally had to join you in throwing in the towel. Why should it squander its intellectual force and resources on you?

At least you'd been paying your taxes. If you hadn't and, say, they'd managed to cure you, you'd have slipped into coma when they sent you the bill. And we also believe, although it's none of our business, that even your unelected government would have lost its head had they been sent the same bill. Maybe it would have replied, 'Take his kidneys. Take his soul. Take his heart and his liver. Take his lungs and his guts. Take his throat and his ankles. Take his pancreas and his marrow and his balls. Take his cornea and his nose and hair and skin and anything else you can lay your hands on as long as we're square. Look at it from our point of view, for Allah's sake! We've protested again and again that we have nothing left to sell except trinkets. Except honour and manhood, which bring no profits on the market of major products that you're after, like oil and gas and heavy metals. What are heavy metals, by the way? Our government's been meaning to ask for a long time but was waiting for the right moment. We think there's no better moment than this. What exactly are heavy metals? Are they perhaps like normal metals, like iron and steel, but need a lot of men to carry them? Please do explain it to us, because if we have none of these metals and can't produce them we could perhaps bury them for you in our desert if the offer's good enough. The desert can take a lot of secrets, as long as everyone keeps their mouths shut and you just cancel the bill for that dimwit. Take all the refugees if you want them. No, not all of them! What are you talking about? You have to leave us some, for charity's sake. For show, so to speak. A protest march, as your dirty West would call it. Otherwise, in whose name would we beg? And who would believe us when we say that these people are truly desperate? Perhaps you yourselves didn't believe us, even though you brought them into being. That's why we kept the camps for externally displaced people in worse conditions than God himself could have imagined. As far as we could, obviously, since we have no control over certain technologies. We would imagine that not even you do. But we've always done our best to keep these EDPs in limbo. A grey limbo about which we had reached an understanding with you. The palace has always said you had an understanding on this matter. At least where food and drink for refugees are concerned, because keeping them in limbo works to our advantage as it does to yours and the other countries, those with oil, who give huge donations to cleanse themselves of sin. A grey limbo. Between hope and desperation. Half happy and half sad. Half naked and half clothed. Half starved and half sated. And in some circumstances we had to treat them as half animal and half human, because that's the only way to keep these pseudo-creatures under control. You've no idea how troublesome they would be otherwise. The government of Jordan knows what it's on about. These aren't things it dreamed up or read about in the *Thousand and One Nights*. These are things it experienced during Black September, and you know it had to slaughter a considerable number of refugees so that calm and order could once again reign in the streets. A number which, as you know and indeed as you recommended, had to be reduced by a significant margin. Our government risked becoming a historical laughing stock because even a pillow fight would have resulted in a higher body count! But what could we have done? Like us, you, too, wanted to maintain calm and order in the region. You know that calm and order in the Hashemite kingdom depends upon calm and order in Tel Aviv. Now we're speaking the same language, aren't we? Do you still want the money to settle the bill for that madman who, after all, went mad in your territory? He was in perfect condition when he left our custody. And yes, 'he was in perfect condition' means he wasn't really. Everyone knows that you can't become an EDP and still be intact. But at least he ate and drank and shat and spoke. He showed appreciation. He swallowed and said thank you, to us and to you and the heavens for providing flour and shelter. We hope you haven't gone and fucked it all up now. You're bringing back the husk of a man. These arid corpses, God himself couldn't keep them quiet. Even though they're mute. We know far more about them than you. We know what we're talking about. There's so much we could tell you about his father and his uncles and his entire family of dummies. Your ears wouldn't be able to cope. But sorry, if you don't even have the conscience to listen why did you create these pseudo-people? Why did you remove them from their land?'

Here we should intervene, since we know for certain that this discussion would lead nowhere and has in any case been repeated a million times, and, another thing, the Jordanian government wouldn't sink to such depths in its use of language. You know that, don't you? It might sink to the most obscene depths, whether or not they were created by God, but it wouldn't lower its linguistic standards to such a degree. Successive Jordanian governments have been known for their decency and civility and their careful choice of vocabulary. This is the school of British cunning we're talking about; let's not tar them with the same brush as the goats they have for neighbours.

You begin to think about the big oval conveyor belt. Wherever you depart from, wherever you run to, however far you go, it still brings you back to where you started from. If not physically, as a skeleton covered in flesh and hair, and not spiritually, then certainly catabolically, the way life takes back its raw materials to reuse them for something else, perhaps something more worth while. What does more worth while mean? Ever since Simon's been gone you seem to have become something of a smartarse. Are you planning to take his place? Is it true that humanity is a failed project, or is it just you and your city friend who are the failures? If humanity is a failed project, it doesn't mean you have to take your own life. But, on the other hand, if you don't take your own life how do you register your protest in a way that is appropriate, and how will you be taken seriously?

Suddenly the luggage starts to appear on the conveyor belt. Your heart starts beating again. It's as if you're afraid to face up to your memories on your own. Twenty years is a long time. Twenty years a fugitive! Twenty years of avoiding and postponing the moment when you stand before the mirror of the past. Twenty autumns away from home. How many sets of twenty autumns and Ammans are there in life? How many faces behind all those autumns are you expecting to recognize or be recognized by when you've stopped recognizing yourself? Twenty autumns postponing and putting off in order to escape the claws of the past? Claws or fangs? Or axes? Or are you afraid that Amman will take one look at you and turn her face away like Nadia and Baghdad and all the others?

Amman, too, has seen the dreams and hopes of its people slip away and be buried under poverty and abandonment, and, like you, it could do nothing to stop the haemorrhaging of its desires that finally culminated in enduring disappointment. Amman and Nadia are similar in the need they have to disavow you. To erase you completely from the pages of their notebooks. One does it so as not to be reminded of its national disappointments and the other so as not to be reminded of the years of uncertainty she wasted trying to break through the prison walls of your strangeness. A city is like a woman. She doesn't appreciate encountering her ex-lover. Especially when she's in the company of another man – her husband, mind you, if this is Nadia we're talking about. We know that several people volunteered to pass the information on to you. Well! You know what Malta's like, don't you? But, listen, it's not just Malta. The whole world likes to eavesdrop and gossip. That's why there's a gossip bulletin every hour. Local gossip and international, too, since intercontinental chit-chat has now begun to undermine us and take its toll on love and bread and the volume and quality of milk in mothers' breasts.

They needn't have come to tell you, since you knew that women are like cities; they know how to fill the absences left by men. They fill them up with whatever's available, with something tangible and within reach, not the void offered by people like you who live in hovels and tombs. Because when the snout of the past comes rooting so aggressively in the present it goes without saying that you feel life pressing in, closing in like the walls of the tomb. Better not to be born. You know that a woman is like a city; she needs to move forward. And only forward. Women don't understand the concept of backwards. That one's for you. Yours alone to choke on. They're not interested. Life for them is all about moving forward. 'Come on, let's go, or we'll get stuck here.' Everyone wants to move forward. The problem is which direction to take. We always confuse our choices of direction even though they're clear and distinct and right in front of us. Who knows, but maybe . . . maybe everyone thinks they're forging ahead. Otherwise there wouldn't be all this lust for life. Did you know there's a biological lust for life? And it's much stronger than you. You see? Even a puny molecule knows which way is forward, let alone a beautiful, brilliant woman like Nadia.

So what did the gossips volunteer to tell you? That she was married? To a friend of your friend's? What difference would it have made? Didn't Halimeh marry your uncle even though she loved your father? Is that why she kept spreading her legs for him? What were those four words you heard that blue night twenty years ago coming from inside the hovel which you don't want to share with us? You're ashamed of the memory, aren't you? Or are you afraid that readers will be ashamed of you? Are you afraid to tell them who you really are? That you are not in fact you? That you're completely the opposite? Your own opposite pole? Because after a few hundred pages of incoherent musings who could possibly understand you let alone believe you? Now we're assuming that the police did, in fact, decide to publish your ranting and raving and didn't just throw everything away to stop their heads and the heads of the other Maltese from hurting any more. You know these people's heads hurt, don't you? Maybe more than you hurt yourself. But this isn't the place for this kind of talk. We know you've had a good chat about Malta elsewhere. Scicluna, the young policewoman, said they found more of your scribblings in which you criticized and even attacked the leadership of the country that welcomed you as people welcome their own children. And you know how insincere the word 'welcome' can be, a diplomatic word, you know, because we, too, exercise caution in our lexical choices. Don't think for one moment that it's just successive Jordanian governments who learned how to get along with journalists and tell-tales. If we really inherited this characteristic from the British, as we believe we did, we might as well cut this discussion short. You know that when it comes to speaking and sounding English we have no equal. Even among the British themselves. Still, all this talk is out of place. We wanted to say that were we able to speak freely without any linguistic sensitivities or cultural intolerances we wouldn't have said 'welcomed' but 'taken in'.

You know what you were like when you got to Malta, don't you? Or have you forgotten, as only the ungrateful forget? Shall we continue with the same frankness? Right, so when you came to Malta in 1990 you were a coward. Literally a coward. Running from a war that was shaking the whole region: Operation Desert Storm. What was that? War number nine? Ten? Eleven? Eighty? For Saddam it was the 'mother of all battles'. Through him the world got to know that wars have aunts and mothers and mothers-in-law – and, obviously, children.

But you were fleeing a bigger war, weren't you? An interior war. The war of a man who has lived his whole life believing he was really himself. Lived it all in reverse. A spectacular reversal of the kind they like to perform so much in your cursed part of the world. It's as if everything has to be in reverse in order for it to make sense to you. On that score, we are in agreement, on the banality and oddity and absurdity of your dazed senses. Nevertheless, Malta took you in, literally picked you up off the ground. From rock bottom. It took you in, dusted you off, washed, clothed, fed and watered and educated you. And so believed in you that it trusted you to handle the blood of its children in the National Blood Bank where you found your first job.

Have you any idea how many Maltese hearts trusted your trembling fingers? What more could you ask for? And then you tell us the world didn't try to take care of you? That Malta didn't do everything it could to make a decent citizen out of you, a citizen who is happy to take his pill and go to sleep until he feels better? Instead of showing some appreciation you insulted its people and called them cats and goats and crocodiles and who knows what else. You let your tongue run over Malta and its new image. You said she'd dyed and straightened her hair. And, worst of all, you said she'd bared her backside to strangers to become part of the Christian family. As if Europe didn't have enough backsides of its own. So what if she exposed herself a little? Well? It suited her, so what? Or did you want her confined to a tent like your women? Once and for all, you need to get it into that dazed head of yours that Malta is not Arab. She never wore a headscarf and isn't planning to start doing so now. Not even if your lot were to reach another peak of civilization and become a model to be blindly emulated by everyone else the way the world followed in the footsteps of the knights of globalization and neo-liberalism.

We don't mean that you're responsible for economic disasters as well, but you can't deny that economic disaster had to have been preceded by a greater moral disaster. You're the last person entitled to talk about ethics and the erosion of morals. You uttered a lot of drivel that you should never have uttered. After all, that's no way to thank people is it? After they opened the doors to their homes for you and treated you like someone who actually had his wits about him? If there's anyone with an identity and personality problem it's you. Yes, you. At least Malta found its parents at last. You remained without an address or a frame, and you don't know, or won't say, what you heard outside your father's hovel shortly before you made your way out of Jordan and probably out of life itself. It was dark and windy and rainy and cold. And, yes, you were a little drunk. And, yes, life can come up with such absurdities that life itself would find it hard to believe them, but on that soaking night you both wanted and didn't want to believe what you'd seen with your own eyes and heard with your own ears.

It was her that you saw, wasn't it? Halimeh getting out of a taxi by your house. She didn't realize you were drinking with your friend Musa in the dark car after you'd been kicked out of the last bar. What the hell was she doing there at that hour? It was getting close to two in the morning. Uncle must have died, you thought. What else could have brought her there that fairy-tale night? It wasn't illusion or imagination. You couldn't have imagined her just then; your head was still screwed on tight to some extent. Musa was there as your witness. She got out of the taxi before your very eyes. Hurried to the gate to the house. Looked over her shoulder quickly and then pushed the front gate and went straight to the hovel. From the crack in the garden wall you saw the hovel door open and the darkness engulf her tall figure. You opened the car door to follow her. Musa grabbed your jacket.

'What are you doing?'

'Leave me alone, for Allah's sake,' you said, flustered. 'I need to see what that owl's gone in there to do with that convict.'

'Hadn't you better stay out of it?' he asked, only half convinced.

You had told him a lot about Halimeh and the stories that had proliferated around her over the years. Like you, Musa had accepted the story that you had been sent off to her house in the summer for the fresh air; he, too, was sometimes sent to Wadi Musa to familiarize himself with his name and become integrated in the family tree.

'Let me go. My heart's about to pack in, it's beating so fast,' you said as if you sensed that a very substantial chunk of the world was about to fall on your head. Why didn't you take his advice that crazy night? Or is that too vague a question? In that case we'll take it back right away, since no one can escape their destiny in any case. Not even if they lock themselves away in a tower. Not even if he's got Vittoriosa and the north wind and the cannon of the Servants of the Cross behind him. And not even if his friend grabs his jacket to stop him from going to listen to the verdict passed on a life that was never his. To stop him discovering that he was not himself and never had been. He was always another. Another who wished to destroy him. Another who could only subsist on his remains and who finds even those irksome. Because they remind him of the other. The other whom he lived his whole life believing he was. Believing he was a refugee. Believing he was a victim. So you pulled away and went to listen.

'What the hell did you come here for? I've told you a thousand times not to come here. Don't you understand we cannot keep grinding ourselves down? Why do you persist?' said your father, the man you believed had become as silent as a block of ice because of Palestine.

'What do you mean persist? Do you expect me to forget that he's my son? Since when is water thicker than blood?'

'He's yours, yes. Your blood has destroyed more than just my family and me. It's destroyed our entire race. What else do you want? Don't you know that everything's long since turned to ice? Why do you persist in dredging up the past?'

'It might have turned to ice for you but not for me. It's all wide open as far as I'm concerned. Everything still bleeds as if the wound was inflicted only yesterday.'

'You have to forgive, Ofra. You have to forgive in the name of Allah. In the name of Elohim. Even Elohim and Allah forgive, or they'd never find rest.'

'Those are the gods of Yusef, and they can forgive. There'll be no rest for us.'

'You're the one who refuses to rest. What are you? A rock? A stone? Even the heart of a stone is softened by time.'

'How can you expect my heart to soften when it's still palpitating furiously as if it all happened yesterday? As if it was only yesterday that I ran from my parents' house to come with you . . . a traitor. Do you remember, Yusef?'

'Your yesterday happened forty years ago, Ofra. How could I keep my word when all of creation came crashing down on our heads? Do you know what's happened during these forty years or do you not?'

'Have these forty years gone by for Nabil, too? Or was he just a casual fuck by the roadside?'

'What do you expect me to tell him? That his mother wasn't his mother? That his real mother's still alive? And that she's his uncle's wife? Do you expect me to tell him I got my brother's wife pregnant? After my brother had long since drifted away from her? What am I supposed to tell him? That his mother's Jewish? That her real name is Ofra and not Rahmeh or Halimeh? And that his grandfather and uncles displaced his other grandfather and uncles? Should I tell him that his brothers are terrorist martyrs and the Zionist wolves are heroes? That he's at once victim and executioner? That he is . . .'

It was late. It was far too late when Musa grabbed your jacket. A jacket that suddenly began to feel like it didn't belong to you. And it wasn't just the jacket. The air and the darkness and the rain and wind and the house and the garden and the hovel and the two ghosts arguing inside it. All of existence. All of you wasn't you. You were the two sworn enemies. David and Goliath. Dr Jekyll and Mr Hyde. Half of you had to die for the other half to survive. You, who thought that you were you. Who thought you were Nabil.

Suddenly two airport officials and a police officer turned up. They came straight up to you with your suitcase. A brown suitcase that had gone grey over time, like the rest of your life. The officer smiled and took you by the arm to lead you away. In his other hand he held a sheaf of papers, and you recognized the Maltese government stamp on some of the envelopes. You were led through various halls and corridors until you finally found yourself facing the last pane of dark glass separating you from Amman. The city of your childhood. What was it teeming with now? The living or the dead? Or phantoms and the ghosts of refugees and prisoners and the tongue-tied? Or the wayward who lived their lives believing they were who they thought they were?

The airport officials and the officer passed you and your grey bag and the sheaf of papers that were about you over to two others who appeared to be medics, or so you thought, judging by their bearing and by the fact that they seemed more interested in the documentation than in you. And maybe also judging by the flicker of the ambulance waiting for you beyond the dark glass that separated you from the city of your death and birth.

Near the wide-open doors of the ambulance stood a large woman in uniform, smoking as she waited impatiently. She had a lot of odds and ends and ballpoint pens in the shirt pocket of her grey uniform. Or was it not grey? As soon as she got her hands on you she shoved you into the back of the ambulance and threw your suitcase in after you. As she shut the double doors to seal your kidnapping, you seemed to catch a glimpse of someone waving and shouting out your name.

Someone with a moustache and a beard. He kept up his antics at the window of the vehicle, waving his hands like an idiot. His face reminded you of things long gone. Maybe of streets and alleys and mountains and valleys and trees and holes and vaults and drainpipes and poles and archways and staircases. Maybe of stones and pebbles and dust and soil and worms and beetles and snakes and birds. Maybe the lizard that stunned you in the mirror in the wardrobe thirty-three years ago after that intimate confrontation with the Arab king who spied on his own people. Maybe the vendor of cold lemonade outside the 'department of fugitives and cowards'. Who knows? After all, that thin bony face did bear a striking resemblance to Musa's.

POSTSCRIPT

For the most part this narrative was written before revolution swept along the African coast and the Arab Spring began.

Musa al-Ghabbadi has published over ten volumes of poetry. He is married to a refugee and lives in Amman. The couple have five boys, all of whom insist they wish to die as martyrs for the Palestinian cause. Their father is constantly in and out of jail because of his long tongue.

Five months after she broke up with Nabil, Nadia married and disappeared from his life.

Simon Anthony De Brincat took his own life in 2007. To this day Nabil doesn't know what drove him to it.

In the process of writing this book, the author should have read the following works:

Azmi Bishara – *From the Jewishness of the State to Sharon*
Adel S. Bishtawi – *A History of American Injustice and the Beginning of the Long Imperial Decline* and *A History of Injustice in the Arab World*
Noam Chomsky – *Human Rights and American Foreign Policy, Pirates and Emperors, Old and New: International Terrorism in the Real World, What Uncle Sam Really Wants* and *Middle East Illusions*
Marc Ellis – *Israel and Palestine – Out of the Ashes: The Search for Jewish Identity in the Twenty-First Century* and *O Jerusalem: The Contested Future of the Jewish Covenant*
Philip K. Hitti – *History of the Arabs* and *Makers of Arab History*
Edward Said – *Culture and Imperialism* and *Orientalism*

The author should also have studied the Bible and the Qur'an as well as some documents in the archives of the British, US, German, Russian and Israeli governments.

All the poems in this narrative are the product of the author's own imagination.

The author would like to thank his colleague, Roberta Cremona, whose knowledge, skill and linguistic precision shed light into many crannies of this narrative, although she might not have been aware of it.

The author would also like to acknowledge the wisdom of his mother and father, who brought him up and provided him with a good education despite the troubles he brought with him into this world.

Peter Owen Publishers

info@peterowen.com

@PeterOwenPubs
Facebook: Peter Owen Publishers

Independent publishers since 1951

www.peterowen.com